ARBUTUS

ARBUTUS

To Geoff
with my very Best
Wishes
Cyril
2012

CYRIL SMITH

Library of Congress Control Number:		2012913841
ISBN:	Hardcover	978-1-4771-5257-7
	Softcover	978-1-4771-5256-0
	Ebook	978-1-4771-5258-4

To order additional copies of this book, contact:
Xlibris Corporation
0-800-644-6988
www.xlibrispublishing.co.uk
Orders@xlibrispublishing.co.uk
304662

CONTENTS

TIMIUS ARBUTUS

The story of a Roman soldier and his companions who fortuitously find themselves active participants in an event considered by many to be the most important in the history of mankind

*

The events in the life of the leading character portrayed are based on twentieth century fact, but are set out here as having taken place in a period of the early Roman Empire.

*

For Patricia—

Thank you, my noble patrician, for all the encouragement and hard work you have undertaken to make a dream become reality.

*

And men will tell their children
Although their memories might fade,
That they lived through the age of Augustus
When the foundations of the Empire were laid

SIBYLLINE VERSE

Primus interparis was the second to enslave the State following the omnipitus, his son, no son no mate.

ACKNOWLEDGEMENTS

The author wishes to thank all the **Xlibris personnel** who have been involved in all aspects of publishing his work. Their help and encouragement is very much appreciated.

In his earlier years he was an avid reader of the classics. These, and Edward Gibbon's epic *Rise and Fall of the Roman Empire,* gave him the inspiration to set the scene for **ARBUTUS** in the Roman era.

CHAPTER I

Mores Puerorum si inter Ludendum Detergent.
QUINTILIAN A.D.14

The characters of boys show themselves in their play.

THE MORNING BROKE once again with a low-lying mist shrouding the little township of Velitrae. It was late summer and the warm day followed by the cold nights gave rise to rather heavy early morning mists.

Timius Arbutus woke early. He had planned to meet his friend Ciatus as soon as he was allowed to go out to play. His elder sister Mena had always insisted that he wash himself properly and eat his breakfast before being able to wander beyond the confines of their humble home. In his mischievous little way, he thought that by rising early and by gently creating a little noise with the metal basin containing water for washing he might succeed in waking his sister who might, perhaps, set about preparing his breakfast which today should be corn cakes and milk. This was a regular breakfast diet in the household.

The reason for the urgency to make an early start was because the boys had planned the previous night to make what was to them a major expedition to the nearby gorge to find some harmless lizards that frequented the neighbouring area, especially during summer time. The excitement the day would bring had made them restless since discussing the plan.

Dawn had already broken on an empire and on the end of an era that was to have a profound impact on civilization for many centuries to come. This was the age that would produce the political, economic, cultural and religious activities and formulate jurisprudence that would mould and shape civilization throughout the known and, as yet, undiscovered word well into the distant future.

Timius met his friend, as arranged, and both boys set out on their jaunt full of enthusiasm.

"Timius, since I am older than you", said Ciatus, "I will lead the cohort against those horrible savages of the Empire, and you can be my chief swordsman".

The boys took a delight in emulating the legionaries of the Empire whenever they set out on their boyish excursions into the territory of the village periphery that was not as yet under cultivation. It was a rather rugged area with wild vegetation and thickets of shrubs scattered here and there. These thickets represented to them the encampments of the barbarians and formed an important part of their make believe world.

Both boys were armed with home made slings and they soon selected a handful of suitable round stones as missiles for their slings. These were enough to fill the rough leather pouches that the boys carried over their shoulders. Thus armed, and overwhelmed with bravery, they sallied forth to meet their imaginary foe. It was some time before they came upon their first lizard basking in the sunshine on top of one of the rocks. They stalked the creature until they were near enough to launch their missiles but, having done so, they missed. Both were disappointed and blamed each other for the distraction, bragging about their prospective prowess and accuracy. The stalk continued for some two hours with each boy missing his prey on every attempt, until one of the boys landed a glancing shot wounding the creature. They ran up to the wounded reptile not knowing whether to kill it outright or to leave it to die or be taken away by one of the swooping hawks that often frequented the area. Timius suggested leaving it to its own fate, but Ciatus was adamant that it should be put out of its misery and moreover, he had been told by someone or other that this type of reptile, when wounded, would follow its assailant to his bed at night. This has been known to happen. Therefore Ciatus' suggestion was the most obvious one although it was fraught with an element of risk. This they did and they named the poor creature Hannibal, although there were no elephants in sight at least not on this occasion.

They made their way to a nearby stream, lay alongside it, flat on their stomachs and drank some of the water to refresh them after their ordeal. Afterall, they had just put an end to Hannibal's ambition. The Empire was once again safe. Again they wandered off amongst the rocks to search out fresh prey and within a few moments spotted another. This time the lizard was rather a gruesome looking creature. Their slings were once more loaded and the stalk began. The lizard, having spotted Timius and Ciatus, ran into a crevice. Both boys moved around the projecting rock in search of the lizard, but were stopped dead in their tracks by a hissing viper that had its eye on them. To kill the serpent required an enormous amount of courage, but which boy had the most courage was hard to tell at this point. The hairs stood up on the backs of their necks and the cold sweat began to run down their backs. If they launched their missiles and missed then this would have angered the viper that would probably have chased them. Ciatus turned and ran leaving Timius dumbfounded and his movement aggravated the viper. The snake slithered towards Timius who realizing he was now alone turned tail and ran too.

After getting away from the rocks he spotted Ciatus, still running, some three hundred yards ahead of him, as though he were running towards the boundary of the eastern provinces. Timius soon caught up with Ciatus as he was probably leaner in stature and a year younger also swifter than his friend. Between them they settled the affair by agreeing that, in such a situation, it was best that Ciatus should have run along for reinforcements. Where these reinforcements were to have come from they did not know because the army had been reduced from about fifty legions to a mere twenty-five, three of which were stationed outside the city to provide a bodyguard to Caesar, and it was not the practice of the Praetorian Guard to engage in campaigns against the external enemies of the State.

During their discussions Ciatus thought he heard the sound of horses hooves in the distance. This was not an unusual sound in the countryside, but this time there seemed to be rather more horses in the troop than usual. They decided to make their way to the road to see if this was the reinforcement that was on its way to help them fight the viper. They would not approach it head-on but would first of all spy through the hedgerow. So they took up their respective positions along the hedge and were able to see, approaching them along the road, a troop of cavalry whose red-plumed helmets glistened in the late afternoon sunshine. Just as the troop approached their position Timius caught his arm in a thorny branch of the hedge and tried to conceal his yelp. This was obviously heard by the officer of the troop who commanded an immediate halt in order to conduct an investigation. The bearers following the front rank of the troop also came to a halt and lowered the litter to the ground and stood at ease. The boys were undecided whether to run or to approach the general and ask for reinforcements. However, since they had run enough that day they decided that the latter course would be the best action, and, when called for, sheepishly emerged from the hedge.

"What are you two up to," shouted the general.

"Nothing sir, we were just watching," said Timius very tensely.

"You two boys should be at home, under the watchful eyes of your parents, not rummaging around here in the open countryside."

"But sir," replied Timius, "we have been on another campaign against the barbarians."

"What barbarians?" the general queried sternly.

"The barbarians over there in those rocks", cried Timius.

As he said that a bearer approached the officer and gestured that the two boys be brought in front of the man who was sitting in the litter. So there they found themselves face to face with an elderly man clutching a notched stick in his left hand and seated on a cushion. He was wearing a straw hat and what seemed like a homespun robe covered with a purple mantle. Both boys wondered who this man was. When he spoke he mentioned that he had overheard them refer to their campaign against barbarians. Once again Timius reiterated the object of the days events. The old gentleman was quite pleased to hear what he had to say.

"As citizens of the Empire I am glad that you are both growing up to be soldiers who will, one day, be called on to defend the frontiers of our illustrious Empire." Tossing them a gold coin each he advised them to go home and devote their time to becoming good citizens.

Timius and Ciatus parted to go home in their respective ways. Ciatus lived in a villa on the south side of the town. His father held a respectable position as secretary to the local senator who represented their district. He belonged to a modestly wealthy family and was therefore never really in need of the essentials of life. Any damage that might have occurred to his clothing or footwear during expeditions with Timius was of no consequence as replacements were easily available, whereas Timius was constantly being grumbled at by his mother and sister for unnecessarily dirtying his clothes, or bringing them to the state of disrepair sooner than necessary.

When Timius arrived home his mother, seated on a stool, was selecting eggs from a basket in readiness to pop them into a bowl of cold water to test their freshness. Crouching on the steps of the veranda were two men from the village and, as Timius approached, his mother enquired of him "where have you been? You always come home filthy as though we were living in a drought-stricken area with no water available to wash yourself. Why aren't you like the other boys in the neighbourhood who keep within the confines of their homes? We can never find you when we need you; you will grow up to be a loafer and make your living scrounging and thieving from other respectable citizens. Come and help me select these eggs for freshness. Eggs that stand up on end in a bowl of water are usually on the turn and should be discarded."

The men from the village farms used to pay a regular visit to the household on the eve of their departure to the town market place. Timius' mother provided them with the facilities to spend the night in a shelter situated in the yard and, as payment, they would always give her perhaps a dozen or so free eggs. Otherwise it would have meant obtaining shelter for the night in a nearby Inn, the cost of which would denude their profits, and the village folk could ill afford this.

"May I have an egg for my supper mother?" asked Timius.

"No you cannot and in fact you will have no supper tonight until you learn to behave like other boys. When your father comes home I am going to tell him what an uncontrollable child you are and this time he may, perhaps, put an end to such behaviour."

Timius' mother was not really cruel to the child but really thought a good deal of him. She was aggravated by the complaints of neighbours regarding his mischievousness and, in addition, she was suffering from an incurable disease that the boy knew nothing about. She was obviously in terrible pain at times and this clouded her affection for him. His father was far from home serving with the Fourteenth Legion in Transalpine Gaul. He had been there on this occasion for nearly twelve months, but the Legion was due to return to its garrison headquarters. Indeed they might well be on the way back now.

Timius crept out again the following morning without anyone knowing where he was going. He called on Ciatus in the hope that they could spend another day on the frontier, but Ciatus said that he was not allowed out today. Timius did not believe him. He was sure that this was only an excuse and that Ciatus was really scared of the viper. That was the real reason. Rather disappointed he wandered off on his own at a loss as to how to spend the day when he noticed just near his foot a grub about the size of his thumb making its way out of a mud mound.

"Ah, I will have some fun with this," thought Timius. So he picked it up, placed it in the palm of his hand and took it under a nearby tree. He crouched down and made a circular endless channel in the soil about an inch deep, placed the grub in the channel, persuaded it to walk and then left it, and the grub walked all the way round and round the channel. This sort of thing fascinated Timius who decided to count the number of times the grub walked round the channel non-stop. It was a question now of who would get tired first, Timius or the grub. At the age of seven he never knew the names of any of the insects, so he called them all *bouchees*. Poor Timius was the first to grow weary because he lost count and the grub showed that it had more stamina than he did, so he left it and made his way home. The poor grub may still be marching in that endless channel.

Wending his way home through the narrow street Timius arrived at the town square in the centre of which was an ornamental carp pond in the midst of which was a fountain in the form of some Greek God, of whom he did not know. Surrounding the pond were grass lawns interwoven with stone pathways. Surrounding the whole area was a circle of young olive trees, evenly spaced. Timius ran up to the pond and with the stick he was clutching he began tormenting the fish. This mischief was soon discovered by one of the Municep workers who chased him. He had seen this man before because it was this man who had reported other acts of mischief, committed by Timius, to his mother. That night, as he was about to snuggle under the bedclothes, his sister dragged him out to his mother who wanted to speak to him urgently.

"Timius, what on earth am I going to do with you? You will be the death of me. The man from the Municep has reported that some fish were found floating on top of the water in the town's ornamental pond, and he reported that you were seen trying to poke them with your stick. Come the morning I am going to cure you of your pranks once and for all. Now go to bed!"

Timius was forcibly dragged to bed by his ear, by his elder sister. His tears made no impression upon his elders. Mena was very fond of the boy but she was also very anxious about their mother's health as it was deteriorating rapidly. Mena felt that these continuous pranks that her little brother kept getting up to would be treated with normalcy if the situation was different but, under these circumstances, it was beginning to aggravate. Of course Timius was wondering what his final cure would be that his mother had promised him.

As Mena was about to extinguish the oil lamp in his room she noticed, laying on top of the box in which his clothes and other belongings were packed, a coin. She picked it up, studied it for a while in the dim light, and noticed it bore the head of the emperor on one side and on the obverse an oak wreath between two laurel branches, and the inscription *Ob Civis Servatos*, commemorating the honours and emblems bestowed on Augustus in B.C.27.

"Where did you get this?" she asked.

"What?" answered Timius.

"What do you think I am talking about, this coin, you silly boy. Did you steal it or find it? If you stole it you had better give it back to its rightful owner. It is a lot of money for a boy of your age and indeed from this household to have in his possession. Did you run an errand for some nobleman who paid you with this coin. Now let's have the truth. Where did you get it from?"

"No Mena, I did not steal it, I did not find it, but was given the coin by an old man who was riding in a litter yesterday. He was surrounded by a cavalry troop accompanying him".

"What did this man look like? Why did he give you a coin?"

"Oh! I do not know what he looked like. He was old. He had a straw hat and wore a purple frock. He gave Ciatus a coin too".

"Why did he give each of you a coin? What had you done to deserve it?"

"We did not do anything. We were just watching the troop pass and when they stopped they asked us what we were doing. We said that we had just been engaged in a battle against the barbarians."

"What barbarians?"

"I don't know. Those I suppose that keep on offending the frontiers of the Empire," replied Timius, yawning.

"Go to sleep now and I will talk to you about this tomorrow morning."

Mena left the room and suddenly realized that she had heard in the market place that the emperor, Augustus, had passed on the road north of the town on his way to Rome from Velitrae where he had a country villa that he often visited. Perhaps Timius is telling the truth after all, as Octavian was reputed to be a generous man, except in some quarters.

*

Octavian was now in the forty-third year of his reign, but to use the word reign would be offensive to the people, as it is commonly associated with kingship, and kingship was abhorrent to the populace. After years of civil war, with a short respite during Julius Caesar's period of dictatorship, a further fourteen years of civil war culminated in the final success of Octavian.

The tyrannical dictatorship of Sulla, who was king all but in name, followed the equally tyrannical Tarquin, the last king of the Roman monarchy. Julius Caesar, after his successful campaigns both in Gaul and during the Punich wars, was hailed as Caesar (Punic meaning head of hair), although ironically he was bald, and baldness was hereditary in the Claudian family. He had crossed the Rubicon and marched on Rome and overthrew Sulla and his associates. Unfortunately, or perhaps we can say fortunately, this repulsion of the Roman people towards a monarchy of any description placed Julius Caesar in a position where he was unable to leave a monarchical heir as his successor. Nor was there an acceptable form of hereditary transfer of power. Julius Caesar, a much loved and respected man endowed with military and literary prowess, was able to, in his speeches to the senate, and through them, to the people of Rome and the provinces, convey his philosophy of a just and secure society which would be rewarded with prosperity. It was popular belief at this stage in the history of the Republic that monarchy was inevitable. The ruling factions were constantly provoking friction. But, although he did not tell the people this, he must have realized that stability and prosperity could only flow provided there was strong government and strong leadership at the centre. The leadership of a group was far weaker than the leadership from one individual. The Roman people grasped this philosophy, but there were several members of the nobility, and indeed his closest associates who totally disagreed with this. They felt that even if one man was elected to endow him with all the powers of the state which he would have inherited as rightful heir to a monarchy would be the return of a monarchy to Rome. Rome was a republic with the ultimate powers of the state in the hands of the Senate and the people. Julius Caesar could not accept this and acquired the powers of a dictator. The eastern provinces, that for generations had bestowed divine powers on their rulers, were about to do so with Julius Caesar and acclaim him a divine deity. This, and moreover his acquisition of dictatorial powers, resulted in his assassination in the Senate chamber in B.C.44.

Octavian was the adopted nephew of Julius Caesar. On the day that Julius Caesar rewrote his will in B.C.45, he named Octavian as his chief heir and, at the very end of the will, he adopted him into his family and gave him his name. At a very early age Octavian realized that he was the rightful successor to his great uncle. However, to assume his rightful position would have meant overcoming far too many insurmountable obstacles to first gaining the confidence of the Senate and the people, unless this could be done by means of bribery and corruption. He was too shrewd a man, even in his early life, to consider adopting this course of action. In any case his finances and his modest background would not allow this. Marcus Antonius, a Patrician of another family, would also aspire to this position if he felt that Octavian's aspirations were similar. Another personality that entered the political arena at this point, vying for power, was Lepidus, an influential and wealthy nobleman and military leader, whose legions under his control defended the frontiers along the Danube and the Rhine.

Octavian had cultivated a lifelong friendship and tremendous respect of the leading military strategist and admiral of the day, Marcus Agrippa. It was with Agrippa that he had defeated the enemies of the state in both Spain and Gaul. Octavian had also seen service at the head of the army in Parthis.

We now have the background to the instability of the situation following the death of Julius Caesar. The only possible solution for the three leading contenders for the leadership of Rome, the mistress of the world, was to combine their forces and activities with the approval of the Senate. Thus we have the formation of the Triumvirate, with Octavian the youngest of the three. The three contenders were elected consuls. This was the highest position one could reach among the Roman rulers. The general agreement was that Marcus Antonius would exercise his consulship of the provinces of the east, including Macedonia. Lepidus, the provinces of Gaul, Illyricum, Germania, leaving Octavian Consul of Rome and the Italian provinces, under whose auspices the provinces of North Africa he would also control through Agrippa. It was only a matter of some two years before this workable arrangement could no longer be workable. The Senate realized that the Republic and its provinces were becoming too fragmented and that there must be more common consolidation of power. However, before a solution could be found for this insoluble situation by the Senate Mark Anthony presented the Republic the means of a solution on a platter. He had joined forces with Cleopatra, Queen of Egypt, with whom he was in love, although he was married to Octavian's sister, Octavia. The Senate realized that they could not tolerate such a situation where the monarch of a client kingdom would be in a position to influence Roman rule in its eastern provinces, and in Rome too. The provinces were beginning to bring wealth to the Republic through its trade and commerce from the already highly civilized nations in the Far East. Octavian marched eastwards with his legions to meet Anthony and at port Actium, on the coast of Greece. He defeated Mark Anthony in a naval engagement thus eliminating him from his contention for the leadership. Mark Anthony and Cleopatra withdrew to Alexandria and were followed by Octavian. It was here that Mark Anthony was killed. His two children by Cleopatra were sent back to Rome for their protection. Cleopatra committed suicide, rather than succumb to the dictates of Octavian.

With a nerve of coolness Octavian rode alone and unarmed into the camp, in the fields of Brindisium, of the rebellious and hostile Lepidus and took his legions away from him without a blow being struck. The legions under the command of Lepidus overnight, so to speak, reversed their loyalty from Lepidus to Octavian. The triumvirate was now scrambled and its decline imminent.

Octavian marched in triumph to Rome where three days of celebration took place. The young Octavian was now supreme after fourteen years of civil war and constant strife, poverty and starvation of the people, since the death of Julius Caesar. This intensely able man was now to begin to oversee an era that would bring peace and stability and the consolidation of the Empire.

The coin given to Timius was a representation of the age of Augustus and, as the little boy dropped to sleep he would not imagine, nor realize, the portent of this symbol. Nor would he, or anyone else for that matter, imagine the effect of an insignificant event, which had taken place in a remote client kingdom of the eastern provinces some thirteen years earlier, was to have on the mistress of the world and her empire. Its eventual outcome would rock its foundations to its very core out of which would emerge an empire much stronger stretching far beyond the boundaries of the known world.

Timius never did find out what his "once and for all cure" was to have been, as promised by his mother. So the next few days were spent trying to behave himself within the confines of his home. He was, on several occasions, tempted to wander off into his old stamping grounds, the cart tracks, the gully, the nearby quarry and the cedar copse. His brother-in-law, Silius, who earned his living in the local pottery, promised Timius' mother to keep an eye on the boy, although he could never understand him and communication between the two never really existed. Silius was more concerned with parochial affairs whereas Timius' imagination took him on travels, in his daydreams, to the far corners of the Empire. From eves-dropping on the conversation of the elders in the neighbourhood he had learnt that there were, what seemed to him, interesting subjects of Greek literature, science, mythology and astronomy, and he had no idea at all of what the subjects even referred to; but he was enthusiastic enough to one day find out what they were all about so that he could converse fluently on any one of these subjects with others too. He overheard on one occasion that the god, Apollo, was the deity of literature and learning, and those that paid homage to Apollo at his temple would acquire the gift of learning without undue effort on their part. Timius often wondered how this was possible because the statue he had seen of Apollo was of stone. He was under the impression that the statue was alive and thought that if this was so it must move, but only when it was quiet in the temple. His curiosity was insatiable, even at this early age, so one day he spent the whole afternoon and early evening hidden in the cloister of the temple in the hope of seeing the statue move. When this did not happen he was disappointed and came to the conclusion that all of it was a sham. He would acquire his knowledge of the learned subjects some other way. There were no scrolls in the Arbutus home and to obtain any from the local library would have meant a donation and that was out of the question so he wandered off and climbed up into one of the trees outside the building. He was brought back to reality when he heard someone calling him.

"Timius, where are you? Are you in the temple Timius? Answer me Timius", came the anxious woman. It was a neighbour's eldest daughter Camilla Maroboduus who was calling him.

"I am here," he yelled back.

"Where is here?" Camilla called.

"Up here in the tree," replied Timius.

"Good heavens, what are you doing in there?"

"I am trying to aim at anything below me."

"Well, you had better come down at once. You are wanted at home. It is extremely important that you come to your home with me right away."

"Why? What is the matter Camilla?"

"We do not know, but you will find out, but you must come now."

Timius climbed down with his sling round his neck, the leather thong hanging in the middle of his chest. They both hurried along from the cedar copse where the temptation to stray was too great that day.

When Timius arrived home and went indoors all was quiet except for the sound of raucous breathing. Mena, his sister, frowning and very red-eyed, ushered him in to the room where his mother was lying on a divan. It looked as though his mother was fast asleep but her breathing was even but loud. Timius had no idea what to make of this, so he turned to his sister and asked if his mother always snored like this. Mena frowned disapprovingly as she felt that this was a ridiculous question. So the boy not knowing what to do, quite naturally, took hold of his mother's left hand and held it to him for a few moments. After a while he placed her hand on the coverlet and decided that the best thing to do would be to let his mother sleep. He wandered off onto the veranda but could not fathom out what all the fuss was about after all. his mother was only asleep. Although he did overhear his brother-in-law, who was talking to the local Greek physician, Theodoret, who incidentally was not very expert on the subject of medicine, say that his mother's body was dead but her heart was very strong and it was only a matter of time now. Still somewhat confused about what was going on he sat on the veranda step and let his mind wander into yet another daydream where he imagined he was marching with one of the legions against the Parthians, his shining armour and brass helmet glistening in the sunlight. His daydream was broken when Camilla ran out to him, sobbing, and clutched him fiercely, saying,

"You poor little boy, what are we to do with you now?" Again Timius had no idea what had happened and was dumbfounded when the Greek physician came to him and said,

"You must be a brave boy now," but did not finish what he had to say because Mena called the physician away to attend to Timius' mother. Timius followed him into the house but did not enter the room. He shyly peered round the door and noticed the physician extract a small mirror-like device from his medical bag and place it close to his mother's mouth and nose. As he did so he shook his head then gently closed Timius' mother's eyelids. The physician came out of the room, reached for Timius' hand and took the boy outside. Crouching down so that he was face to face with Timius, he said, "yes, as I was saying, you must be a brave boy now because your mother has gone away to join the gods who live among the stars."

Timius could not comprehend how his mother could go away and live among the stars. He felt very sad and wandered out on to the veranda very pensive and confused. After a while he spotted a bullfrog hopping along the edge of the nearby wall. "Ah," he thought, "I'll catch him and put him in my box." The bullfrog was too quick for him because every time Timius tried to snatch at his legs the frog would hop a yard away from him, and so this went on until he arrived at the gate of the house still in pursuit of the frog. A horse and cart pulled up at the gate and the driver threw down a lambskin bag. From beneath the canopy of the cart emerged Timius' father. Timius ran up to greet his father and was greeted and hugged by him. His father was not as cheerful as he had been on all other occasions when he returned home. He must have sensed that there was something tragically wrong and spent little time with Timius before striding brusquely off into the house.

Night had fallen by this time and Timius continued to wonder what that old Greek doctor had been doing with that mirror object. An idea struck him and he made for his room, rummaged through his box of clothes and other little treasures and came upon a piece of broken mirror that he had found and kept among his souvenirs. Taking the piece of mirror, he made his way stealthily into the room in which his mother's body had been placed. All was quiet and, in the light of the four flickering candles, he noticed lying beside her some tiny bunches of flowers. Taking the piece of mirror he placed it under his mother's nostrils and then near her mouth. Not knowing what it was he was looking for, he then put the piece of mirror to his own nostrils and then to his mouth and discovered that the mirror clouded over. It had not done this when he performed the same act on his mother. This was very strange, but then the Greek physician must have some magic powers about him. He returned to his room and replaced the piece of mirror in his box. He could not understand since he had been alone in the room with his mother why she had not spoken to him, or indeed grumbled at him, as she had done on many occasions just recently. His mother never used to be like that. He could remember the days when she taught him to make a sling and use it the proper way, also the art of jumping off a low wall or fence or bough of a tree without hurting his legs when he landed. He wondered if she was really dead and then suddenly realized that if this was the case then he must have been the cause of it, because he did recall her saying that age old expression:

"You will be the death of me, Timius."

This worried him, so he ran to his father who was in the next room where the family and close neighbours were assembled, to try and derive some comfort from him. Sejanus Arbutus put his arm round his son and half sobbing said,

"If only I had arrived earlier Timius."

Sejanus, a lean athletic figure, in his late forties, had spent the best part of his life in the service of his first Consul. Until recent years he had been occupied in the service as a combatant but was now employed in the ordnance company of the legion. The ordnance company was responsible for provision of armaments, clothing, footwear, food supplies and tents, to the legionaries. The older members of the legion would invariably be stationed at garrison headquarters, usually situated in the provinces of Italy, but Sejanus Arbutus had several years of serviced to complete before he would be eligible for a home posting. It was only rarely that those employed in a front line ordnance capacity would be called on to take up arms and with the other combatant companies. This was only in situations when the strength of the legion was overwhelmed but this situation rarely arose because the highly trained legionnaires were able to successfully stand their ground because of the strict discipline and hardiness, no matter how large a number a disorganized enemy force pitted against them. Sejanus had reached a point in his life when he could look forward to the day of his retirement. His service would be terminated with a large gratuity and a piece of land donated to all veterans by the personal decree of Octavian. When Octavian reduced the number of legions to twenty-five the large numbers of men that were made redundant by this action would have posed an enormous problem to the stability and security of the system. Octavian realized that without generously rewarding the veterans in this fashion, their services would be apt to be enlisted by other ambitious noblemen, with their lust for power, with the ultimate view of resting the vestment of the 'purple'. The loyalty of the existing men at arms was therefore secure.

"Varus, give me back my legions!" This expression was well known throughout the legions and helped to maintain their loyalty to the first Consul.

The Bodegas, the family of the local magistrate, were celebrating the eleventh birthday of their twin daughters. Each year on this day, the family gave a party for the local children in honour of the occasion. Timius had never attended one before because, on the last occasion, he conveniently lost his way. He did not really want to go the party. But this time Mena thought it would be a good idea for him to go along to help take the boy's mind of the events of the past few days. Her main worry though was that the boy had so little clothing in a good state of repair and suitable for the occasion. It then occurred to her that with so many attending whatever the boy wore would go unnoticed. Mena arranged for her friend Camilla to escort Timius to the Bodegas villa. He was unenthusiastic but decided that he would go.

On their arrival at the villa they could hear a small troop of musicians playing. Camilla bid Timius farewell and conveyed her hope that he would enjoy himself, and off she trotted home. He could not find an excuse to change his mind so he entered the hall of the villa where the merriment was taking place. One of the matrons officiating greeted him and took him over to a table on which was an array of sweetmeats and other delicacies, where he could help himself to whatever he fancied, including fruit juices in the earthenware beakers provided. Timius bashfully picked up a beaker and helped himself to one of the juicy drinks, sipped it and began to study the celebrants, composed mainly of children slightly older than him. Above the hubbub he could hear the excited voice of his friend Ciatus, and this put him at ease immediately. He was a very sensitive boy and seemed to lose his nerve when surrounded by company of any description. But here was Ciatus whom he knew well and perhaps in whose company he could spend the evening. He made his way through the crowd of children and approached the place where Ciatus was relating to a group of girls and boys his and Timius' exploits in the gully a few days earlier. Timius was shocked to find that Ciatus had twisted the whole story. Ciatus was showing off to his audience by telling them of his bravery with the viper and went on to relate how his friend Timius was so scared of the reptile, that, on catching sight of it he immediately turned and ran. Timius was dumbfounded by the way Ciatus had twisted the truth. Ciatus was also quick to relate to them that an old man, who was being carried along the road in a litter, was so impressed with his bravery that he gave him a gold coin and one to his friend Timius as a consolation. Timius had gradually edged his way to face Ciatus.

"You are a liar," Timius exclaimed. "You were the one that ran and left me alone with the creature, and I had an awful job catching up with you. Also, it was I who explained to the man on the litter what we had done. You were too scared to say anything. You were still trembling from shock, so don't tell lies!"

The girl nearest to Timius who appeared to be one of the twin daughters of the magistrate Bodegas, disdainfully looked at Timius and turned to Ciatus, saying,

"Who is this ragamuffin Ciatus? Is he the one who left you in the lurch when he ran away from the viper? He must have been because you can see from his clothes that in his haste he had torn them on thorn bushes and he had been so scared since that he hasn't even changed his clothes, or washed himself properly to come to our party."

Timius was so hurt and disgusted at what he had heard. He put his beaker down on the table and rushed out of the hall, fighting back the tears. He thought to himself, "if only Ciatus had told the truth he would not have been so insulted in this way". He vowed he would never go to that sort of party again. He would rather spend his evenings with the lizards in the gully. After all, although they were imaginary enemies of the state and barbarians, they were better friends than those precocious people at the party. He didn't go the same way home as the route Camilla had taken him. Instead he wanted to kill time until sunset when he could go home safely and pretend that he had enjoyed the evening. He made his way to the cemetery because it was the longest route home but, by the time he reached it, it was nearing sunset. He half-ran and half-walked to the spot where his mother had been buried some three days earlier. There was a mound of earth over her resting place on which were the few bunches of by now withered flowers, with a name-plaque which he could not read. He knew this was his mother's grave because he had attended the funeral and was nearly given a terrible spanking by his father for punching two men in the stomach for shovelling the soil over mother's remains. After walking around the mound a few times, Timius ran over to the wild rose hedge that served as a perimeter of the cemetery and picked a few roses, pricking his fingers on the thorns, then ran back and placed them on the mound. These looked rather good he thought, better than those other withered flowers. I will get some more and off he went.

"What are you doing there?" bellowed a voice.

Absolutely startled, Timius looked around to find the keeper walking towards him. "I had better not get into any more trouble," thought Timius and off he ran with the keeper in hot pursuit. There had often been vandals tampering with the statues and other artefacts on the graves. But the keeper could not believe that the rascals were as young as this fellow. Darkness had just fallen when Timius arrived home.

"Did not enjoy the party?" asked Mena.

"Oh, yes, I had a lovely time".

"Did you have plenty to eat and drink?"

"Yes, as much as I wanted, thank you Mena."

"Oh, well, then you will not be in need of any supper tonight."

"After you have washed, do not forget to say goodnight to your father."

"Very well, Mena, I will not forget," and with this Timius ran to where his father was seated.

"Goodnight father."

"Goodnight son. Oh Timius come over here for a moment, there is something I wish to talk to you about."

"Yes father."

"Did you go to the party this evening."

"Yes father."

"Good, I am sure you must have enjoyed it."

"Yes, I did, father." He hated to tell a lie but he did not want to blacken Ciatus' name.

"Mena tells me that you wanted to borrow a scroll from the public library, but she reminded me that you would not be able to, firstly because you are too young and secondly you cannot read!"

"Ah, but the scroll I wanted to borrow has pictures in it which I wanted to see so that I could try and draw them myself."

"Anyway, forget about that for the moment, I wanted to tell you that in two days time you will be coming away with me for a few days, and I will show you the place that had many buildings with rooms full of scrolls where you will also see many boys of your age learning to read them."

"Oh, smashing father."

"Will I need to bring any clothes and any other of my bits and pieces?"

"Oh, yes, son you will need them all. Don't leave any of your possessions behind."

"Very well father, I will go and start packing now," Timius said excitedly.

"There is no need to do that tonight; there will be plenty of time in the morning."

"Is this place far away father?"

"Oh, yes it is, several days journey in fact."

"Wonderful! I shall be able to see lots and lots of countryside and rivers."

"Yes, you will indeed son."

"Father, is it anywhere near the frontier, along the Danube or Rhine?"

"No, my son, not as far as that, goodnight now and go to bed."

"Goodnight father."

Timius hopped off excitedly, half-forgetting his hunger. The boy had not had anything to eat since midday. But if he had told Mena the truth he would have got into further trouble with the family.

CHAPTER II

Quid Romae Faciam?

JUVENIL

What am I t o do in Rome?

THE SUN HAD already risen when father and son left Velitrae the following morning. The sky was heavily clouded, but as the day progressed the clouds lifted giving way to a bright sunny afternoon. They alighted from the carriage and with the other four passengers awaited the horseman to hand them their baggage. The baggage had been stowed for the duration of the journey on a rack suspended beneath the floorboards of the carriage and between the front and rear axles. It was very much an open carriage sufficient only to accommodate six passengers and, in times of inclement weather, a makeshift canopy would be erected with the aid of some lengths of yew canes bowed over from one edge to the other. The carriage, drawn by two ponies and each sporting brightly coloured plumed harnessed to their foreheads, and a warning bell hung around the neck of each animal, was a common form of transport over long distances. It meant that there were stages on any long journey when the carriage would have to stop to either change horses or allow the animals to rest. In the cities there was a restriction on the number of common carriages that were allowed to ply the streets. The restriction was probably understandable because throughout the day many of the streets in the city would become congested with pedestrians. Rome was the commercial, political, cultural and business centre of the world. The population of the city was intensely cosmopolitan, citizenship being bestowed on all nationalities that inhabited the city as permanent residents and freedmen.

Sejanus Arbutus and his son Timius were to spend the night at a rest house in the courtyard of which they had alighted from the carriage. In the morning they would go through the city on foot till they reached Porta Collina. From there they would arrange seats on another carriage en route to Narnee. The rest house proprietor was a kindly old soul. He provided them with their evening meal and was able to rent them a room for the night. Both travellers were tired, although the journey had been quite uneventful. Timius was absolutely absorbed throughout the day with the sights he was able to see during the journey. Many fired the imagination of the little boy and especially when the carriage travelling along the Via Ostiensis enabled them to see the wall of the city and the Ostiensis Gate in the distance. The rest house was situated some fifty yards from the Getae Ostiensis.

They had finished their meal and Sejanus Arbutus instructed his son to quickly drink up the remains of his coarse wine that he was unused to drinking. This Timius did but, as they were about to leave the table, Timius, with his enquiring mind not satiated, looked at his father who was collecting their bags so that they could make their way to their room and asked,

"Father, why were those two men tied to those crosses of wood alongside the road we have just travelled along?"

"I have no idea son."

"What had they done?"

"I really do not know," replied Sejanus, "but we had better get you cleaned up for the night, so hurry along."

They entered their room, which was in darkness, and Senajus immediately walked out to the recess, helped himself to a taper and, protecting the lighted taper with the palm of his left hand, returned to their room and lighted the oil lamp. The room was very sparsely furnished. A mattress, made from Calico stuffed with coconut fibre lay in the centre of the floor on which was neatly folded some woollen blankets. Standing against the adjacent wall was a rudimentary stand on which was an earthenware basin and jug containing water. Sejanus poured some water into the basin for the boy and placed the basin on the floor because Timius couldn't reach it on the washstand and he promptly set about washing himself.

Meanwhile his father spread the blankets out over the mattress under which they would crawl for the night. Having completed his ablutions Timius sat himself on the bed with his feet crossed underneath him while his father took his turn with the fresh water. Timius was not satisfied with the answer his father had given him to his question about the two men on the crosses. So he thought he would try again.

"Father, does that sort of thing happen to everyone who gets old?"

"What on earth are you talking about?"

"Those two men who were hanging from those crosses, were they old men and therefore time for them to die?" Timius thought that there was perhaps some religious custom that dictated this sort of action.

"No, they were probably criminals and executed for their crimes and, if you continue to be a naughty boy and grow up to be a wicked or evil man, the same thing will happen to you if you are caught."

It was the practice in Rome that the supreme penalty for crimes committed against the state would be death by crucifixion. Many of the condemned ended their lives hung on a cross on the outskirts of the city wall and especially along the highways leading to the City gates. This was to exemplify to the public at large the severity of the penalty. Many who had committed such crimes were, either stoned to death by the crowds if they were dragged away from the protection of the court officers, or else were condemned to years of servitude in the galleys of the Roman military vessels or merchantmen. Those who had committed lesser crimes and, especially foreigners in the capital, were returned to domestic slavery from whence many had originated.

Timius covered himself with the blankets because he was now beginning to feel a tinge of the cold night that was setting in. Turning to his father he again asked, "Where are we going tomorrow, father? Are we going back home?"

"No, we will be walking through the city until we reach the Porta Collina, where we may have to spend another night before moving on."

"Oh! Goody," Timius thought aloud.

"Yes, and it's a long way there, so you had better get off to sleep quickly when I put out the lamp."

"Will we be going near the palace father?"

"No, why do you ask that?"

"I thought we might go and see the emperor."

"What nonsense," replied his father, and continued "he wouldn't want to see us and there is certainly no chance of either you or I ever seeing the emperor, let alone come face to face with him."

"Have you ever seen him father?"

"Of course not; why do you ask?"

"Because you might have been able to tell me what he was like. Perhaps you have heard what he is like."

"Well they say he is an old man that doesn't have much to do with anyone these days."

Thus ending the conversation, Sejanus Arbutus extinguished the lamp and lay alongside his son, bidding him goodnight. The room was in darkness, and through the open window Timius could see the stars mirrored against a midnight blue sky. Although he found his surroundings strange the bed on which he was lying was very little different from his bed at home.

They breakfasted on a wholesome meal before setting off on their trek through the City, having bid the rest house proprietor farewell and thanked him for his hospitality, which was certainly not free of charge. Father and son had passed through the Ostiensis Gate and were now making their way into the city: not just any city but the city that was the centre and mistress of the world, Rome.

It was here that the cut and thrust of power politics, which affected the civilised world, were to be played out hour by hour. Sejanus Arbutus strode along slightly ahead of the boy who was carrying the two bags and observing as much as he could of the city sights.

"Alms for the poor," wailed a beggar.

"Alms for the poor sire," wailed another.

This chorus seemed to greet all those who entered the city gate, and Timius wondered why his father had ignored them until it was explained to him that many of these beggars were not truly needy but merely professional beggars making a living in this manner. This was a common sight throughout the city, although it must be said that among these were many genuine cases, especially those with disabilities sustained through either disease, for which the medical profession could not extend a cure, or through disabilities as a result of war wounds. Their only means of obtaining a livelihood was reliance on the charity of the aristocracy and the middle classes, and there were many war disabled in the City, especially after years of civil war and subsequent campaigns in defence of the frontiers.

They rested for a while, after some two hours of trekking, at a stall vending fruit juices and other light refreshments. This was cited near beautifully laid out gardens. Formal gardens were a feature prominent in the cityscape of the capital and were tended zealously by the City Municipality. Trees and shrubs from Italy and imports fro other parts of the Empire were prominent decorations in the City gardens. The use of water also played an important role in these gardens, in the form of ornamental fountains that cascaded into picturesque ponds.

The next part of their City trek took them into the central area of the city, where Sejanus was able to point out to his son some of the lavish buildings and the triumphal arches that were representative of a gateway to the various forums. Bathhouses were on his list because the main idiosyncrasy of the Roman was his devotion to bathing, not only for cleanliness sake, but mainly for health reasons and the sheer delight the relaxation offered by such practice. Many of the houses they passed had been built with a view to coolness, boasting patios, pools and gardens. One would think that behind the locked doors of these beautiful villas there would be a natural addiction to intemperance to eating and drinking coupled to natural idleness. This was not so as the Roman was a naturally active-minded individual. The centre of the City was monumental in appearance because it had received much attention of embellishment from Sulla, Pompey and Julius Caesar. The discovery of new building materials opened up fresh possibilities for Roman architecture, and this was very much in evidence here in the heart of the capital. The discovery and use of concrete three hundred years earlier was modest, but it did pave the way for revolution in construction methods. It made possible great domes and vaults in Rome and other cities of the Empire. Architects began experimenting in masonry and had busily engaged themselves in seeing to it that the building of amphitheatres and auditoria made use of the new materials. This accepted method of building had its fruition about two hundred years ago. The city was also brightened by the use of attractive limestone from Tibur known as Travertine and white marble from Carraro. Coloured marble was imported in large quantities from abroad, especially Numidia. The poorer quarters of the City remained squalid. The Romans were inveterate protectors of the environment and many disused and baron areas within the precincts of the City were developed into beautiful gardens and attractive public parks.

Our travellers had now entered the Forum of Boarium, which boasted a variety of commodities. One could see from their different modes of dress that many had come from the far corners of the Empire, or were representatives of their merchant masters abroad. Silks, exotic perfumes, carpets from Armenia, fruits from Greece and Cyprus, leather goods from Egypt and extensive variety of oils at their various stages of distillation were on sale. The oils used by the populace for lighting purposes and right through a range of other purposes to medicines. Dotted among these stalls, where the bargaining and haggling over prices were a common feature, were the market magicians plying their trade in providing sideshows for the shoppers. Sejanus Arbutus suddenly caught the eye of an army veteran with whom he had served during the Illyricum campaign and on doing so strode up to this friend and greeted him. While the two men were exchanging pleasantries and reminiscing on old times, Timium noticed, quite nearby, rather a jovial exchange of views taking place between an eastern merchant and two off duty soldiers. They must have been soldiers because of their manner and bearing. The salesman had handed one of the soldiers a piece of foodstuff, which the soldier accepted and promptly put in his mouth. Since the boy felt a tinge of hunger he, quite unwittingly, found himself attracted to the scene and heard some of the argument.

"That was very good wasn't it, sir," said the salesman.

"No, I didn't think so."

"Ah, you Romans are all alike, very hard to please, this dhol dhol only arrived this morning at Ostia, and it had come over from Alexandria on a fast galley by my special orders," stated the salesman, and turning to the other soldier, he continued, "what about you sir? You are a very clever man, I am sure, and you must have very good taste; why don't you try some?"

The second soldier accepted a piece of the dhol dhol for tasting and after he had eaten it, with a wry smile on his face, said jokingly to the salesman, "that wasn't enough for me to smell, never mind taste. Give me another piece to taste."

The salesman reluctantly did so, adding, "If you have too many tastes of the dhol dhol you will not want to buy any, because this is the trick all you Roman soldiers play on me. You fellows always want to taste and keep on tasting my dhol dhol until you have had your fill then you won't buy any; and I can never make any profit from you stingy fellows."

Feeling a little sorry for the salesman, the soldiers each bought a piece of the sweetmeat for about two dinarii, tossing the coins into the man's money basket. One of the soldiers spotted Timius from the corner of his eye. The boy was sucking his thumb while he watched them chew on the sweetmeat. One of the soldiers offered him a small piece. Timius reluctantly put his hand out and accepted, thanked them and ran back to his father who reprimanded him for accepting food from strangers, but he thought that on this occasion he would let the incident pass. He handed the boy his handkerchief to wipe the grease away from his mouth, and they continued their wander through the Forum. Many men and women, some very elaborately dressed, just seemed to be idling away their time in the Forum and a stranger to the City would often wonder how such a race of people could be masters of the world. Some had their slaves accompanying them to tend to their needs and carry any merchandise that might be purchased. The stranger could not overlook the fact that there was tremendous affluence in the City. Their day would be spent at public libraries or baths, time wasting in the forum, attending public orations in the temple squares, and public shows appeared to be the chief recreation for both rich and poor alike. These shows, it is true, grew yearly more brutal and bloody in their extravagance. Promiscuity was prevalent because the religions of the City and Empire were either formal or political, and rarely did they extol the virtues of morality. Materialism and immorality had killed the very morals of their religions and, consequently, Greek philosophy filled the gap that was left by the absence of religious feeling. This was the impression that any stranger from an outlying district coming to Rome, or to any of the other major cities, would get, but underlying all these outward signs of affluence, apathy and complacency was a strong spirit, if the stranger wished to look deeper into this race of people, of patriotism and a high degree of responsibility. The Roman or full citizen of the Empire from whatever corner of the World he might have his origins, had cultivated a sense of responsibility for the well being of their civilization and their Empire. It was no mean race of people that were able to take their form of civilization and implant it on the foreign nations that were now under their control. In so doing they refrained wherever it was possible to impose it on their foreign subjects. Instead the introduction was subtle in its entirety in as much as they adopted and inculcated the culture, religion and custom of the foreign nations and fused it in with their own. Many of their subject nations were autonomous although this autonomy was subject to the pleasure and approval of the Pontifax Maximus Caesar Augustus. While there were many objections to Roman rule, which often resulted in uprisings and local wars against the security forces of the Empire, nevertheless these nations that were now within the protective ambit of the Empire owed their continued prosperity and stability to the unified beliefs and projects of Rome, needless to say, under the very real protection of the Roman Legions and their local auxiliary forces.

Sejanus and son were making their way towards the exit area of the Forum, but were suddenly attracted to a small group of people who appeared to be intensely interested in a public exhibition or performance of one sort or another. They could not tell immediately what this group of people found so interesting but they could hear, above the whispers and quiet mumblings of the group, the sound of what seemed to be a shepherd's pipe played in a wailing manner. They edged their way into this group and young Timius was quite fascinated with the display that had aroused the interest of the others. Seated cross legged on the ground was an eastern gentleman, wearing a white turban and a loose fitting loin cloth with a necklace of many coloured beads around his neck, playing rather an unusual type of instrument. This instrument had the appearance of the conventional shepherd's pipe with the exception of a round-ish bulge on its audible end, which had a tendency to make its tone sound rather mellower than its counterpart. He gave the impression that he was playing while in a trance, but obviously the object of his tuneful rendition necessitated the full use of his mental faculties. Just rising up out of an open shallow basket, placed on the floor in front of him, was the head of a snake, and, as this reptile raised itself further into the air, its head gradually bloomed a hood with a distinctive rounded **V** that could now be clearly seen in the skin which covered the hood and it gave one the impression that it was an inverted omega. The snake was a cobra, one of the deadliest snakes and a common inhabitant of the Indian subcontinent. As it emerged out of the basket to a height of some three feet, it started swaying to and fro and side to side in rhythm with the tune being played. The snake charmers from the East were a rare but interesting one man spectacle that one could often see in the City in places where large groups of people assembled for past time activities. Timius was absolutely enthralled with the sight of what was going on before his eyes, and very soon the audience tossed the odd coin into the basket lid, which was set slightly apart from the basket. The young boy's imagination ran riot and what a good idea he now had. Sejanus clutched the boy's hand, tossed his donation into the lid of the basket, and off they strolled.

They were now out of the Forum and on one of the central streets of the City.

"Will you buy me a pipe, father?"

"Come on, now, you're not going to grow up to be a snake charmer," came the reply from his father. "That will be too tricky a job for you."

"I do not want to become a snake charmer. I just want a musical pipe."

"Oh, very well, if we see any on the stalls that we pass on our way I will buy you one," replied Timius' father, hoping that the boy would soon forget the idea.

They were now passing, to the right of them, a small rectangle beautifully adorned with a low marble wall with four statues of early Roman noblemen in each corner. Sejanus recognised the one nearest to him as being that of Pompey, but he could not recognise who the others were. Laid within the marble wall was a lush green lawn through which grew nothing else but an olive tree, a fig tree and a vine. The vine was suspended on an ornamental bronze trellis. These three trees, suitably pruned, were symbolic and were treated with natural respect by all Romans. The object of this display was to remind the Roman constantly of his early country beginnings, and he was never to lose sight of this.

Here in Rome we have a profusion of sculpture. The style has been adopted from the Greeks, but, unlike Greek work which is chiefly bland and rather expressionless, the Roman sculptors advanced much further giving it expression and lifelike shapes and sizes. Military and religious personnel found themselves reproduced and very often in God like attitudes which they may not have commissioned. The personages did not approve but acquiesced in the hope that their dedication to public service or exploits in the cause of Republican ideals was passed on to posterity. Roman sculpture and art was full of vitality; movement was one of the finer points of their artistic work, whether in sculpture, metal work, or their artistic inclinations reproduced in mosaic, an art in which they excelled.

"Don't forget you promised to buy me a musical pipe father," said Timius anxiously as he noticed the stalls were fewer as they walked through the City.

"Oh, I had forgotten, but we will get one as soon as we see some."

Timius' idea was that if he could be the proud possessor of such a musical instrument, he would practise a tune day and night until he was able to master the instrument as well as the snake charmer. He would then be able to take the flute with him to the gully, or the nearby gorges back home in Velitrae and attempt to charm some of the vipers that he had often seen when on his campaigns against his imaginary barbarians. He might even be able to acquire a basket and then keep one as a pet, but the first step was now to persist and persuade his father to buy him a pipe.

"Ah, there are some, father, over there on that stall," cried Timius taking his father's hand and pulling him in the direction of the stall, delighted that he was now going to be the proud possessor of a musical pipe.

"I suppose now I shall be pestered all the way to our destination with the noise of that pipe," thought Sejanus, but never mind, he wanted the child to be happy.

What seemed to be the last stall in the stretch of the road was given a wide berth deliberately by Sejanus because the merchant was selling a good number of scrolls of the latest poetry and oratory that was popular in the City. The end of each scroll was affixed to pieces of wood in the shape of narrow dumbbells, and they were arranged on the stall in order of merit dependent on the popularity of the orator or post. The purpose of giving this stall a wide berth was because Sejanus felt, in view of what he had heard from his daughter Mena, back home in Velitrae, that young Timius had expressed a desire to borrow a scroll from the local library, if he were to see the drawings and pictures on the stall it might prompt him to want one now if he saw the selection of scrolls. Sejanus felt that not only could he ill afford to buy one for the boy because of his recent expenses, but where he was taking him there would be ample opportunity to fulfil his desires.

The Romans were inveterate orators and took an absolute delight in debates of various descriptions, no matter where it was. They were extremely able and just administrators, and this founded its zenith from the many days, weeks and indeed months of constant debate on policies suitable for their administrative zeal. Almost every street corner, squares and public parks were suitable places for debate and argument on current policies and events, with the culminating force of the debates in the Senate. Public opinion, thus moulded, not only affected the tenor of the senatorial debates but assisted in the decision making that would provide an acceptable public solution to an event or problem of the day with final endorsement from the Emperor. Intended edicts of the Emperor were invariably communicated through Senate and to the populace before final intelligent debate in the Senate and final ratification. In this way the Roman felt that he was very much a part of the ensuing government policy. Of course, there were many who would argue for the sake of argument, and there were many orators who would expound their views on any given subject in flowery terms and for the sake of oratory. But, nevertheless, each opinion, each argument played its part towards final, if sometimes, reluctant acceptance of policy. Indeed one would get the impression that Caesar's edicts were autocratic, and many were. However, edicts were issued in an emergency in order to meet some urgent situation, but topics of a similar nature that had publicly been debated previously would be acceptable to a large measure by the Roman populace.

Orations found their way into the literary works of the day, both in literature and in poetry. Perhaps no notice would be taken of these published works, but they did provide literary media. The well known poets of the past and present day, men like Cicero, Horace, Pliny and Ovid, propounded their theories and views through their literary works. The Roman was not a realistic person, but rhetorical; and solutions, especially those concerning the provinces, were hardly ever dealt with pragmatically to begin with. They always felt that the right solution would emerge after rhetoric and debate, and this lack of pragmatism was evident when quick solutions could have been found in many instances whereas a period of unrest and indeed bloodshed was the result of invariably military solutions. The Roman was not a bloodthirsty individual; yes, they may have attended bloody sports in the Arena, but under this veneer of bloodthirstiness, if they were able to solve a problem through sensible debate and its resultant policy, they would preferably choose this course. But there were so many events and situations where this high ideal was never possible and therefore never given a chance.

Father and son now entered one of the main streets on the northeast part old the City, lined with Acacia trees, and Timius, in between practising the odd note on his musical pipe and also trying to keep up with his father, observed all the goings on around him. There were aristocratic ladies and gentlemen being carried about in litters; their slaves immaculately dressed for the occasion. The senator, or civil servant, was making his way to attend to government business on the Palatine Hill. He saw a troop of smartly dressed soldiers who were obviously marching to take up their posts as guards in the many civic and government buildings, dotted in and around the Capitol; there was a cart pulled by six strong horses conveying marble and granite slabs to the stone masons who would shape them, as required, for the task in hand. Greetings were exchanged between many of the passers by but these greetings were rather more exaggerated from those, like the dozens of fortune-tellers, who had some service to sell. Timius noticed a group of four priests dressed in flowing white robes and matching hoods, reverently on their way to the temple; today was probably a sacrificial day. The two main religions of Rome were those of Isis and Dionysis and these religions embraced the rites and devotions to many of the imported gods of Greece, Etrusca, as well as the Roman's own, such as Mithras and Diana. Sacrifices of animals, birds and reptiles, very often in large quantities, were offered to these deities in the hope that the fortunes of the nobility or the people could be favourably altered. It is interesting to note that the institution of the vestal virgins, which found its inception in early Republican times, was still extant. The sanctity of the vestal virgins was most zealously guarded. Aside from their religious functions, these women, who at a very early age took the vow of chastity, were entrusted, among other things, with the responsibility of guarding the secrets of the State and of individuals, private wills of the nobility and secret state documents. Documents that would be of a controversial nature were placed in their hands for safekeeping, and without such an institution the States would have been reduced to perpetual civil war. The Patrician families were the most devout guardians of this institution, whereas under the present circumstances the Plebians would not find much use for it.

The business quarter of Rome was a hive of industry. This is where the commercial and banking interest of the Empire had its fortress. Roman millionaires studied commercial values rather than artistic qualities. This was the heart of the Empire's banking system. Immense quantities of merchandise and loot had crossed the Adriatic and Rome was the home of the connoisseur and the collector. Rome was a consuming society, and very little was ever manufactured there. There was no industry of any consequence, as the Roman could always rely on the imports from the Empire and commonwealth. Therefore, the commercial interests of the Empire must lie here in the City, and it was from these houses of commerce that the commercial undertakings blossomed abroad.

Philosophy abounded in the City but was rarely adhered to. The philosophy of the early Greeks was augmented here, and many of the well-known philosophies from North Africa, the East, and some from Druid Britain assisted in the augmentation of the Greek philosophy, and it was this augmented philosophy that filled the gap of morality that was absent in the religions of the day.

There were several intellectuals hurrying along the road with expressions of seriousness on their faces as though arguments in favour of, or against, the criminal and civil cases that they were to deal with today had burdened their consciences all night long. The greatest intellectual achievement of the Roman people was in the domain of law. They were endowed with a sense of equity that was devoid of all sentiment. They had an instinct for order and justice, with as its base, the twelve tablets that were treated like the two tablets of Moses. The basic statues of the twelve tablets were built on and developed with an invaluable abundance of case law. The civil law of Rome was handed down from praetor to praetor, and the magistracies enacted this case law that was to form the foundations of jurisprudence for the whole of Europe well into the yet unforeseen future. The civilized world owed the jurisdiction of every state to the law makers of Rome.

The weary trekkers finally arrived at Porta Collina at the northeast wall of the City. The birds above their heads were flying home to roost as night was falling fast, while the lamplighters were busily engaged in lighting the oil torches along the walls that led outwards from Porta Collina. Sejanus was anxious about finding a room for the night. Mucas, an old army colleague who had now joined the ranks of the veterans, had assured Sejanus that should he ever be in the vicinity of Porta Collina he would be welcome to sojourn at Mucas' home. He had only visited him there once.

"Timius, I think you had better stop making that noise on that pipe of yours you will have plenty of time in the morning to play. So hand it to me and I will put it away in the bag."

"Very well father," Timius replied, and went on to ask whether Mucas kept any snakes in his house; because if he had, Timius would like to practice his pipe on the snakes early the following morning.

"Don't be silly, why would Uncle Mucas want to keep snakes? He has better things to do," retorted Sejanus, rather aggravated by the boy's question.

The veranda of Mucas' house was lit with a torch hung at an angle from the pillar nearest the entrance. Just in line with the front doorstep was a small mosaic obviously laid by Mucas himself from chippings of coloured marble with the word *'HAVE'* inlaid with darker chips meaning *'welcome'*. They knocked on the door and were greeted by a delicate lady in her late fifties.

CHAPTER III

Omnes Immemorem Benefici Oderunt.

CICERO

All hates one who's forgetful of kindness.

THE TOWN OF Narnee lies at the foothills of the appenines, the range of mountains that runs from north to south of the Italian peninsula and geographically forms the backbone of Italy. It is not a town of much importance but is situated at the meeting point of two important and busy highways. The road from Narnee leading northeast spans the Appenines to become the famous *via Flaminia*, reaching one of the important Adriatic sea ports of Fanum Fortunae, and thence the road would travel both north and south along the peninsula coastline serving as an arterial roadway to all coasts along the eastern shore of Italy. To the north, it would reach out to and beyond the important trading port of Ravenna. This northern route also was the gateway to the *via Aemilia*, which was the main service route to Transalpine Gaul and the northwest corner of the peninsula. The other highway that was to find its starting point at Narnee fed the many towns and villages that abounded on the slopes of the central part of the Appenine chain.

Narnee was used as a recuperation point for the legions on their return from the provinces after either disembarkation at the many Adriatic ports from foreign service or from their long marches from the northern provinces which led them either through the terrain of Transalpine, or Cisalpine, Gaul. Recuperation from these long marches was necessary for the soldiers and auxiliaries as it provided them with the respite to enable them to not only refresh themselves but, see to it that their equipment and uniforms were properly in order before their triumphal march on the last leg of their two-day journey to Rome. The legions, of course, were able to make final preparations to their dress and equipment before entering the city to receive honours and gratuitous awards for gallant service under acute hardship for the sake of Rome and their first Consul. Sacrifices would then be offered by the Tribune of the Cohorts on behalf of the men under their command in the temples of Mars and Jupiter: Mars, because of homage and sacrifice to the God, was appropriate from successful fighting men, and equally appropriate to the God Jupiter for providing them with the pleasure of absolute relief after their ordeals on the battlefields.

The town was therefore a lucrative situation for the small merchants. These merchants earned a profitable living, albeit of some infrequency, when the legions took their respite here in Narnee. The profuse sale of baubles, trinkets, imitation jewellery, and, for the thrifty soldier, the genuine gold and silver jewellery was a common practice here on these occasions. There was a good selection of bathhouses in the town that made full use of the refreshing waters that flowed down from the Appenines in an abundance of streams and rivulets. Gambling dens and wine houses were also a common feature and were never short of patronage from the soldiers when the Legion called a halt at Narnee. Military discipline, as stern as it was, was relaxed on these occasions. Prostitution was rife and totally spurned by the local inhabitants because many of the women would make their way to the towns, such as Narnee, which were on the main military routes to the capital, that served as sites for recuperation for the Legions, and the vast majority would be those who had found their way from the City itself.

Their obvious aim was to relieve the soldier of his salary and other items of loot which he might have accumulated and acquired while in foreign lands. The local population of Narnee were people who were quite content to carry on their daily work in the numerous woodwork shops that were dotted about the town. Being in close proximity to the forests that lay on the slopes of the Appenines, the carving and manufacture of household furniture was the main industry of this region, and many fine wooden carvings that were to be found in the capital originated both here in Narnia and other towns similarly situated along Appenine foothills.

Timius and his father had not planned to arrive at Narnee at such a time when the ninth Legion were in encampment after their long and arduous campaign under Tiberius and lately General Germanicus, in Germania. The Legion had lost nearly five hundred men fatally at the hands of the German tribes, while in their awesome duty of defending the Rhine frontier. But this situation was inevitable when it was firmly established by Augustus Caesar that the frontiers would be fixed and no further conquests into the heartlands of the barbarian territories, German and others, would be permitted under his policy of consolidation.

Timius had thoroughly enjoyed the two-day journey by open carriage from the Porta Collina in Rome to Narnee. His father had informed him that the journey was not yet over, and they would now have to hire a horse to take them to a place on the Appenine slopes, where his father had promised him he would see and learn wonderful things. Timius had never experienced anything so exciting as the past few days. He felt so proud and fulfilled that he had seem so much countryside and, above all, the city of Rome. To add to his fulfilment he was the proud possessor of a musical pipe, even though it was only a length of hollow bamboo cane with a series of air holes carved out to give variations in the sound that it would produce, when played properly.

He had never been given anything like this previously. Indeed, apart from the clothes he wore and the odd pair of cheap sandals, his food for sustenance and a bed to sleep on, he could not remember ever being given anything in the past by either his family or friends that he could treasure and call his own. He always had to improvise and use discarded articles like broken pots, well-worn basketry, and other bits and pieces to play with in his world of fantasy. A thought just struck him and, searching deep into the pocket of his tunic with his right hand, he was breathlessly relieved to find, wrapped in a small soiled piece of papyrus, the gold coin the distinguished old man, whom he had met and spoken to, needless to say in fear, on that dusty track back home in Velitrae, had given him. This is something he would never give away, and after inspecting it a while he quickly put it back into the pocket of his tunic, so that his father wouldn't see it and perhaps confiscate it, as his sister, Mena, nearly did, or even take it from him for either safe keeping or in payment for meals or the hire of a horse, which they would need for the rest of their journey. After all he thought, this might be a symbol of good fortune, or perhaps be a bad omen. That old man might have even been Jove, who had come to life for a short while as this was a possibility because all the other gods came to life from time to time, or so he was told, but this still left him very sceptical.

After alighting from the carriage that had brought them from Rome, they had walked through the town of Narnee in search of a livery stable from where Sejanus could hire a horse. But they had not come across any where the proprietor was in a position to oblige them. The town was now full of soldiers mingling with the inhabitants and frequenting the many stalls, rest houses, wine houses and so on. Some of the soldiers hired horses for the pleasure of a ride out into the surrounding countryside, and therefore it was not a suitable moment for their arrival at Narnee. Without the presence of the Ninth Legion, at any other time, it would be quite easy to obtain a horse on hire. Sejanus had left the boy and had asked him to remain where he was and take charge of the baggage while he made further enquiries nearby. Timius had made himself comfortable alongside the wall of a local pottery where his father had left him. He looked up from having a blow on his pipe to see his father striding towards him with a look of disappointment on his face.

"Come on, son, we had better try elsewhere, as I don't seem to be having much luck around here."

Clutching the bags, Sejanus Arbutus led his son down one of the side streets of the town, and, as they went along he made enquiries with the local passers by, but they only shook their heads in their inability to advise him. The road led out onto the courtyard of what seemed to be a luxurious villa, and perhaps one of the very few in the town. It was surrounded with a low-lying wall, marble in appearance, with the odd bust of some public figure with surmounting balustrades evenly spaced to give it an appearance of some importance. To the left of the villa was some common ground on which the grass was beautifully kept and trimmed. It was the job of all the local barbers to spend the first hour of their morning attending the lawn prior to making use of their keenly sharpened razors. Here and there, dotted in the lawn, sprang trees proudly displaying their leaves in the mid-morning sunshine. There was a gentle breeze rustling the leaves, which must have had a cooling effect on the travellers who were encamped in gaily-coloured tents beneath their branches. These people were of course the close relatives of the senior officers and other military officials who often accompanied the legion on its tour of duty in the field. Since the legions were stationed for very long periods away from their Italian cantonments it was normal practice of the hierarchy to accompany their men on such excursions. The lower ranks were unable to practice this discriminatory luxury. Not only did the families travel with the officials, but they also enjoyed the luxury of having their slaves and freedmen, who would attend to their every need, accompany them.

The villa itself was a facility for meals, baths, and wine saloons, patronized mainly by the hierarchy of the legion. The common soldiers would have to make use of the more meagre facilities that the town had to offer. Father and son approached the villa, and Sejanus looked about him wondering which direction he should now take in search of a place from whence he could hire a horse. A man, dressed in a rust-coloured, knee length toga with a jute rope tied round his waist in the form of a belt, entered the gateway of the villa and was about to make his way up the steps and into the front entrance when he was spotted by Sejanus.

"Excuse me, can you help me, please?" enquired Sejanus.

Stopping rather abruptly and turning round, the man immediately approached Sejanus obediently, obviously sensing that the man who had spoken to him was a militaire. Sejanus realized from the man's expression and obedience that he was either a slave or a freedman in the pay of the proprietor of the villa.

"Are you very familiar with this town?"

"Yes, sir, I know it quite well."

"Perhaps you could help me then."

"By all means, sire."

"I am trying to find a stable from which I could hire a horse for the day."

"Well, sir, many soldiers like yourself would probably have had the same idea in mind and perhaps beaten you to it, because they always get to the stables early to give them maximum time before noon to indulge in the pleasure of riding; and since there is only a small cavalry troupe with this legion, most of the others being foot soldiers, your chances, therefore, of getting one are not very good. However, if you would like to go right through the town until you come to its eastern edge there is a stable owned by a man who calls himself Mercator, who is also a wealthy Jewish merchant, and I am almost sure that he will be able to help you."

"How long would it take me to walk there?" enquired Sejanus.

"Oh, perhaps a good half of the hour, sire."

"Perhaps you would give me directions."

"Certainly." and crouching down, the man, with his index finger, started drawing directions in the fine sand edging the street.

"Thank you very much," said Sejanus.

The man, acknowledging him, continued up the steps to the Villa.

Meanwhile Timius had wandered some yards away from the father and was watching something going on in front of him, near one of the larger tents that were pitched on the lawn. Four men carrying a litter with what looked like white sailcloth to shield the occupant from the rays of the sun laid it to rest. Out of the litter emerged a stocky young man with a prominent limp as he approached the tent. The young man hesitantly stopped in front of it, and Timius noticed that he also twitched his head every so often. Almost as though they were playing hide and seek, a young curly headed boy ran out of the tent and as he did so began to pull faces at him. The young man tried to speak to the curly headed boy, but Timius could see that he was having a devil of a job trying to say something. He then heard the young man say

"H-h-h-hello, G-G-G-Gius, h-h-how are you? H-h-how, is your m-m-m-mother?"

"Oh, stop stammering, Uncle, and speak properly," retorted the boy, and again he started poking fun at him by pulling faces and making various insulting gesticulations at the young man. He then immediately, and what seemed to be playfully, chased him round the tent with his limping gait and twitching head.

"Come here, Timius," called Sejanus.

"Father, I have just seen a funny man over there, and he is still playing around."

"What's funny about him?" queried his father.

"Well, he cannot walk properly and speaks in a funny way and cannot keep his head still," replied Timius, who was quite amused at what he had seen.

Sejanus looked across and was able to see for himself the frolicking that was going on between the crippled young man and the curly headed young boy. Turning on his son he said to him, rather firmly,

"Now Timius, you must never make fun of people who have an affliction like that poor man over there. It is very wrong to amuse yourself at other unfortunate people's expense, as you will realize, my boy, that some of these people are extremely kind and gentle and very often cleverer than you; even so, you must never, never, do it."

"All right, father, I will never do it again."

Sejanus was sincere in his advice to his son, because during his many travels in his service with the legion he had come across scores of such people who were similarly afflicted through no fault of their own, and very often their afflictions were caused by their dedicated service to their Emperor and he felt there were far too many people in this world who were quick to mock the misfortunes of others, never having experienced any of the hardships of life themselves. He always felt that those who were quick to mock, humiliate and criticize others were exceptionally narrow in their attitudes to life and very often had led lives of a parochial nature. If they themselves had been faced with the adversities of life as he had, on many an occasion, both in the battlefield and in the conditions required of a Roman soldier, they would be the first to weaken and perish with the least adversity.

Having given Timius this sound advice, trusting the boy understood, as he was sure he had, he said to him that it would be rather better if Timius could stay here beside the wall of this villa while he made his way to Marcator's stables. He thought it would be advisable, otherwise it would mean walking the boy all the way through the town carrying the heavy bags, whereas this way free of any baggage he would walk there much more quickly, alone, hire a horse and come back for Timius and the luggage. Sejanus, placing his hand under Timius' armpits, picked Timius up and sat the boy on the low wall and placed the bags beside him.

"Now, I will not be long. Don't go anywhere! You will get lost. Just sit here quietly and I will be back, as quickly as possible, with a horse to take us on our way. If you get hungry while I'm gone here is an orange to eat," and taking one out of his pouch he gave it to the boy and strode off.

Timius looked around him, and he could still see the curly headed boy and the young man fooling around. The young boy seemed to have taken something from the young man, who was desperately trying to retrieve it, stuttering, twitching and limping. Timius placed his pipe to his lips and started blowing it, making an awful noise with the flat notes, and since there was nobody around to disturb him he was blowing it rather loudly, moving the pipe from side to side as he did so as though he was charming a thousand and one cobras. He stopped and looked up and standing before him was the curly headed boy who was screwing a gaily-coloured handkerchief or neck scarf in his hand as though it was his intention to tear it apart.

"Where did you get that horrible noisy instrument from?"

"My father bought it for me."

"Where is your father?" enquired the curly headed boy cheekily.

"He had gone to try and hire a horse", replied Timius, "and is coming back to collect me soon."

"What is your name?"

"Timius Arbutus."

"What a funny name you have."

"What's yours then?" queried Timius.

"Gaius, but the officers and the soldiers call me Caligula."

"What does that mean?"

"Oh you must be as stupid and as hollow as that pipe you have been playing if you do not know what that means. It means *Little Boots*."

This was the title given to Gaius Caesar by the troops during their campaign in Germany because the boy was looked on as a mascot to the legion, and they seemed to get a delight in dressing him in specially tailored soldier's uniform and suitably hammered helmet with boots having rather pronounced spurs. Seated on horseback and dressed in this fashion, he was spoiled and cheered on in whatever he wanted to do by the officers of the Ninth Legion and many of the senior soldiers. He was the son of Germanicus and the great-grandson of Caesar Augustus. Looking at Timius rather disdainfully, he succeeded in tearing the handkerchief, or scarf, whatever it was, in half. Hearing the limping footsteps of his uncle, the cheeky lad ran off into the villa. The young man saw Timius sitting alone on the low wall and, breathing rather heavily, approached him and sat down beside him to recapture his breath.

Timius placed his pipe down beside him and gave a sidelong look at the stranger. The stranger's head continued to twitch every so often and, turning to Timius, asked,

"H-h-h-hello, h-h-how are you, young man?"

"I'm all right," Timius replied shyly.

"A-a-are you on your own, or are you w-w-w-waiting for your friends?"

"No, I am waiting for my father who has gone to the stable to try and hire a horse, so that we can carry on with our journey."

"W-w-where are you going to?" the stranger enquired

"I don't know; my father didn't tell me the name of the place. He only told me it was a nice place where I would be able to see lots of scrolls with drawings in them," replied Timius.

"A-a-are you interested in books and reading?"

"Yes, but I cannot read. I like looking at drawings."

"W-w-w-well, you must learn to read quickly, because you will then be able to read about lots of interesting things. W-w-w-what is your name?" the stranger stammered, his head still twitching.

"Timius, Timius Arbutus, w-what—Timius just stopped himself in time because he was about to mimic the stammer and stutter of the stranger—what is your name?"

"Cl-Cl-Claudius, but my friends and family call me Clau'Clau'. C-c-c-can I call you Timmy?"

"Yes, of course you can," replied Timius, smiling shyly.

There conversation continued for several minutes during which time Claudius found himself interested in why the boy was here in a strange town and his father's occupation, and he expressed his view that such an occupation was considered a noble one. Timius discovered that Claudius had come all the way from Rome to meet his sister and nephew and to greet them on their return from Germania. When Timius enquired whether Claudius was connected with the Legion, Claudius was rather amused and replied that a 'useless cripple like himself would never be tolerated within the gates of an encampment let alone be a serving member of a Legion'. He also found out that Claudius' presence was only tolerated here where the Legion had encamped in a dispersed manner for recuperation purposes, because he was related to General Germanicus. Perhaps he did not tell Timius this because it would have made him feel a little humiliated knowing that his brother was the most respected and best loved general in the whole of the Roman army, whereas he was only an unwanted, useless, idiotic, cripple.

However, during their conversation, despite the difference in age between the two conversationalists, there had grown up a deep understanding between them, even though it was only some brief moments ago that they had met for the first time. Timius almost immediately felt that this man, sitting beside him, whom on his father's stern advice he had not mimicked and indeed was glad that he had not done so, was a sincere person and one in whom he felt if there wasn't this age difference would be a friend to him, unlike Ciatus, whom he had discovered was a shallow friend. On the other hand Claudius felt the same way about this young boy because he realized from the outset something rather strange which he never experienced before. In the past when Claudius had been introduced to anyone, no matter whom, he had made them feel so embarrassed with his stuttering and twitching that they either could not be bothered to enter into conversation with him or would go away slyly laughing and giggling; or they would attempt to mimic him. But this was the first time that he had ever met anyone who had not done this, and he expressed his feelings by saying that Timius would grow up to be a man of fine character and understanding—and he meant it; but he didn't really think the boy was old enough to appreciate his sincere feelings. He also invited Timius to come along and pay him a visit provided of course his father would bring him, knowing that the boy couldn't do this on his own, the next time they were in Rome.

"But where would I find you, and where do you live in Rome?" asked Timius.

"W-w-well, a-a-ask your father to make enquiries in any of the offices situated on the P-Palatine H-Hill and ask to speak to C-C-Claudius. If you insist, they will tell you. Y-y-you can both have supper with me and I will order the best wines, and we can talk for hours."

"That would be marvellous," said Timius, "I would love to come, but I will not drink a lot of wine because it makes me become sleepy, and I will not be able to talk then."

"N-n-n-never mind, we'll give you a short ration. I must go now, because I think that is your father coming along in the distance on a horse."

Timius had by now peeled his orange and, breaking it in half, offered one half to Claudius.

"N-n-no thank you T-T-Timmy; you eat it to help you grow strong."

"Oh, go on, have a piece of the orange, I want you to have half," insisted Timius.

Not wanting to disappoint the boy, Claudius accepted the piece of orange, shook hands with Timmy and limped off, twitching his head while he sucked his portion of the orange, juice running down his chin and onto his tunic. Timius watched Claudius limp his way up the steps, half tripping as he did so, and, before entering the doors to the villa, he turned and gave Timius a cheery wave and disappeared.

Sejanus Arbutus drew the horse to a halt and dismounted. He looked as though he had been under some tension.

"Are you all right, son?"

"Yes, father, I am fine."

"I had a devil of a job trying to hire this horse, and the old Jew, Mercator, has overcharged me, I think, for the hire of this wretched animal."

"Don't speak about the horse like that, father," retorted Timius. "It is not his fault if his owner has robbed you."

"You're quite right, son, forgive me for having vent my feelings on the horse."

Securing the bags with leather straps to the hind haunches of the horse, he lifted Timius onto the saddles and mounted behind him, tugging at the reins and turning the horse around. They trotted down the street and out of the town of Narnee. They were now making their way through a well-worn track up through the foothills of the appenines, passing only the odd horse and cart on their way up. They acknowledged the compliments of the drivers as they progressed. They now arrived at a spot where there was rather more activity and which occupied one of the many glades. Well-tended shrubs and a grassy lawn surrounded a small temple, and Sejanus drew the horse up to a halt, dismounted and hitched it to a rail outside the temple. This was another one of those minor temples that abounded in the countryside throughout Italy, and this particular one was dedicated to Juno. Sejanus lifted his son off the horse and looking rather red-eyed asked the boy to keep an eye on their belongings, so that he could go and pay his respects to Juno.

Timius wondered why his father looked so sad. Perhaps he was not enjoying the trip, or perhaps he was missing some of his comrades back in the army. It hadn't occurred to Timius that he was probably still feeling very deeply the loss of his wife. But anyway Timius thought he would try to cheer up his father by stroking the horse gently on his neck which he could only just reach so that the animal would give them a smoother ride. Sejanus entered the portals of the Temple, picked up a small piece of incense, placed it in a dish, lighted it with a taper from a three-wick oil lamp that was suspended with bronze chains from the ceiling, and when the incense began to smoke, he entered the temple to perform his obeisance. The temple was not as elaborately decorated, or as magnificent as those to be found in the cities, but these temples provided a place of worship for travellers in the area because there were few settlements in this district. The statue of Juno had been sculptured from Carraro marble whereas the stonework of the building had obviously been hewn out of rocks from the nearby quarry. There were no elaborate carvings in the temple, nor was the stonework unique in any way. Simplicity seemed to have been the overriding factor here because the place of worship served the purpose of individual worship only. Sejanus had not invited Timius to join him in the temple because it was customary for young boys to only enter a temple when they reached the age of twelve. However, had anybody found out that Timius had on one occasion in the recent past entered the temple of Apollo at Velitrae to see if the marble statue of the God Apollo really moved he would have found himself in serious trouble and may have had to pay penance for the rest of his life but his clandestine excursion went without repercussions. When Sejanus emerged from the temple he found the boy gently stroking the horse, reaching for the lower part of its neck on tiptoe. They remounted and continued their journey.

Timius excitedly pointed to a group of stone white buildings he could see through the trees lying further up on the hill.

"Oh, look at that place father? I wonder what goes on there."

"That's the place we are going to, son. That's Larcia, and what you can see through the trees is the collegiate, and that is where you will be staying the night."

"Is that the place where they have plenty of reading material and drawings?"

"That's right, son," and you will have plenty of opportunity to browse through all of it when we get there. You must try and remember everything you read and see and everything that the college elders might tell you."

"Oh, I will father, I certainly will," expressed Timius. "Will we be there long, father?"

"Yes!"

"Will you be there with me?"

"No, I am afraid not, son, because they do not accommodate travellers in the collegiate."

"Oh, what a shame," replied Timius. "But anyway I'll come and see you every evening and tell you about all the things I have seen and read. No, I won't do that," thought Timius aloud, because I won't know where to find you, so you had better come and see me every sunset."

"Very well, son," responded Sejanus.

"May I take the horse with me, father?" the boy requested.

"Oh, no you will not be able to do that. If you did it would take up all your time looking after it and then you will not have the time to study any of the literature in the college, so I'll keep the horse."

"Yes, I suppose you are right," answered Timius.

They arrived at the entrance of what appeared to be the main building. The horse was again tied to a stone pillar that supported the patio roof and father and son walked into the entrance hall of the building.

CHAPTER IV

Si Domi sum, Foris est Animus sin foris sum, animus est Domi.

PLAUTUS.

If I am at home my mind is abroad. If I am abroad my mind is at home.

THE INTERIOR OF the hall, the ceiling of which was supported by six narrow stone columns equally spaced and positioned centrally in two rows of three, was rather spacious. Leading off from the wall that surrounded the hall were heavily carved large timber doors. These doors were entrances to the principal's office and two other offices from which the administration of the institute took place. The other doors led to the library and reading rooms. Sejanus Arbutus was met by an assistant in the hallway and, after greeting one another Sejanus expressed the purpose of his visit and was politely ushered into the principal's office. Timius was politely asked to seat himself on one of the wooden benches that stood along the empty space of the surrounding wall. He sat down obediently. While sitting there he was able to study some of the paintings that hung on the walls that divided the doorways. These were portraits of people who had been associated with the institute and had distinguished themselves in life in some field or other. Hanging from the centre of the ceiling, and suspended on a heavy iron chain, was an elaborate iron chandelier which formed the support for thirty candles. Timius had sat there and counted them, because he had been taught to count up to one hundred by his mother, who had promised to teach him how to multiply, subtract and divide, but this would not be possible now.

Three institutions had been founded, for orphan boys and for those whose fathers were unable to take care of them whilst they were serving in the legions, by Octavian in the year 24 B.C. when he accepted the purple mantle of Emperor. The object of this inception was a noble one. Without proper care and attention those boys who were either bereft of parents or relatives or friends to foster them would, if neglected, fall into the clutches of the world of crime at a very early age, and the Emperor felt that if a legionnaire was assured that his son or daughter would be properly cared for in a well-run establishment, then it would lift the burden from the minds of a legionnaire who had this kind of responsibility to carry and would thereby make him a more loyal and better fighting man. There were institutes at Brindisium, Florentina and here at Larcia. The pupils invariably entered the institute between the ages of six and twelve. Beyond the age of twelve it was not felt practical to accept applicants because the childhood grounding and character building necessitated a start much earlier. Character building, among other things, was the prime purpose of the institute, because it was felt that this would be the basis of any subsequent motivation that would enable a young man of ability to progress in life. Many past pupils had since distinguished themselves in the army, or in administrative positions throughout the Empire. There were many failures too, and an education in such an institution was not a guarantee of success in later life. The institutions were financed from the central treasury but were under the control and administration of the Praetorian Guard, and it was practice for an officer of the Praetorian Guard, whatever his background might have been, to be appointed to the praetor-ship of the institution for a five year term as reward for distinguished service. The academics were nearly all Greeks, whereas the masters in charge of sporting activities were appointed from those men of Rome who had achieved some sporting accolade during their athletic lives. Military discipline, which the boys were cruelly subjected to, was in the care of members of the Praetorian Guard who were approaching retirement from service, which carried a monetary award greater than one they had been used to as their reward for long and loyal service to the Emperor.

Sejanus Arbutus came out of the principal's office accompanied by a smartly dressed man in a toga, and they were finalising some discussion or other on their way out. Timius was called over to meet the principal, who welcomed him in a voice that seemed to be underlined with a measure of sternness. This gentleman instructed the boy to go outside with his father and say his farewells and then return and report to the assistant who had first met them on their arrival.

Timius and his father proceeded outside to the place where the horse had been tethered. Sejanus off-loaded Timius' bag from the horse, put it down beside him, crouched down in front of him and grasped Timius by the shoulders, and as he did so, he said to the boy, "well, son, I must be on my way now, as it is nearly sunset, but I shall be back to pick you up. Look after yourself and be a good boy and do just as you are told. You must be obedient to all the seniors here and when you get notes to study, or pictures to draw, you must do so diligently."

"When will you be back father?" asked Timius.

"I cannot really say, son, but it will not be long."

"Will we be going back through Rome father?" queried Timius.

"Yes, of course we will, why do you ask?"

"Well, father, that crippled man I met when we were in Narnee, when you left me to get a horse, remember?"

"Yes, why do you ask?"

"Well, he invited you and me to supper, when we next go through Rome. He told me he lives on the Palatine Hill, and if we go there and ask at any of the buildings for Claudius, he said, we will be sure to find him; and I would like to meet him again and I would like you to meet him, because he was ever such a kind man. So do you think we can do that, father?"

Not answering straight away, Sejanus agreed. But his agreement was very, very half-hearted, because he realized that the young man that Timius had just spoken about was in fact one of the members of the Julio Claudian family and the grandson, through marriage, of the Emperor. Whatever invitation the young man Claudius had extended to his son Timius could not be taken at all seriously because it was an anathema for any of the lower classes and, in particular, for a serving member of one of Caesar's legions to associate with a member of the ruling house. Hugging Timius close to him for a while, Sejanus patted the boy on the on the head, showed him to the door of the hall, mounted his horse, waved and rode off.

Sejanus felt quite broken hearted to have left his son at the college, but he had no alternative. He could not expect his daughter Mena and his son-in-law, Silius, to provide the boy with a home because, firstly, Mena was expecting her first child in some seven months time and her hands would be full tending to their house as well as making preparations for the addition to their family. Secondly, his son-in-law, Silius, who was an exceptionally unassuming man, lacking ambition, could not be expected to take advantage of any opportunity to better himself beyond the occupational confines of the pottery. This was not in anyway an ignoble attitude or one to be despised but, unfortunately, such people, in whatever meagre contribution they might make to society, was an essential one because the enterprising and ambitious would never be able to achieve their goals without the supporting foundations of ordinary men like Silius. For this reason Sejanus could not add the responsibility of his son's upbringing onto the shoulders of Mena and Silius, especially as he was away from home for such lengthy periods, in the service of his Emperor, very often hundreds of miles from home. Of course, he could send them adequate financial assistance helping them in this task, but this would have just been shedding the real responsibility of a father. Since he was now committed—and had been for many years—to service life, there was nothing else he could do at this stage. So however depressed he felt at the moment about leaving the boy in the care of strangers, nevertheless he could feel assured that Timius would not only be taken care of, but he would be assured a manly upbringing that would forevermore stand him in good stead for later life. It would help him to become totally independent and, moreover, he would receive the basis of a good education, not only academically but socially. Any big ideas the boy might cherish would soon be stifled, and he would have to learn to rub along with others perhaps more greatly endowed, or indeed of lesser ability and intelligence, and adapt to it whether he liked it or not.

He had no idea what line of work Timius would enter when he became a young man, but he felt that with an education in a military controlled establishment Timius would either, enter service in the forces and follow in his father's footsteps, or he might even enter one of the fields of administration. With regard to the invitation Claudius had extended to them Sejanus again thought about it and once again realized that even if they were able to accept this invitation it would be rather silly of him to follow it through, because poor old Claudius, the reputable idiot of the Palatine Hill, would have most probably have forgotten all about it now and was probably only making conversation with the boy. Claudius had a reputation for idiocy, and to have supper with him, as was suggested, according to Timius, would be to sup in a fool's company. What would his friends back in the legion think if he related to them that he a had supped with Claudius. They would obviously consider him to be as idiotic as Claudius. Never mind, he must put such thoughts out of his mind and concentrate on getting back to Velitrae and from thence to legion headquarters. He intended to write to Timius as soon as he settled down, to explain the situation. 'Timius perhaps will never forgive me', he thought, 'but he will not grow to regret what has happened. When he reaches an age of realization, he will then come to know the meaning of it all and perhaps not judge me too harshly'.

*

Timius was ushered into the hall again by the assistant who took him through a corridor, still struggling with his bag, and the assistant then ushered him through a door into an assembly room where there were other boys around his age seated on benches with a slate, resting on each of their laps, scratching what appeared to be letters of the alphabet onto their slates. These were being sung out by a middle-aged gentleman who was standing on a small dais in front of them. When the man had finished, the assistant caught his eye and nodded towards the boy. The gentleman beckoned them forward and, as they approached him, he stepped down from the dais and Timius was introduced to him by the assistant. Our young friend's name is Timius Arbutus, sire.

"How do you do Timius Arbutus, my name is Doronyd?"

By this time there were mumblings going on amongst the other boys. Doronyd turned to them and instructed them to "keep quiet and get on with writing the alphabet once again, from memory." Turning back to Timius, Doronyd said, "You have come to join us, eh? Welcome, we are very pleased to have you with us." Dismissing the assistant, he advised Timius, "I will be your master, and I am sure before long you will get to know me as well as the other boys. But before we get acquainted I will take you over to the store room, where you will exchange your tunic and, in addition, you will be issued with other clothing and bedding and we can then proceed to the dormitory. By the time we get to the dormitory these other young fellows will also be there and you can make your acquaintances with them.

"Thank you, sire, but I will not be staying here long. I shall only be here a few days, and then my father will return to take me home."

"How right you are," responded Doronyd, "but nevertheless we must still see to it that you are properly settled in."

Doronyd had had this sort of reaction from other boys in the past. So many of them had been left under the pretence that it was only for a few days, and year later, on their discharge, strangely enough, none wanted to leave. He was sure that the end reaction would be the same in young Timius' case.

"I will see you all in your dormitory in half an hour," he said to the other boys and departed, taking Timius along to the store room.

In the store room, Timius was told to undress while Doronyd fumbled through Timius' hair to see, rather quickly, whether he was carrying any lice around with him. Meanwhile the store keeper selected three straw-coloured tunics, a pair of sandals, and two pieces of linen to serve as towels; wrapped a bar of soap in one of the towels; took a short cloak from the rack; added this to the tunics, and then proceeded to count three blankets from the pile and a straw mattress. Timius was also given a cotton scarf which looked as though it had been washed several times because the green in it had faded. He lay the scarf out flat on the low-lying counter and, apart from the clothing that Timius had worn all his small personal belongings were put into the middle of this scarf and tied in a bundle. Before Timius let his own tunic be taken away by the store keeper, he was able to grab hold of it and go to the pocket of the tunic to retrieve his gold coin. He clutched this in the palm of his hand and was able to hide it from the store keeper and Doronyd. Doronyd picked Timius' pipe up from his personal effects and said he would carry it for him to the dormitory. Now that he was in the straw-coloured tunic and had slipped on the sandals, he was ready to go. His own personal bag, brought from home, was labelled and placed in a pigeon hole in the rack.

"Come along, boy, we had better go on our way."

Timius carried the clothes while the store keeper carried his bedding for him.

On their way to the dormitory they passed through a hall. This hall was used for dining purposes, with wooden tables and benches arranged at the southern end of the hall. At the opposite end it was clear of all furniture and gave a spacious appearance. The only item of any significance in this part of the hall was a large wooden podium which stood about three feet from the stone floor with three wooden steps leading to its platform. Behind the wooden podium there was a sculptured bust of the Emperor, Caesar Augustus. Above the sculpture, and suspended from the highest point of the wall behind the bust, was an ethereal painting of the same person. Two, floor standing, candle sticks, about four feet tall, made from heavy bronze with lighted candles gave the appearance that the subject's face was naturally illuminated. This appearance of reverence to Caesar Augustus was quite understandable. Firstly, it was through his decree that institutions such as this one at Larcia, was founded and, secondly, by an overwhelming vote of affirmation from both the Senate and the people of the Empire, Caesar Augustus had not joined the ranks of the Greek and Roman gods. His case was different from that of the other Gods. He was the only living god in the Empire and he had been deified some ten years previously. The podium was used for announcements, lectures, and other matters requiring the ears of an assembly.

On the wooden tables in lines which gave the appearance of regimentation, were pewter plates and mugs. On either side of each plate was a roughly cast knife and two-pronged fork. Leading off from the assembly hall were four large doorways each one leading to a dormitory. Doronyd and his two followers entered into one of the dormitories, and, as soon as they entered, the boys who had already found their way there hustled around quickly to get to their respective beds, neatly placed along each wall of the dormitory. Doronyd placed his hand on Timius' shoulder and ushered him forward and, as he did so, he introduced the boy to his new peers.

"Good evening, junior citizens, I have the pleasure to introduce another newcomer, junior citizen Timius Arbutus. He will be living among you from now on, so I will leave you to make your acquaintances with him and gently guide him into the routine of the College."

There was several spare bed frames intermittently placed on either side of the central corridor of the dormitory which were not occupied. These frames were made from stout lengths of bamboo and stood about one foot from the stone floor. Criss-crossing the frame was waxed lengths of thick twine made from coconut fibre. The assistant who had helped carry Timius' mattress placed the mattress on the frame with the blankets and, going over to the far wall of the dormitory, where simple wooden chests were stacked, carried one over and placed it at the foot of Timius' bed.

Doronyd had by this time returned to the room and said to the boy, "There you are Timius, you can put your bits and pieces in that box. You must take care of your own possessions and, as a word of warning and advice you must never touch the possession of any of your room-mates here without their express permission. If you do so you will be severely punished and you will never forget it. Do you understand?"

"Yes, sir," said Timius.

"Very well, I will leave you now and I will see you in the morning with the other boys. Take care to be up on time because the college rises and starts its day at the sound of the first cockerel."

"Very good, sir," replied Timius.

Handing Timius his musical pipe, Doronyd turned round and strode off with the assistant.

Immediately after he had gone, all the other boys in the dormitory gathered around Timius, jabbering with one question after another. All of them wanted to know where he had come from, how he had got there, how was his mother or father killed, how many countries of the Empire his father had served in, how old he was, and so on. The questions were endless and Timius just could not answer them all at once. The poor lad was quite confused. One of the boys posed what seemed to Timius a rather cheeky question.

"Did you say your father was a slave or a freedman?"

Timius did not know how to respond to him because he wondered what had prompted this question.

One of the other boys replied on his behalf. "You had better have your wash tonight, instead of tomorrow morning, because you obviously didn't hear what he said. He quite clearly said that his father was a soldier and a Roman citizen."

"Yes, I thought he did," retorted the other boy, "but I wondered why he wasn't wearing his Bulla."

A Bulla was a golden amulet worn round the neck of all freeborn Roman boys from their birth to the age of sixteen. This was customary lest they should be ganged into more menial jobs.

"Very well," said Cyrus, and turning to Timius asked, "tell us, where is your Bulla?"

Timius was quite lost for words for a while, because he didn't quite realize what a Bulla was until some of the other boys began waving theirs in front of his face. Timius quickly thought that he would have to tell a lie as a way out of the situation.

"I know what a Bulla is," he said, "so you don't have to show me. I lost mine on the way up here, and when we stopped to look for it we couldn't find it, and my father has promised to get me another one, and I shall have it in a few days."

Timius never had a Bulla because his father could never afford to buy him one, and even in situations where he might have been able to spare the money, either he forgot or more important expenses had to be met. Anyway, he had got out of this one quite easily, he thought to himself, and he hoped they would never raise the subject again. He was a free-born Roman, but there was no way of proving it without his father being there, but he hoped they would forget the whole matter in due course.

Cyrus, who had spoken up on his behalf, came over and introduced himself properly. My name is Cyrus Vinicius. I live in Rome. "Where do you live," asked Cyrus.

"I live in Velitrae."

"Oh, is that so," said Cyrus, "that's where our glorious Emperor was born."

"That's quite right," said Timius, although he didn't know this and this was brand new information to him and this made him feel inwardly proud that he was born in the same town as the great Augustus.

Cyrus then proceeded to help Timius unpack his scarf bundle and place all his bits and pieces into the box. He then showed him how the beds were required to be made. He then showed Timius the washroom, which was at the other end of the dormitory in which were metal basis on a roughly made wooden stand with recesses in which the basins snugly fitted. These were filled from copper urns that were, in turn, filled by the boys themselves from light metal buckets. It was the boys' duty to keep the urns topped up from the college well. As the boys arrived back at their respective beds, the door opened and a stern looking official, dressed in military attire, entered. He was the one military man seconded from the Praetorian Guard who was in charge of this dormitory for the general routine, discipline, and other purposes, except academic training. He recognised Timius, because his was the strange face among the boys, and came up to him. In a stern voice said, "You are the newcomer, I see. I am the officer in charge of you and the other boys in this dormitory. I will be taking care of your interests from now on. So if there is anything you want to know, you come to me. But I hope you don't come to me very often. In fact I hope you don't come to me at all, because I haven't got time to mollycoddle and wet-nurse you—understood? I see you are settled in now, or aren't you?"

"Yes, sir, I am," Timius timidly replied.

"Very well, join the other boys and come down for your evening meal. Come along boys," he called to them and led the way out of their dormitory and into the dining sector of the assembly hall.

This is the moment that all the boys had been waiting for. They always loved meal times, and Timius could not understand why they all rushed to get out of the door, but he was soon to find out the reason. They all took their places set aside for them along one of the rows of tables. They were soon joined by other boys from other dormitories. Many of them were much older. When they had all assembled a hush came over them as another Praetorian official, the more senior official of all those who had been seconded to the college, mounted the podium. He stood straight to attention facing the boys and raising his right hand straight and smartly in front of him, he bellowed, "Hail Caesar."

The boys responded similarly. He then turned around to face the painting of Augustus, and with his eyes gazing on the face of the Emperor, gently bowed in obeisance. All the boys followed suit. This done, he turned to face them again, raised both arms in front of him, and indicated to them to sit down and commence the meal. Assistants from the cook house then came into the dining sector carrying large bowls of broth and baskets of bread, filled each boy's plate with the boiling broth and gave each one a small loaf of bread. Cyrus sat beside Timius, as by now it seemed that he had decided to become the newcomer's keeper. He was two years older than Timius, and in another year he would be moved to the next senior dormitory. There were about a hundred and fifty boys in the college, and they were split up into four dormitories by their age groups. Roughly from the ages seven to nine, ten to twelve, thirteen to fourteen, and fifteen to seventeen. In each dormitory one boy was selected to be a prefect.

The prefects were usually chosen from one of the boys who had been a member of the dormitory the longest and who was perhaps one with a dominant nature. Any whim or wish of the prefect, however slight, had to be adhered to. The college had several punishments in line for any boy who disobeyed instructions from seniors, whether prefect, praetorian officials, or academy masters. The obeisance to Caesar Augustus was a ritual that was paid at the commencement of each meal throughout the year. After all, Caesar Augustus was the founder of this institute, and it was at his pleasure that they existed at all.

Timius thoroughly enjoyed his meal because he was quite ravenous. At the end of the meal, the boys were marched out of the dining section and back to their dormitories where they were to spend the next hour on the interior cleaning of their living quarters. The prefect of the dormitory to which Timius now belonged was the senior boy in the dormitory by the name of Vasius. Vasius took Timius aside, and at the same time beckoned Cyrus to join them and then began to instruct Timius about the cleaning tasks, a nightly routine throughout the college, in which he would now be expected to participate. Timius thought he was going to enjoy this and very enthusiastically agreed, somewhat obediently, to all the instructions and advice given to him. He was rather pleased that Vasius had asked Cyrus to show him what he had to do and the high standard that was expected. Timius' enthusiasm seemed to show through his countenance and Vasius, as many a senior before him, realized that any enthusiasm at this early stage would be short lived. Vasius was a bragger and, as Timius later learned for himself, was one who constantly tried to create an impression, and perhaps that was why he was chosen to be a prefect. Any conversation or argument Vasius might have been engaged in with his other colleagues invariably ended up with a form of recital which boasted of his father's exploits. Vasius' father, according to Vasius, must have fought and survived in so many battles for the Empire and won innumerable honours, that surely he must be only second to Mars in the field of war.

However, it was common among all the boys to praise and boast about their fathers' achievements, and it was very often a case where many of them had to lie knowingly just so that they would not lose face among their companions.

Timius job this night was to help clean the metal wash basins in the washroom. They were just finishing the task when the praetorian officer, Paulo, entered the dormitory and instructed them, after doing a cursory inspection of the building, to return to their beds and start preparing to retire for the night. Timius did just this, but before getting in between the bed clothes he felt he ought to make sure his two prized possessions, the gold coin wrapped in a piece of papyrus and his musical pipe, were safely tucked away in the chest he now called his kit box. The gold coin he made sure to tuck well into a corner, and he concealed it with other clothes that had been issued to him. He was much more relieved that his possessions were safe and in his box at the foot of his bed.

The Praetorian officer, Paulo, extinguished the oil lamps, shut the door of the dormitory and left the boys for the night. All was now quiet. Before dropping off to sleep Timius thought what a wonderful experience all of this was, and above the silence he could hear in the distance a mournful hoot from what sounded like a shepherd's horn intermittently breaking the still of the night. Sleep soon overcame him.

He was awoken the following morning with the banging of a stick on the box lids by Paulo who was forcing them to make haste out of their beds and to prepare themselves for the first part of their daily routine. Timius awoke quite startled, and it took him a few minutes for realization to take control. When he first awoke he had no idea where he was, but after rubbing the sleep from his eyes and looking around him soon felt quite happy that he had another day of enjoyment to look forward to. After their early morning ablutions the boys were hastily mustered outside the dormitory and a role call was made. All the boys in the school assembled in the rectangle nearby, under their respective Praetorian officers. They were then told to strip to their waists and leave their tunics on the ground where they stood, properly folded, of course. The cold early morning air sent shivers down the boys' spines, but after getting used to it they found it quite bracing. They were then taken for a run by one of the athletic sports officers assigned to the college for physical exercise purposes. This was absolutely thrilling for young Timius, although many of the other boys moaned and grumbled all the way. The run enabled Timius to acquaint himself with the precincts of the college and he concluded that this was quite an attractive spot to be in, and he was grateful to his father for bringing him here.

It was totally different to anything he had seen at Veliltrae. Beyond the precincts were dense woodlands that rolled down into valleys and dales and beyond these on the slopes of the near distant hills he could see field upon field of cultivated land which looked lusciously green from where he stood. He thought, 'one day I would like to go up there to see what it is really like,' and he was curious to know what sort of crops were grown in those fields, because he was now beginning to feel a tinge of hunger brought about by the morning exercise.

Physical training was now over, and the boys dashed to the nearby well and, as if in a race, hauled buckets of water up to refresh themselves before collecting and donning their tunics again. Then they were mustered for their breakfast, which consisted of tiny bread loaves, one per boy, with a dash of newly collected honey. This was washed down by a lukewarm fruit wine. Again before the meal started there was the salutation to Caesar and the obeisance to Caesar Augustus. After their first meal of the day they were mustered, in a regimental fashion, and handed over to a respective academician, the man who took charge of Timius and the other boys in the same dormitory, who walked them to the far end of the college complex and into a room that was used for study purposes.

Doronyd was there to receive them and after they were seated he began to lecture and digress on the religious faculties that were predominant in the Roman world. He began moralizing and drawing their attention to the conduct and worship codes, as espoused by the established religions. Timius found this interesting. Perhaps part of all of this would give him a chance that he had been waiting for, for a very long time, of seeing one of the statues of the Gods actually move in the manner to which they were accustomed in whichever religious sect that was their domain. He gazed around discreetly and saw that the expressions on the faces of his colleagues to be somewhat rather bored. Timius could not understand why this was so as he found it fascinating. He did not realize that the boys had heard this all before many times over. However, Timius was not going to be deterred from taking an interest in all the things that he would be lectured about here, because he remembered his father's words advising the boy to pay attention and digest everything he was taught. After all, he would have a lot to learn in the very few days he would be here, and time was not on his side.

The religious lesson was now over, and Doronyd commenced going through the alphabet and the primary numbers of their arithmetical tuition which was repeated over and over again in parrot fashion by the boys. Timius was eager to go on to something more interesting because with only a few days to sojourn in the college he felt that his time was being wasted in going over this repeatedly. The day wore on and when the position of the sun, in the autumn sky, indicated that it was mid-afternoon the academic lessons were over. The boys were now led out in an orderly fashion back to the dining section of the assembly hall where they were treated to light refreshments. This completed they were again mustered under their respective Praetorian officials who then commenced their very early and extremely basic military training.

In the case of the younger boys, with officer Paulo in charge, the basic training consisted of marching in step. Timius found this very difficult because he was keen to get on with it and get into a march-like walk at the fastest speed. Paulo bawled him out on several occasions during the next hour and, in doing so, used quite a lot of insulting language to the boy. The other boys in the company thought this was great fun, having their laughs at the expense of somebody else. But then it was not really cruel or too humiliating for any one of them because they had all been through the same experience themselves. However, Timius did not take any of this to heart and he thought to himself that when he returned home he would be able to march his own imaginary legions around Velitrae much more sternly and in a much more polished fashion than he had done in the past.

The elder boys' military training was comprised of the basic use of the lance, the bow, and the art of parrying the sword and defensive use of the shield.

The next hour was spent in the care of athletic officials, who were responsible for the physical fitness and training of the boys. Again, while the younger boys were confined to the basic jogging, walking, and running around the sports field which was in close proximity to the college, the elder boys were trained to use the discus and the javelin. They also participated in other athletic events, such as running wrestling, boxing, long jumping and high jumping that were included in the more advanced activities. Timius always enjoyed running and outdoor activities. He could not quite understand why the other boys appeared to find this rather irksome. After the physical activity all the boys in the college were split up, under the instruction of the Praetorian officials, into groups of about fifteen boys and each group was then given the task of general cleaning of not only the college but the surrounding grounds.

Metal bowls of water were given out, with cotton cloths, to some groups of boys. Their job was to wash the floors of the school assembly hall, lecture rooms, and corridors. Some groups were given the task of scouring the school grounds where falling autumn leaves had to be gathered and placed in heaps at pre-selected pickup points where slaves, who belonged to the municipality of Narnee in which district Larcia fell, were able to bring their rubbish carts each day to collect and take away the leaves for disposal. One group of boys was directed to the school cookhouse where they were to help the cooks and assistants to clean the utensils and assist in the basic preparation of the meals for the following day. There was one very large group of boys of all ages whose task was considered rather special, whereas the other groups of boys went about their daily tasks on a rota basis.

The special group had the same task consistently. Their job was to clean out the school latrines. They not only had to wash the latrines but it was also their job to carry the buckets of sewage to a pit receptacle and dispose of it. Having done they would sprinkle powdered lime over it to assist in decontamination. This was naturally the most menial task in the college and any boy who needed a dose of punishment for any wrongdoing was seconded to this group for one, two, or three weeks, depending on the seriousness of the punishment. Another task that was necessary in the college was the cleaning out of the college communal bath. This bath was about twenty feet by ten feet wide with a depth graduating from three to five feet. It was heated by a metal boiler under which were burned logs and twigs that were collected from the nearby woods. One morning per week was devoted to the job of collecting and cutting the logs by all the boys in the college under the control of the Praetorian officers. The water from the boiler was channelled by a series of lead pipes to the bath and then, after use, was drained away into one of the near ravines, and thence into a rivulet. There was never any shortage of labour for this job because it was confined to boys who had committed any kind of minor offence and served as a suitable punishment. However much a boy tried to keep out of trouble, it was virtually impossible, to avoid being accused of some minor mischief or other either, real or fabricated, and the object of this was primarily to keep the bathhouse well established with labour. It was not a pleasant task because it did mean cleaning the mosaic surround and stone interior of the bathhouse and the marble walls and flooring of the bath spotlessly clean. This was achieved by the regular use of cotton cloths and cold water, and it meant working on ones hands and knees. In winter months it was a cold job and in the summer an unpleasantly sweaty one but overall a miserable one which was not confined to any one age group of boys.

The general cleaning tasks now complete meant returning to the dormitories and continuing the cleaning of the respective living spaces. The thought crossed Timius' mind that anyone who had to do this sort of cleaning for a number of years would soon find that he would have no hands left. He would have his hands worn down to his wrists. But then, of course, this was no concern of his, as he wouldn't be here very long, but nevertheless he felt sorry for the other boys in whose company he now found himself.

Today was Sunday and a day devoted to worship in the college temple of Mars. This temple was rather like the temple his father entered to pay his respects when they were on their route from Narnee. Timius began to wonder what had happened to his father. After all, he had been here five days now and the daily routine had not changed at all except for today, but even so they still had to start their day with their physical training early in the morning, and he also wondered, although he thoroughly enjoyed it, what the purpose was for all this physical training. Cyrus had told him that it was on the orders of the Emperor, and if the Emperor ordered it, so be it. Cyrus had now become quite friendly with Timius and their friendship was joined by another young boy a year older than Timius whose name was Marcus. Both Cyrus and Marcus had informed Timius, during their conversations, that their fathers' were both centurions in the legion, and Timius did not want to feel too humiliated, so he led them to believe that his father was also a centurion. In truth, his father was a mere trooper, but never mind, they would never know, he thought. Even if they did, it would make no difference as the college was a great leveller.

The principal of the school, whose name was Artimeses, led the boys to the temple of Mars. Those boys above the age of twelve were allowed to enter the temple, whereas the younger boys assembled outside in the courtyard, under the strict scrutiny of a praetorian official, and they had to remain silent for over two hours while Artimeses offered sacrifices at the altar of Mars in the Temple. Sunday was a customary day of worship throughout the Roman world. It had been set aside in very early Republican days for religious practice.

The sun god, Ra, the supreme deity, was allocated one day a week for worship, and Ra was imported into the heart of the Empire from the province of Egypt. The god Isis was also an import from Egypt, although Isis was worshipped on a much higher plain and much more regularly than Ra, but, nevertheless, Ra was the sun god, and Sunday was devoted to his worship. There were no temples of any consequence to Ra, either here in Italy or in the provinces. But the day of worship of any of the other gods was found to be most convenient on a Sunday. The Egyptians felt that this was rather patronising of the Romans but then the Romans were their lords and masters now, and any practice they may institute was deemed to be proper for them. There was no other temple in the college except this one to Mars; and since this was a military institution, the worship of Mars was appropriate.

After the service of worship had finished, all the boys who had taken part in the service within the temple began filing out and took up their respective places outside in the courtyard. Artimeses then bellowed some sort of garbled prayer from the steps of the temple and instructed the Praetorian officials to march away their respective dormitory groups. They had now arrived at the assembly area outside the great assembly hall. The Praetorian official, Paulo, in keeping with his other colleagues, gave order to his troop of dismissal, but before doing so called out, "junior citizen Arbutus, when I have dismissed you all, would you come here to me right away?"

He then gave the command for the dismissal. Timius wondered what this was all about and thought that perhaps he would be given instructions on the arrangements made whereby he could collect his personal belongings from the storeroom and hand in his college kit, and feeling quite happy, he smartly trotted up to Paulo, who towered above him with a frown on his forehead.

"Now, young man," said Paulo, "I want to have words with you. There is something I noticed today while we were in the courtyard outside the temple of Mars." Paulo was one of the Praetorian officers who had remained outside the temple during the period of worship.

"You were not wearing your Bulla today, were you?"

"No sire," Timius replied.

"Well, why not?" queried Paulo, because all the boys were compelled to wear their individual Bullas throughout the day of worship. This was a college regulation.

"I have not got it, sire," responded Timius.

"Where is it then?"

"I lost it on the way here, when my father brought me from home."

"Are you sure you had one?"

"Yes I am, sire."

"Well, describe it to me," said Paulo.

Timius was now completely flustered because he had no idea what one looked like, and he had not had an opportunity to study the Bulla of one of his peers, so he could not bluff his way out of this situation.

"Are you the son of a slave, or are you the son of a freedman?"

"No, sire."

"If you are the son of a freeborn Roman, you would have a Bulla, and I am sure your father would not have let you lose it and, in fact if you did, he would have replaced it by now. You understand its significance, don't you?"

"Yes," replied Timius, although he had no idea what it was all about.

"I am sure you are lying."

"I am not, sire, and when my father comes I will ask him to get me one, and I will bring it and show it to you."

"Very well," said Paulo, "but meanwhile, tomorrow mid-afternoon when we assemble for our cleaning tasks, I want you to report to Praetorian officer, Carpus, and you will remain in his charge for the remainder of your time here until you are able to produce your Bulla."

"Yes, sire, I will do as you say."

Timius had no idea who Carpus was, but when he returned the dormitory both Cyrus and Marcus and some of the other boys asked Timius what Paulo's inquisition was all about. When he told them they began sniggering and informed Timius that Carpus was in charge of the cleaning troop that were responsible for cleaning out the latrines. This was the most menial job in the college and one permanently allocated to the sons of slaves who had served with the legions in a military capacity or freedmen who had also served with the legion. The sniggering was caused through the boys' realisation that Timius was not, after all, the son of a freeborn Roman that he had claimed to be.

Timius went to bed that night feeling rather dejected because his father had led him to believe that he was a freeborn Roman, which indeed he was; and he thought that his two friends Cyrus and Marcus were much more worthy characters than the types that would poke fun at him. Naturally he was disappointed that he had been wrong about them. As he lay in bed, he thought that it would be rather good to return home to Velitrae because he was now beginning to miss not only his father, whom he had got used to being away from home but, more so, his imaginary legions and his imaginary barbarians down at his favourite gorge at Velitrae. He now wished he had not been brought to the college because he was beginning to feel quite disappointed; everything he had imagined this place to be was nothing like it in reality, and if his father did not come soon to take him away, he had no idea how he could adapt himself to this situation. He now began thinking about all the common places in Velitrae, which he often frequented during past times. He thought about the temple he sneaked into; about his favourite trees which he used to climb, his sling dangling round his neck. He was thinking about the carp pool when he eventually dropped off to sleep.

CHAPTER V

Ne libeat tibi quod, non licet.

CICERO

Let that not please you, which is not lawful.

WHILE THE BOYS were beginning to make their early morning ablutions, Cyrus came up to Timius and apologized for the humiliation he helped bring about the previous night and assured Timius that whether or not Timius was a freeborn Roman or the son of a slave it was of no consequence to him and that he would still remain his friend. Cyrus also assured Timius that Marcus' affections would not be altered either. Timius brushed this gesture aside, rather lightly, but could not help feeling more reassured that his two friends had probably realized the folly of their ways and could henceforth be held in some trust. When mid-afternoon arrived, Timius duly reported to praetorian officer Carpus as instructed.

Carpus did not know that there would be an addition to his troop of latrine cleaners, and when Timius approached him, while he was glad that the strength of his cleaning group would now be increased by one to nineteen he did not think the boy would be of much use to him because he did not appear to be endowed with any strength at that early age, nor could he believe the boy had any resilience, but he secretly felt that it would give him some pleasure to knock him into shape.

"So you've come along to join my body of cleaners, have you?" asked Carpus

"Yes, sire," replied Timius.

"Well, you had better not shirk the job, or else I will have your nose rubbed in the muck, and that is no idle threat," said Carpus rather sternly.

"No, sire, I will do my best."

"Very well, you had better go along and join the others, and you can begin by helping them carry the latrine buckets down to the lime pit. Go along then; don't stand there looking at me," bawled Carpus.

The latrines were surrounded by a modest wall covered with a tiled roof. Along the centre of the structure was a long wooden plank about eighteen inches wide in which eight suitably shaped apertures were cut out, serving as seats. With constant use, this plank had now become shiny and smooth to the touch. Beneath each aperture was an iron bucket and the plank was supported by the sides of the bucket, and kept rigid in place at either end by wooden stakes driven into the floor which slotted into the ends of the plank through suitably fitting holes. Access to the buckets merely meant lifting the plank at either end, and placing the plank against the wall. This had been done by the time Timius joined the other boys, and they were now beginning to dispose of the sewage in the buckets. It meant four boys having to lift each bucket down to the sewage pit that was situated some seventy yards away. The buckets were made from beaten iron and each was fitted with a loose handle which came to rest on either side of the bucket when not being carried. The other boys were quite happy to see a newcomer in their midst because aside from the arrival of a newcomer, their task was one of constant monotony, and when Timius offered his assistance to a group of four who were lifting a bucket, they all immediately placed the bucket back on the floor and invited him to take their place. However, without much ado only one was able to extricate himself from this task and, by doing so, he could opt for the much more pleasant task of swilling the floor with water. The other boys knew that Timius was a newcomer. They waited for a moment, rather impatiently, to see the expression on his face when the odour of the contents of the bucket penetrated his nostrils. They were to be disappointed. Timius did not flinch at the stench. He had been used to the smell of rotting rubbish because some of his wanderings back home in Velitrae took him to the rubbish heaps in the town. It was there that he could salvage bits and pieces and other curios with which he would amuse himself for hours. The kind of play things that other boys of his age—from perhaps better-off families were used to in their hours of enjoyment, Timius was not fortunate enough to have himself. So the strong smell from the sewage buckets was not to have any adverse effect on the boy, but he did find it a strain when he helped to lift the bucket, because it was quite heavy. The bucket was half-dragged and half-carried down to the lime pit. The boys had to take care not to allow the contents to slop over the top of the rim and splash onto their clothes. With a mighty heave from all four porters the sewage was tipped into the lime pit. As the contents dropped onto the sewage from the previous clean-outs, a small swarm of flies buzzed up almost to the edge of the pit, eventually settling down after being disturbed. Back the boys went to the latrine for another collection and so it went until all eight buckets were emptied. Then each of the boys grabbed handfuls of lime which was stored in baskets on the edge of the cesspit and sprinkled it all over the sewage in the pit, making sure that much of the surface area was properly covered. Each handful disturbed the flies and it was considered fun to keep the sprinkling in a continuous motion so that the flies had to constantly hover above the surface of the sewage. This daily routine was to become second nature to Timius henceforth. He couldn't see why this job was always one of derision, particularly when he considered that had he been given the job of tidying the shelves of scrolls in the library, or some of the classrooms, he would have become very bored, whereas here in the latrines they did have their moments of fun, especially when, out of carelessness, the contents of a bucket splashed on one of its porters. They would then have to sneak the unfortunate victim out of sight of Carpus' watchful eye to the fresh water rub in order to clean him up.

Timius had now been at the college three months and the festival of Saturnalia was approaching. During his stay here, apart from learning the alphabet, which had found its way into the Latin language of the state from Phoenicia, and learning to assemble words out of letters, in the way of fun Cyrus and Marcus, joined by other boys from time to time, had taken him to the orchards which he had seen in the distant hills on the first day he arrived at the college. They also took him to the small lake which was in close proximity to the college boundaries. Any places beyond the college boundaries were strictly out of bounds to all the internees. Their Sunday afternoons which were free for them to participate in their own activities, in the case of this group with which Timius had become associated, lead by Cyrus, meant venturing into areas beyond the school boundaries stealing apples and pears from the orchards; digging up raw carrots and breaking off cabbage leaves from nearby fields and trying to catch fish in the shallows of the lake without any conventional tackle were all considered worthwhile activities by these boys. Fortunately, they had not yet been caught.

It was now Sunday again and Timius, together with the other boys in his group, was feeling high in spirit because he and the others had planned to sneak down to the lake to try their hand, literally, at fishing. Their only means of catching tench or carp was to use the swiftness of their hands in trying to trap the fish, in the shallows of the lake and throughout the past week each boy had bragged that he would be the first to do so.

After the midday refreshment in the assembly hall, Paulo, the Praetorian officer, announced from the Podium that junior citizen Arbutus was required to report to him after the rest of the assembled boys had been dismissed. Timius wondered what all this was about. All kinds of things raced through his brain and he naturally thought that someone had told tales to his superiors that he had been out of bounds in the apple orchard the previous Sunday. He wondered why Cyrus had not been called too, but then he thought that the person who had told tales on him was perhaps a little scared of Cyrus who was not lacking in strength or dexterity. Anyway he had no choice but to obey the command and find out what it was all about.

"You sent for me sire," said Timius.

"Yes, go along to your master Doronyd's study, as he wishes to see you straight away."

"Yes, sire, but will it take long?"

"Why do you ask?" enquired Paulo. "I suppose you do not want to lose any time because you are up to some trick this afternoon. Am I right?"

"No, sire," responded Timius, half lying.

"Well, don't waste time; Doronyd hasn't got all day to wait for you."

Timius felt a little upset because the afternoon was sure to be ruined, and after all the plans of the week he would be very disappointed if he was not able to join Cyrus, Marcus and Tacitus. He entered Doronyd's study and noticed him seated at his desk.

"Sire, you sent for me," Timius called.

"Yes, young Arbutus, come over here," and taking a piece of folded papyrus from the shelf underneath the desk, he handed it to the boy.

Timius was reluctant to accept it but did so, not knowing what to do with it.

"Go on, don't just stand there, open it," instructed Doronyd.

Timius promptly broke the seal and opened it. He gazed at it awhile. It was full of writing that he did not fully understand because he was not fully able to read it.

"Have you read it?" asked Doronyd.

Looking up from the piece of manuscript, Timius replied that he had not because he couldn't read it.

"Would you like me to read it to you?" suggested Doronyd.

"Yes please, sire, but what is it?"

Timius' eyes lit up, and for a moment he forgot all about his plans for this Sunday afternoon's adventure. Doronyd took the piece of papyrus and moved it around until it was the right way up and began reading:

My dear Timius,

I am sorry I was not able to call back for you as I told you I would, but when I returned home to Velitrae instructions had arrived from my legion headquarters telling me that I was to report back on duty immediately because the Legion was moving for service to Noricum on the Danube frontier. This being so I shall be away quite some time and there is no telling when the Legion will return for service in Rome. Therefore you will have to remain at the collegiate at Larcia until the Legion returns.

I am sure you will be very disappointed but I am also sure that by now you have made many friends at the collegiate and that your instructors and superiors are taking good care of you. You must remember my advice to you which was 'to learn as much as you possibly can and to do exactly as you are told by your superiors.
You will then grow to be a sensible and strong young man and be able to take your place in this glorious Empire of ours. I will be writing to you again to keep you informed of my whereabouts.
Be a good boy and behave yourself.

Your loving father
Sejanus'

Timius thanked Doronyd for reading to him his father's letter as Doronyd handed the letter back. He was disappointed now with what his father had told him, because he had given up hope of his father ever returning weeks ago, and he had made up his mind to make the best of things here at the collegiate. But he was much more relieved to know that his father had not forgotten him and that the only reason his father was not able to come and take him away was because of his duties as a legionnaire. After all, his was a noble occupation, and he was proud of his father. He ran back to the dormitory, opened his kit box and laid the manuscript letter right at the bottom of the box. He did this in a great hurry because he wanted to catch up to Cyrus and his other friends who, presumably, would be halfway to the lake. In his haste he must make sure, of course, that he did not allow anyone to see him sneak out of the boundary fence. So, his mind fully concentrated on what he was to do next, he ran out of the building and, at the carefully chosen spot, he hopped over the fence and made his way down the track to the lake.

He ran down the track for all he was worth, and his footsteps clumping through the wood disturbed some of the birds that were reposing on the branches for their early afternoon rest. The track wound its way downhill and, some two hundred yards from the lake, he came upon Cyrus and Marcus who were busily chatting to each other excitedly. Timius stopped alongside them, breathless, and Cyrus greeted him by saying,

"Ah, there you are. We thought you had deserted us for the afternoon. What did old Paulus want?"

Timius did not reply straight away because he was still out of breath but, after a while, he told them that it was for him to see Doronyd who had handed him a letter from his father.

"What did the letter say?" queried Marcus. "Did your father say he would be coming for you shortly?"

"No," Timius responded. "He said that his Legion was going to Noricum and that he had no idea when he would be returning."

"Oh, I am pleased to hear that," said Marcus, his little face lighting up, and Cyrus joined him in his own expression of pleasure.

"I do not know what you are pleased about," said Timius. "I am not very pleased about it."

"I am sorry, but I do not want you to leave now. Cyrus and I enjoy your friendship and we are very glad you aren't a sissy like some of the other boys."

"Why did you join the other boys the other night, when they jeered and poked fun at me for not wearing my Bulla?" asked Timius.

"Well, we didn't mean anything," explained Cyrus. "We just wanted to test you to see if you could take some leg-pulling."

This made Timius feel quite overcome, to know that his friends did not join meaningfully with the others in their humiliation of him. They continued on their way to the lake, and Timius realized that since early afternoon there had been the regular tooting of a horn in the distance. This seemed to continue even now while they were approaching the lake. It occurred to him that he should ask what was making the noise.

"Cyrus, what's that tooting we can hear some nights, and even now, because I heard that the first night I arrived here at Larcia?"

"Oh, that's just the farm folk who blow through a cow's horn to try and frighten the wild boars and wolves away from their crops and their poultry."

"Does it work?"

"I don't know, but it certainly works on me because it keeps me awake some nights," responded Cyrus.

Wild boars and wolves were a nuisance to the farmers in this district because the wild boars would cause considerable amounts of damage to the root crops with their burrowing and crops, such as carrots, turnips, parsnips and arrowroot, which is grown profusely in this part of the country. Wolves were common predators in the area also, and were constantly harassing the farmers' poultry. Blowing through a cow's horn intermittently, had a tendency to warn off both the wild boars and the wolves, but was not always successful. Nevertheless, this was the only real precaution that the farmers could take. However, they had, as yet, found no way of warding off the human predators from the collegiate, because these predators made a habit of sneaking over their fences during their off-duty hours in order to steal the root crops and, indeed, sometimes chickens, to satisfy their pangs of hunger. The food at the collegiate was monotonous and inadequate. Coupled with this was the constant exercise that the boys were put to and this played no mean part in giving them a healthy appetite. It was these pangs of hunger that was driving our three friends down to the lake, which was strictly out of bounds. Unfortunately for the boys the off-duty hours were not frequent enough, whereas for the farmers, the off-duty hours were quite sufficient. The farmers would have been much happier had the boys had no off-duty periods at all. There were constant complaints from the farmers, in the surrounding district, to the school authorities about the boys denuding them of some of their livelihood. Whatever restrictions were placed on the boys were to no avail, because they continued to scrump and poach. The school authorities had tried increasing their food ration but this was not always possible because of the shortages in the corn supply from North Africa. In addition the incidents of earthquakes had increased, both in Rome and areas in close proximity, which meant that supplies of food from cultivated lands became a desperate need for Rome and other cities of the Italian peninsula.

They arrived at the water's edge, and Cyrus would now show Timius how to catch fish with his bare hands. Cyrus had been in the college for two years and had learnt all the tricks of making life pleasurable during his time at the academy. It was Cyrus who had taught Marcus the art, and even at this early age the tendencies of leadership were beginning to emerge. He was the product of a broken marriage. His mother and father had separated some three years earlier, while he was still very young, because of an accusation of adultery on the part of his father, and he knew not where either of them were. He had then been placed in the care of his uncle and was obviously unwanted. The collegiate at Larcia was his only home.

Marcus was an orphan. He had lost both his parents during the riots of A.D.13 in Rome when, because of the shortage of corn and before the ensuing rationing, by an edict of the Emperor Caesar Augustus, people fought each other in the streets in attempts to acquire their share of the meagre corn supply. The riots were mainly the cause of unfairness and corruption by the municipality, whose responsibility it was to ensure that corn was equally distributed irrespective of a household's needs. It was only the Emperor's edict that put a control on the grossly inflated price of the corn and a rigid control on the amount sold per household. The available corn during the period of short supply was bought for the people of Rome and the provinces out of the personal purse of the Emperor. For this and many other things he was constantly held in the highest esteem. Both Cyrus and Marcus were sons of legionnaires. Cyrus knew not the whereabouts of his father. He might, by a quirk of fate, be rubbing shoulders with Timius's father somewhere in Noricum. He may even be at Illiricum, or Darcis, Syria or Egyptus, in the service of his Emperor, whereas Marcus's father came to a tragic end while he was on an extended leave of absence from his legion, after five years service, in the province of Lucitania where the local provincials were restless towards Roman rule.

All three boys removed their sandals and woollen socks and Timius, being the shortest of the three, was advised by Cyrus to tuck the hem of his tunic into the top of his pants. Cyrus then advised Timius to gently step into the water and go along very quietly through the reeds until he came to the edge of the open water of the lake. Timius found the sludge under his feet a little uncomfortable, but he soon got used to it and, when he arrived a the edge of the reed area, the water was lapping the top of his thighs

"What do I do now?" called out Timius.

"Sssssshhh!" Cyrus said, in a hushed voice, and reprimanded Timius for making a noise. "You'll damn well disturb the fish if you don't keep quiet."

The other two then joined him and took up positions about ten feet away on either side of him. Cyrus advised Timius to stoop over until he was able to see, without the reflections of the water obscuring his view, the fish swimming beneath the surface. Cyrus advised, "You keep very still and quiet, and when you see a fish within easy grasp you snatch it out of the water and hold on to it tightly, because these slithery creatures will soon wriggle out of your hands." As he said this Cyrus snatched into the water for a fish but missed.

"That was bad luck," whispered Timius. "I'll have a go now."

"No, not yet," advised Cyrus. "Wait until the surface had settled."

Just as Cyrus had finished speaking, Timmy took a grab at a fish and caught it. He raised it out of the water most excitedly, but it escaped back into the water and swam away. When the water had settled again Cyrus made another attempt. Again he missed. He made yet another and again was unlucky.

Marcus, meanwhile, had got his eye on rather a large carp which was swimming freely around his knees, and determination welled inside him. With a quick snatch he grabbed the brute but in doing so his foot slipped on the muddy bottom and he fell back on is backside. His two companions, for a moment, could only see Marcus's arms rising from the surface of the water with his hands clutching a carp as though he was offering it to the gods in sacrifice. His head was beneath the surface of the water. They paddled to his rescue and lifted him up by the armpits. Fortunately he had not let go of the carp and, after spitting out the water and recapturing his breath, Timius and Cyrus gently lead him back to the shore. Marcus was soaked.

"Well done, Marcus," chorused Cyrus and Timius as Marcus placed the fish on the grass. It was a brute of about ten inches and weighed about a pound. After a final wriggle for life, it lay still.

Cyrus said, "We will soon have him roasted and eaten before we return to the college."

"But what are we going to do with you. You are wet through. What a silly fool you were to fall into the water," added Timius.

"I couldn't help it," said Marcus, "I slipped."

"For your effort and your success, you can have the biggest portion," decided Cyrus.

They then crept back into the clearing in the woods, collected a few sticks and some fern which they placed in a pile. Cyrus set about getting the fire lighted. He did this by producing two flint stones from his tunic pocket, which he always carried with him when they went out on such excursions, and with these he showed Timius the trick of lighting a fire with flint stones. As soon as a spark caught the end of the dried fern, it began to burn and all three boys crouched around it and blew at it profusely to get it going. Once this was done they then fed the fire with more sticks. Timius was advised never to use damp sticks or fern, or indeed any that were not properly dried, as this would cause unnecessary smoke which might be seen billowing through the woods from a distance and arouse the suspicions of the masters and superiors. They then found a suitable stick and, with its pointed end, pushed it into the gullet of the fish and Timius was instructed to hold the fish by the stick, a few inches above he flames, to roast it, and, at the same time to keep it turning slowly so that the roasting spread evenly throughout.

Marcus was beginning to feel the effects of his damp tunic and pants. The cool breeze made him shiver. Cyrus noticed this and advised him to take his tunic and pants off so that they could attempt to dry them by the fire. Marcus did this, but as he crouched by the fire in his nakedness, with Cyrus holding the tunic above the fire, having wrung out most of the water, he continued to shiver. So Cyrus advised him to run around the clearing to keep warm.

"Yes, I think that is a good idea," Marcus said, teeth chattering, as he immediately set out on a trot around the clearing.

After a while Cyrus shouted to Marcus, "Hey Marcus this tunic is not drying very quickly, but I have an idea to speed up the process; while I take my turn to roast the fish, you and Timius run round together with the tunic with each of you holding a sleeve"

"What will that do," chimed in Marcus.

"Well, if you hold the garment taught between you the air travelling through the spores of the garment will dry it out, but don't run too fast with it, otherwise it will not have much affect."

The two boys began to do just as Cyrus advised and round and round they ran along the edge of the clearing until they were both completely exhausted. They finally collapsed at the edge of the fire and were pleased to know that the fish was now ready to eat. Cyrus walked over to the edge of the clearing, selected three rather large leaves from an Arcacia tree and then divided the fish into three portions and kept his promise to Marcus by giving him the largest portion. Timius thoroughly enjoyed the fish. He thought this had been a most enjoyable afternoon, and he looked forward to many more. He felt most enthusiastic about doing this again. Perhaps next time he would be lucky enough to have the largest portion, because he was going to try very hard to catch a fish. Perhaps if they all caught a fish they could have a whole fish each.

"When will we come here again?" queried Timius.

"Oh, fairly soon," responded Cyrus. "I think we ought to come here again when the collegiate closes down for fifteen days during the festival of Saturnalia."

"When will that be?" asked Timius excitedly.

"Not very long, as it is only a matter of weeks away."

"What happens then," Timius asked.

"Oh, we will have fifteen days of freedom when we will not have to partake in any academic or athletic activities. You will be a little unlucky because you will have to continue with your job of cleaning the ablutions everyday. Whereas Marcus and I will not have to be involved in any corridor scrubbing because they allow us to forget about that during the festival days. It is only the boys who work in the cookhouse and the latrines who have to continue with their work during the holiday periods."

"Oh, well, that will not be too much of a hardship as I will still be able to join you both for most of the day," replied Timius feeling a trifle dejected.

Marcus continued to shiver although he was less cold after eating the roasted fish. Cyrus was rather concerned about him because the tunic wasn't quite dry, so he suggested that they now collect as many dried leaves and twigs that they could possibly find, to build up the fire so that they could hold the tunic near to it and try and dry it that way. His idea of drying it in the wind had helped but it would have only been completely successful if there had been a full relay team to continue to keep the garment moving. Drying it by the enlarged fire was not totally successful either, because time was not on their side and sunset was drawing in fast.

"I am sorry, Marcus, but you will just have to put this back on damp. We will get back up the hill as quickly as we can so that you can stand in front of the open fire in the dormitory and get yourself thoroughly dry before supper."

"Very well," agreed Marcus, "I will do as you say, and while I am dressing perhaps you two will put out the fire."

The fire was quickly damped down with the water they had collected in a broken pot, which they had found earlier, and the dying embers scattered, our three friends trotted up the winding path and through into the school perimeter. When they entered the dormitory the other boys present were inquisitive to ask why Marcus looked so bedraggled and cold.

"Oh, it's nothing," said Cyrus. "We were playing around outside the cookhouse when one of the kitchen assistants threw a trough full of water out of the window just on the spot where Marcus was standing. That's the reason for him being soaked through."

"You have been unlucky," said one of the other boys, "but it's a pity you weren't drowned," he continued spitefully.

Marcus was not a very popular boy in the dormitory because he was most reluctant to communicate any of the tricks of fun that he and Cyrus had got up to in the past. Now it would seem that Timius was to be treated as a reluctant outcast too, in the dormitory, because of his association with Marcus and Cyrus.

It was time for the boys to assemble for supper. Marcus was seated on the edge of his bed with his head between his knees. Timius and Cyrus approached him and sat down beside him. Timius put his arm around Marcus' shoulders, saying, "come on Marcus, it is time for supper. You will feel better after you have something hot to eat."

"No, Timius, you and Cyrus had better go along without me. I do not want any supper tonight. That piece of fish has filled me up."

Cyrus knew that this could not possibly be true, and he became concerned for his friend, because this reaction from Marcus was most unusual. He was usually one of the first to get to the assembly square for fear of missing some delicacy that might be served up.

Cyrus and Timius left Marcus and promised that they would be back as quickly as possible. At supper, Timius ate his bowl of broth but deliberately refrained from eating his bread roll. He was hungry enough to eat and relish it, but his thoughts were on Marcus. He decided to take a terrible chance by hiding his roll in the top of his tunic. After the boys were dismissed from supper, Timius ran back to the dormitory as quickly as he could, arriving there breathless, only to find Marcus snuggled under his blankets. Timius wanted to get there before any of the other boys except Cyrus because he wanted to give Marcus the bread roll to eat before being caught. If any of the other boys were to see him, the incident would be reported to one of the superiors so Timius gently nudged Marcus to wake him and offered him the bread roll, but Marcus refused, insisting that he was not hungry. No knowing what to do with the bread roll, Timius quickly tucked it under his own blanket just as Cyrus came running in.

"What have you been up to?" asked Cyrus. "You didn't wait for me after supper."

Timius explained what he had done and added that Marcus did not want the bread roll. He asked Cyrus if he would share it with him. Cyrus agreed but suggested that they should wait until after the lamps were turned out before they ate their portions of the roll under their bed clothes. They certainly could not eat it now as the other boys had started entering the room. Timius secretly broke the roll in half and passed one piece to Cyrus who nodded to him in thanks. Marcus was still shivering, even though he had his three blankets over him. Timius felt quite sorry for him and wondered what he should do to help. He decided that the only thing he could do was to put one of his own blankets over Marcus to give him added warmth. Cyrus, noticing what Timius had done, did the same thing with one of his blankets much to the consternation of the other boys.

"What's the matter with him?" asked one of them.

"He is not very well," replied Cyrus.

"I hope he hasn't picked up a disease which might be passed to us others," replied one of the bumptious characters.

"No, nothing like that," Cyrus answered, "he has just got a chill and so would you have if a bucket of water had been thrown over you."

Thus ending the conversation, the boys crawled into their respective beds, Timius and Cyrus to enjoy their late-night feast of dried bread roll.

CHAPTER VI

Arbores multas serit agricola, quarum fructus non adspiciet.

CICERO

The farmer plants many trees many of whom do not see the fruit.

YOUNG MARCUS FOUND it difficult to drop off to sleep that night because he now felt quite ill. In his wandering thoughts, he longed for the comfort of his mother and the protection of his father, whom he could clearly remember. He remembered his mother being a kindly person who had a knack of understanding his every need, and he wished that he could leave this place for the company of his parents. He longed for this desperately but was sufficiently mature in mind to realize that this could only be a dream. Despite this adversity, and comforted with the thought that his two friends, Timius and Cyrus, would take care of him, he finally managed to drop off to sleep. Timius had proved to be a loyal friend by virtue of the fact that he had taken a personal risk and had also deprived himself by sneaking his bread roll out of the dining hall for him. Marcus also felt a deep gratitude to Cyrus for offering to help him up the hill back into the college boundary when he was beginning to feel so cold and weak.

Marcus was roused, together with the other boys, the following morning by Paulo. Before Marcus could bring himself properly to his senses out of his fitful sleep, both Cyrus and Timius were at his side, enquiring after his state of health, and urging him to make an extra effort to get out of bed before Vasius, the prefect of the dormitory, reached his bed to remand him. They were not successful, and on Vasius' arrival Marcus complained of his illness to him.

"Well, you had better not just lay there like a weakling, you had better get on with your ablutions and then make your way to the sickroom and have yourself treated properly," ordered Vasius.

Marcus half-agreed and, with what seemed to be a tremendous effort, dragged himself from his warm bed still shivering, and most reluctantly did as he was told. He was not fit to attend the morning roll call or physical training; nor was he inclined to eat any breakfast. At the sickroom, the Greek physician gave him the once over and then made him drink a glass of bitter-tasting liquid. It was a purgative in the form of diluted medicinal salts.

"I am sure that will clear up any complaint which you might have. Be sure now to report to your master and carry on with your lessons," instructed the physician.

Marcus felt quite low and dejected at this, and again he had to do just as he had been instructed. To disobey would have meant punishment of the severest nature. He well knew that if the physician had not excused him from routine academic studies for the day then he was automatically considered fit and capable by the masters and the Praetorian officials. Any other excuse for non-attendance was considered shirking. However, several times during the lessons that day the purgative he had taken began to have its effect to the extent that on each successive occasion he had to make his way to the latrine more hastily than the last time. The other boys in the group all knew the cause of his short and frequent absences from class and this caused considerable amusement. Many of the boys had been through this kind of thing themselves and it was common knowledge among them that the only remedy the old Greek physician offered, no matter what kind of complaint, including toothache, was always a dose of medicinal salts. They had nicknamed the physician 'salty medici'. During the physical exercises that evening, Paulo reprimanded Marcus for breaking away from the group in which he was running in order to make his way to the latrines. His reprimand was rather mild and injected with a modicum of humour as he added, "Well, I suppose you have had sufficient exercise for today, running to and from the latrines. I think it would be a good idea if all you boys were administered a dose of medicinal salts each day in order to enliven you up."

Marcus was by now feeling much better, and he was able to treat the remarks good humouredly. Tossing his red cloak back over his shoulder, Praetorian officer, Paulo, strode off to continue his other duties.

Roman civilization was extremely fortunate in that it was able to draw on the intelligence and experience of Greece. The majority of the learned Achemedians, sculptors, geographers, and highly qualified men of the medical profession were Greek. In these domains they were unequalled. Rome provided statecraft and administration, whereas Greece provided the Empire with the intellect that was necessary to sustain the civilization. Therefore, academies throughout the Empire were staffed in the higher echelons by Greeks. This was true also of the medical profession. Many of the physicians seconded to Roman institutions or the legions, and indeed those in private practice were also Greek. The medical institutes of Antioch provided a constant supply of Greek physicians and medical consultants. The older physicians invariably found their way to more settled institutions, such as this one here at Larcia, after perhaps many years of service with the more active institutions connected with the legions. Thus our old physician, Desmosis, here at Larcia, now led a settled life in the collegiate and was perhaps beginning to lose touch with the innovations of his profession. However, his remedies on the young active inmates always worked and, therefore, there were never any real complaints from the collegiate authorities.

Both Paulo and Carpus, the Praetorian officials, were happy to be seconded to this collegiate. They had both seen active service in Spain, under Augustus, and because of their meritorious service had been offered positions in the Praetorian Guard. After some eight years of Guard service they had been transferred here to Larcia with complete acquiescence. Some of the rascals they had to contend with here and Marcus and Cyrus were two of them, added spice to their lives. Timius Arbutus, they both recognised, was another rascal in the making. They realized, as did their other Praetorian officer colleagues in the institution, that it was very often mischievous boys who were later to grow into mischievous men that were always the most reliable types, especially in times of adversity, as they had often found during their service.

These fellows never let adversity weaken them. They would always come back for more punishment. However sternly these boys were admonished or punished, they never bore any animosity towards their persecutors. Paulo always seemed to have a sly glint in his eye when he had to administer a reprimand to one of the rascals. He knew full well that this was the real stock that made up Rome. Quite naturally there always seemed to grow up between Paulo and the mischievous type of boy a mutual respect, and Carpus also found this to be the case. They would often discuss a certain boy's mischief-making, or some trick that a boy might have got up to, in their off-duty periods.

That evening, as prearranged during the day, Paulo summoned Marcus and Cyrus and questioned each boy separately to get behind the truth and the reason for Marcus' illness, which both he and Carpus had heard was the result of Marcus' tunic being wet through. Vasius had reported, as was his place so to do, that Marcus' tunic had become soaked when one of the assistants had inadvertently thrown a bucket of water, which showered Marcus, out of the cookhouse window. This was a likely tale but obviously not the truth because it was forbidden to throw water out of any of the windows. Marcus and Cyrus stuck to their story when questioned. The cookhouse assistants were each questioned on the matter but categorically denied doing so. Carpus in his turn summoned Timius after they had completed the chores of cleaning the latrines. Timius told the same tale, but he was not a very good bluffer. He had not yet learnt the trick of the trade from Cyrus, and he could not help blushing when questioned. He was immediately taken to Paulo's office by Carpus, and, as they entered, Timius was not too surprised to see his two friends in the midst of being questioned. Carpus reported to Paulo that Timius had told him the truth. His two friends immediately turned on him and accused him of being a terrible sneak. Paulo intervened and now asked them to relate the truth themselves, which they did. Timius blurted out to both his friends that he had done no such thing, that he had told Carpus that water had been thrown through the window of the cookhouse. All three realized that they had been tricked into admission and were now to await their punishment. Paulo, grinning all over his face, then said to them, "Not one of you is clever enough to bluff me. But I confess that I respect each of you for being loyal to one another and dishonest to us. Tomorrow morning you will be awakened before dawn, at the hour of 4.00 a.m., by the night Praetorian officer whom you will work under until the hour of 6.00 a.m. scrubbing the floor of the assembly hall on your hands and knees. You will do this for three days. You will not be sparing with the water, and I shall instruct the night Praetorian officer on duty to make sure that you do the job right. Perhaps after three mornings of making good use of water, you will all learn to keep away from that big expanse of water which is so conveniently situated at the bottom of the hill and which you know is out of bounds to you."

It was now the evening of the third day of their period of punishment, and, as they entered the assembly hall for their evening meal, they noticed how unusually clean the stone floor looked due to their efforts. They also realized how fatigued they were, and it was in the mind of each of the boys that any further fishing expedition they had planned during the retreat at Saturnalia could be forgotten at the moment, because next time, if they were caught, the punishment would be for at least a week or even longer. All the boys, who had assembled for the evening meal, felt that there was an air of expectancy about this evening. The Praetorian officials and Achemedians were all gradually beginning to assemble alongside the podium, and this was indicative that a major announcement was to be made after the meal by the principal, Artimeses. Cyrus called out to Pallius, with whom he was acquainted, across the table, "Hey, Pallius, do you know why the officials are all assembling today?"

"No, I do not know," Pallius replied. "Perhaps we will be told about the arrangements that have been made for attendance for worship at Saturnalia."

Cyrus had queried this with Pallius, because Pallius was the sort of fellow who had a unique way of getting to know what was going on in the campus before any announcements on the subject had been made.

After the meal the boys remained seated as instructed until Artimeses arrived and mounted the Podium. He raised his arms as an indication that he wanted them all to stand. The assembly rose and stood silently. There was a natural air of expectancy about them. Artimeses began his announcement with these words:

> *'Pretorian officers, masters, ancillary staff and junior citizens of the Empire, I have a sad announcement to make to you all. I have received a confirmed report from Rome which informs us all that our generous and well-loved Emperor, Caesar Octavian Augustus, is dead.*
>
> *I am informed that he died yesterday before sunset and that he will be cremated tomorrow on the military field outside Rome. His loss will be felt throughout the Empire, and we will greatly feel his loss here at this Augustan collegiate which was established at his will and will continue in his honour. Tomorrow will be a day of mourning and worship at the Temple, when we shall offer a sacrifice to the gods that they may accept his spirit among them, as a living deity beside them. I am pleased to announce to you also the succession of Tiberius Caesar, who was the natural chosen and considered heir of Augustus. The day of Caesar Augustus' birth will, henceforth, be recognised as a Holy Day in our calendar, when we will, each year, worship and*

offer sacrifices to Augustus the God. I will make arrangements that this beautiful bust we have of him, standing here beside me, be moved to its rightful place in the Temple. His portrait which you also see hanging behind me will be moved to the Library.'

Timius' eyes immediately fell on the portrait that was hanging on the wall above Artimeses head. The portrait was dimly lit by the flickering flames of two candles. He had looked at this portrait many times before but did not know who it was, and he did not dare ask for fear of showing his ignorance. Somehow he vaguely seemed to recall certain features of the face in the portrait, but he could not remember where or when he had seen that face before. Suddenly, as though a bolt from the blue had struck him, he remembered. It was the old man who was being carried in the litter which stopped to enquire why Ciatus and Timius were hiding in the hedge and who had tossed to each of the boys a gold coin. Could that old man have been the Emperor, thought Timius. No, never. After all, what would the Emperor be doing in Velitrae. No, it must be, he came to the conclusion, another person who resembled the Emperor, and he put further thoughts out of his mind immediately.

Artimeses then dismissed the assembly asking them to pray to the gods that the spirit of the Great Augustus be conveyed unto their heavenly bosoms by the noble eagles that flew as protectors over the wonderful city. He instructed them that all normal duties be relaxed for one day. Timius was excited about this because he could have a one day respite from his latrine chore. His hopes were soon to be dashed because Carpus was quick to remind each boy of the latrine group, as they came out of the assembly hall, that the relaxing of duty did not include latrine cleaning.

The death of Augustus left Rome and the Empire with a feeling of uncertainty about the future, the anxiety being that there might be a return to the pre-Augustan era. Tiberius had now succeeded Augustus. He was not the natural or expressly chosen heir because it was well known in senatorial circles that Augustus had an intense dislike for him and treated him with no respect. It was only through his marriage to Livia that Tiberius, who was Livia's son by her previous marriage to Drusus Nero, was to succeed him.

His chosen successor was initially Marcellus who was Augustus' natural nephew by his second marriage to Scribonia. His first marriage to Claudia broke up because there were no children. Marcellus was killed in battle so his second choice was Postumus who was the son of his daughter Julia by his second marriage to Scribonia. Julia's second marriage was to Agrippa, and it was their son, Postumus, who was his second choice. Unfortunatelly, Postumus met his end and, it is alleged, by deliberate assassination while Augustus was on his deathbed, by the hand of Livia. Livia's one aim was to have her son Tiberius succeed Augustus and this she succeeded in doing. Tiberius had been granted a consulship and magistracy, but he was not competent in either office. His main achievements were that of a general, particularly in the many campaigns in which he was engaged along the Rhine/Danube frontier against the German barbarians alongside Germanicus.

Germanicus was the grandson of Livia and Drusus Nero, and he was at this time on one of these campaigns. Had Augustus lived longer he would have undoubtedly chosen Germanicus to be his successor. Augustus in all his actions, all his statements and all his desires, did not choose and did not want Tiberius to succeed him. It is probable that he realized Tiberius' total incompetence for this high office. His last hopes, on his death, were that the restored Republican order would be truly practiced, whereby Tiberius' consulship would be an elective issue of one year at a time until a rightful successor would emerge. The rumour that Augustus was poisoned by Livia can easily be discounted because we are aware of the fact that his health was failing, and it could well have been that he died a natural death from contracting pneumonia. The continuation of the Augustan order now depended largely on whether these foundations were properly set out. If they were the emergence of Tiberius or any other tyrant, assuming of course that Tiberius would become a tyrant, would have little or no affect on the established Augustan order.

The ceremony to adulate their dead god, Augustus, at the Temple, took place as arranged. It was very similar to the routine Sunday worship except that, on this occasion, two lambs and a calf were sacrificed at the Temple. All schoolboys gave heir full attention to the sacrificial rites and outwardly treated the occasion sombrely. Inwardly, of course, their feelings were much different. Many of them had feelings of some delight because they realized that the bodies of the sacrificial lambs and calf would be taken to the cookhouse to be prepared into a tasty evening meal, but, naturally enough, they did not like attendance of worship on these occasions even though it provided them with a meal of a difference. Unfortunately sacrifices to the gods were only made on religious days of observance, which in the boys' estimation was not often enough, but because of the infrequency these days were looked forward to for the cuisine treat they provided. Their very routine and sparce meals drove many of them to breaking bounds and trespassing into the fields of the surrounding farms in order to steal edible root crops, raw cabbage leaves, and fruits from the orchard to satisfy their constant hunger. The authorities were aware of the boys' needs but deliberately refrained from overindulging them in fattening nourishment, this being the means of instilling the much-relished discipline of Rome.

At the midday meal, which, as previously explained, was the usual one of light refreshment, Timius noticed, for the first time since he arrived at the collegiate, that there was a group of eight boys who were standing at a table, which was set apart from the other tables. These boys were not permitted to sit down. Timius noticed also that there was no pewter dish in front of each boy on which to place a crusty bread roll. The only utensil that was placed on the table for them was the regulation pewter mug. These eight boys stood throughout the meal, and Timius enquired of Cyrus, very discreetly of course, why these boys had not been given anything to eat and why had he only seen them drinking from their mugs. Cyrus very briefly explained that these boys were obviously being punished for some offence or other. They were absent from the ceremony that morning at the Temple. The punishment was that they would be deprived of their routine meals throughout the period of three days, and their only sustenance would be a portion of a bread roll for their evening meal. They would be given no other liquid to drink except water during this period. This was another punishment which was instituted here at the collegiate. As in any other establishment or institution, the punishments were made to fit the severity of the crimes. At the end of the meal, the Praetorian officer on duty in the assembly hall instructed the assembled boys to remain seated, and on the entry of Artimeses into the hall, they were instructed to stand. He mounted the podium, as he had done the previous evening when he announced the death of Augustus, and the boys immediately expected another important announcement to be made. They were to be disappointed. In a high-pitched voice he called out the name of Gaius Menon.

"I am here, sire," Gaius Menon replied obediently.

"Come over here this instant," ordered Artimeses, and the fourteen year old boy half-shuffled, half-ran to the foot of the podium. Artimeses then made an announcement.

> *Junior citizens, you can see standing before me one of your colleagues Gaius Menon. He had the audacity to not only absent himself from paying his respects to our glorious Emperor, Augustus, who had so sadly left our midst to join the gods, but he also had the audacity to return to his dormitory and crawl back under his bed*

clothes and pretend that he was sick. He knew, as well as all of you know, that before permission to absent oneself from a college ceremony, or any other arranged activity, one must first obtain permission from the physician. He did not obtain permission from any of his superiors and therefore my sentence is that he shall receive twelve stiff strokes of the cane on his posterior. You will all remain standing while you witness this punishment being carried out.'

Artimeses turned to face the praetorian officer who was standing on the other side of the podium with a cane, specially selected for this purpose, poised in his right hand. Artimeses nodded to him indicating that he could proceed with the punishment. He strode to Gaius Menon, stopped alongside him, clutched him by the back of the neck with his left hand and bent him over. He then lifted up the part of the tunic that covered the boy's posterior and commenced applying the cane until twelve strokes, loudly counted by Artimeses for all assembled to hear, had been administered.

They could hear the swishing and landing of the cane onto Gaius' flesh very clearly, but they could not hear any whimper or murmur from Gaius. When the punishment was over Gaius stood up and faced the assembly. They noticed his eyes were red with the need to conceal the pain, but he dare not cry because he would never live it down if he cried publicly. He desperately wanted to rub his backside to alleviate the stinging. He dare not do this publicly either. However, he did not have to wait very long and when dismissed rushed out of the assembly hall. Artimeses then granted the assembled boys permission to leave. Since this was a special day of mourning the rest of the day was free, except for the usual latrine cleaning, which took place just before sunset. When they were outside the assembly hall, Timius remarked to both Cyrus and Marcus that he would hate to have to experience such humiliation and punishment, because what he had witnessed had made him feel fearful. Marcus' response to this was, 'your turn will come one day because nearly all of us have had the cane sometime or other.'

Timius felt a little with-drawn, and he went on to ask if twelve strokes were always administered. He was informed by Cyrus that the number of strokes depended on the severity of the crime. They were about to make their way to the dormitory to make plans for the afternoon when, in the distance, they could hear the incessant sound of horns being blown by the farmers.

"I wonder what has caused them to blow their horns so loudly at this time of day," mused Marcus.

"I have no idea," Cyrus responded, "but I'll soon find out." Spotting a wood chopper busy with a tree trunk on the perimeter of the collegiate, Cyrus ran over to him to enquire. He came back to inform them that a pack of wolves had been spotted in the area. They all looked at each other questioningly for quite a while, when Marcus broke the silence by saying that their afternoon could well be spent tracking the wolves. Timius and Cyrus were quick to jump at this suggestion and agreed that this would be a most fruitful way of spending the afternoon. Cyrus teased Timius by implying that, since he was the youngest of them, if the wolves captured him perhaps he would be lucky enough for the leader of the pack to be a 'she' wolf, and then perhaps he would not have to return to the collegiate because the 'she' wolf would undoubtedly suckle him like the 'she' wolf, in the old days, suckled Romulus and his brother Remus. Timius took this jokingly and shrugged the comment off although he was aware of the legend that the founder of Rome, Romulus, had been suckled by a 'she' wolf and, thereafter, the age-old symbol of Rome was the wolf suckling the brothers Romulus and Remus.

The trio sneaked out through the perimeter and quickly darted for cover in the nearby trees. Once under cover and out of sight of the campus, they each selected a sapling tree, the branches of which they broke off at the lower end of the stem, clearing the upper end of its leaves. These now provided them with a staff each, and armed with what they considered to be suitable weapons against the wolves, they set off into the wooded valley keeping watch for the wolves. They knew not where they were going, because they did not know where they would find the wolves. If they did come across the creatures their weapons would be of no use to protect them. The only weapon that would put a wolf out of action was the pilum, which was a spear about six feet long, and even then the hunter would have to be very accurate in its delivery. At their tender age they were not to know this, and going out in search of a fierce pack of wolves was a means of satisfying their bravado. Timius noticed a little wren fly out anxiously from its nest. He crept over to where the nest hung by the top end of its matted hood and peeped into it. There he could see three little eggs.

"Hey, Marcus and Cyrus, come over here and see what I have found," he shouted to the others.

They came over to take a look but were disappointed that it was only a nest. Timius could not understand the reason for their disappointment, but it was obvious that they had seen many such nests here in the wooded valleys. They half-suggested that he should take the eggs and blow them out so that he could keep the shells and form a collection. A lot of the boys in the college did this although it was illegal and not in accordance with the college rules. Many of them had clandestinely collected a fair selection of bird eggs which they had hidden in the bottom of their personal boxes. Marcus then went on to explain how one blew out the embryo from the shell. He advised that all Timius had to do was to select a good strong sharp thorn from the Hawthorn tree or any other tree that produced thorns, pierce the egg at both ends, very carefully, so that the shell did not break, then blow hard through it until the contents flowed out through the other hole. Once cleaned, it could be stored away safely without going rotten. Timius thought he would like to try this some time, but on this occasion he did not do so because they were supposed to be going after wolves. However, he did wish that he had known this trick earlier because he could have tried it on many occasions when he was asked to help his mother select eggs that had been given to her by the farmers who called at their house on their way to town. Anyway, he made a mental note of this because it would be an enjoyable hobby collecting wild birds' eggs.

They had not been very long on their excursion when they were suddenly startled by a wild boar which had been suckling its young. The animal grunted angrily and made a charge towards them. Cyrus spotted what it was and called to the other two to run like mad as he headed back to the school perimeter. In their state of fright, they each dropped the staffs they were carrying and, hot-footed for all they were worth, back to the school. There was no well-worn path that they could follow, so they had to make their way back the way they had come. The grass beneath their feet was damp, and they kept slipping every so often. Fortunately the animal kept turning back and retreating a few yards to make sure the piglets were still following. Timius was the first to reach the perimeter and make his way through the opening because he was much more nimble-footed than his companions. When they were through the perimeter, they ran up the bank and into the compound of the college buildings. They were still not safe because to their astonishment the wild boar, followed by its piglets, continued to give chase. When they reached the compound other boys who were in the vicinity saw what was going on and joined in the excitement. Some tried to capture the piglets but were prevented by the piglets' mother. Praetorian officer Lictus heard the rumpus and came to investigate, saw what was happening and quickly ran into the building to grab a pilum. He ran back to the scene at the far end of the compound where the wild boar at this point was beginning to give chase to another group of boys. He launched the spear which had gone through its body just at the beginning of its hind quarters. The five piglets were grabbed up into the arms of the other boys squealing furiously. The Praetorian officer, Lictus, calmed down the situation by ordering the boys who had been clutching the piglets to take them to the butcher in the cookhouse. He then withdrew the spear from the wild boar, after it gave its last kick, and instructed some of the other boys to drag it to the cookhouse.

"What will happen now?" whispered Timius to Cyrus.

"After it has been butchered, drawn and quartered, we will have the wild boar and its young served up for our evening meals in two or three days' time."

"Oh!" exclaimed Timius, "that will make a change, but I wish they would let those piglets go free, because I wouldn't like to see them slaughtered. In any case, if they are, I will not eat any of it."

"Don't be foolish," was the response from Cyrus. "You'll not know the difference after the cooks have prepared and cooked the meat, and by then you will be so hungry that no doubt you will relish the meal".

"I don't—,"

Timius was unable to finish what he was about to say because at that moment Lictus approached them. He gazed at them for a moment, with the pilum still held firmly in his hand and a twinkle in his eye said, "I am told that thanks to you three we can look forward to some tasty dishes for our evening meals very soon. I am sure we will all be grateful for that."

Our trio felt quite proud that they had done their colleagues a service by providing them with a delicacy, and quite modestly brushed aside the compliment. Lictus eyes lit up.

"So it was you three that had originally been chased by the wild boar?"

"Yes, sire, answered Cyrus, "but we didn't do anything to it. The sow saw us and chased us, presumably to keep us away from the piglets."

"Is that so?" queried Lictus.

"Yes, sire," Cyrius replied.

"Well, then you must have disturbed it in the out of bounds area beyond the school perimeter, because the wild boar never come inside the boundary."

"No, sir," lied Marcus. "We were just walking alongside the perimeter when it saw us, found a large enough opening in the fence and took up the chase."

"I do not believe that excuse. Before sunset the three of you will report to and wait outside Praetorian officer, Paulo's office.

"Very well, sire," they replied in unison.

Timius then remembered that he had to attend to the latrine chores before sunset, and when he explained this in a mutter, Lictus then instructed them to report after sunset and before their evening meal.

The table that was set aside for wrongdoers in the assembly hall at mealtimes had now to accommodate a further three patrons. The eight boys who had been punished for three days on bread and water were now joined by Cyrus, Marcus and Timius. Officer Paulo had sentenced them to four days of bread and water, and on the third day of their punishment, there were only the three of them left at the punishment table, the other eight boys having served their punishment rejoined the assembly for their meal. The meal this night consisted of the delicacy of pork, and the aroma from the dish made our three friends' mouths' water.

During the meal some of the other boys, from time to time, although repeatedly admonished by the Praetorian officer on duty in the assembly hall, cat-called and called out in a jeering fashion their thanks to Timius, Marcus and Cyrus, for providing such a delicacy. Cyrus at one point lost his temper and threatened one of the cat-callers with his pewter mug. This led to a challenge for a fight. The Praetorian officer on duty this night overheard the argument, and Carpus instructed both boys to report to the college gymnasium the following morning, where they could settle the argument in a wrestling match under proper supervision of the gymnast. Cyrus agreed and was confidently supported by his two companions who were absolutely sure, without any doubt, that he would win the match.

The day of mourning that had begun so well for our three friends had now ended in a period of punishment, but Timius, who was still optimistic, began straight away to enquire whether their plans to go fishing again during the week's holiday of Saturnalia was still their intended plan. He was assured that this was so and was also promised by Cyrus that if the wolf pack was still wandering in the vicinity of the collegiate, they would find time to go after them. But Timius had noticed that the blowing of horns had ceased and drew this to Cyrus' attention. Cyrus suggested that as the pack must have moved on they would have to plan some other excursions for the holiday period.

Timius was very eager to know what these plans would be, but Cyrus was not able to tell him because he had not thought of any yet but said to Timius, "don't worry about planning now. You may be too weak after four days of bread and water to want to do anything, and in any case we may well have to spend most of the time stealing cabbage leaves, carrots, and turnips from the fields, and fruit from the orchards, to build up our strength again before we can plan anything else."

The thought of raw cabbage leaves and freshly plucked fruit from the orchard sent pangs of hunger through Timius, because even though he had just eaten his crusty stale meagre portion of bread and had drunk all the water from his pewter mug, he still felt terribly hungry. The thought that he had another whole day to go before he would receive any other nourishment left him very depressed and dejected. Since his companions were able to find the whole episode amusing he joined in the light-heartedness of it in an effort to forget his hunger.

CHAPTER VII

Primus Interparis

The first among equals

IN 29 B.C. Caesar Octavianus had finally triumphed. He had defeated Mark Anthony and the Egyptian queen Cleopatra at the battle of Actium in 31 B.C. In 30 B.C. Lepidus had been disposed and was no longer a threat to the stability of the republic. The second triumvirate, of 43 B.C., formed by Mark Anthony, Octavian and Lepidus, was now at an end. The formation of this triumvirate was a temporary expedience, which was formed by the agreement of the three parties concerned in an effort to bring about stability.

After the death of Julius Caesar, in 44 B.C., Mark Anthony assumed the control of Rome, but having disposed of Julius Caesar by assassination, it was not prudent to hand over the powers of state assumed by Julius Caesar to yet another individual, however worthy or noble his ambitions might be. Thus the way out of such a situation was the recommended formation of the triumvirate, which enabled the powers of Lepidus, Octavian, and Anthony to be unified for the good of the State. Rome might have known that this coalition would not last, especially when it was found that Mark Anthony was becoming more allured to the affections of the Egyptian Queen, and if their relationship had developed to a natural conclusion the result could not be acceptable to Rome. Rome would not be a slave to Egypt. Marcus Agrippa and Caesar Octavian decided, after the defeat of Anthony, to conquer Egypt and this they did. Cleopatra committed suicide, and her two daughters were brought back to Rome as hostages.

The glory of the day was Agrippa's but the good fortune was that of the young Caesar. He was now proclaimed, by popular consent, First Consul of the Republic and he was able to inaugurate his consulship at Rome by presenting Rome with Egypt, which was the richest country in the world. This was in 29 B.C., and it was in this year also that he came to Rome to celebrate a triple triumph and to open a new era as the first Roman Emperor.

Octavian accepted the consulship with Marcus Agrippa, and their first task was to return the constitution to Republican practice. Their next task was to put an end to the civil disorder which resulted after the death of Julius Caesar. At this point, the Senate was overwhelmingly inflated in numbers. There were over one thousand senators; because Julius Caesar had admitted into the Senate, possibly as a reward for past services, among others, centurions, soldiers, scribes and the sons of freedmen; Gauls were also allowed to enter the Senate and these were more at home in barbarian garb than in the Roman tunic. Octavian decided to reduce this number drastically and install, in the main, members of patricians and like the old Republican order, he reintroduced the conciliation powers of the tribunes, who were elected representatives of the plebeian tribes.

The elections were by plebiscite and through the tribune communications between the wishes of the Senate or, indeed, the patricians and the plebeians was on a much more sound footing. Octavian can be granted the supreme tribute of his impartiality. He fully propounded his theory that all citizens of the restored Republic would have access to his personal office, where complaints of a most trivial nature were given a hearing. Thus he ensured that ostensibly he would be truly representative of the people. But, in fact, his aim was to subtly control the Senate. However, this noble theory was infrequently practiced.

The Senate was ruthlessly purged, and again there was a much deeper reason for doing so. It was not just to purify the Senate of the body of foreigners but also to purge it of the supporters of Mark Anthony. Over three hundred Anthonians were discredited. Hundreds of others who had gained their office through bribery and corruption were expelled and Agrippa made it his business to publicly record their degradation. Complementary to the purge of the Senate, in 28 B.C., Octavian issued an edict for a full scale censor of Roman people throughout the provinces of the Italian peninsula. His pretext here was to have on record details of all the citizens of the Italian province, but the real purpose was to register citizens of all classes and of all public standing for the purpose of an orderly collection of taxes. This exercise was so successful (in that its aim of bestowing citizenship on all registered people and in its acceptance by the people, apart from the few breakaway groups) that it was later extended, in 4 B.C., to embrace the colonies and client kingdoms of Rome. Again the purpose of doing so was for the collection of taxes. The effect of this edict, both in Italy and the provinces, was readily accepted as a gesture and as an advertisement of the return to order and legality.

In 27 B.C., having been elected Consul for the seventh time, Octavian appeared before the Senate and resigned all his powers, and all his provinces to the disposal of the Senate and the Roman people. The Senators pleaded and urged him not to abandon the Republic, which they claimed he had saved. At length, Octavian, with ostensible reluctance and indeed one can call it cunning to a remarkable degree, consented to assume the command of Provincia, which consisted of Spain, Gaul, and Syria, for a period of ten years. A few days later the Senate met again and, as a reward for his succumbing to their plea, they voted him exceptional honours and endowed him with the title of *The Saviour of the State*. They decreed that wreaths of laurel were to be placed on Octavian's doorposts and on the lintel, because he had saved the lives of the Roman citizens. A golden shield, suitably inscribed with his virtues, was set up in the Senate chamber. Copies of this were widely distributed throughout Italy and the provinces. To make the new dispensation, Octavian took a new name, but this was after many hours of arguing and debate.

Julius Caesar, just prior to his assassination, was on the verge of being proclaimed a god throughout the Republic, but the final honour was not be his. It was common practice throughout the provinces, and particularly those of the Eastern Mediterranean, which embraced the client kingdoms of Rome, that the head of their State should automatically assume the powers of a deity. Since these kingdoms were now part of the Roman Republic their own kings and princes could not be endowed with such titles. Had Rome had a monarch, this monarch would have automatically been proclaimed the deity of these client kingdoms. But here in Rome there was a group of ruling senators working in unison. Therefore, to continue this custom and practice it would have been necessary for nearly three hundred senators to be proclaimed deities throughout the Republic. This practice would be impossible. Maecenas argued at length in the Senate the impossibility of such an action, and then it was proposed by Munatius Plancus that Octavian, by decree of the Senate, become Augustus. This title did not indicate the superior powers of a monarch or a dictator, but in deed and in practice was much more supreme and powerful in its extent to any other title previously given to an individual employing autocratic powers with the approval of the

Senate. The subtle difference here meant that any edict of Augustus would only be promulgated with the approval of the Senate. Maecenas went on to argue that since Octavian had accepted, albeit reluctantly, the supreme powers of Augustus therefore the first consul of the Senate, it was now quite in order for him to be granted the powers of a deity, and thus satisfy the needs of the provinces and client kingdoms for a living god to whom they could direct their gratitude and worship.

The month of Sextilis, the sixth month of the year was renamed August, just as Quinctilis, the fifth month of the year, had earlier become July in honour of Julius Caesar.

As first consul and soon after with the adoption of the administrative title of proconsul, Augustus now found himself in a delicate situation whereby if he was to keep the powers bestowed on him by the Senate and the populace, it would mean that he would have to exercise a balance henceforth. He would have preferred the title name of Romulus, the founder of Rome, but since Romulus had been recorded in Roman history as one who had slain his brother Remus and thereby wrenched the powers of the early citizen states for his own ambitions, Augustus realized that if he had urged the Senate to grant him the title of Romulus, he could undoubtedly have given the Senate, the nobility, and the populace the very real impression that he was desirous of monarchical powers. Therefore, the acceptance of the title of Augustus, as suggested by the Senate, and also the lofty position accorded him of that of a deity again by popular vote in the Senate, he could have all the powers of Romulus and of Julius Caesar; that is, powers of a monarch and of a dictator without blatantly prostituting them, but this would mean a balancing act of the most keenest delicacy. It was only the astute and extremely intelligent mind of this rather physically puny individual that would be able to practice this. No resolution, no instrument of policy, no edict, was ever given ratification although ratified invariably by popular vote from the Senate without the express approval and final authority of Augustus. Thus as proconsul, the impression given to the citizens of Rome and her conquered and client provinces was that of a man who was merely chief spokesman of the Senate and the populace. By adopting this stance throughout his lengthy consulship of forty-four years he was able to lead Rome and consolidate the Empire in a fashion that was very much of his own formulation.

Having given Rome the gift of Egypt and then later resigned the consulship, when he was re-elected to position of first consul by popular decree, he accepted on the condition that Egypt would remain a province under his control, and this request was fully agreed to by the senate. He did this in the full knowledge that the wealth of Egypt would provide for him the personal financial wealth that would be needed from time to time to maintain the position he had now acquired by extremely subtle means, that of the Emperor, nay not Emperor, this title was anathema to the roman world whereas the title Augustus was supreme and superior to that of Emperor. This title would come to be regarded as the supreme title throughout the world, and it was only he that truly deserved it, and it was only he that could acquire it without bloodshed, without wars, without civil strife, but by popular vote of the Senate and popular acceptance by Roman citizens. This title was not inherited by him. It was granted to him, and no other ruler henceforth would ever find himself in such a lofty position and with such enormous control over the daily lives and customs of Roman citizens and subordinate clientele of the rest of the Empire.

After purging the Senate his next task was that of consolidation. The past two centuries had seen the lifeblood of the nation drained through lengthy periods of conquest. There was to be no further conquest for the sake of enlarging the empire during his period of office. His aim was to strengthen the Empire by extending orderly administration to all its far-flung corners, a task in which the Romans were extremely adept.

He was to institute a period of rebuilding and widespread development. Townships throughout the peninsula of Italy and the provinces developed and prospered. Systematic trade between provinces was fostered. Roman jurisprudence came to be the accepted yardstick throughout the Empire, and education academic, cultural, and in the crafts, was now enthusiastically encouraged. Freedom of the many religions was tolerated and, in many cases, expanded. In order to achieve these aims Augustus, having accepted the purple mantle of responsibility for the Empire, the frontiers would have to be arrested and strengthened. There had been the aim, even before the death of Julius Caesar, for the conquest of Britannia because it was felt that the assistance given by the Celts and the Druid tribes of Britannia to the barbarians of Germanica was considered a thorn in the side of Rome. But Augustus had decided that this thorn could remain until it was his pleasure to deal with it finally.

However, he never took this action because the frontier along the Rhine-Danube which was the northern extreme of the Roman world, was well guarded by legions under the brilliant generals, and since they were able to keep at bay the German barbarians (although suffering set backs from time to time) the assistance given by the natives of Britannia was of no consequence at the moment. The eastern extremity of the Empire was settled up to the Syrian border, and there was no border that required the defence by large numbers of legions in the vast area that lay behind the Roman settlements of North Africa because beyond this frontier lay the impenetrable Sahara Desert. His next task was to take a hard look at the number of legions both under the financial control of the central treasury and those that were personally financed by members of the nobility. If the frontiers were to be fixed without any further conquest, he was prudent enough to realize that, with over fifty legions in the field, manned by men who were thirsty for the spoils of war, many would become restless. Not only would the legions become restless, but so would their commanders; and commanders of legions were always ambitious individuals. If they were to refrain from further conquest and merely exist to guard the frontiers or deal with local disturbances, fighting machines of this nature would become tired of this kind of existence. May they not then direct their attention to supporting the ambitions of their commanders and may not the commanders ambitions be that of deposing him and the resting the people for themselves. Yes, Augustus was shrewd enough to realize this. The problem he was now faced with was one of enormity. Certainly he could recall most of them and still keep the frontiers safe; but having done so, what was he to do with them. Faced with this problem, he was to emerge from it once again successful after putting his plan to the test. He now began to form three legions in Rome of skilled soldiery and, paid from his personal purse, he named these three legions the Praetorian Guard.

Here was a man who had acquired the powers of the supreme prince of the Republic, by popular consent, finding that it was necessary to form a personal body guard of three legions. He was astute enough to recognise the kind of impression that this act would give to the Senate and the populace. He was not going to make the same mistakes of his grand uncle Julius Caesar by flaunting dictatorial powers on the Senate and the people, backed by an army of legionnaires, nay, that would be a big mistake. He was to have the Praetorian Guard encamped outside Rome. Except when on official duty in the capital, no member of the Praetorian Guard was allowed to enter the gates of the capital in military uniform, nor bearing weapons of any description. His explanation to the Senate for the maintenance of such a force was that they were to be in reserve in case they were called on to go to the aid of a frontier legion that would at any time come under undue pressure from barbarian enemies.

The Praetorian Guard, paid from his own purse, ensured personal loyalty to him. Any would-be ambitious general or leading member of the nobility would refrain from ousting him from his position by fair means or foul, as they did with Julius Caesar, or have the Praetorian Guard to reckon with. Thus his own safety and position were ensured. The remaining Roman military force was reduced to a maximum of twenty-five legions. These were augmented where necessary by auxiliaries who were recruited from members of the local population, but under the control of Roman generals and senior officers. The problem of the demobilized regions after their numbers had been reduced to twenty-five, was overcome by offering them demobilization in the provinces in which they were stationed together with financial gratuities and a gratuity in the form of land. Since many of the veterans had cultivated a fraternity with the local population their acceptance of the settlement was widespread and successful. This action achieved two ends; firstly, it satisfactorily resettled the veteran in his country and area of choice; secondly, since the vast majority of these veterans were of Roman stock and citizenship, their subsequent presence in these settlements in foreign provinces helped to stabilize the local situation and greatly assisted to Romanize the respective areas. This was another important factor towards stabilizing the Empire.

Augustus established a military chest thereafter to provide pensions for his veterans, in place of the farms to which they had become accustomed to expect, and he was successful in reducing their enormous rates of pay, to which they had also become accustomed during the years of the civil war. He was able to do this by offering them proper careers in the legion. Twenty years service is the established period of service required of them and an oath of allegiance taken yearly to serve their Emperor was instituted. The Praetorian Guard, of which there were nine thousand men, enjoyed a shorter service of only sixteen years and double pay. The twenty-five legions are for the most part stationed along the northern and eastern frontiers, and were deployed as follows. Upper and Lower Germania were protected by four legions each, Pannonia three legions, Dalmatia two legions, Mosia two legions, Syria four legions, and Egypt two legions. Three legions were necessary in Spain where there was constant local unrest, whereas one legion was considered sufficient in the remarkably peaceful provinces of Northern Africa. The Praetorian Guard had to be genuine Italians, whereas the legions that protected the rest of the Empire could accept genuine volunteers from members of the local population, and by doing so were automatically granted Roman citizenship. The legions themselves were stationed in great fortified camps along the frontiers of various provinces. There were thus huge spaces of country totally without military forces. For example, for warfare on the shores of the Black Sea troops had to be summoned from Syria. This did present an inconvenience and a danger, but Augustus did not intend or mean to organize a military monarchy. The creation of a standing force of twenty-five legions under his direct control was a tremendous achievement of Augustus, yet his creation of a standing fleet was not one of his better achievements. The Italian navy was divided into two flotillas, one for the western Mediterranean and one for the Adriatic. The Mediterranean was now properly policed and commerce was free to circulate and prosper. Great artificial docks were constructed for the navy.

The loyalty of the troops to Augustus was surprising. It was because of the rumour that spread like wildfire throughout the Roman fortifications, that their Caesar had so much concern for them that he would focus his affection for them in his nightmares. *'Varus, give me back my legions.'* And yet again he would yell,*' Varus, give me back my legions,'* until he was woken up by his slaves. Three legions, under the command of General Varus, had been ambushed in the Tuterburger forests of Germany and totally massacred. General Varus also lost his life in this debacle. This event had a tragic effect on Augustus, and is said to have been the cause of a very severe illness which was nearly fatal, but his nightmares continued because he could not forgive the incompetence of one of his generals in losing three legions and three revered Eagles. These nightmares were aptly interpreted by all military personnel as his sincere affection for his troops. This might have been a misinterpretation because having reduced the legions to such a small number in comparison with the extent of the territory they were to police, it probably had an acutely worrying effect, so much so that he began to wonder whether he had made a great mistake. Fortunately, the interpretation of his nightmares and his cries of loss were misinterpreted. His adopted nephew, General Tiberius, was given the task of reforming the three lost legions from the remains of the previous legions to march back to the Rhine frontier in an attempt to deal a final blow on the German chief, Hermann Armenius.

Augustus had now assumed tribunicial and censorial powers, which gave him complete control of the central treasury. Although he was a man of immense wealth which was continually replenished from his dominion of Egypt, he needed additional wealth to put his economic plans into action. The powers of tribune and censor were again granted him by popular consent, and although registration had already been made for the orderly collection of taxes, this did not include the fiscal facet of income tax. A tax on landowners imposed and adhered to and death duties became an accepted fiscal practice throughout the Italian peninsula. The provinces rendered taxes in the form of a *tributum* to the central treasury without the express authority of the August Princep. He was now in full control of the central finances of the Empire.

The inseparable ability of law and order is a very Roman concept. The sole guarantee of ordered social life is an effectively forced system of law. To legislate men into virtue may seem a useless occupation, but it was not so to the Romans. The more society lost its moral bearings, the less assured became its discipline; the less assured its discipline, the more certain the collapse of internal stability; and with the collapse of internal stability went loss of Empire. Thus was explained the failure of the Republic prior to Augustus.

He believed that is men were not moral by nature, they could be coerced into morality by law, for if the individual citizen was corrupt then the whole Empire was in danger. The establishment of peace and security in Rome and her Empire was an important task. Therefore, the restoration of the Republic meant the regularization of law and order. First **Lex Iulia de Adulteriis Coercendis**. This made adultery a public crime. The law assumed that marriage and parenthood were the natural state of men between the ages of twenty-five and sixty and women between the ages of twenty-five and fifty, and this imposed disabilities upon those that abstained from marriage and subsequent parenthood. Husbands and fathers gained promotion quicker by parenthood, and those who had many children increased their seniority in their application to public office. The second law, **Lex Iulia de Maritandis Ordinibus** liberalised the law of marriage by recognising the validity of marriages between freeborn citizens and men and women freed from slavery. But senators were forbidden to marry freedwomen. This moral legislation proclaimed a return to traditional moral standards. Admission to the Senate now rested not only on wealth and noble birth, but on moral standing and ability, and this led the way to the acceptance in the Senate of citizens from other parts of the Empire. It is unfortunate that Augustus was unable to set an example on the question of morality; he had already committed adultery and experienced divorce twice. Despite this, the law on adultery was fairly successful.

The main occupation in Italy was in agriculture of all types. Stability and greatly increased wealth under Augustus resulted in a considerable improvement in horticulture and farming. For example, wine production developed in quantity and quality; but the main problem still remained the production of corn. An insufficient amount was being grown in Italy to feed the hungry mouths of the large numbers of immigrants ceaselessly attracted to the capital. Therefore, Rome had to rely largely on the grain tribute from Africa and Egypt. His fear at one time was that the population would rely too much on the corn dole from abroad, and this would create a situation where production of corn in Italy would remain largely static. Therefore, with large sums of money from his own personal wealth and the central treasury, he encouraged the cultivation of corn in Cisalpine Gaul, which was part of northern Italy, but even this cannot satisfy the demand of the capital now saturated with a large population. Augustus was fairly confident that by fair jurisdiction of North Africa and Egypt from whence the much needed corn was imported, stability could be continued and he tried to project his belief onto the Senate that these colonies could be satisfactorily and favourably administered—much more so than the other provinces of the Empire—the status quo, or indeed the Pax Romana could be maintained without any undue local upheaval which could have brought the corn supply into a precarious situation. There was an occasion, during the many debates that took place in the Senate chamber, on the question of corn supply when he sternly admonished the Senate in that they were more concerned with the amount of the corn dole than in the just administration of the land supplying the corn, which was vital to the well-being of the capital.

'Why, oh, why a I surrounded by incompetent politicians when I desperately need statesmen,' was his reproach to the Senate. This admonishment guided the Senate into taking a more serious view of the situation that was extant in the corn-supplying colonies. Prior to the Augustan era, the delicate wines of Italy were mainly imported and the majority of the supply came from the Hellenes, but now Italy produced moderately large quantities of wines of an equally good quality. Large tracts of land around the capital came under cultivation of the vine. The breeding of cattle was a growing concern, and large quantities of sheep were bred solely for the purpose of the local woollen industry. Homespun fabrics were the main produce of the local industries and, in addition, this stable period resulted in a growing prosperity with a measure of affluence as its natural culmination. Affluence gave a gradual development to a number of urbanised industries.

There were growing demands for various forms of materialism and to supply the materials of affluence demands a growing body of craftsmen and labour in the industries that are engaged in a productive capacity to meet its needs. Immigrant labour was drawn to the urbanised townships for employment. But in order that this labour could be harnessed properly it was necessary to introduce codes of conduct among work forces and this Augustus encouraged.

There were now several technical innovations in the production of glass, and this had the effect of making glassware extremely cheap. The result was the growth of new factories where considerable skill was still required.

The smelting of iron ore was already a well-established industry, but another industry that seems to have developed a real factory system was bronze and copper, wares of all descriptions, from ladles, kitchen utensils to artistic objects and elaborate metal furniture. These industries, where the production of vast numbers of uniform articles which required much more elaborate and specialised techniques than in the iron industry, can only have been achieved by heavy investment and considerable division of labour. As we have already said the development of these specialised industries, which also included the fabric industries, resulted in the formation of guilds of spinners, weavers, glass makers, iron ore smelters, bronze copper and silversmiths. We must not forget at this point, one of the largest industries in Italy. That industry was brick making, and although Augustus later boasted that he gave Rome marble instead of brick, the majority of buildings in the capital were brick-built, although many were embellished with marble. Of course, the most important buildings were constructed to give the appearance that they were wholly of marble. The restoration of peace and the fixing of the military frontiers under Augustus enabled the products of Roman ingenuity and the craftsmanship of the commonwealth to be transported throughout the world.

Augustus did not have the gifts of soldiery or military craft, but his intense ability lay in the much more mundane field of statecraft. He was endowed with the peculiar gift of pragmatism, and he was able to put this to use at a time when Rome and her provinces were badly in need of such an endowment. His pragmatism can again be seen in the way he approached the problem of overcrowding in the capital. The very prosperity he was instrumental in developing resulted in the immigration of people into the capital from other parts of Italy resulting in the obvious problem of accommodation. The problem was solved by the existent landlords in their exploitation of this situation. Buildings in their ownership that were originally constructed two or even three storeys high, with family dwellings within them, were now utilised to accommodate more people. Land in the capital was not readily available on which new housing construction could take place. Therefore, many existing buildings were increased in capacity by means of additional construction on top, making them five, six, and sometimes seven storeys high. This brought about overcrowding in many sections of the capital—and slums. The danger of fire was now a very real problem, and during the earthquake, one of many that took place about 7 A.D., these poorly built constructions collapsed even at the slightest tremor and were the cause of untold loss of life. The resulting reconstruction programme was therefore guided by a code of building practice which was enforced. This act stemmed from Augustus' concern for the well being of the capital. In addition to this fire hazards were now to be the concern of the landlords and hierarchy themselves. He has made it their responsibility to provide voluntary fire brigade forces paid out of their own purses. The policing of the capital is totally absent because it was his belief that, since he was the true representative of the population at large in his capacity as first consul and tribune, their loyalty lay entirely with him, and that any offence against the State by one of his citizens would be an offence against his person. This would not be permitted by the populace at large. In fact groups of part-time volunteers known as vigils were automatically set up among the people without any prompting from Caesar Augustus or the Senate. Naturally there had been many occasions when disorders had to be dealt with by army guards while on civil duties. But the people made it their business to bring offenders before the courts. This situation of order and control was to last for many years. But what would happen now that he had gone to take his rightful place among Jupiter, Juno, Jove, Apollo and the other deities. Time alone would tell.

It was now merely in Rome that the Augustan principate stimulated building, as had previously been done throughout Italy. The communities concerned were responsible for the expenses of public construction of town walls, local roads, bridges, water works, and sewers, numerous temples and baths, theatres and amphitheatres. Frequently part or even the whole cost of a particular project was contributed by an individual citizen. Civic pride was very strong in Italy and some of the wealth acquired by the Augustan nobility was spent on the adornment of their native towns. Augustus had given generously to many of the towns in Italy. In 20 B.C. he established a Senatorial Commission to maintain the great highways in Italy. Those in the provinces remained the responsibility of the provincial Roman governors. One notable feature was a Golden Milestone engraved with the distances of the main cities of the Empire measured from the gates of Rome. The individual towns were made responsible for the upkeep of their local roads, streets, and bridges, and even for this there were many wealthy contributors.

When Augustus returned to Rome from Spain and Gaul, after his successes in those provinces in 13 B.C., the Senate decreed that an altar of the Augustan Peace, the *Ara Pacis*, should be consecrated in the Campus Martius in honour of his return. They ordered the magistrates and the priests and the vestal virgins to offer there a sacrifice every year to commemorate its consecration. In the sculptured freezes of the altar can be seen standing among his friends, family, freeborn citizens and the nobility, Augustus with little to distinguish him from the others, but in which he is depicted in the same standing as his associates; equal to all of them but, nonetheless 'first among equals.'

The *forum* of Augustus was constructed as a complement to the *Ara Pacis*. Both these monuments denote a continuity of the past, in that the Augustan Principate was the natural successor to the Republic and that the Republic had indeed been restored. The Forum presents this claim in the military sphere indicating that Augustus was the great general, the servant of Rome's imperial mission, the other heroes of old, following the duties imposed by heaven to fulfil the decree of Virgil's Jupiter, in which he says, *'On the Romans I place no limits, either of space or of time: I have given them imperial power without end.'*

The *Ara Pacis*, Alter of Peace, denotes the theme that peace and homecoming was proclaimed, but this could not exist without the imperial mission of Augustus and Rome. The orator Horace constantly returned to the theme that it was the military power of Rome and Augustus which assured peace, and the Sybil—the oracle—in the sixth book of Virgil's *Aenid* closed the great review of Rome's heroes with the words ***'Do you, Roman, remember to rule the nations with power as these shall be your arts and to impose the ways of peace, to pardon the humbled and to destroy the arrogant in war.'***

This theme would now guide the destiny of the Roman people for many centuries into the distant future. Slavery was rife during the period of the Republic but, whereas previously the ownership of slaves was mainly the domain of the aristocracy, with the increased affluence of the Augustan period, the domain was extended beyond these bounds. Slaves were transported from nearly all the conquered territories to Rome and the other major cities of the Empire. Augustus took no major steps to alleviate slavery; indeed, he was a slave owner himself, and the philosophers argue that a civilization supported by slavery cannot last. After the episode of the last century when the slave rebellion under the slave leader Spartacus finally succumbed to the military might of Rome, slaves never again were given the slightest opportunity to organize themselves into a rebellious force. However, there was now more opportunity for the slaves to earn their freedom from their masters, and the increase of freedmen in the cities became much more prevalent.

*   *   *

This, then, was the new Roman world in which young Arbutus and his generation would grow up, a world bequeathed to the Roman people and their client kingdoms by the benevolent, autocratic leader, Caesar Augustus, in the opinion of many an informed mind the greatest ruler that mankind had ever been worthy of.

The impression that was gained by the young Arbutus and his generation of their beloved Emperor was that of a man who was soldiery and heroic in all aspects. Here was a man of great physical strength and personal courage that in defence of the Empire could easily and in person smite down all his enemies. This was not true.

Augustus was born the son of a small-town Italian banker and passed by adoption into the patrician Iulii clan and by marriage into the heart of Roman nobility. He went to Rome at the age of eighteen, in the middle of one of the most murderous epochs of European history and spent the next thirteen years in the most remorseless pursuit of his own ambitions through cajolery, bribery, fraud, treachery, murder and civil war until he emerged, at the age of thirty-two as the sole master of the Roman world. The last forty-five years of his life were spent in the consolidation of his personal power to the establishment of peace and stable order. He thus laid the foundations of the form of government which would rule Rome and practically the whole of Europe for many centuries. His achievements stand on record and are a cause of wonder and surmise. He was a handsome man and most graceful at all stages in his life, although he cared nothing for finery. When talking and in silence, he was calm and mild. His eyes were clear and bright and gave one the impression that there was a sort of divine power in them. His teeth, widely separated, were small and dirty and his hair was slightly yellowish and curly. His ears were small and he had rather a protruding nose. He was a short man, but his height was disguised by the good proportions of his figure and was only apparent if somebody taller stood beside him. He was badly birth-marked all over his chest, and his left hip, thigh and leg were not strong. He walked with a limp. The malfunction of his bladder caused him constant pain of which he hardly ever complained. Physically, it is clear,

Augustus was a coward. He was terrified of wars and battles, and his fear of thunder and lightening is well known; at the first sign of a thunder storm he would make his way rapidly to some near underground cavern.

He had a weak constitution, and his life was constantly debilitated. But it has been said that his illnesses were the product of a nervous and timid temperament, which in his capacity of first consul placed quite an extraordinary strain upon him. He lacked glamour and did not have the vigorous masculinity of Mark Anthony. Although he was puny, sickly and cowardly—ruthlessness often coexists with cowardice—his high moral courage and a firm grasp of reality commanded admiration. It was no weakling who progressed from obscurity to a position as the father of the Roman Empire. He had given the world peace, the Republic was restored, and at last tranquillity and prosperity prevailed. He had hoped for children that which fortune had withheld.

He knew, above all, that the whole Roman world yearned for peace in which children would be longed for blessings not causes of worry and sorrow. Rome was no longer inward looking and in its new outward stance, it had unified the whole of Italy and had created for the first time an Empire as an entity. The Empire was not now merely held together, but was fused into a new unity.

CHAPTER VIII

Utroque vestrum delector.

CICERO

I am delighted with each of you.

DURING THE SHORT period between the cessation of early morning exercises and the commencement of breakfast, Cyrus, accompanied by Timius and Marcus, made his way to the campus gymnasium. On arrival at the building he found it locked and the area deserted. After deliberating what they should do next, they decided to report to Praetorian Officer Paulo, to whom Cyrus would explain that his instructions of the previous night, 'to be at the gymnasium that morning to take part in the wrestling contest', had been carried out by him, but his opponent had failed to make himself available. Moreover, he explained that the gymnasium was closed. In these circumstances he approached Paulo for his advice because, as he also explained, he did not want to be punished yet again for disobeying an instruction.

Paulo looked at him rather indifferently and informed him quite casually, as though this were information he should have the common sense to know, that the gymnasium was closed for three days on the instructions of the principal as a mark of respect to their glorious Emperor Augustus. It was Artimeses instruction that no sporting activities, or those of a combatant nature, were to take place. Paulo advised Cyrus to obey the instructions given him and report to the gymnasium on the fourth morning. Cyrus felt a little embarrassed that he had not known this, but then nobody told him. He was not the kind of boy who mixed very freely with the other boys because he had found that his interests, outside of those academic activities in which he was interested, lay in other directions than those of the vast majority of the boys at the college. These wider interests of Cyrus attracted to him some boys who were of the same mind as he. Consequently, everyday, campus information that was considered common knowledge was always late in arriving as far and, because of this, Cyrus had been placed in many an embarrassing situation.

On the fourth morning, again during the period between exercise and breakfast, our three friends made their way to the gymnasium. Timius was a little excited about the event he was soon to witness, and Marcus was happily giving him an account of two other matches between other combatants which he had the pleasure to witness. When they arrived at the gymnasium, the big wooden doors of the building were flung wide open and they nervously entered it. The gymnasium contained very little in the way of furnishings. Aside from the boundary of a square marked out in the boards which made up the flooring of the gym there were three vaulting horses standing along the outer walls and along these walls were positioned, at equal intervals, exercise bars.

There were also, to the far end of the gymnasium, a wooden structure which provided parallel bars and a single horizontal bar raised about nine feet off the floor. There were also scattered here and there heavy coconut fibre mattresses which were used to provide a softer landing for vaulting gymnasts. These furnishings were common and could be seen in any of the gymnasiums in any part of the Empire, and had their origins in Greece, during the hay day of Spartan glorification. They also saw, in a group to the left of them as they entered, the boy whom Cyrus had threatened in the assembly hall during their meal four days earlier. Pilpius had a group of about eight supporters around him because he was a very popular boy in the school and the gymnast Demetrius, a Greek from Antioch, was in the middle of discussing something with them, and it seemed the discussion was taking an amusing turn because after a few minutes they all burst out laughing. As they did so Cyrus was spotted by Pilpius who pointed him out to Demetrius. Demetrius beckoned him over and after telling both the combatants' supporters to stand alongside the walls and not to interfere in the contest ushered both the boys to the centre of the gymnasium and to the centre of the marked out square. He then instructed them on the essentials of making this a clean match and then gave them the signal to commence. Timius had never seen a wrestling or boxing match before and Marcus, in between moments of excited cheering, informed Timius of the finer points of wrestling, as though he was a past master of the art. He pointed out actions that were considered fair play and those that constituted fouls. Cyrus's two supporters, although cheering loudly, were drowned out by the supporters of Pilpius. After some fifteen minutes had expired, the excitement was beginning to wear thin with both Timius and Marcus because they could now plainly see that Cyrus was getting the worst part of the deal. It was only a matter of a few minutes before Cyrus conceded defeat. He lifted himself up with what seemed like tremendous effort, and as a gesture of gamesmanship, shook hands with the victor and returned to join his companions. They could see he was not only very dejected but also very weak. This weakness had been brought about through lack of proper nutrition over the past three days. He, like Timius and Marcus, were absolutely famished and weak with hunger. Cyrus did not lack stamina and there would probably have been many others faced with the same situation who would have given up much earlier. He knew that he had not got the strength to defeat his opponent although it was evident during the contest that Cyrus far excelled in what little basic skill he had of wrestling. Timius and Marcus consoled him by giving him hefty pats on the back.

"Never mind, Cyrus, said Timius. "When you have had some good food down you for a few days and have gathered your strength you can challenge him again, and we will come and support you."

"Of course we will," rejoined Marcus, "I think you did very well. We had better get back quickly to the assembly hall otherwise we will not even get our bit of bread and a mug of water. I do not think I can go any longer without something to eat and drink."

The festival of Saturnalia was now here, and the boys could look forward to a whole week free from academic, physical, and other cultural activities. The first day of Saturnalia was spent in worship and sacrifice at the campus temple and during the remainder of the week, so that the boys would keep at arms length from mischief, less formal activities were organised, but these were purely on a voluntary basis. Walks and hikes around the surrounding countryside would be arranged, and minor sporting events where competition was virtually absent were arranged. The boys were encouraged to participate in these activities, and many of them did so to refrain from boredom. Others amused themselves in less energetic games, such as knuckle bones and dice, while the more studious types were able to spend many leisurely hours in the collegiate library.

Those boys who had been assigned to groups for essential chores, such as the latrines, were not excused their attendance at these chores at the appointed times daily. This caused them to feel discriminated against but there was nothing they could do about it. It had been suggested from time to time that on such occasions as these that these essential chores be shared equally among all the boys, but the Roman dogma of each person to their class persisted although there was every opportunity for an adult person to move up the class scale in society. The slave could earn his freedom, and the plebeian could earn his place in the higher echelons of society.

The Romans acquired their religions mainly from their predecessors, the Etruscans and the Greeks. The more centralised worship of Rome belonged to the household, and most households had their beginnings in agriculture and horticulture. The father in the household, in early days, was considered the priest, and his principle deity was Janus, who was the God of the Doorway. His sons were the subornate flamines and his daughters were given special charge of the goddess Vesta, who presided over the family. The gods, Saturn, Ops, and Vesta were agricultural deities and attracted their worship in the hope that the coming spring and summer would provide abundant crops and a good harvest. These were Etruscan deities which had now passed into Roman religion. They also developed this tendency towards the Etruscan trinity of gods, Jupiter, Juno and Minerva. The adoption of the Greek gods, such as, Mercury, Ceres, and Diana, came after the Etruscan deities had established themselves.

Rome had little to elevate or inspire in religion. Their only virtue to belonging to a religion was their strict sense of duty and to the Romans, religion meant a binding obligation. They had the fear of the unseen and, therefore, their main concern was to be punctilious in their worship. They felt that gods confronted men as the creditor confronts the debtor. The only true Roman deities that emerged from the beginning of Roman predominance were gods like Flora, Fortuna, Verilis, and Anna Perenna, and these native deities had a native licentiousness all of their own. Blood sacrifices are constantly prevalent, and the gladiatorial schools reflected this. Much of Roman worship was therefore directed to an "unknown God." The extent of worship to any one God depended largely on the needs of the day. If, for example, the Romans might need victories over their adversaries, the god Mars attracted special attention to their worship, and since the importance of the legions and their necessary task of defending the Empire was always necessary; so the god Mars attracted constant worship. The god Saturn was also worshipped annually, and this worship gave rise to a festival because the agricultural and horticultural requirement of the Roman people was equally as essential to the military one. They were great people for blending work and leisure, and the deity Jupiter, who could make their moments of leisure so pleasurable, attracted constant attention. There is a thirst for learning and general knowledge, hence Apollo is never forgotten.

Juno the God of Love, had to provide them with this necessary requirement, and Venus—as the Romans have clothed her on her arrival into their religion from Greece, where she was known as Aphrodite—provided them with the licentiousness which was generally part of their daily lives. Many families of the aristocracy chose and focused their worship on other deities, such as Diana. On arrival at the frontier posts, the first and most important task of the legion before taking up the duties in the fortifications was to pay its respects in worship and sacrifice to the god, Terminus; the God of the Boundaries.

It was the third day of Saturnalia. Marcus and Timius had not volunteered to participate in any of the organised leisure activities of the day. Instead they were diffident in what their plans of the day would be. They both sat on the mounds of the embankment some thirty yards from the perimeter and passed the time generally chitchatting. They now heard the sound of hooves approaching, and coming along the approach to the school was a horse and cart fully loaded with bulging sisal sacks. These sacks contained the supplies of vegetables and other fresh produce which was on a routine delivery to the college cookhouse. The driver pulled the horse to a halt outside the rear entrance of the cookhouse, which was in their view from where they were sitting. The animal reared and the startled middle-aged driver fell backwards over the sacks but was able to recover quickly and take control of the animal. This incident amused our friends enormously, and they could not stop laughing. Behind them down the bank and near the perimeter fence was a woodman chopping medium trunks of trees into logs. He did not seem too experienced at the task and kept missing the log with the axe. This also amused our two friends and held their interest for some time. The woodman, not knowing what his onlookers were laughing at, carried on doing his work quite nonchalantly.

It was time for him to take a breather, because he struck the log with the axe and let it rest with the blade still in the trunk. He mopped his brow with his handkerchief and strode along the edge of the bank towards the latrines as he was desperate to use the toilet.

"Hey, Timius," Marcus said, "that's a smashing axe that the woodman has been using."

"It is," replied Timius, "but it will not be any use to us. What could we do with it?"

"Well, if we had an axe like that we could easily cut nice long staves when we go wolf hunting, and we could also point them like a spear. When we go down to the lake with Cyrus tomorrow, we could also use it to make a small raft to float out onto the water and then do our fishing from the raft. I am sure if Cyrus were here he would agree with me that it would be useful to us."

Timius answered, "I think they are good ideas, Marcus, but we cannot take that axe because it would be stealing and besides, if we did where would we keep it?"

"Well," said Marcus, "I know it would be stealing, but the other boys steal things, too, and if we took it we could easily hide it in some bushes beyond the perimeter, where only you and I would know its whereabouts, and we could also show Cyrus where it is hidden."

Cyrus was not with them on this occasion; he felt he would prefer a walk so volunteered for one of the organised walks that had been arranged.

"If you go and get that axe Timius, I will keep watch for anyone approaching and, if anyone comes, I will give you a shout," suggested Marcus.

"Why me?" asked Timius.

"Because I have better eye sight than you, so you had better be quick before the woodman returns."

Agreeing to the plan Timius ran down the bank to take the axe, but when he pulled at it he could not dislodge the blade. He put his left foot on the log into which it was firmly stuck, and heaved. The implement moved slightly. As it did so, he heard Marcus' voice shouting in a half-whispered fashion.

"Quick, Timius, the woodman is coming!"

Timiuss heaved and tugged at the implement with all his might and finally dislodged it, but the momentum of his last heave threw him on his back. Marcus was by this time urging him on in desperation because the woodman was getting nearer. Timius recovered himself, grabbed the handle of the axe which was now lying on the ground and tried to run with it although he found it rather heavy to lift. Meanwhile, the woodman spotted him, shouted and ran after him, and caught him.

"I've caught you in the act of stealing my axe, you young rascal."

"I wasn't stealing it," replied Timius, "I was only trying to see if I could use one."

"Then why were you running?" asked the woodman.

At this moment, Marcus joined them and vociferously supported Timius's allegation that he was merely trying to see if he could use the axe.

"I don't believe that," said the woodman and, grabbing both boys by the arms, marched them into the school building and into Praetorian Officer Paulo's study.

Paulo was sat at his desk as usual, studying the programmes for the next session of the academic term. He looked up from his papers and was surprised to see the two rascals meekly standing in front of him with the towering woodman behind.

"In trouble again I suppose," said Paulo.

"No, sire," the boys replied in unison.

"Oh, yes they are," retorted the woodman. "This rascal on my left I caught stealing my axe, and the other boy was in collusion with him."

"Very well," said Paulo, "you can leave the matter to me," and he thereby dismissed the woodman.

Paulo took the two boys to Artimeses' office. Artimeses was disgusted to hear the report from Paulo and, on questioning the boys, found they both denied the allegation.

"Very well," said Artimeses. "You can both go now, but you will both hear more from me on this matter later."

When they emerged from the building, neither boy knew what to say and they half-jokingly convinced themselves that the incident was now over, and the least said the better.

The boys spent the rest of the day playing dice, because the sky looked rather ominous and the winds were beginning to freshen up. They thought it would be foolish to go beyond the confines of the campus lest they be caught in a rain storm. The set of dice Marcus put on the floor had been given to him by his parents some two years previously. Timius had never seen a set of dice until now, and after Marcus described the game to him he began playing with enthusiasm to a point where he did not want to break off from the game. It began to rain late in the afternoon and Cyrus returned, in the company of other boys, to the dormitory, having just returned from the organised walk. All the boys were delighted that they had just missed being caught in the rain.

Cyrus joined Marcus and Timius in their game of dice until the appointed time when Timius had to break away to report to the latrines to carry out his usual chores. Naturally they both related the incident of that morning to Cyrus, who found it most amusing and could not stop laughing about it. He promised that he would see to it that Timius became swifter of foot and to run away quickly when danger approached in the future. That is, of course, the kind of danger that he did not necessarily have to face, and

from which he could safely extricate himself. It was still raining that evening
when the boys entered the assembly hall but this did not bother the boys
because tonight they were to enjoy a meal of fish, instead of the usual variety
of broths. It was only fish that had been boiled and flavoured with salt and
some spices; nothing very appetizing but certainly a welcome change to
the assembled boys. Timius enjoyed every morsel and the meal was washed
down with a mug of warm milk, which was diluted with water. At the end
of the meal Praetorian Officer Carpus who was on duty that night in the
assembly hall, instructed the boys to be seated, as their principal had some
business with which he wished to attend, and no sooner had he said this
than Artimeses entered the hall wearing his usual flowing rust toga. He
mounted the podium. An air of anticipation now hung over the assembly,
as Artimeses silently cast his eyes over the assembled boys. All the boys
began to wonder what special announcement was to be made. Artimeses did
not beckon to them to be seated which indicated that they should remain
standing, and whenever this occurred they all knew that they were to witness
a punishment. Artimeses called in a shrill voice,

"Junior citizen Timius Arbutus and junior citizen Marcus Piritus, come
over here at once."

The two boys were shocked to hear their names called out and
apprehensively obeyed the command. Artimeses then continued with the
indictment.

"Junior citizens of Rome, you will see standing before you here, at the
foot of this podium, two of your colleagues who have today committed an
unspeakable crime. Timius Arbutus was caught red-handed stealing the axe
belonging to a woodman, and he was ably abetted by your other colleague
Marcus Piritus. This is something that we will not tolerate in this institution.
Stealing is a most dishonourable crime and one which we view with the
greatest severity. I therefore sentence junior citizen Arbutus to six strokes
of the cane, and junior citizen Piritus to six strokes of the flat pad. You can
carry on with the punishment officer," instructed Artimeses, turning to the
Praetorian officer Lictus.

Timius did not know what to do, because he was suddenly overwhelmed
with terror, but fortunately the sentence came as a complete surprise to
him. Before he could come to his senses he had been forcibly bent over by
Lictus, and had felt the first stroke of the cane on his posterior. He winced
a little but suddenly remembered that it was dishonourable and cowardly to
cry out, so he immediately clenched his teeth until all six strokes had been
administered. He was then up-righted and at this point he did not know

whether he wanted to run or jump. Tears began to well in his eyes, and he was absolutely dying to rub his backside with his hands, but he dared not make a move. However, this situation lasted for only a few moments although it seemed like a lifetime to Timius, and he was instructed to quickly make his exit and return to the dormitory. He shot out of the hall like a thunderbolt, and as soon as he was out of sight, he began to cry bitterly and rub his backside vigorously with the palms of his hands.

Marcus Piritus took his turn next, but being as he was not the culprit his punishment was much less severe. The flat pad was a piece of flat wood about twelve inches by nine inches attached to a handle in the shape of a paddle. On one face of it was smooth and shiny, whereas the reverse was engraved with Caesar's seal with a laurel chaplet surrounding the initials **S.P.Q.R. 'Senatus Public Que Romano'**. The object of the punishment, using this implement, unlike the cane, which had the tendency to cut into the flesh, gave the recipient a nasty stinging sensation on the part of the body to which it was applied, but again, unlike the cane the stinging soon wore off. Marcus received his sentence of six strokes from the flat pad soon after which he was dismissed to the dormitory.

Timius did not hear Marcus enter the dormitory because he was still sobbing and rubbing his backside with the palms of his hands while kneeling beside his bed. Marcus entered, rubbing his backside too. He knelt down beside Timius, placed his right arm around Timius' shoulder with his left hand, still rubbing his own backside, and very poetically and full of feeling said,

"Poor little Timius
Poor little swine,
The cane has cut across your b . . .
· And Caesar's seal 'cross mine."

This little poem amused Timius for a moment, and in-between his sobs he laughed. A moment ago he was wishing he was at home in Velitrae and especially in his favourite gorge, chasing those lizards that frequented the place. He would have liked to have been with his mother because he remembered that on an occasion such as this his mother would put her arms around him, comfort him, and sweetly sing him a lullaby, but then this was not possible any more because she was now dead and he remembered being told that it was his fault for being such a wicked boy and that he had been the cause of her death. Perhaps he now deserved all the punishment

that was coming to him. However, Marcus' arrival soon made him forget
all thoughts of being back at home and indeed even running away from
the college which he had contemplated, because he felt he couldn't leave
Marcus and Cyrus behind and go it alone. They were very much part of his
life now. Cyrus entered the room with some of the other boys and although
they all felt rather sorry for the two wrongdoers, they accepted this sort of
thing as a matter of course and soon began joking and trivialising the whole
episode. Timius and Marcus were much more cheerful now, and when Cyrus
pointed out that during Timius's very short stay in the institution he had
been initiated with nearly all the punishments that were practiced there, he
could now consider himself a well-worn veteran, and there was now nothing
to fear in the future. This statement of Cyrus' brought the spirit back into
the boy, and he was practically back to normal.

Next day Marcus and Timius once again were in a quandary about how
to spend the day. They were back in the same spot on the college boundary,
near where they had seen the woodman the previous day. They were not
doing anything special, except to have unwittingly entered into a little game
of trying to identify the various calls and chirrups of the birds that inhabited
the wood beyond. Neither of them was in a position to judge the correctness
of their guesses because neither of them was familiar with all the birds'
sounds, but they just continued their game of guessing as a means of passing
their time. Marcus looked up from pondering the state of repair of his
sandals while still trying to guess the call of a bird he had just heard, when
he noticed a few yards away coming towards them the principal, Artimeses,
and their master, Doronyd. Although these two gave the impression that
they were directly approaching the boys, this was not so because they were
on their way to other business and were merely in the course of passing the
boys. Marcus drew Timius's attention to the approach of the two officials
and when they were near to them the two boys stood up, as was customary
when officials passed and approached inmates, and paid their respects to the
two superiors by wishing them a polite good-morning. Both Artimese and
Doronyd returned the greeting and passed by. They had only walked a few
yards beyond the boys when Artimeses turned around then said,

"Junior citizens Piritus and Arbutus, I am delighted with you both."
Neither of the boys knew how to reply and merely grinned shyly.
Artimeses bowed slightly to them and walked away to join his colleague.
They had no idea what Artimeses meant by his remark, but it is correct to
say that while the effects of Marcus's punishment of the previous night had

worn off completely Timius still felt the effects of the cane on his backside. It still felt very sore, but the effect was slowly wearing off.

Arimeses, while he continued his walk with Doronyd, explained to Doronyd, when he noticed his enquiring look, the reason for having expressed his pleasure with the two boys, and went on to say,

"Do you know, Doronyd, I find it an honour to serve in this institute as principal. Those two young rascals whom we have just passed both received punishment last night for quite a natural boyish prank. Both the young fellows took their punishments extremely well without whimpering, crying out, or otherwise. These boys represent the calibre of the young generation we have in our care. If these boys are representative of the young generation throughout the Empire, then our glorious Empire will live forever, because in my humble opinion this is just the kind of stuff our Empire is made of, and we shall have nothing to fear in the future while we have young men of such a high standard, playing their full part as citizens in our Empire."

"I agree entirely and share your sentiments completely. I, too, feel honoured to be working here among them," replied Doronyd.

The two officials continued on their way.

That same evening, while Timius was busy with colleagues in the group cleaning out the latrines, a thought struck him. He suddenly remembered that he had not had a chance since getting to Larcia to do any practice on his musical pipe. The reason for this was not only because the boys were constantly kept busy, but even in the odd off-duty periods that they had he was not able to find any privacy to enable him to do so without irritating or disturbing others, because he well realized that, with the very short practice he had, he was still only able to play notes that were off key. He thought that, after his evening meal, he would collect his pipe and come down to the latrines and, seated on one of the pedestals, with the light of the torches that burned all evening in the latrines, he would do a bit of practicing in privacy. He might even ask Cyrus and Marcus to come and join him, because he felt sure that they would also be glad of an opportunity to play his pipe, but he would try it on his own this evening after his meal.

Timius made the excuse to Cyrus and Marcus, as soon as the meal was over, that he had to dash down to the latrines to do some usual business. Cyrus and Marcus found this rather amusing and joked with him about the turnip broth which they had just eaten not agreeing with his constitution. Timius laughed this off without letting them into his secret. He dashed away to the dormitory and was the first one back; he ran over to his wooden box, lifted the lid, rummaged under the clothes and found his musical pipe.

When he got it out of the box, he found that it had some how become shortened in length; rummaging again he found the other half. It was broken completely in half. He knew for a fact that the instrument was in one piece the last time he went to his box, which was yesterday, because he always put his hand to the bottom of the box to make sure the pipe was safe. It was always put at the very bottom of the box, but he found that the two halves had been placed between the bottom layers of his clothes, so he immediately knew that somebody had tampered with his belongings and in the process had broken the pipe. Timius was absolutely broken hearted and just about able to fight back the tears before he dashed to the door of the dormitory. He had heard the other boys approaching, and he did not want to make a public exhibition of his grief. He ran out of the building and realized the only place he could go to where he could weep in private was the latrines. As he ran through the wide open door of the latrines he stopped abruptly because there were two other boys already seated on the pedestal chatting away to each other surrounded by an unpleasant odour. Timius turned back and then ran out into the darkness towards the lime pit. He arrived at the edge of the pit, flung himself on the ground, and sobbed his heart out with only the crickets screeching around him for company.

He could not understand why anyone would do such a mean thing as this. Had any of his colleagues asked him if they could have had a blow on his musical pipe, he would have willingly let them; but to take it without his knowledge and then to break it in the bargain was a dastardly trick. It was a possession that he prized because it was the only gift that either of his parents had ever given him, and he did so want to play a musical instrument—now his chance had gone. He was now contemplating whether he should report the matter to his superior and perhaps the culprit would have the courage to own up, but then he also realized that telling tales to superiors was an anathema at the college.

If he did so he might even lose the respect and friendship of Cyrus and Marcus, so he decided to let the matter rest. Possibly, when he saw his father again, he would ask him for some *gum arabic*, so that he could repair it. He wiped away the tears and walked around the lime pit very slowly to give himself time to recover fully before he went back so that he did not enter the dormitory with reds swollen eyes, which would give away the fact that he had been weeping.

Another thought just struck him, and he remembered his gold coin and hoped desperately that it had not been stolen because he had planned to buy his father a little present with it the next time they were both in Rome.

He would also buy that crippled man whose name was Claudius a present to take to him when he and his father visited Claudius. He sped away from the lime pit leaving the crickets to screech in their own world and back into the dormitory. The other boys did not notice him because they were busy talking among themselves or reading. Again he rummaged through his box and found the gold coin intact, wrapped in a small piece of papyrus. He felt his fingers round the inner bottom edge of the box and found that it had a slight cavity where the upright side joined the bottom. This cavity was just wide enough for him to wedge the piece of papyrus containing the coin, and this he did. He lay on his bed still feeling very downhearted.

Cyrus was the first one to approach him, and as he did so, he said to Timius, "What's the matter with you, aren't you feeling very well?"

"No, I feel quite alright, thank you, Cyrus," replied Timius.

Cyrus could see that he was upset and pressed him to tell him what had happened. Timius eventually did, and what he said angered Cyrus. He promised to get to the bottom of this and agreed that it was a horrible act on somebody's part. Cyrus called Marcus over and relayed to him what had happened and Marcus, too, was very upset that somebody should do such a thing, but again had to be pressed by Timius to say and do nothing about it. Timius made them both promise faithfully that they would leave the matter to rest, because he did not want any kind of unpleasantness to result from the incident.

Tomorrow was the last day of Saturnalia, and Cyrus cheered him up by telling him that he and Marcus had planned, during Timius' absence in the latrines, to go fishing down at the lake again, and it was now Timius's turn to promise not to whisper the plan to anyone lest some of the others might have the same idea and spoil it for them. Marcus had forgotten about the flat-pad punishment he had received and was now wishing that they had been successful in stealing the axe. Building their own raft with the aid of an axe would have made the day much more enjoyable, but Marcus' imagination always seemed to run riot, especially on things that were impractical. Timius now felt much better because he had something to look forward to the following morning. He asked Cyrus if he could have a try at igniting the fire, with the flint stones, on which they would roast their catch. Cyrus half-agreed but reminded them not to tempt providence because they may not have the luck to catch any fish.

Timius now began to count the hours until daylight.

CHAPTER IX

Castra sunt in Italia contra rempulicam collocata.

CICERO

A camp has been formed in Italy against the Republic.

TIBERIUS DRUSUS NERO had now firmly established himself in the position of first consul, on the death of his step father Augustus. The lifelong designs of his mother, Livia, had now materialised. The supreme title of Augustus was not granted to Tiberius by the Senate, and as much as he would have liked to have acquired this title it was not bestowed on him. The majority of the Senate had not planned deliberately during the lifetime of that august prince that an acceptable successor would establish himself during the twilight years of Augustus' life, because many could never contemplate the time that was bound to arrive when he would not be present to lead and guide the Senate. Even in his advancing years, it was difficult for them to accept the fact that even Augustus would one day depart from their midst. When this tragic event did occur they were left helpless. Since Tiberius was serving the Empire here in the Senate as a consul and magistrate, the fact that it had been divulged to them that it was Augustus' will that he should succeed him fulfilled a natural process, and he accepted the purple mantle of office as first consul.

Tiberius did not need any persuasion in accepting the purple. All persuasion, planning, and cajolery had already been done and taken care of by his mother, Livia, and there were powerful elements in the Senate who had also been bribed for their support of Tiberius. Tiberius was not the popular choice of either the Senate, the majority of the aristocracy, nor of the populace. But the powerful elements in his support were not easy to oppose. He had acquired all the powers of first consul and all the additional powers that his stepfather had possessed, and although his stepfather had the title of Augustus, it had now come to be accepted as merely another title for that of Emperor. The Republic and its provinces had now gradually come to be referred to as the Empire, and therefore there was little opposition when the title of Emperor was spoken of when referring to Tiberius.

Rome now had an Emperor, both in fact and in name, but the supreme title of Augustus was still the sole possession of Octavian. From Tiberius' early days as Emperor, intrigue surrounded the court on the Palatine Hill, and reached a point where the edicts of the Emperor raised little opposition. This is very much the result of fear and distrust. On the surface the administration gave the impression that all was calm and well, but the intrigues that now began would have far reaching effects for many years. If there was a popular choice, or, indeed, if an Emperor could have been elected by plebiscite, it is without any doubt that Germanicus Drusus would have been the popular choice.

Rome loved heroes, and their heroes were military men. Tiberius enjoyed heroism and an amount of adulation after his successes as a general in Germania, but that had been some years ago, and memories soon fade. His place had been taken by Germanicus and Germanicus was still the hero of the day. It is argued that the place for heroism is in the battlefield and not in the central government of the Empire. Therefore Germanicus was in his rightful place on the battlefield. This was an accepted philosophy of the Romans, and since they were practical people, there was little or no opposition to this argument.

Since the early days of the Republic, committees had been set up known as comitia from Senators within the Senate. The purpose of these committees was to represent the views and wishes of various sections of the public. These views were debated between committees and the rest of the Senate. Before legislation was passed by the Senate the public could feel that their views on whatever subject had been properly considered in the Senate chamber, even though the outcome of the registration might run counter to those views. Tiberius found that there was no purpose that these committees usefully served which could not be met by open debate and, therefore, his first major act of reform was to disband the comitia. His powerful supporters in the Senate were thus able to stifle any opposing view before it had been properly aired and therefore the established practice now was that any legislation placed on the statutes by the senate must be meekly followed throughout the realm. The early indications of tyranny had now become noticeable. The strengthening of the Praetorian Guard had since taken place and the supremacy, by means of donations from the central treasury, placed them in a superior position to those of the rest of the armed forces. They were now properly considered to be the personal bodyguard of the Emperor, and woe beheld any faction that wished to openly oppose the legislature. We now had a period of acquiescence.

The law of the Delatio was also firmly established within the administration. There was the odd occasion, during the Augustan era, when the informant was suitably rewarded for his service. But under Tiberius the informant became part of the establishment with no limits to its confinement. It is accepted as proper practice that information derogatory of the Emperor or his close associates be brought to the Emperor's notice. If any subsequent charges are proved to be accurate then the culprits are severely dealt with through degradation and death and, ultimately, execution. Tiberius has given avid support to the practice of Delatio.

The main reason for this was possibly the fact that Tiberius was not entirely confident. While Germanicus was still alive, he was constantly fearful that on his return from his successful campaigns in Germania his popularity would be a threat to Tiberius' position. There were also other popular generals and public figures that might clandestinely gather support and overthrow him, therefore a means had to exist whereby men with such ambitions could be frustrated in their attempts at arresting the people from him. The donations that were given to the Praetorian Guard far exceeded the value of the guard as a purely military formation, and their loyalty was bought to imbibe them for their political support.

In recent months, it had been rumoured that Senator Gaius Mucianus was driven to commit suicide by the invidious position in which he had been placed after making an undignified retreat from his enthusiastic proposal that work should commence on the redevelopment scheme at the Port of Ostia. Some years ago, Augustus had instituted a commission to survey and report on the facilities that existed at Ostia. The commission submitted that Ostia did not have the facilities to cope with the increased trade and, in particular, the vast imports from other parts of the Empire. Ostia was the gateway to Rome and through Ostia passed many of the supplies of raw materials, including grain, wine, oils, spices, and so on. Rome was becoming a consuming society, and the needs of its inhabitants, especially in basic consumables, was growing at an extremely rapid rate. Heavily laden ships from all parts of the Empire constantly off-loaded their cargoes for consumption by Roman society. These ships spent many wasted hours anchored in the bay at Ostia awaiting port facilities. Many of them returned empty to re-load their cargoes from the major ports of the Empire.

The commission reported that the facilities at Ostia were not totally inadequate, but were also the cause of time consuming wastefulness, and it was their suggestion that if a proper survey of the facilities could be taken by engineers the result would be concrete proposals for redevelopment and expansion. Soon after engineering survey plans were drawn up on various projects that would facilitate redevelopment. Unfortunately, these plans were shelved by Augustus, partly because there were other matters of prior nature that needed his attention. In order for ratification by the Senate to proceed with these plans, many hours of debate in the chamber were required; the expenditure required was of rather enormous proportions and when the Senate was asked to ratify expensive projects there was the tendency for the debates to be spent on minor details and minute scrutiny of the expenditure, before ratification. In his advancing years it is felt that Augustus did not have the patience, or indeed the will to sit through endless hours of debate.

Senator Mucianus had some twelve months ago resurrected the proposed redevelopment of Ostia. When his proposal was first put forward there was enthusiastic support from the majority of the Senate, but Tiberius and his close associates acted diffidently. Mucianus had enlisted support from local dignitaries at Ostia to the extent that many of them had even offered contributions towards the cost of this vast project. They were fully aware that such an expensive project would bring its rewards when completed. As the increased trade through Ostia would expand the commercial activities in the area of the port the local population of Ostia were also agreeable to the scheme, because they knew that it would not only bring employment during the reconstruction of the port facilities but subsequently the expansion of other facilities, such as warehouses and lading offices and it would continue to provide employment for the area. Large sections of the population that had been attracted to Rome because of its growth and prosperity were fully aware that if this situation was to continue the gateway to Rome would require expansion.

Ostia was the gateway to Rome for merchants who came to Rome from across the sea. When Mucianus' proposals were given an unenthusiastic hearing in the Senate, had he been a prudent man he would have let the matter rest with a view to raising it again when the climate was favourable. But his enthusiasm for the project caused him to summon the support of certain sections of the nobility and the populace that were resident in the sector of Rome through which direct access to Ostia existed. Petitions were filed, speeches were made by his supporters at various public venues and Mucianus was now the focus of attention by the chroniclers of the day.

Tiberius and his supporters became alarmed at the situation: the support that Mucianus was getting was increasing daily. They could not by any legitimate means stifle this support, nor could they find worthwhile excuses to have the project shelved through lack of finance, because the central treasury—and they knew it—would not have to support the whole expenditure of the project. Wealthy persons were now beginning to pledge financial investment, and had the project been shelved merely on financial grounds it would not have been an acceptable excuse. Tiberius needed money to reward his supporters because he was not confident of their loyalty. He still found himself in this invidious position. There was also the question now that if Mucianus' proposals had been ratified by the Senate his position in the Senate would be strong, and this strength might lead to demands of a higher nature which may have, in time, weakened the position of the Emperor. There was also a situation developing in Germany where Germanicus had gained tremendous popularity. His exploits during the campaigns against the Germans and the heroism of his legions was daily news among the populace of Rome. A situation was therefore contrived where Mucianus was accused by some of the close supporters of Tiberius of having ulterior motives, and he was accused of using the popularity gained for his proposal for the start of the project at Ostia as an excuse to further his ambition. This indictment of Mucianus grew daily more vicious. Mucianus had decided in these circumstances to resign from the Senate. His act of doing so did not lose him the popularity which he had gained. Consequently he was maliciously pursued with rumour and blackmail through his compromises until he finally decided to end his own life by suicide. When news reached Tiberius that Mucianus had committed suicide, he was able to expound to the Senate that his suspicions of Mucianus's ultimate ambitions had now been vindicated. There was no other Senator who dared to step into Mucianus' place and pursue the argument that the projected scheme at Ostia should be continued.

Senators Vellius and Tetricus also mysteriously lost their lives through sudden illnesses which are a matter of conjecture. These two Senators were pressing their colleagues to raise a further four legions with the aim of annexing Britannia. The Celtic and Druid tribes of Britannia were causing harassment to Roman shipping off the coast of Spain and Gaul. Piracy on the high seas has become an inconvenience and a nuisance and, in addition to this, the tribes of Britannia sent raiding parties to points along the coast of northern Gaul, and their expeditions gave encouragement to protest and uprising in the settlements in those areas. The two Senators concerned argued endlessly that the total annexation of Britannia would put an end to this situation. Tiberius and his supporters argued that this was merely a storm in a wine goblet and was of no consequence to the stability of the Empire. The proposals of these two Senators were misinterpreted deliberately by the staunch supporters of Tiberius as indicating their greater ambitions. Again the two men were degraded in the Senate. They resigned and mysteriously died from unknown causes. This was indicative of the situation of the Roman administration, and gave support to the theory that in present circumstances it was better to acquiesce with the Emperor than to make new proposals and never oppose the proposals of Tiberius and his close associates.

Although this situation existed in the government of the Empire, nevertheless stability still reigned and the prosperity of the people continued to flourish. The arts, the culture and the religion of the Empire were fostered. The legions were loyal and were officered by generals who made it their military duties. They were unaware of the cajolery and corruption going on at the heart of the Empire. So far as they were concerned, the Republic had been restored and Republican ideals now existed, even though the first consul had adopted the title of Emperor, which they treated merely as a title of expedience. Periodically, there were opposing factions among the client kingdoms subservient to Rome, but can there ever be a situation where total subservience would be tolerated and accepted meekly and without any opposition whatsoever. The indoctrination that progress and prosperity would follow under the protection of Rome would take many years to be imbued into the lifeblood of these nations. Meanwhile the situation such as existed had to be tolerated and dealt with as and when it occurs. Those legions that are stationed along the Rhine Danube fortifications enjoyed a much less hazardous existence. Germanicus, who was very popular among his troops, spent many days, weeks, and months ensuring that the legions along the Rhine frontier were fully trained and at their highest peak of fighting fitness. The training he had imposed upon them was of the most severe nature. The penalty for the weakness of any of the troops was even more severe. In a forceful and sometimes maniacal manner, he demanded absolute and total loyalty from these troops, and the discipline he instilled into them was second to none. He was obsessed with the need to defeat the German chief Hermann Armenius, and even when he had been recalled to Rome with the purpose of being granted the powers of a magistrate, he declined this offer until he had achieved his aim of thoroughly defeating the German chief. Even though the German chief had not, as yet, been defeated, Germanicus was nevertheless hailed as a hero by his troops, and the three eagles under which the legions served were not in their possession. They had been lost to the German tribes by General Virus, some years previously. These symbols of the legionnaire's loyalty to his Emperor and country through his immediate general needed a determined effort if they were to be revenged. It was humiliating that symbolic emblems of such tremendous reverence should be in the possession of the enemy, and any amount of sacrifice was worthwhile in the pursuit of recovering these emblems. Germanicus knew this, and he exploited the passions of the troops. Therefore, any instruction of his, no matter how severe, was obediently carried out. He was now ready to face the German tribes, not just with sufficiently well armed and highly trained troops, but moreover with a body of troops whose morals and spirits were of the highest order.

On the morning of March 27, after a respite, celebrating the Ides of March, the scouts of the eighth legion reported to their headquarters that they had observed the assembly of some five thousand German barbarians at a place called Idistavisus. It was reported that Idistavisus was situated on the western banks of the river, in a semicircle on a bend on a bank of the river. The barbarians had crossed the river on rafts with their supplies and equipment during the past week and were now assembled and poised for an attack. They knew that there were Roman troops assembled nearby, and they knew that the roman general had been seen among these troops. Hermann Armenius' plan was to cause a surprise attack on these troops and capture General Germanicus alive, to be held as hostage. The reports he had received over the previous months were correct in that Germanicus was popular not only among the troops but among the populace particularly those at the heart of the Empire, and he felt that by holding Germanicus as hostage his demands that the legions leave Germania completely would be met, even though it would mean months of haggling. He was prepared to do this because time was on his side. He had no visions of settlement or the lofty concept of civilization. Freedom was his only concept, and this was shared by all the tribes in Germania. However, when Germanicus learned of the situation at Idistavisus he decided to attack the barbarians without any delay. He knew that they were in a precarious position with their backs to the river and if he could ambush them at this point, he could set them to flight without much loss of life to his own troops. Time was

very short, and Germanicus knew that he had to act quickly. He summoned
all his commanders at the greatest speed and put forward his plan which he
insisted would be carried out to the letter. The main attacking force would
be the cavalry but he would keep two cohorts of cavalry in reserve in case
the first troops were successfully fought off by the barbarian chief. The next
part of his plan was that the attacking cavalry should be quickly called off
after causing the utmost chaos, and then they would be followed by as many
cohorts of bowmen as were possible. If the barbarian existed after this attack
the bowmen would be followed by infantry men armed with spears which
would be launched from very short range. These infantrymen would then
follow up rapidly with a sword attack. His plans also included that each type
of arm would have cohorts kept in reserve and concealed well below the
brow of the hill which overlooked the river. He was determined not to make
the same mistake as General Varus and put all his forces into the attack in
the first instance, although it must be said that General Varus had no option
under the circumstances in which he found himself, because the German
barbarians had, on that occasion, ambushed him.

It was midday before all the troops were ready for the attack, and when
it did occur, it was a complete success. The Germans were taken unawares,
and although they put up a remarkable stand, they were no match for the
highly disciplined and trained troops of General Germanicus. Hundreds
of barbarians tried desperately to cross the river on their rafts but were
slaughtered in the process. However, the captured Roman eagles were still
in their possession and were successfully landed by Hermann Armenius and
his associates onto the far bank of the river, but Germanicus was determined
to retrieve these. He ordered that the rafts left on the west bank of the river
be put to use quickly by his own troops, who were now in hot pursuit of the
barbarians. He personally led the pursuit and the bewildered barbarians, not
expecting pursuit, were at their wits end trying to take cover. The Roman
military machine relentlessly followed, urged on by Germanicus. Hermann
Armenius met his end when a Roman spear was thrust through his chest.

He had fought against the Romans for countless years and was quite
convinced that if he should meet his end other than through natural causes,
it would be at the sharp end of a Roman weapon. He was a respected enemy
of the Romans, and when news reached the Roman troops that Hermann
Armenius had been killed there was no jubilation as one would expect,
because the Romans realized that although they had profound faith in
their own Empire and their own ability that an enemy with the abundant
thirst for freedom as had possessed Hermann Armenius, was an enemy that

commanded their admiration and respect. They had often expressed their
thoughts in their conversation that Hermann Armedius should have been
born a Roman. They would then conjecture that a Roman having the spirit
and tenacity of Hermann would be the ideal general to lead the legions
against the Persian monarchy. The leadership of a man of this calibre would
find the Persians hard pressed in their efforts to defeat them. However, cries
of jubilation were rendered by the troops when word reached them that the
revered eagles had been retrieved.

Many prisoners were taken that day, but Germanicus decided not to send
them back to Rome to be placed in bondage as slaves. Instead he kept the
prisoners under his control in Germany and put them to work on renewing
the fortifications. He knew they were a, hardy, motley band of men and
this hardiness he could make full use of in his building programme. More
fortifications were thus constructed along the frontier, with the aid of nearly
two thousand German prisoners. It was his strict instructions that these
men were on no account to be humiliated nor treated as serfs.

During the battle, Germanicus had sustained a wound at the base of his
spine and the first effects of this wound appeared to be of no consequence,
but as the days progressed the effects started to weaken him. The army
physicians did their very best to overcome their leader's malady. When news
reached Rome of Germanicus' glorious victory, his grandmother, Livia, felt
that the least Rome could do was to send their best physician to Germania
to take care of Germanicus' injury.

Polybius was in the pay of Livia and was considered to be the most
brilliant physician in Rome. Germanicus had suffered from his spinal injury
for nearly eight months, and his health gradually deteriorated to a point
where it was felt major surgery was necessary. Livia despatched Polybius
and his medical assistant to Germania and instructed him that he was not to
return until Germanicus had recovered. The magnanimity of Livia was the
subject of admiration on the Palatine Hill, but it had been rumoured, and we
must remember that there is no smoke without fire, that if Germanicus had
fully recovered and returned to Rome as a conquering hero of the day, his
popularity thus further enhanced weakened Tiberius's position. It had also
been rumoured that Livia had spent many years arranging matters at Court
whereby her son, Tiberius, would become the obvious successor to Augustus.

Her change of heart at this stage, in that she relented in sending Polybius
to Germania and thus save the life of that popular hero Germanicus, was
treated with the utmost suspicion. It was only weeks after Polybius' arrival
at Idistavisus, that Germanicus died even though Polybius had done his

very best to impress all concerned that he, Polybius, had done everything he could possibly do to save the life of their hero. Tiberius had instructed that the remains of Germanicus be brought back to Rome for a ceremonial funeral but the Eighth Legion, that was considered his personal bodyguard, put forward various excuses as to why this was not possible. The barrenness of the area and the lack of proper medical facilities did not enable them to properly embalm his remains. The weather was also constantly inclement and would have taken many months of embalmed remains to be ceremoniously transported to Rome. His remains were therefore cremated at Idistavisus with full military honours. The territory to the west of the Rhine was named Germania in honour of this brilliant general. Previously it had been merely the northern extension of the Gaelic province.

Germanicus's successor, General Julius Gallus was not a magnanimous leader. He could not readily accept Germanicus' attitude that the German prisoners should be treated with respect and fairness. As far as he was concerned, they were dastardly enemies and a constant threat to the safety of the Empire. In his opinion countless worthy legionnaires had lost their lives through their belligerence, and he ordered that the tasks that they were given now to be those of the harshest nature and that their treatment was to be that of complete and total servitude. His attitude was not easily accepted by the troops. Because of his attitude he did not receive the full cooperation of their guards. This resulted in many escaping over the months that followed to eastern Germania and freedom. It was felt among the legions that if Germanicus's attitude of magnanimity had continued it would have benefited not only the prisoners who were in Roman hands, but also those scattered tribes that were coming under the jurisdiction of Rome.

It would have led to an accommodation between the two parties, and the warlike attitude of the German tribes would have gradually been subdued. Unfortunately this was not to be so. Many of the escaped prisoners who were bitter about their recent harsh treatment formed themselves into warring gangs to harass and murder groups of legionnaires at irregular intervals with their surprise attacks. These people were determined and they would not be subdued, no matter how strong the Roman legions grew. It was now Roman policy that these warring groups should be given a chance to congregate and organise themselves into a much larger force. Harassment now persisted on both sides. On the one hand the Romans were harassed in the hope that they would give up and return home. On the other hand the Romans harassed the tribal factions so that they would not have the opportunity to congregate and organise themselves.

We now had a stalemate in Germania, and this situation gradually spread into the heart of Gaul. These people looked across the sea to Britannia where they saw where their own ultimate hopes lie. They were avaricious of the freedom enjoyed by the tribes in Britannia. There was growing concern in the capital at this situation, and constant proposals from leading members of the Senate for the annexation of Britannia. But Tiberius' disregard for the policy only lead one to believe that he would do so at his pleasure, like his august predecessor.

*

Sejanus Arbutus prepared himself, together with his colleagues, to take up duties for the night patrol. They were to relieve the day patrol at sunset and, in turn, would be relieved at dawn. Their duties were to patrol the frontiers along the banks of the Rhine and keep a watch out for German raiding parties. These patrols had met many raiders in the past but were sufficiently trained to beat off any attack. It would perhaps be the same tonight. He was confident, as were his colleagues, that any raiders that might appear tonight would be given short shrift. The Maniple assembled in routine formation and was then split up into smaller groups to move along the frontier perimeter at intervals of about half a mile. No sooner had the patrol to which Sejanus Arbutus was detailed arrived at the point from which their night patrol would begin when they were surprised by a group of Germans, yelling loudly and flaying at them with their swords. They appeared to be in a drunken stupor but this behaviour was probably the result of their savage enmity towards the Romans. Their bison skins and faces were daubed with yellow and red dyes, which was to add to their ferocity.

The Romans fought back gallantly and were able to despatch their attackers within a very short time, but some of them in the group became casualties. Eight of them died instantly, whereas about fifteen were seriously wounded. Sejanus Arbutus was one of them. He had received the thrust of a German sword at the base of his stomach. He was not dead but there appeared to be little hope of his recovery. However, his two colleagues, Pollio and Drusus, carried him to a point where the wounded would be collected and taken for medical treatment back at the Cohort sub-headquarters. A message had been sent to the sub-headquarters requesting stretcher bearers be despatched immediately to collect the wounded.

Sejanus Arbutus found himself lying on the floor of a medical tent at these makeshift headquarters. Of the fifteen seriously wounded, four had already died while a further ten had very good chances of recovery. This was the opinion of the military physician. But so far as Sejanus Arbutus was concerned, they paid very little attention to him because in the opinion of these physicians there was little hope for him; he should be left to pass away peacefully. He was in terrible pain, and although Pollio mopped his brow and tried to comfort him in the hope of resurrecting his spirits, even if only a trifle, this effort seemed to be useless.

Drusus entered the tent clutching a folded and sealed piece of papyrus. It was addressed to **Legionnaire Senajus Arbutus** marked **PERSONAL**. He knelt down beside Sejanus and said to him very quietly, "Sejanus, I have something for you."

Sejanus opened his eyes slightly and tried to lift his right hand to accept the document, but was unable to do so. Drusus therefore suggested that he place it in his pouch so that Sejanus could read it when he felt better. Drusus also suggested that it might be a citation direct from the Emperor and tried to cheer him up by saying so. The document had arrived with the weekly despatches from Rome that accompanied the supply trains. Supplies arrived at legion headquarters each week from Rome by way of carts drawn by mules which were laden with replacement arms, footwear, clothing, and rations that were unobtainable locally. Medical supplies also formed part of the consignments.

Drusus had only just placed the document in the pouch of Sejanus Arbutus when Sejanus gasped and his head drooped to one side. On examining Sejanus more closely Drusus found Sejanus to be dead. His two colleagues were completely saddened by the event. It was now their task to report his death to Cohort sub-headquarters. One of the Centurions in charge instructed them to collect his belongings, which were very meagre, and bring them to headquarters at daybreak. They were also instructed to see that his body was properly buried. At daybreak, Pollio and Drusus did as they were instructed and buried Sejanus Arbutus. They prayed to the gods that his soul be considered courageous enough to be placed in the protective care of the god Augustus. His pouch was taken to subs-headquarters and the Centurion Tullius took charge of it. In their presence he checked through its contents to find that the legionnaire, like the vast majority of the others, had few possessions to pass on to his relatives. There were a few coins amounting to sixteen denarii. There was a pocket knife, two gold emblems that were given to him by his commanders for service beyond the call of duty, on previous occasions in the campaign. These were in the form of medallions, one was silver and one was bronze. There was also the document which had arrived the night before, still unopened, and Tullius decided, that since it could have been an official citation which would have to be entered in the legions records, to break the seal and open it.

He immediately realized that this was not a citation document and although he could not read the writing he recognised that it must have been written by a very young person. He summoned a scribe who took the document and read it. He informed Tullius that it had come from the Augustan Institution at Larcia. Tullius asked him to read it aloud. The scribe read out the letter as follows:

'My dear father,

I was very pleased to receive your letter three days ago and my schoolmaster Doronyd has given me permission to reply. He has assured me that this will be sent to you through the Army communication facility. I am delighted to hear that you are keeping well and that you are bravely fighting off all the German barbarians that have the audacity to attack our honourable Legion.

I am very glad to hear that you will be coming to see me soon and I have told my friends, Marcus and Cyrus, about it and I would like you to meet them. I am getting on quite well here and I only wish you could be here to join Cyrus, Marcus and myself, with some of the other boys when we go wolf hunting and fishing, because I am sure you would be able to kill the wolves quite easily. I am also sure that you have a special knack of catching fish, and you could teach us how to do it.

When you come could you please hire a pony as well, because I would love you to teach me to ride a pony. We could then go around the campus so that I could show you lots of places.

I am sorry to tell you that the musical pipe you bought me in Rome was accidentally broken in half. When you visit could you also bring some gum-arabic so that we can mend it.

I look forward to seeing you and until then don't let any of those horrible barbarians lay a hand on you.

Your obedient son,
Timius'

Pollio immediately ran out of the tent and made his way to the supply tent. He was able to persuade the storekeeper to give him a handful of gum-arabic which was wrapped in a small piece of linen. He ran back to Cohort sub-headquarters and, as he entered Centurion Officer Tullius' tent he spotted Sejanus Arbutus's pouch being sealed with a cord. Pollio asked Tullius to reopen it so that he could place inside the little linen bundle, saying that it was another item of his dear friend Sejanus's that he had remembered and ran out to collect. This Tullius did, and the pouch was then placed among others items ready for despatch to their various destinations.

CHAPTER X

Democritus dicit innumerabiles esse mundos.

CICERO

Democritus says that there are countless worlds.

THE MOST PERSONAL possessions were carried by the legionnaires in a leather pouch and it was sacrosanct that these should remain personal. On the untimely death of a legionnaire the leather pouch was handed down through proper military channels to the legionnaire's eldest son of no matter what age. If he did not leave a son then the pouch would be placed in the safekeeping of a military records office until it was established, at even some distant future date, that a male heir had come into existence to take possession. Any salaries, donations, gratuities that might be owing to the legionnaire at the time of his death were automatically passed on to his next of kin, irrespective whether the next of kin was male or female.

Sejanus Arbutus had quite a large amount of accumulated salary owing to him. He knew this before his death because it was his plan that the money should be accumulated to mature at his retirement as a lump sum saving, added to which he could fully expect a handsome service gratuity.

The object of accumulating his hard-won earnings was to enable him to buy a small plot of land to work for agricultural or horticultural produce. Before his tragic death in service to his Emperor, he had a mere four years ahead of him before demobilization. Wrapped up very much in his plans was the full intention that his son Timius, whom he hoped would by that time be a reasonably educated young man to ably assist him in his project. His aim was to provide a comfortable home for the lad and to commence a small business in which he could include his son as a partner. He had realized that with his long service and many years away from home, which denuded him of natural parental responsibility, that this was the least he could do the for boy. His aim was most noble. Unfortunately it was not to be. The accumulated money would be passed through the military establishment to his daughter, Mena, as she was the eldest of his next of kin, but as is policy his pouch of meagre personal belongings would find its way again through military channels to his son, Timius. The vast majority of legionnaires planned a similar future for themselves, on retirement, and Sejanus Arbutus and his colleagues often discussed the technicalities and obstacles that they would have to face when setting up these businesses on their eventual demobilization from the service.

Young Timius had read his most recent letter from his father several times over during the last eight months. This was the second letter he had received since being at Larcia. He wanted to read it again but refrained from doing so because each time his colleagues in the dormitory saw him reading the letter, they were inclined to be jeering, and often remarked that he was treating it as a love letter from a young maiden. Before going to bed that night he secretly tucked the letter, which was now well soiled with his finger prints, into the bosom of his tunic and ran with it down to the latrines. He was relieved to find the latrines empty. He sat himself on the pedestal and by the light of the burning torches read his letter again. He was trying to read between the lines in the hope that there would some indication that his father might surprise him with his arrival at the annual summer athletic meeting which was to take place the next day. He had trained hard for the events and he thought that, by some means or other, word might have been sent to his father that he was participating and his father might have decided to surprise him with his attendance on that very day. He opened the letter and read it again although he knew the contents by heart.

'My dear son Timius,

Very soon our Legion will be relieved of duties here in Germania and we will then return to Rome. When this happens you can rest assured that I will make it my first priority to come to Larcia to spend a few days with you. I am looking forward to seeing you very much because I am sure you have now grown into a fine young man. I am extremely proud of you.

Circumstances have prevented me from coming to see you these past few years because the Legion has been engaged in constant frontier duties from which we have had no relief. You are probably quite disappointed with me for leaving you at Larcia in the way I did, but I can promise you that my motives were completely honourable because of my care and affection for you.

I have often been comforted in the thought that you are well looked after and that you are learning all the many things that a young man growing up in our glorious Empire should know. Whatever your feelings are toward me now, which would be completely understandable, I do sincerely hope that as you grow older you will come to appreciate that my wish, after your mother's death, that you should receive a good all round education has partly been fulfilled.

I cannot tell you when I shall be arriving because I do not know, and should I surprise you with my arrival, please do not think too harshly of me. There are many things for you and me to talk about, and I am looking forward to the day enormously.

Until then, I hope that you are in the best of health and happy with your school friends.

Your most affectionate father
Sejanus Arbutus'

When Timius came to the end of his letter, tears welled up in his eyes, and he began to read it again but had to put it back in the bosom of his tunic quickly because he could hear some of the other boys approaching the latrines. He acknowledged the other boys as he went through the door and back to the dormitory. Marcus was already in his bed and Cyrus was lying on top of his bed across the other side of the room, pulling faces at him.

Cyrus had just beaten him for the umpteenth time at a game of dice, and when they made a quick calculation of the imaginary bets that were laid, Marcus, if he were to properly repay his debts to Cyrus, would be a slave to him for the rest of his life. This situation did occur to Cyrus, and he teased Marcus about it, informing him quite glibly of all the tasks he would ask him to perform as his personal slave. Marcus was humiliated, but Cyrus thought it was great fun having a laugh on Marcus. When Timius arrived, Cyrus related his good fortune to him and suggested that he should not be averse to Timius sharing his slave, Marcus. Timius agreed wholeheartedly with the idea, making Marcus feel more dejected.

"You cannot make a freeborn Roman a slave," retorted Marcus.

"Oh, yes you can," replied Cyrus, "especially if a freeborn Roman becomes bankrupt and, at the rate you are going, you will be bankrupt before you are much older if you continue to lose at dice."

"I won't be if you don't cheat so much," Marcus accused Cyrus.

And so the argument continued until lights out.

In some three months time Timius would be fourteen years old. He was growing into a lean, energetic youth and had now begun to take a keen interest in athletics, particularly the track events. His friend Marcus was also an athletic youth and each of the boys gave encouragement to the other in any training sessions in which they participated for the popular track events in the school. Cyrus, on the other hand, was a much more sturdily built lad and was one of the school champions in the field of gymnastics. His dexterity as a wrestler was extremely good and over the many years they had been friends, although there were many moments of argument and difference, they continued to remain loyal to each other. This kind of relationship to remain loyal to each other was common among all the boys in the school, and our three friends were no exception. When Timius first arrived at Larcia, he only accepted the situation in which he found himself because there was the constant hope that his stay would be of short duration. But as the months, and now years, had gone by, he came to live with his fate and made the most of the life. His childhood years at Vellitrae were now a distant memory whereas the life he was leading in the college was the only one he really knew. He had seen many a newcomer arrive, and they all had the hope that their stay would be of a short duration. He knew differently, but dare he tell the newcomers for whom he could not help feeling a tinge of sorrow. He comforted himself with the thought that he had gone through it all and had emerged unscathed.

Practically all the inmates at Larcia were a mischievous breed, and again our three friends were no exception. Over the years they each received the cane and the flat pad. They were committed to cleaning chores that were considered punishment; they had what amounted to weeks on bread and water, and they spent numerous hours worshipping at the temple which they considered was an absolute bore;—indeed, punishment in itself. The practice of religion and the ritual of worship at the temple was part of the daily curriculum of the inmates and whether they liked it or not, worship to the Gods must continue. Our three friends often discussed their boredom with the whole religious ritual, and Cyrus even expressed the brilliant idea that it was time that somebody, somewhere, invented or conceived another god, as this would perhaps break the monotony of ritualistic worship. This suggestion was shrugged aside by Marcus because he was quick to point out that it took many years to create a new god and, after they had created a new one, he was convinced that it would take even more years for the practice of worship of any new god to be more interesting and enlightening. The boys could not change the established religion.

Timius was quite fluent in reading and writing, but he was not very quick to grasp the intricacies and calculations of mathematics. It was a subject for which he would gladly have given up his most prized possession to the oracle if the Sybil would only grant him the magic powers to grasp and fully understand the subject. He had learnt the geometric axioms of Euclid and found the science principles of Archimedes thoroughly interesting. The theorem of Pythagoras remained a constant fascination to him, and he spent many hours alone trying to grasp the proof as expounded by Pythagoras. He fully understood the principle that *the length of the side of the right triangle and that since the sum of the squares of the lengths of the legs is equal to the square of the length of the hypotenuse (the side opposite the right angle)* but the mystery of proving this fascinating theorem occupied his innermost thoughts. He would draw the parallel line from the apex of the triangle through its base and beyond to the outer side of the largest square parallel to the perpendicular side and then form congruent triangles to proceed with the proof. This was all done in his imagination. Pythagoras' explanation of the universe in terms of numbers also set his imagination alight. He was not a poor pupil of maths but he wished he could properly grasp this magical academic subject. The philosophies of Plato and Aristotle were also of immense interest to him. Oratory was a popular subject at the college, and the oratories of Cicero, Livy, Ovid and Julius Caesar were some of the subjects of which he had now attained some knowledge. The campaigns of Julius Caesar he read over and over again, and he would continue to do so because Julius Caesar had now come to be his favourite hero. He only wished that Julius Caesar had been alive to put an end to that horrible Cyclops that had nearly caused the death of Ulysses and his band of wanderers in Homer's Odyssey, another subject he was in the midst of studying. Homer's famous Iliad is another of the epic poems, which, among other things he was in the midst of learning. It describes the climax of the siege of Troy.

In the next two years, advanced Latin would be prominent in their curriculum, and they would also move into a more advanced stage in their learning of the Greek language. Doronyd almost daily reminded them of the importance of learning Greek. Perhaps he had an axe to grind, because he was a Greek, although he had explained to them many times that his

Greek nationality had nothing whatsoever to do with it. He stressed the point that knowledge of Greek would be of immense value to all of them in the class should they ever find themselves in the fortunate position to travel their glorious Empire which, he was quick to add, was nothing but an extension of the earlier Greek Empire. Many of the boys in the class treated Doronyd somewhat contemptuously, but Timius could neither understand, nor accept, their attitudes. He always admired Doronyd and respected him for the immense amount of knowledge with which the man was endowed. Timius only wished that he could be half as clever as Doronyd because he felt that if he were then when he reached manhood, with half the knowledge of Doronyd, he would be able to make many friends and interest them with his conversation. The knowledge would also help him take up a profession, which would enable him to travel the Empire. He had often thought that he would like to hold an ambassadorial office, but when he considered the idea further, he rejected it, because he could not accept a situation where he would probably be negotiating with barbarian chiefs. He would be very reluctant to negotiate with barbarians. In past history the end of a sword was the only resolve when dealing with them.

The history and background of the calendar, which Doronyd was at pains to explain to the boys, he tried to impart with enthusiasm; still many in the class found it boring, but not Timius. There had been many an occasion on a clear night and before making his way to bed, when Timius would go out of the college building and look up at the sky and try to pick out the stars, some of which Doronyd had told them about. He imagined the difficulty of the early astronomers in their efforts to try and record a systematic cycle of the universe and the positioning of the various constellations at different times of the year. Doronyd had explained to them that over eight hundred years ago astronomers in Babylon, on the banks of the Euphrates River, had studied the sky. They had deduced that the sum visited twelve groups of constellations every year, each for about thirty days. Seven hundred years ago Numa Pompilius, who was the successor to Romulus, gave Rome a calendar based on the lunar system brought from Asia Minor by the Etruscans. This calendar had twelve months which began with *Martius*, named after the god, Mars, *the god of war*. This was followed by *Aprilis*, which means *the opening of the buds*. Aprilis was followed by *Maius, the Goddess of Growth*. The *Goddess of Marriage* came next, who is *Juno*. Following Juno, we had *Quintillius*, which was changed by Julius Caesar to the month of *July*. *Sextilis*, the sixth month became the month of *August*, in honour of Augustus. August is followed by *Semptembris*, the seventh month, *Octobris* the eighth month, *Novembris* the ninth month, *Decembris* the tenth month. *Januarius*, named after the god *Janus* became the eleventh month. Janus signified a two-faced god looking back to the old year and forward to the New Year. The last month of the year *Februarius*, marked the feast of purification and was known as the month of purification. In 46 B.C. Julius Caesar brought the Egyptian astronomer Sosigenes to Rome, and replaced Pompilius's lunar calendar by a solar calendar derived from the physician Thoth. Sosigenes divided his five extra days, with six every third year, among alternate months. The alternate months were increased to thirty one days beginning with March. Other months stayed at thirty days, but February was reduced to twenty nine, with thirty in every third leap year. This calendar began at the first new moon after the winter solstice, which was the shortest day in 46 B.C., to start the first new calendar year on the first of January.

When the Senate renamed Sextilis in his honour, Augustus gave it an extra day to equal Julius Caesar's month of July, and he thereby cut February to twenty eight days. Timius thought Doronyd was very clever to be able to explain such a complicated subject as the calendar, and he made many notes on the subject so that he would eventually be able to learn it by heart. He thought it was important to know how their calendar was derived, especially since it was something everybody now took for granted.

Praetorian Officer Paulo had not changed very much over the years. He was as strict and firm as ever in ensuring that discipline was properly imposed. Timius had come to realize that this man's bark was worse than his bite. In fact he found this to be very much the case with the other Praetorian officers who were seconded to the college as part of their service assignment. He could never understand what kind of indiscretion had been committed to cause the authority to keep Praetorian Officer Carpus continually in charge of the latrines group, because aside from the times that Carpus was absent on retreat, he seemed to be as much a part of the latrine group as the boys whose task it was to carry out the endless daily routine.

The cleaning of the latrines had now become second nature to Timius and indeed many of his peers in the group, and he was now living with the hope that very soon his father would arrive, and he would make a point of asking his father to give him a gold bulla in order that he could signify that he was a true freeborn Roman.

His interest in athletics had rather a fortuitous beginning. Cross-country running was an event that was constantly encouraged in the college. In order that this event could properly take place and that training for the event could take place on a regular basis, the school authorities had negotiated with the farming folk that owned the land and woods beyond the college perimeter that certain tracks that led through their grounds could be used for this purpose. The negotiations included tracks which comprised three-mile, five-mile, and seven-mile circuits, and the age group of the boys governed the distances run by them. The younger boys would run the three-mile circuit, whereas the elder boys would be trained for the seven-mile circuit. All three of these circuits had two strategic points which passed through a pear orchard, which the boys nicknamed *pastimes*, and also through a large field in which root crops were grown.

The Sunday afternoons provided many of the boys with an occasion to satisfy their constant hunger and it was Cyrus who had first discovered the most useful excuse of the cross-country circuits, which enabled them to spend some moments over the fence in the pear orchard, or in the field, whichever crop was in season. He was cunning enough to obtain permission from Praetorian Officer Paulo, although there was some haggling over it, for the three of them to train for the cross-country event. This ostentatious training session provided them with the opportunity of either stealing the pears when the track on which they were running led them alongside *pastimes*, or the opportunity of stealing carrots, turnips, or parsnips, when they were running in the vicinity of the field.

By using this excuse they were not detected by any of the school authorities, nor could anybody accuse them of being out of college bounds. This trick had gone on year after year, but the training the boys received in their so-called self-inflicted dedication gradually brought to the attention of the Praetorian officers the athletic talents of Marcus and Timius. This talent became nurtured by the gymnast Demetrius in his regular coaching and training of the two boys who were now part of the college athletic group. Cyrus, on the other hand, being the most agile of the three, was always automatically considered to be the best one to either hop over the fences and climb up the trees, or swiftly pull up the root crops by grabbing hold of their bunches of leaves on the surface. He was also the strongest of the three. He was also in the athletic group being coached by the gymnast and his assistant in gymnastics. He was very good at vaulting the horse and extremely dexterous on the parallel bars.

Timius was very excited today because he was going to represent the **Blues** in both the one-mile and the three-mile races, and his excitement was given a further uplift with the hope and thought that his father might be present. He would run his hardest today against the opponents in the **Green**, **Red**, and **Yellow** teams. As each boy prepared for his respective event, the spectators started assembling on the opposite side of the track. There was a canvas awning suspended by stout poles to shield the spectators from the sun. Among the spectators, which included of course Artimeses the Principal, were all the other college authorities, who were accompanied by their wives and families who were quartered in individual villas at the north end of the college campus. To the left and to the right of the dignitaries area row upon row of wooden benches had been placed for all the other college boys who were not entered in the events of the day.

It was time for the one mile race, and the competitors took up their places on the start line opposite Artimeses who would give the signal to commence. It was his honour to signal the start of each of the races, and it was also his honour to give out the prizes to the first three winners. The prizes consisted of natural laurel chaplets of three varying amounts of leaves which were placed on the heads of the winners at the end of each race. There were eight competitors in the race consisting of two representatives from each of the **Red, Blue, Green** and **Yellow** teams. As the competitors got on their marks, Timius looked over to the spectators stand to see if he could spot his father, but there was no sign of him, and Marcus noticed the disappointed look on his friend's face. Marcus was to run alongside Timuis as he was one of the other representatives of the **Blue** team. As the race progressed, Timius' disappointment began to gnaw at him, and he was gradually losing distance on the front runners despite the hearty cheering from all the supporters of the **Blue** team and guests. He could see in front of him Marcus, leading the field, but it was too late for him now to attempt to catch up. He finished the race in sixth place but was delighted that Marcus had received the prize chaplet, and was the first to congratulate him on his success.

It was mid-afternoon when, with tremendous pleasure, he heard that Cyrus had succeeded in becoming the prize gymnast. He had also won the discus event and the throwing of the *javelin* and by doing so had gained valuable points for the **Blue** team, which was running level in the points system with the **Yellow** team. Timius had been the firm favourite in the college to win the one-mile event and by not doing so had left him extremely dejected. He was consoled by his two friends, Cyrus and Marcus, who were both enthusiastically confident that he would have success in the final race that afternoon, the three-mile distance. It was mid-afternoon when Timius joined the other competitors on the starting line for the three-mile race. Again Marcus was beside him, and Marcus offered his advice by telling Timius to slightly loosen off the blue cord which was tied around the waist of each competitor to signify the team they represented. Timius did this, and when he looked up from retying the knot, his eyes once again glanced over to the spectators' stand.

There was a good deal of chattering and general merriment going on among the spectators, which indicated that they were enjoying the day. Standing at the rear of the spectators he noticed a tall dark-haired man standing upright with his arms folded across his chest. From a distance he thought that his father had at last arrived and his heart immediately skipped a beat. The adrenalin began to flow through his body at high pressure, and he was determined to win this next race. The outcome of this race would determine the outcome of the day's events in deciding the winning team of the day.

Artimeses gave them the signal to start, and Timius took up a leading position straight away. After three laps of the field, he was now some twenty yards ahead of his nearest rival. The excitement brought about by believing that his father had arrived moved him to call on all his reserves. In doing so his mind began to wander onto greater events. He was now dreaming while his slender legs padded around the track as quickly as they could carry him. In his imagination, he was leading a troop of legionnaires of which he was the leader and the bravest one, and he was urging them on in pursuit of the barbarians, who had caught the legion napping and killing many good legionnaires in the fracas. His sword was held out in front of him, and he had dispensed with his shield. He was approaching the fleeing barbarians swiftly, jumping from rock to rock, leaping over streams and climbing up the hillsides. He was racing the stragglers to the top of the hill hoping to beat them there and then do battle with them at the summit. His mind was completely involved in his daydream and the cheers from his peers were not heard by him, especially when he had overlapped five of his rivals, including Marcus. He was now at least three quarters of a lap ahead of his nearest rival, as he passed the finishing post. He did not even feel out of breath because in his excitement he could have run all day.

The first thing he would ask his father was whether he had remembered to bring some gum-arabic. Marcus was third in the race and arrived some minutes after Timius, but this was understandable since Marcus had spent a lot of his energy earlier in the day winning the one-mile race. The three winners now calmed down and received their respective winners' chaplets, but Timius could not take his eyes off the tall man who was still in the same position as when he first spotted him. He was absolutely certain that this was his father, although it was nearly seven years since he had last seen him, and Timius could only vaguely remember what he looked like.

He remembered he was a tall man who stood very upright, and he also remembered his father's habit of standing with his arms folded across his chest. After receiving the chaplets competitors were instructed to assemble in the middle of the athletics field where Artimeses would announce the winning team of the day. A tremendous cheer went up from the spectators while the competitors exchanged congratulations and commiserations. The spectators began to leave, and the competitors started making their way to their respective dormitories. The **Blue** team were the winners of the day, and it was Timius and Marcus who had made certain of the prize. Timius hung behind in the middle of the field and asked Marcus to go along without him. His eyes were still gazing on the tall spectator but he casually turned around and walked away, never to be seen again. Timius was heartbroken because he was absolutely certain that had that man been his father he would not have left without speaking to him. The following morning Artimeses sent for Timuis. Timius immediately thought that Artimeses would inform him of the arrival of his father but this was not so. Artimeses merely informed the boy that an article, which was a small leather pouch, had arrived for him, but that he had decided that since it contained very little of any importance it would remain sealed and in his study until he felt it time that it should be handed over to the boy. Artimeses merely reminded Timius that when he eventually did leave the institution here at Larcia he must not forget to ask for it, to which Timius agreed. He soon got over his disappointment because shortly afterwards Demetrius, the gymnast, whom he met in the courtyard, enthusiastically suggested that he should now, even at this early age, take his training much more seriously with a view to one day being selected to represent Rome in the Olympics. This helped bring the spirit back into the boys, especially when Demetrius went on to describe the importance of the Olympic Games.

Demetrius was extremely impressed with the way young Arbutus had run the three-mile race yesterday. He had never, throughout his career as athlete, gymnast, coach, and trainer seen a performance like it from a boy of his age. He was quick to realize the tremendous talent displayed. He explained to Timius that every four years competitors from all over the world assembled at Olympia in Greece, and had been doing so for nearly two centuries, to partake in athletic games. These games were really only open to athletes of the highest calibre, and the games were held in honour of the god Zeus. Apart from the games, sacrifices to Zeus were offered and the games were treated as a sombre festival.

Timius found it quite amusing when Demetrius informed him that all competitors at the Olympic Games had to compete in the nude. He felt he would never be able to do that although he would love to go to Olympia, and he questioned Demetrius about the reason for nudity being one of the conditions participants had to meet. Demetrius explained that this was the established practice at Olympia simply because no women were allowed to attend the games. There had been an occasion many years ago, at one of the meetings, when a woman, whose son was to partake as a competitor in a boxing match, was so enthusiastic of giving her support to him that she disguised herself as a man and entered the arena wearing a man's cloak—and paraded as one of her son's coaches. When he won his event, she was so excited that she yelled out to him giving her disguise away. This was totally against the custom and spirit of the Olympic Games, and from that day onwards, all competitors and their coaches and trainers entered the arena in the nude. In addition, all spectators were also naked. Timius understood the purpose now and promised Demetrius that he would henceforth take his training as a runner more seriously, provided of course that Marcus join him.

*

The tall dark stranger whom Timius had seen among the spectators was a military courier who had visited the college in order to deliver a leather pouch. Artimeses had invited him to stay and attend the athletic events of the day before proceeding on his mission of other deliveries.

CHAPTER XI

Senatus Populusque Romanus.

Roman Senate and People.

MARIUS ARIOVISTUS HAD retired from public life. He had spent many years in the Senate and was a keen supporter of Republicanism. He held very strong views about autocratic powers of any one individual. He had had the honour of serving in the Senate during the latter part of the Augustan Era and felt that in such a situation—where an autocrat was able, conscientious, and astutely persuasive in his leadership—Marius could tolerate a full measure of autocracy. But when autocratic powers were grabbed and flouted, as they were by Tiberius, he felt that enough was enough, and the spirit of Republicanism surged back into his veins. He was an ardent opponent of autocracy and constantly debated the subject with his senatorial colleagues. His private business was centred on the Port of Ostia, where he was the major shareholder in a firm of merchants. He was a man of advancing years whose family had grown up and gone their various ways, and he now lived in a modest villa in Rome, with his wife and two slaves.

It was mid-July and Marius had decided to take a gentle walk through the grounds that lay on the eastern side of the Forum of Boarium. On his way, he had passed by the Theatre of Marcelli, where he was able to see groups of people making their way into the theatre for a performance of the popular play of the month. He was not very interested in the theatre, nor was he interested in the circus, because he often mused to himself that the many recent scenes he had witnessed in the Senate chamber could only be akin to a circus or theatrical farce. There had been so much meaningless argument and debate over meaningless subjects; subjects that he considered to be trivial in comparison with the earlier days when Augustus was first consul and many matters of real importance needed serious debate and swift ratification. He had witnessed the demise of many conscientious colleagues, who took their senatorial responsibility very seriously, and the absence of worthwhile debate, which hastened his decision to retire, also.

When he arrived at the grounds which were laid out as a small public park he found the atmosphere there most pleasant and refreshing. As he strolled through the grounds he inhaled the first morning air in deep breaths. His walk took him along neatly laid pathways which wound in and out of beds planted with a variety of shrubs, many of which had been imported from other parts of the Empire. The grounds were well tended and the chirrup of the birds added to the pleasantness.

As he arrived at the southern exit of the small park he noticed, sitting quietly on a stone bench, his old friend Livius Maas. Livius spotted him approaching and stood up to greet him. The two men shook bands and exchanged pleasantries and seated themselves on the bench. Marius thought that this would be a good time to take a well-earned breather. There was no hurry for him to return home as his wife, Diana, had arranged to entertain a few friends, which amounted to a general gossip. As they seated themselves on the bench they could hear, in the near distance, the footsteps of marching soldiers, and very soon a maniple of Praetorian Guards passed by their helmets, shields, and javelins gleaming in the sunlight. After they had passed by, a thought occurred to Marius and, turning to his friend Livius, he quite casually comented,

"Do you know, Livius, we in Rome, and indeed all of us Romans, bear a terrible responsibility for the rest of the world."

"I agree entirely with you, Marius, but let us not forget that it is a responsibility that we have wholly snatched for ourselves and not a responsibility that has been thrust on us by anyone."

"I cannot agree with you," replied Marius. "Rome has been fated to this responsibility, but I sometimes wonder whether providence has not been anterior in its purpose. I have often wondered," he continued, "whether Rome is mature enough to accept such a responsibility, but have been comforted with the thought that maturity is a never-ending situation. It grows and keeps on growing and the more experience we have the more mature we will become."

"You're a very patriotic man, Marius, old friend," said Livius.

Livius Maas was a man of seventy-two, four years older then his friend Marius. He had also retired and enjoyed his retirement these past three years. He had spent thirty years in Antioch, where he had been a lecturer in philosophy at the University Institutions, which had been set up in that city. While he was in Antioch, he was extremely pro-Roman in his attitude, and this was determined by the fact that he was surrounded by Greeks who were extremely patriotic and proud themselves, but he had come to recognise that the Greeks were right to be proud, particularly in that they had given to the world the basis of all culture. During periods of contemplation he recognised the fact that the city states of both Rome and Athens could be likened to the parents of the civilized world. Rome was the masculine and robust parent which had given the world security and protection and the laws by which society would be governed. Rome was a very harsh taskmaster.

Athens, and its extended territory of Greece, gave the world charm and loveliness; to her could be credited the culture, medical, and scientific discoveries, religion and art. Although she was conquered by Rome as any women is eventually conquered by man, having done so her charm and loveliness now basically controlled Roman attitude. Let us not forget that during the height of the Greek Empire, Alexander the Great had virtually extended the frontier of his empire to the borders of India. And in those days Greece was very masculine in her attitude and poise.

Livius pondered for a moment and, with a twinkle in his eye, continued the discussion by agreeing again with Marius about his observations on the maturity of estate and went on to ask, "Do I understand you correctly when you talk about maturity, that the more mature a state becomes the more its need for slaves has to be satisfied?"

"Not at all," replied Marius abruptly, "slavery has nothing to do with it."

"Then why are we surrounded by so many slaves? Is it a weakness in our system that without slavery the very fabric of our society would collapse?"

"Of course not," retorted Marius, "many of the slaves we have, have been shackled because of either their contempt for our system of law and order or, in many cases, direct opposition to it. You know as well as I do that many of the slaves were captured on the field of battle during the days of the conquest, and you are fully aware that the majority can earn their freedom by proving their loyalty to our system of civilisation through their loyalty to their masters."

"Yes, I am aware of that, Marius, old friend, but it is my belief that if the system we glorify as civilisation was one of character and substance, there would be no need for slaves, and then every individual could live freely to cherish their own personal hopes and ambitions, however lofty, or however humble these might be."

"Come along now, Livius, you don't believe, surely, that the system you are advocating would in fact work. After all, let us compartmentalize society for a moment; we have the nobility who are in need of very little in life. All their whims and fancies are there for the taking and their only ambition is to gain more power. Having gained this power, what would they do with it? They would become greedier, which would be the eventual ruination of them and in their ruin untold number of innocent people would be included by fighting their battles for them to satiate their greed to conquer new territories.

They are aware of this and keep their ambitions within bounds, but once they have done this their ambitions are fired in other directions and the main direction in which it appears to be going at the moment is in to the immoral province of licentiousness. Fortunately, their move in this direction does not involve the lives of many innocent people who can stand aside as spectators. It is common knowledge among the nobility that there is this trend, but they foolishly take no steps to arrest it. In fact, they indulge in more perverse acts of licence. You know as well as I do, that incestuous marriages are commonplace, and if it continues in this fashion we will arrive at a stage where intermarrying will not only be among close relatives of the family but will even extend to brother marrying sister, with the eventual result of physical weaknesses in their off-springs and absolute ruination of the noble families of our fair empire will surely result. I think though they are becoming aware of this and are possibly now striving to reach other goals, but what they are I do not know. Now tell me, dear Livius, my honourable philosopher, why do you think that we have such a situation among our nobility?"

Lilvius thought for a while and answered, "Well, Marius, you have already said what the reason is. Surely you do not want me to repeat it to you."

"Yes," replied Marius. "I have given you the reason for it, but I am asking you for the basis of my reasoning."

"I don't quite follow," replied the old philosopher.

"Well, let me tell you," said Marius. "Those people of whom I have spoken have little in life to which they can direct their hopes. They've no need to hope for anything and, as I have already said, their every wish is granted to them. Do you agree?"

"Yes, I do entirely," responded Livius. "But I still do not see what this has to do with slavery, and, in fact, as I have contended to you on other occasions, it is my belief that slavery should be abolished and the Plebiscite should be extended to all members of the populace to elect their own representatives to the Senate, and each representative would be elected on his merit and ability alone, and nothing else."

"Ah! My dear friend," Marius replied, stroking his beard, "you cherish such noble thoughts, and you command my admiration, but I am afraid such noble thoughts would only be acceptable in another age."

"Come now, Marius, you are only avoiding the issue, and you know very well that this system could be introduced without much trouble, even in this age in which we are living."

"I cannot agree with you at all on that score, Livius, so let me continue with my pet theory of compartmentalization. Let us now take the ruling classes, the Senate, and the administrators: these people endeavour to carry out their public duties as efficiently as they can. Many do it out of conscientiousness, it is true, but let us be perfectly honest they are primed with the hope of gaining higher rewards, with a view to entering into the nobility themselves. We can apply this maxim through all strata of life. The slave cherishes the intense hope of gaining his freedom; the artisan and craftsman improve their artistic bent with a view to gaining promotion and thereby increasing their rewards; the management of our noble enterprises and even our merchantmen and bankers endeavour to make their businesses more prosperous with the hope of increasing their rewards. It is human belief that the greater one's rewards are, and if properly applied, the greater the measure of security. You will find, dear fellow that people, at all levels, live in hope and subconsciously or consciously their every effort is directed to this end. I have contended continuously the old, old saying that *it is better to travel in hope than to arrive.*'

Livius was rather amused at his friends contentions, because he had not overlooked this philosophy himself but, nevertheless, it was still his own contention that the philosophy of hope could be applied equally well in a free society where people gained position on merit and ability. He felt that political electioneering should be extended to all classes and expressed this view with the utmost conviction. Marius could not agree with him and was quick to point out that if this situation was to be the accepted norm, then for it to work properly, all individuals would need to be disciplined, responsible, and properly educated politically, otherwise a situation would arise where agitators would be quick to inculcate the merits of a true democracy but with a view to merely serving their own ends.

He was convinced that such people would cleverly indoctrinate the populace to support their views. Then, having been popularly elected they would be no different in their behaviour to the present day nobility, except that they would have arrived at these lofty positions out of pure hypocrisy and, in his view, hypocrisy was the lowest state to which one could stoop. Moreover, Marius also drew the attention of his learned friend to the fact that discipline was the first maxim that had to be achieved in a civilized society, and this could only be achieved by the inculcation of respect for one's superiors of whatever class or position and respect for one's neighbours. He was also convinced that respect was always reciprocal. It was his belief that if a society was disciplined and respectable in all its attitudes, all the other benefits and advantages and progressive modes of life would follow in due course. His learned friend, Livius, could not really fault this argument but insisted that a society supported by slavery was doomed to failure. It was his view that oppression was not the right way to discipline a society, to which Marius argued that some form of oppression was necessary in the early stages of a developing civilization to act as a deterrent. Total freedom and licence would lead to anarchy and chaos. He was quick to point out to his old friend that one only had to travel to the boundaries of the Empire to witness such a state of affairs among the barbarians, but even they, in the barbarism, used the tools of oppression as a means of instilling discipline which they were fully aware was absolutely necessary in order to maintain control over the lives of their various tribes.

Livius accepted the fundamental argument propounded by Marius but, with a smile crossing his lips, felt that here was an opportunity for him to gain the advantage of the discussion and continued, "Quite so, dear Marius, but you haven't convinced me why it is necessary to keep large foreign territories under our control because, if you are going to use the excuse that it will be necessary to do so otherwise they will turn their attention, out of complete avarice, to our Italian peninsula, then I must ask you why we have fixed our present boundaries. You contend that the barbarians have focused their attention on Rome and its provinces out of avarice. So, therefore, to follow your argument through, we should really extend our frontiers even further so that within them would be included the barbaric territories. If we did just this, then where would the policy of expansion end? You would have a never-ending policy of conquest on your hands, purely for the sake of dispensing with the avarice of peoples that may lie beyond those frontiers. You know very well what problems this would cause."

"This is precisely my theory, Livius, but I am also aware of two very important factors that require consideration."

"Oh, and what are those, Marius?"

"Firstly," answered Marius, "we must consider the question of finance, and a large amount of finance will be necessary to pay a vastly increased number of legions that will be required to fulfil the task. Once they have completed the task of extending the frontiers well beyond the margins of prudent safety, then we shall require a constantly sound financial base in order to follow through many years of settlement, redevelopment and eventual civilization of these newly won territories."

"You are aware, as I am, he continued with a snigger, "any additional finance gained through increasing taxation would be hurriedly spent on pet projects by our beloved Caesar. Secondly, we cannot view, at the present moment, the expansion of the Empire while there are still large pockets of unrest within our existing boundaries. These territories must first be brought to heel and thoroughly civilized before our sights can be set on new horizons."

"Precisely, Marius," replied Livius. "This task is made even more difficult when our client kingdoms and provinces look with envy at the freedom enjoyed by the barbarians, and the free territory of Britannia is a fine example of this; and I contend that if we gave our provinces total freedom and increase our moral standing and civilized status to a degree where it could be held out as an example to them, I think they would strive to reach the same standards. Their own frontiers could be guarded by their own provincially raised legions."

"Yes," responded Marius, "that is a sound proposal but unfortunately one that could not be put into effect at this stage. Maybe some day, in the future, this might be possible, but certainly not now because there are still, in all the territories, certain people with ambition who would fight each other in civil wars to gain supremacy, just the same way as we Romans did ourselves during the years of civil wars that we experienced. This is happening at the moment in Spain where we have constant unrest—to use just one province as an example."

"Yes, yes, I agree," Livius said impatiently, "but you cannot compare the attitudes of our provincial people to those of us Romans. Remember many of them have reached a much more advanced state of maturity than the noble Roman, and I cannot accept that this situation would be the natural outcome if Rome withdrew from these territories."

"That might be so," retorted Marius. "But, my dear friend, please remember that while we are endeavouring to impose our form of civilization on these territories, we are also adopting many of their cherished customs and forms of culture."

He continued, "it is a give and take situation, you know, and allow me to add further that while the provincials are in an oppressed situation, as you believe they are, their enmity is at least focused against Rome and not among themselves. But let us also not forget that while they might harbour an enmity towards Rome, they readily accept Roman protection from foreign invaders of their shores, so that they can partake in the activities of their daily lives in security. And they must be aware that their growing civilization can only be accomplished with the bounds of security. If this security was taken away from them they would fight among themselves, not because of any internal differences, but through anxiety, anxiety caused through a feeling of insecurity."

"No, I'm afraid-."

Livius abruptly stopped speaking because he saw coming towards them their friend, the nobleman Terrence Curtius. Curtius approached them with a smile which seemed to fill his whole face. He was so pleased to see again two friends whom he had given up for lost. It was over six weeks since they had last met, but Curtius should have remembered that his two friends could never lose themselves simply because they were retired gentlemen. On the contrary, he was the most likely one to be lost from them because of his vocation. He was an administrative advisor in service to the Roman government, and his most recent assignment in this capacity had taken him to the distant province of Judea.

He was a member of a government commission set up to monitor tax assessments in this client kingdom which was ruled by King Herod. The assessment was necessary in order that the tributum, levied on the kingdom, could be properly assessed and he had arrived back in Rome some four days ago. Curtius was a very tall upright man in his late forties, with many years of administrative work behind him. His work had taken him to other parts of the Empire: Illyrycum, Dacia, Greece, Parthia, Egyptus, and Morrocco were some of the provinces which he had visited in many cases for months on end. He was an unmarried man with no domestic responsibilities who thoroughly enjoyed his vocation, to which he was extremely dedicated. He was an observant man who did not miss the subtleties of local gossip because he always felt that from local gossip he could always rely on acquainting himself with a measure of truth, and the kind of gossip that aroused his keenest interest was that of a political nature. By this means he was able to assess the feeling and the ambitions of the provincial populace, which enabled him to keep the Senate aware of the changing attitudes in the provinces. He was extremely popular among senators and they invariably took heed to any information he was able to disclose, even though much of it might have only been local rumour.

The three companions exchanged hearty pleasantries, and Curtius enquired what the intense discussion was all about between Marius and Livius. He could not help but notice, he informed them, that they had been involved in a serious discussion, and he asked them what it was about out of pure curiosity. Both Livius and Marius brushed their discussion aside as being of no importance, and Marius added, "Surely you know, my dear Terence, that when two old men get together on a sunny morning such as this, they enjoy reminiscing about old times. But never mind us, what news do you have?"

"Not very much," said Curtius, "except that I have just returned from the most godforsaken land of Judea, and I hope never to return there. Those Jews are the most conceited and cunning individuals one could ever meet, but their nature is probably determined by their horrible surroundings. They appear to be constantly at each others' throats. Duplicity is too kind a word to use in describing them, and it isn't any wonder that our gods have forsaken them.

Terence Curtius' description of the Jews and the client kingdom of Judea amused Marius and Livius immensely and they laughed among themselves for quite some time. He continued to tell them that he had heard a rumour that some of them had found another god whom they were hailing as their long awaited Messiah.

Marius then went on to ask, "I am sure you took no notice of the rumour, because those Jews have for years and years been looking forward to the coming of this great and wonderful Messiah, but I am sure that when he does come he would not linger very long among them and would hasten to get back to whence he came.

Livius nodded in agreement, and they all laughed at Marius' remark. Neither Marius nor Livius accepted the views of Curtius in his regard for the Jews because they were both fully aware that although the Jews were a people constantly plagued by one form of unrest or another, this was probably because they had for centuries been seeking an ideal that never seemed to be within their grasp.

They had spent decades in their endeavour to establish themselves and develop a form of ideal unity which was promised to them by their patriarchal ancestors. Their indoctrination, which began with the early patriarchs, that there was one god and one god alone, and also the more recent prophecies of their many prophets that the coming of this god on earth in the form of man was nigh was probably the basis of their restlessness. There were Jewish prophets continually on the Judean scene, and each one at sometime or another attracted the attention of a few of their followers to be raised in their religious enthusiasm to being that of the Messiah. This enthusiasm, in each case, was always damped because the prophets that bestrode the country were later to be seen to be mere mortals.

None of the prophets claimed to be the Messiah, and the Jewish people were generally in a constant attitude of expectancy, in which they expected their Messiah to arrive, with all the glory and finery of a powerful noble king. He would be followed by a vast army of angelic soldiers, whom they believed would finally drive out the oppressive Romans and their own oppressive administrators in the Court of Herod. Aside from this, they were also a people of tremendous literacy and enterprise, and given the full opportunity to pursue these talents, it was felt, by both our aged and learned friends, Livius and Marius, that they could be of tremendous use in further development of the Roman Empire, but alas, they had also been indoctrinated to being anti-Roman, although their opposition to Roman jurisdiction was not of a violent nature.

The subject of the Jews had been discussed on previous occasions by our learned friends. They were naturally anxious to learn more from Curtius of the recent developments in Judea, particularly on the question of their religion, which was a subject of intrigue among not only Marius and Livius, but also other scholars in the Empire. They could never understand how the Jewish religion had been extant for so many centuries, especially in their belief of one god, and that this god insisted that no other god would be worshipped by them in any shape or form. They pressed Curtius to tell them more.

Livius began asking Curtius, "Tell me Curtius, this most recent contender to the aspirations of the Messiah—what do you know about him? Does he act like a king? Does he have a tremendous army of followers, and are these followers armed?"

"No, not at all," replied Curtius, "all we had heard was that he was a very ordinary fellow who lived off the land and on the benevolence of his followers. Apparently he has not claimed to be the Messiah, although many of his closest associates appear to acclaim him as the Messiah."

"What name does he go by?" queried Marius," and what has he been preaching to his followers?"

"Oh," thinking for a moment Curtius replied, "I think his name is John, and in his preaching, so I am told", continued Curtius, "he merely communicates the message that he is the one who has been sent by heaven to prepare the way for the Messiah. I am also told that he is practicing a religious ritual which they call baptism."

"Baptism!" both Livius and Marius exclaimed. "Prey, tell us more," requested Marius. "Is baptism a ritual in which the Jews sacrifice to Jehovah, and if so what do they use in their sacrifices? Do they sacrifice animals? Or do they merely go through the motions of doing so? I ask this because, as I understand it, the country cannot support an abundance of livestock, and if they constantly sacrifice during the ritual of baptism, then I am sure Herod's administrators will soon put an end to it, because it would deplete the country of one of its essential commodities."

"No, I'm afraid not, my dear friend. Baptism is not a sacrificial ritual. We were told," said Curtius, "that this John merely ushers the faithful down to the shallow banks of the River Jordan and immerses them in water for a few seconds and recites a prayer as he does so. It is believed, among the faithful, that this cleanses them of all their mortal sins. But if one could be cleansed of all one's mortal sins by such a totally inexpensive and unceremonious ritual, such as baptism, then I am sure that if the aristocracy who live on the Palatine Hill heard of such an inexpensive means of forgiveness from their sins they would surely be converted to becoming followers of the Messiah overnight. Moreover, they may even find it worthwhile, in the long run, to build special baptismal baths in which they could bathe each morning after the licentious night before, and so be purified in a most cheap and easy way."

Again, Curtius' two aged friends were thoroughly amused with this remark and both laughed loudly. Yes, they agreed Curius was quite a character with a terrific sense of humour, and this was probably the reason why he was so popular.

An expression of seriousness began to form on Livius' face, and Curtius noticed this and asked, "Is something troubling you?" dear Livius.

"No, not really," replied Livius. "But one or two questions have just crossed my mind.

"Well, what are they?" asked Marius eagerly.

"Well, it's concerning this one-god religion of the Jews. Would you consider that it is a religion that could spread to the rest of the Empire?" asked Livius.

"No, not at all, old friend," replied Marius.

"And why not?" asked Livius, "especially when, as Curtius has described, many of their rituals are quite inexpensive and do not require the facility of a temple. They merely practice it in the open air, according to our dear friend here."

Curtius nodded in agreement, and Marius continued, "In my view it is not a religion that would spread to Rome and her illustrious empire, simply because we in the Empire like to focus our worship on several deities and, moreover, those deities that are worshipped by the Nordic provincials among the peoples of our northernmost territories are representatives of the male gender, like Thor and Woden, whereas the Celtic races of our Empire not only feel secure in the worship in a variety of gods, but among this variety are those of the female gender. It is a possibility that the Nordic races would accept one male God, but I am absolutely convinced that our Celtic colleagues would miss focusing their worship from time to time on female goddesses and, as regards the acceptance of the Jewish religion, the Celts would be most difficult converts to a one-god religion."

"But, my dear friend," replied Livius, "you are so narrow in your reasoning, and you lack vision, I am sorry to say. Had it occurred to you," he continued, "that if this one-god religion was to become accepted throughout the Empire, then our Celtic brethren would automatically invent female attendants of this one God whom they would acclaim as having powers verging on the supreme deity to whom they would also pay homage. These female, and indeed male, supreme beings would of course be second in line, or indeed third, fourth or fifth in line to the supreme deity, who will be a masculine deity, and given this set of circumstances, and this type of situation, everybody will be happy in their religious affairs and, who knows, it might be an acceptable situation. They then will not have deviated from the maxim of one god, because all these other attendant deities would be subordinate. Moreover, circumstances could be arranged by the noble religious advocate, that the teachings and the simple rituals of the one god could remain undisturbed."

Thinking aloud Curtius said, "Yes, I can fully see your point, but there is one important factor which you seem to ignore."

"What is that?" asked Livius.

"Well," replied Curtius, "the religion of our empire demands ceremony and ritual with all its attendant regalia, but that of the Jewish god seems to ignore ceremonious forms of worship.

"Come along, now," countered Livius, "don't try and tell me that if this Jewish religion spreads throughout the Empire, then our religious masters would not add some of the ceremonious refinements of our existing religion and combine them into that of the Jewish religion; and they can do this in a most subtle manner without offending the basic teachings and principles of the Jewish religion., whatever they might be. What I am trying to say is that the religious activities which you may have witnessed or heard of in Judea in connection with the teachings of the prophets and the teaching of this messenger fellow John, who tells of the coming of the Messiah, could easily be made attractive to the population at large by practicing it in specially built or converted temples and adding a few of the refinements of our present religions. You cannot tell me that the Jews do not believe in temples, after all, their ancient King Solomon built a golden temple to his god in the heart of Jerusalem."

Both Curtius and Marius nodded their heads in agreement because they could now see the logic of Livius' argument.

Terence Curtius expanded the logic of Livius by adding that it would be essential at some stage or other, that this one-god belief of the Jews would have to be augmented, in his opinion, by some of the existing rites of the practiced religions of the day and also the creation, or invention, of attendant deities of both genders to be attractive to the enormously large Celtic element of people that inhabited the Empire. He realized that the Celtic inhabitants, when in their practice of religion, were extremely devout and if they were to be successfully converted, and no matter from whence a one-god religion sprang, that religion would have to embrace mystic figures to whom they could also focus their attention.

The question was, 'how were these mystic figures to be conceived' and, moreover, 'what form would they take?' He could not accept there being a situation where a one-god religion would be supported by their existing Greek, Etruscan, Egyptian, Roman and Celtic gods and goddesses. He felt sure that the so-called one god and supreme-being commonly referred to as the Messiah, commonly referred to as Jehovah could hold the supremacy over these other deities without causing religious upheaval. Therefore, he argued, that when the Messiah did in fact arrive from heaven above, he would either have to bring attractive attendants with him in the form of assistant gods and goddesses through whom the faithful could use as mediators, who would in reality take the place of Juno, Jove, Dianna, Mithras and the many other gods which were representative of particular functions, or the religious followers of this messiah would have to pontificate and build up legends around his closest associates in the form of either his friends or relatives, be they male or female gender. This combination would then stand a fair chance of replacing the present-day religions.

It would be fairly easy for the religious pontiffs—and not beyond their imagination—to weave legends around the close associates of the Messiah, in order to elevate them into positions of prominence within the one-god religion. The views of Terence Curtius were found to be most agreeable by both Marius and Livius. Having said his piece, Terence enquired what his two aged friends were discussing when he arrived on the scene. Marius then went on to inform him of details of their discussion about Roman attitudes to government and jurisprudence.

Terence was more inclined to agree with the views expressed my Marius, to the slight disappointment of Livius.

"What are your views my dear Terence?" asked Livius.

"Well," replied Terence, "as you both already know, I am a pragmatist. I'm firmly of the belief that before we could enjoy the benefits of a society that is the vision of Livius, all our citizens in the Empire must learn to accept authority and respect it and, moreover, react to it responsibly."

He continued, "I cannot accept a situation where authority is eroded and flouted. There must be a deterrent to irresponsibility and the deterrents can only be lessened as and when society grows responsible and mature because if, as you suggest, dear Livius, we dispensed with slavery and all other forms of so-called oppression, it would not be very long before there would be a demand that the death penalty be removed because it was uncivilized. If we met those demands then there would be further demands for the removal of other penalties. If these demands were successful then we finally arrive at a chaotic state of affairs where there were no penalties imposed on law breakers and wrongdoers—because the view would then be held that any form of penalty would be oppressive and uncivilized."

He carried on by saying, "We would then have a state of anarchy. The laws would be interpreted to suit each individual circumstance and broken at will by any individual, without any respect for one's fellow man, and the whole fabric of our society would break down. Out of this situation we would see the rebirth of insecurity, discontent, and total disorder, resulting in civil war, out of which would emerge a dictator with more oppressive powers and so the cycle would begin again. I will admit that our present constitution which is supposed to fall within the ambit of the wishes of the Senate and the roman people whom they are supposed to represent, leaves a lot to be desired, but in the world as it is it is all we have, which of course could be refined and developed. In fact, dear friend, in my opinion with all its shortcomings the constitution is the best we have and will remain so until somebody comes up with something better."

"Those are exactly my sentiments, my dear Terence," replied Marius. But Livius shook his head from side to side in disagreement.

"I see you still hold your own views," said Terence, turning to Livius.

"Yes, I do indeed," replied Livius, "but I won't bore you with the finer points of my argument."

"You will never bore me," replied Terence, "and I am acutely aware of the fact that you are a complete visionary, and very often I have wished that I could also have such an intense visionary attitude to life. Although I do not agree with your views, my dear Livius, I respect you for them and woe-betide any man who may ridicule you for holding such views in my presence."

"Thank you, thank you," replied Livius, "but I must be getting along now, so I must bid you farewell, trusting that I will see you both again, very soon." Turning to Terence, Livius said, "may the gods go with you if your travels take you abroad before I am able to see you again."

"Thank you, Livius," replied Terence, "but I trust you do not mean the gods that will accompany this so called Messiah."

They good humouredly shook hands, and all three characters departed to go their separate ways.

The controversy of the Roman constitution was a constant subject of discussion among the intellectuals of the Empire. Many propounded Republicanism, while others argued its disadvantages in comparison with the present arrangement, whereby the people's wishes were ratified through the senate by Caesar himself, but the Republicans argued that this was not what happened in practice. It is their conviction that the situation had now developed to a point where it was Caesar's wishes and the wishes of his very close associates, that takes precedence over all others—at the expense of ignoring the real wishes of the people. However, the controversy would linger until the weaknesses of the system now practiced—ostensibly within the terms of the constitution—came to the fore, and the Republicans felt that it was only a matter of time before Republicanism would follow in the wake of the chaos and discontent that the present system was bound to leave, in their view.

Religion was not a popular subject of discussion because, even among the intellectuals, the status quo of religion and its practice, in its many forms would remain undisturbed because there was no indication from common people of dissatisfaction of the religious rites, which they were free to practice, as and when they wished. It was not a compulsory duty imposed on them by the state. It was left very much to their own conscience. Naturally the Patricians were the most zealous worshippers, whereas the Plebians did not take the subject too seriously. The arguments in favour of monotheism and polytheism did not arise, and there was no major faction outside of Judea where monotheism was propounded with any zealousness. It was accepted that even the Jews had, at times, during their long history, passed through phases where monotheism was abandoned in favour of polytheism, although currently they were about the only race within the Empire that were monotheist in their ideals.

CHAPTER XII

Fit ut nemo esse posit beatus.

CICERO

It is the case that no one can be happy.

"NEVER MIND ASKING so much about myself," said Cyrus, "but pray, tell me, how have you been getting along lately? Have you had many exciting wins on the athletics field; how many punishments have you experienced these past two years; have you been out wolf hunting; and what about fishing? Have you caught anything larger than the two-pound tench of three years ago; are you still working in the latrines."

"So many questions from my old friend Cyrus whom I am so very pleased to see, after his two years of absence," said Timius. "Yes, I have had several wins especially over the three-mile events plus a few failures of course, but I'm afraid this has not helped to boost my position here in the college, where the authorities have not felt it prudent to reward me by excusing me from the latrine chore. It seems that every success I have had on the athletics field has soon been marred by the troubles that I have brought upon myself by being stupidly caught fishing or wolf hunting in the out of bounds areas."

"Ah," Cyrus said, "you really need me around you I can see that plainly because when I was with you, I knew just how to trick them into not being able to catch us, but I'm afraid, old pal, we cannot turn the clock back now, and you will just have to do the best you can and learn from your mistakes. Anyway, it will not be long now before you will be leaving the college."

"No, I suppose not," replied Timius.

"What will you do when you leave here?" asked Cyrus.

"I've no idea", Timius replied, with a far away look in his eyes, "I have no idea," he repeated faintly. "I did so very much want to join one of the legions, but after the description which you have given me of legion life I feel a bit dejected because I don't think I could stand the pace and the harsh treatment which you have told me about."

"Of course you will," retorted Cyrus, "and we can certainly use a person like you in the Fourth Legion. You might look puny, but you're a resilient fellow, and in my experience of legion life, it is the thin, puny fellows that are the hardest and the most able to stand adversity, whereas the big strong-looking fellows are invariably the first to weaken."

Timius laughed shyly and went on to say, "Cyrus, you are talking like an old veteran legionnaire, but even so, I am absolutely delighted to see you again, and it was extremely good of you to pay us a visit. I'm sure old Paulo was also surprised and pleased to see you."

"Oh, yes he was," replied Cyrus, "at least he gave me that impression during our conversation although there were a couple of occasions when he referred to me as an old rogue and said that if he was my commander, he would post me to some distant desert frontier and that, he felt, would be my ultimate cure."

Both young men amused themselves in their reminiscing of Praetorian Officer Paulo's admonishments to them.

"You were telling me about Marcus," said Timius. Where did you say he is, now?" he asked curiously.

"Well," replied Cyrus, "I heard from old White Sandals and the other fellow Jacobs Boots that he was now in Velitrae working in a pottery. I have no idea what he was doing in Velitrae, but these two fellows, whom we always used to quarrel with and tantalize, I met again in the Fourth Legion and it was from them I gleaned this information."

And so the conversation progressed while the two young men sat on the southern bank of the college boundary. Their meeting came to an end when it was time for Timius to report to the latrines. Cyrus and Timius bid each other a most hearty farewell and promised faithfully that they would keep in touch. When Cyrus left, their was a hint of a tears in both lads' eyes and it was a grave pity that providence had decreed that they should be separated by a mere two years of age.

Cyrus had left the college some two years ago, and after wandering about the streets of Rome, most dejected and lost, he had found himself in the company of some other young men who used to spend their time with the merchants who owned and operated the market stalls where they would help them replenish stock and carry out other menial chores to earn a few coppers. After a while the realization came to Cyrus that this was not the life for him, and when he broached the subject of joining the army to his companions, they did everything they possibly could to dissuade him from doing so. They had painted a most awesome picture of the life of a legionnaire, although none of the pictures were tainted by experience.

Cyrus flew in the face of their persuasion and advice, and joined the army. Life in the army, as life is in a closed community, he found to be not very different to his boyhood days at Larcia, and he was now back home, so to speak, because the four months of disorientated life around the market stalls had been quite upsetting to him. He was now happy albeit faced with a much tougher existence. Larcia had prepared him for this life into which he was able to adapt to much easier than other newcomers who had come straight from living a very ordinary life with their families at home. The harshness of army life and its strict discipline was something with which he could cope because, overriding this, there was the complete satisfaction of comradeship, a comradeship similar to that he had experienced at Larcia. The army also provided him with a bedroll and a bag and box for his personal belongings.

When he was working in the stalls, he had neither comradeship, nor anywhere to sleep, and his personal possessions were nil. It was a life where he lived from day to day, and even though the young men he worked with were companions of a sort, each one of them behaved selfishly, and it was a case of every man for himself, irrespective of the trials and tribulations of the other. Cyrus, although a loner from a very early age, nevertheless relied strongly on comradeship and the kind he had experienced at Larcia he could only find in an army environment. He was not acutely intelligent enough to follow a vocation other than that of a soldier. He fully accepted this situation, although Cyrus did not lack the quality of leadership. It must be said that the only persons that he had ever led, and very often into the realms of mischief, were his two most loyal followers at Larcia, Marcus and Timius, and now that he was no longer with them they were at a loss; so was he, because he had not found anyone else to lead. He was thrilled to have seen Timius again, and he was now looking forward to making a trip to Velitrae to see the other member of the triumvirate, Marcus, before his end of basic training vacation expired.

*

Timius was now the senior member of the latrines group and one of the senior members of his dormitory. He had seen many colleagues, both in the

latrine group and in his dormitory, come and go, and he often felt that his
stay at Larcia, as an inmate, was never ending. He was now beginning to
wonder whether his father had realized that his education at the institution
was in fact coming to an end, and he also wondered whether his father
would come along to collect him. He had kept his father's last letter to him,
which he had received nearly seven years ago among his belongings and
treated it preciously even though the days, weeks, months, and years rolled
by with his declining hope that his father would ever return.

He felt it very strange that the one man all his hopes and realizations
for the future rested upon had apparently let him down, but Timius was an
optimist, and through his mind ran hundreds for reasons why his father had
not paid him a visit nor, indeed, written a letter to him. It was seven years
ago since his name was last called out at supper time to come and collect a
letter sent to him. Nobody had communicated with him since, and although
he had the feeling of imprisonment, he had now come to accept that the
school authorities like Praetorian Officer Paulo, Carpus Lictus, and his
master Doroynd, the principle Artimeses, and the gymnast Demetrius, were
the heads of his family, and his family were his colleagues in the institution.
As he told Cyrus when he visited, in the past two years, he had experienced
several troublesome moments because he had not had the quick wit of Cyrus
to lead his new-found companions out of tricky situations when they were
up to mischievous acts.

As a result, he had experienced the cane on more than one occasion, and
several days on bread and water, and he always felt that all these number of
days on bread and water was the reason why he was so lean, and had helped
him in his enjoyment of athletics. He comforted himself with the fact that
he did not have to carry around a bulky body when running the three miles,
or the seven-mile cross-country run. He had remained school champion in
both events since that triumphant day seven years ago.

The previous year, because he was a senior member in the school, he had
been promoted to the position of a prefect, but his natural bent for mischief
very soon denuded him of this position and he was demoted promptly because
Artimeses felt that he was insufficiently stable to set his junior peers a good
example. This did not bother Timius very much because, although Marcus
had left the college a year earlier, he wanted to maintain good relations
with Marcus right up to the time of his leaving, and Marcus was always one
who was derisive to people, of whatever rank, in authority. Marcus detested
authority of any description, although he did try tremendously hard to keep
to rules and regulations himself. That is obviously the reason why, as Cyrus

had told Timius during his visit, Marcus was now working in a pottery, where authority would be at its minimum. He could never imagine Marcus becoming a legionnaire. But anyway, Timius had hoped that when his father did eventually come to collect him and take him home to Velitrae, his arrival there would have the added excitement of seeking out Marcus and spending happy hours in his company chatting over old times.

*

When Marcus' education was complete and he had left Larcia, he was delighted to be free of the shackles of the institution and he was so overwhelmed with his freedom that on that day he could not remember any part of his journey to the town of Narnee. While he was resting on the step of a doorway, along the high street at Narnee, a horse and cart passed by and the driver had trailing from the cart a young pony. The pony came loose from its tie, turned around and trotted off in the opposite direction. Marcus noticed this and quickly drew the attention of the driver to the incident. The driver was startled and pulled the leading horse to a halt and ran after the pony. He was not swift enough and the pony was gaining on him, although it was only trotting. Marcus realized that if this state of affairs continued, the driver, who was a man in his early fifties, would never catch up with the pony. Marcus then got up from where he was sitting and took up the chase himself. He caught the pony but quite unaware of what was about to happen: the pony kicked him in the stomach. Marcus rolled on the ground in agony for a moment but soon took up the chase again and caught up with the animal. This time he would be more careful.

Marcus gently stroked the animal's nose once he had brought him to a stop, and was able to keep it from running off until the driver caught up with them. The driver then gently ushered the pony back to his cart and fettered it fast. The driver then asked Marcus his business and on learning that he was not heading anywhere in particular but was trying to find work, asked the young lad if he would like to accompany him on his trip to Velitrae, which was where he was heading. Marcus readily agreed, most enthusiastically, and jumped up alongside the driver and sat down. Marcus was to learn from the driver, Sosmus, that his business was to ply earthenware pots from the pottery at Velitrae to Narnee, Rome, and other commercial centres. Marcus had asked Sosmus if he could provide him with a job as his assistant in his business, but Sosmus was not able to offer such a post, purely because the business did not earn enough profit to enable him to pay the salary of an assistant.

Marcus had offered his services free of charge, but was soon to discover that Sosmus was a man of high principle and would not accept the labour of any one individual without proper payment. However, Sosmus did inform him that if he was looking for a job, he was certain that there would be an opportunity of one at the pottery, and when they arrived there he would try and introduce Marcus to the works manager in the hope that there was a vacancy. This was indeed what happened, and when Marcus had been working at the pottery for nearly twelve months the works manager, Dodimus, was soon to discover that Marcus was capable of some commercial work and elevated him from the job in the pottery to one in the commercial section of the business where he was engaged in work of a clerical nature. He is now learning to assist in the accounts department of the business and Dodimus had also been able to rent him a room, with meals provided, in his own household, for which Marcus paid over three-quarters of his monthly salary. Marcus did not find the environment very conducive, and if he were to tell the truth he felt like a duck out of water. Although he was delighted to leave Larcia, he yearned for the companionship of the school colleagues, especially the comradeship of his two friends, Timius and Cyrus. Moreover, not a day passed by without his thoughts turning to Larcia. His yearning to be back with them grew stronger, although he fully realized that Cyrus had now left and Timius could not remain there forevermore. Nevertheless, if they would accept him back, he would carry out the instructions of the authorities explicitly because he looked on the authorities at Larcia as the true replacement for his parents. However, he fully accepted the fact that he has a lot to be grateful for, in that he had a job and a roof over his head and without living quarters what could he do. The thought of what else he would do he soon rejected from his mind.

*

It was once again sun-set and Timius Arbutus was, as usual, engaged in his chores at the latrines. The job had now become second nature to him and absolutely boring, and it was at moments such as these that his thoughts turned to his two companions, Marcus and Cyrus, even though he was fully aware that they were both now leading lives of their own elsewhere. However, he thought of them quite a good deal, and over the many months of their absence he gradually had come to yearn for their company. He was carrying a sewage bucket ably assisted by his dormitory colleague Platius when he saw Praetorian Officer Paulo approach Praetorian Officer Carpus, the latter still being in charge of the group. Both men talked earnestly for a few moments after which Carpus cast a glance over to where Timius and Platius were, nodding his head, as if in agreement, as he did so. Both Praetorian officers saluted each other, as was customary, and Paulo strode off in the direction of the school buildings while Carpus approached Timius.

"Citizen Arbutus," called Carpus.

"Yes, sire," responded Timius. Both boys stopped in their tracks and lowered the bucket to the ground.

"I have had instructions that you are to report to the Principal Artimeses' study immediately after your evening meal, do you understand?"

"Yes, sire, I will," acknowledged Timius, and then both boys lifted the bucket again to carry it to the lime pit.

"I wonder what he wants to see you about," enquired Platius.

"I've no idea, only Jupiter would know," replied Timius.

"I hope it isn't too serious," said Platius.

"I hope not, either," agreed Timius, "but I haven't long to wait before I find out."

Platius was about a year younger than Timius, but had only spent six years here in the institution at Larcia. He was the son of a freedman and came from the Adriatic port of Ravenna. His father was freed from the shackles of slavery in the household of a Ravenna merchant, after years of loyal service, and was now an employee in the business of the merchant. The business had taken him to the province of Morocco, where he had been for the past six years.

Timius was anxious throughout the meal as to the reason why Artimeses wanted to see him. He remembered that the last time he had had been instructed to report to Artimeses was when Artimeses had sent for him to personally thank him for his brilliant effort in winning the three athletic events in a competition between the military institution at Larcia and the civilian counterpart at Narnee. He knew that on this occasion it would not be for the same reason that Artimeses wished to see him, because there had been no recent athletic competitions in which he had taken part.

His conjecture continued, and he thought perhaps that his master Doronyd had reported the fact to Artimeses of his interest and diligence in the classroom deteriorating, especially during the study of the work of Homer's Iliad. Timius did not dislike the study of the Iliad, but he found it difficult to grasp the fundamental reasoning behind it and was constantly admonished by Doronyd and accused of being disinterested and sluggish. He knew this was not so because he had tried very hard, and he had planned to tell Artimeses this as straightforwardly as he could.

He knocked on Artimeses' door, and after a moment he heard the principal's voice instructing him to enter. Rather fearfully he entered the study and found himself standing before Artimeses. Artimeses promptly beckoned him to take a seat on the stool that was placed against the wall. Timius did so very nervously and sat upright and rigid, with his hands clenched tightly in his lap. Artimeses looked over at him and with his head slightly leaning to one side, began to speak.

"Now, young man," he said, "I am sure you are aware that your education has now come to an end here at Larcia. You are now seventeen and a half years old, aren't you?"

"Yes, sire, that is so," replied Timius.

"Well, have you thought what you will do when you leave here," enquired Artimeses.

"Not really, sire, but I have hoped and have been expecting, these past few months, my father to come and take me away, and he will probably have plans for me."

"I see," said Artimeses.

The principal now found himself in a somewhat difficult situation and remained silent for a while, and Timius could see by the expression on his face that all was not well. He detected something and broke the silence by asking.

"What is it, sire?"

"Well, young Arbutus," replied Artimeses, as though he had been awakened from a trance, "I have some disappointing and very sad news to tell you."

Artimeses was normally a serious and stern man, but in his reply Timius detected a note of understanding. Artimeses continued: "It's very hard for me to have to tell you that some five years ago we had word that your father had been brutally slain in battle on the frontier in Germania. He was a very brave and courageous man, and a man who you can be very proud of, who served his Emporer and Rome with distinction."

Artimeses then paused for a while to allow Timius a moment of realization before continuing. Timius was astounded to hear this, and his mind became a complete blank momentarily. He looked into the eyes of Artimeses and was about to ask, when Artimeses appeared to have read the thoughts of the young man and immediately broke the momentary silence, by saying, "Yes, I know what you are going to ask me, and I will tell you. The reason why this has not been made known to you previously is that we did not wish this news to have an adverse effect on your education. We felt that it was wise, under the circumstances, to keep it from you but if we were wrong in our judgement then all we can ask is for your forgiveness. Our motives were entirely honourable.

"I understand, sire," replied Timius choking back the tears and swallowing hard to try and rid himself of the lump which had welled up in his throat.

The young man was overwhelmed with sorrow and disappointment and a feeling of utter loneliness. There was no Cyrus or Marcus, either, on whom to lean for comfort. Artimeses then stood up and went across to a wooden cabinet behind his desk. He opened it and took out a small leather bag and handed it to Timius, saying, "Take this, young man, it is the personal belongings of your father, which were brought here by an army courier, and they are now yours. We have not inspected its contents because we treat such articles as personal and private."

"Thank you, sire," said Timius hesitantly, accepting the bag.

Artimeses then reseated himself and went on to tell Timius that he had better collect all his own personal belongings from the storehouse the following day and he was to hand back, the day after that, all the articles and bedding, etc., on loan to him from the institution, before his departure.

"Before you leave, Arbutus, let me leave you with a few thoughts on which you can ponder, if you please. Our job here at Larcia has been to educate young men like yourself, but over and above this we try to build character into all you boys. We try to make useful citizens out of you and I am sure, in your case, we have been most successful.

He continued by saying, "Whatever the future may hold for you, never forget the lessons you have learnt here. You must be loyal to Rome, her glorious institutions, and her Empire. You must not be afraid of defending whatever you know to be right at whatever cost. If there are laws and regulations which you abhor or disagree with, as an individual, try and remember that invariably they have been framed and formulated in the light of experience for the benefit and preservation of Roman society as a whole. You will find many things in life that are most disagreeable to you, but try and treat them with the utmost tolerance and understanding. Be loyal to your comrades and your superiors; respect the wishes of your elders, and, above all, respect your neighbours and never forget that there have been many others in the past who have passed through our institution here, and we trust that if the gods allow it, there will be many more in the future."

Timius listened intently to Artimeses lecture and felt he understood what the principal was trying to tell him.

"Very well, sire, I understand, and I will try and remember what you have said. May I go, now?"

"Yes, of course you may, and I will see you before you leave Larcia."

Timius came out of Artimeses study feeling very crestfallen and, clutching the bag, made his way back to the dormitory. He was in a complete state of disillusionment.

Timius went into the dormitory and sat on the edge of the bed. He felt extremely depressed and was about to open the leather bag that Artimeses had handed to him when his fellow student Platius noticed what Timius was about to do, which prompted him to call out, "What have you got there, Timius? Did Artemeses give you that leather bag? Open it up quickly, and let us all see what it contains?"

The attention of the other boys in the dormitory was now focused on Timius and they gradually gathered around him. Timius did not want to open the bag in their presence, although they urged him to do so. He had to quickly come up with an excuse for not doing as they asked and told an untruth by informing them that the bag did not belong to him, but that Artimeses had merely asked him to give the bag to the gymnast Demetrius in the morning, when he, Timius, attended the gym for coaching and deep-breathing exercises under Demetrius, tuition as part of his training in athletics. This was a plausible excuse, which the other boys in the dormitory accepted without any further argument, because they were well aware that on some mornings, before they breakfasted, it was the habit of Timius and the other athletes in the college to attend the gymnasium to receive physical training and coaching. The embarrassing moment had passed for the time being. Timius was most annoyed that there was absolutely no privacy afforded to him, or any of the other boys for that matter, and his bursting curiosity could not be satiated until an opportunity to open the bag arose. He began to think how he could arrange such an opportunity. Many ideas went through his mind, but were promptly rejected as being unsuitable. The only idea he thought might work in order to give him the privacy he craved would be put to the test later.

After lights were extinguished in the dormitory, Timius lay awake for a period that seemed like hours. The events of the day and what the 'morrow and the day after might hold absorbed his thoughts. He felt a little pleased that he would very, very soon be leaving Larcia. But he also felt it would be with mixed feelings because he was apprehensive of what lay ahead of him. He now realized he would have to make his own way in the world, just as many other graduates had done in the past. He was comforted in the thought that Cyrus and Marcus had successfully done so and felt that there was no reason why he could not also succeed. These thoughts began to make him feel a trifle enthusiastic about the unknown events that lay ahead of him. He began to hear the snores and deep breathing of his colleagues in the dormitory. He could also hear the hooting of the owls in the nearby woods and, in the distance, the intermittent sound from the farmers who were blowing on horns.

These sounds were commonplace to him, as there had been many occasions in the past when he had heard the horns in the distance and, in many instances, intermingled with the hoots from the owls and occasionally the baying of the wolves also could be heard. The stillness, apart from the snoring, indicated to him that his pals were asleep. He quietly slipped out of bed, donned his tunic, clutched the bag in one hand and his sandals in the other, and tiptoed out of the dormitory.

He continued to tiptoe through the adjoining corridor until he came out of the building and was standing outside in the cold night air. He slipped his sandals onto his feet and trotted down to the latrines. When he arrived there, the place was empty and completely silent. There was only one torch burning; the other had been extinguished as only one torch was kept lighted throughout the night for obvious reasons. Timius sat himself on a pedestal that was nearest to the flickering torch and nervously opened the bag to inspect the contents. He drew out a folded piece of papyrus, and when he looked at it more closely he recognised his own handwriting; it was the last letter he had written to his father.

"I am so happy he received it," Timius said quietly to himself, and continued to forage in the bag.

"The next article he removed was a small muslin bag tied at its neck with a thin cotton cord. He carefully opened this and, to his astonishment, discovered that it contained a small handful of gum Arabic globules. An expression of pleasure crossed his face. His father had remembered, he thought, to get him the glue. He also thought that his father must have been a wonderful man to have remembered, even though he was engaged in bloody battles with the enemy.

When the opportunity arose he would set about and repair his musical pipe, after all these years, it was still tucked away in his wooden box back in the dormitory. The rest of the contents he did not find too exciting; there were a few beads, four medallions, and a handful of silver and copper coins. He knew not the value of the latter because he had not handled a coin for years. He selected two of the coins, one silver and one copper, and placed them in the pocket of his tunic. He then repacked the bag and told himself that he must remember to go to the library tomorrow and from the papyrus wall charts that hung framed in the library, he would try to establish the value of the two coins in his pocket. He left the latrines and returned to the dormitory, entering it on tiptoe and very, very quietly opened his wooden box and put the bag in it, making sure to hide it at the bottom underneath all his clothes. He would have to make himself inconspicuous in the morning when he went down to the gymnasium so that he would not draw attention to the fact that he was not taking the bag to Demetrius, otherwise his secret about the bag and truth would be discovered by his peers.

The other boys in the college were in their dormitories on this morning preparing themselves for their daily attendance of worship at the temple before the commencement of their studies, as Timius knocked on the door of Paulo's study. Paulo opened the door and invited him in, saying as he did so, "Well, young, man, I suppose you are now ready to leave."

"Yes, sire," replied Timius, and I have come to bid you farewell."

"I see," said Paulo. "Have you said your farewells to the other masters and Praetorian officers, and have you seen the principal," asked Paulo.

"Yes, I have, sire, but I haven't as yet seen Praetorian Officer Carpus."

"Well, you must promise me that you will see him before you leave."

"Most certainly, sire, I do want to see him," replied Timius.

Paulo continued by saying, "Well, young man, we are all sorry to see you leave us, but you cannot remain here for the rest of your life. There is a big wide world beckoning you to serve it, and serve it well you must in the highest traditions of this our beloved institution. I know you have the personality and character to see you through all the trials and tribulations that lie before you, and I trust that you will always have time to spare a kind and noble thought for all of us here."

"Yes, I will, sire," responded Timius.

Going over to a shelf, Paulo picked up a cotton sack and handed it to Timius.

"Take this, young man," he said, as he did so, "it is a present to you from all of us here at Larcia. All the officers and masters have contributed towards it. It is not very much, nor is it very valuable; but it contains something that you will find most useful to you, for a little while anyway," he added as an afterthought. "Praetorian Officer Carpus is the only one who hasn't contributed to this. Your mischief in the past must have placed you at the top of the list in his bad book!"

Timius accepted the present, smiling shyly, acknowledging it gratefully. Paulo thrust out his right hand and clasped Timius firmly by the forearm of his right arm as a gesture of farewell and said, "Farewell, young Arbutus, and the gods go with you. Moreover, thank you for the contribution you have made to this institution.

Timius returned to the dormitory to collect his other belongings which were wrapped up in a bundle, the dormitory being empty, as the other boys had gone to the temple.

On the previous day, he had handed in all the college articles that had been on loan to him except his bedroll. Hid bedroll was handed in earlier in the morning. He had also paid his visit to the library to check on the value of the coins he had in his tunic pocket, and he had also spent the rest of the day saying his farewell to all the other members of the college staff. Each of his farewells was touched with a note of sadness, especially on his part, because he was leaving Larcia with mixed feeling. Added to this was a feeling of apprehension for what lay ahead of him—and a feeling of sorrow when the many happy times he had had at Larcia crossed his mind throughout the day. However, he felt he was now setting out on a wonderful adventure, and he would try and enjoy every moment of it. Artimeses had also expressed his gratitude for the contribution he had made to the institution and was sincere in his hopes that he would do well. After all these years, his suspicions that every member of the college authority was very human underneath their veneer and their harsh indifference were vindicated. Carpus was the only one he could not place in this category because he always gave the very strong impression of a man of very cold indifference, especially now that Paulo had told him that Carpus had refrained from contributing towards his present. Timius was very surprised to have received such a present which he was not expecting, but it was practice here, at the institution, that very long serving internees received a presentation which was the contribution made by all members of staff.

Timius very excitedly opened the sack that Paulo had given him. He loosened the cord at the neck and pulled it open and found inside a homespun cotton tunic of an oatmeal shade, together with a brown cord to tie around the waist, a muslin scarf and a pair of sandals. He was thrilled with this because when he tried on the tunic and the sandals, they fitted perfectly, and the sack was something he really wanted. He would be able to use it to pack his few belongings out of his box, which he promptly did. He picked up the sack, slung it over his shoulder had one last look around the dormitory and strode out for the last time. He went down to the latrines to see Praetorian Officer Carpus, because he had promised Paulo that he would not forget to say his farewell to him, before leaving. He knew not where to find Carpus, and after searching around the buildings, without success, he thought he should try in the vicinity of the latrines. As he approached the latrines, he saw Carpus leaving them after his morning inspection. He ran up to the officer, and when he caught up with him, Carpus stopped in his tracks and a smile crossed his lips. This was the first time Timius could recall Carpus ever smiling, and a little breathlessly Timius said, "Sire, I have come to bid you farewell."

"I know," replied Carpus. He continued, "I am glad you did not forget me. After all, young Timius, You and I are the veterans of the latrine group. You have served with me longer than any other boy, and it is from the first day of your arrival, isn't that so?" Carpus asked.

"That is correct, sire," responded Timius, but I have had the odd absences when I was too ill to attend, but you knew about that."

"Yes of course I did, but you and I have seen the others come and go; but it seems that we have gone on forever."

"Yes, it seems so," Timius agreed shyly.

"Well, young man, as a small token of my appreciation and gratitude for the loyal and obedient way in which you have performed your duties each sunset over these past ten years or more, I would like you to accept this."

Out of his pocket of his tunic he produced a small papyrus packet and handed it to Timius, saying, "The gratitude of my wife and two children are also included."

Timius accepted the gift, nervously, because he was astonished. He realized that his estimation of Carpus was very wrong; very wrong indeed.

"Go on, open it," said Carpus.

Contained in the package was a bronze coin in the form of a medallion to which was attached a small bronze ring through which passed a bronze chain. Timius could not understand the meaning of this and immediately thought that it was a Bulla, and asked Carpus if this was so, thanking him profusely as he did so.

"No, it isn't a Bulla, young man, it is only a medallion made from a sestertius coin, and you should wear it around your neck. It may bring you good luck, and I sincerely hope it does, but, if nothing else, it will help to remind you of the many nasty and smelly hours we have spent here together doing our daily duty."

"Yes, it will, sire, indeed it will, and words cannot express my gratitude." Laughingly, Timius continued, "the odour from the latrines will remain in my nostrils for evermore, I am sure."

Timius placed the chain on which hung the medallion around his neck and looked down at it admiringly.

"I had better be on my way now, sire, or I shall not want to leave."

They shook hands firmly and Carpus said, "If you should ever find time to come and pay us a visit, we shall be delighted to see you and my wife, and I will be very pleased to accommodate you in our humble quarter for however long you wish to remain. You will be most welcome, so have no fear about accommodation when you decide to visit Larcia."

"Thank you very much indeed," replied Timius gratefully. "Farewell, sire, and would you please convey my grateful thanks and best wishes to your wife and children.

"Thank you, Arbutus, I will," and as Carpus spoke these words Timius saw a tear roll down the Praetorian officer's cheek, as he quickly turned his head away.

CHAPTER XIII

Miratur portas strepitumque et strata viatum.

VIRGIL

He marvels at the gates and the noise and the pavements.

AFTER TIMIUS HAD said farewell to his father on the first day of his arrival at the Augustan military institution for boys, Sejanus Arbutus was to meet his old friend in whose company he had spent many hours in the army, before Praetorian Officer Carpus was posted to the Praetorian Guard. Sejanus Arbutus was leading his horse away from the school grounds when to his astonishment he recognised Carpus walking briskly to the buildings. He recognised him and called out to him, and the two veterans were undoubtedly very pleased to meet each other again after a spell of three years. Naturally, they enquired after each others health and prosperity before parting once again.

Praetorian Officer Carpus had, throughout these years, been aware that Timius Arbutus was the son of his old and dear friend Sejanus Arbutus, but he could never understand why Sejanus had not provided the boy with the customary Bulla, indicating that he was the son of a freeborn Roman. Carpus knew very well that Sejanus Arbutus was a freeborn Roman and that his dear wife was also freeborn. He felt that it was a sad oversight on the part of Sejanus for failing to provide his son with a Bulla. Consequently, the boy had been subjected to the most menial chore in the institution, which he had carried out diligently and uncomplainingly these many years.

There had been occasions when Carpus had discussed the matter with his wife and was on the verge of buying a gold Bulla to give to the boy on one occasion in the distant past. On advice from his wife he refrained from doing so. Carpus' wife had very rightly advised him not to do so because he would have had enormous difficulty in explaining to the authorities, particularly Artimeses, how young Arbutus came to possess a Bulla without the knowledge of its arrival. This was sound advice and, on reflection, Carpus realized the complications that could have occurred had he let his heart get the better of his head.

Carpus' wife also advised him not to make it known to the boy that he had been a very close acquaintance of his father, because, as she pointed out, under the circumstances the boy might have expected the odd favour or two from his superior. To grant the odd favour would have been grossly unfair to the other boys under his control in the latrine group. Thus Praetorian Officer Carpus had kept his secret to himself, the only other person knowing about it being his wife. When Timius had finally left, Carpus suddenly realized that he had now lost the only link that connected him to the happy times he had led many years ago, in the legion. He was more heartbroken to see this young man leave whom he was unable to elevate out of the latrines group at any time during his internment at Larcia, however much he wished so to do. His only hope now was that the young man would not think of him too harshly and would indeed one day return to see him. If he did, the situation might be right for him to disclose his secret to him.

*

It was a glorious morning, as Timius half-ran and half-walked down the track leading away from the grounds of the institution, and as the track began to wind its way down the slope and through the woods he felt exhilarated. He had never been beyond the bounds, in this direction, since the day of his arrival and as he progressed down the track he noticed the gradual change in the kind of vegetation and the types of trees that were growing in the woods. Every new tree and new shrub presented to him an adventurous discovery. Sometimes he stopped and studied them closely, and by midday he had reached the foothills beyond which lay the town of Narnee. Artimeses had given him directions on how to reach his home town of Velitrae. He had made a mental note of the directions and planned to follow them explicitly. Artimeses had also, at the young man's request, counted the money that was left to Timius by his father, and which he had found in his father's leather pouch.

Artimeses had assured him that although the amount of money was only a pittance in relation to present day standards of living, it would be sufficient for Timius if he spent it wisely to provide him with two good meals a day and also the fare on a passenger cart from Narnee to Rome and from there to Velitrae. It would also provide him with the rent of a room for two nights of his journey back home, but he would have to be careful not to spend it on useless articles in the market places he would see at Rome, or else he would find himself financially embarrassed. Timius accepted the advice and decided that now he was getting hungry. He would not hurry along to reach Narnee before sunset and have a evening meal, but he would try and find some fruit trees along the journey that would help satisfy his appetite and save him some money. He decided to keep a look out for fruit bearing trees from which he could help himself. He did not have to wait long because lying down the track in front of him he could see a fenced-off olive grove. This was just what he was waiting for. He hurried along to the fence, placed his sack at the foot of one of the upright posts to which the fencing battens were fixed and promptly climbed over the fence. Quickly he helped himself to a bunch of deep brown ripe olives.

He ran back, hopped back over the fence, and sat himself down beside his sack and made a meal of them. He enjoyed the olives and felt much stronger now and thought a drink of water would help wash them down and quench his thirst. He now began searching for a stream and in this type of terrain there was no shortage of them. Having quenched his thirst he sat himself on a rock near the stream to take a rest and watch tadpoles darting around on the surface of the water. He was fascinated with what he saw and the many birds that fluttered from bough to bough, above him in the trees, also fascinated him. After a while the realization came to him that, apart from the wild life that surrounded him he was now all alone in the world. He had broken off his relations with Larcia and was wondering whether he would be successful in cultivating, or even renewing any relationships with the very few people he had known as a young boy at Velitrae.

He did not think this would be possible, because the few people who had known him as a boy would by now have forgotten him. If he reminded them of who he was they would only remember him as being a dirty, mischievous boy whom they would want to forget rather than rekindle a friendship. He was not even sure whether his sister, Mena, or his brother-in-law, Silius, would want to know him now, because so many years had passed, during which time he had not received any communication from either of them. He had often wanted to write a letter to his sister, but did not know what her married surname was, so there was no way of him contacting her. He was in a predicament but decided that he would let matters take their natural course and pray that the gods would allow the outcome to be favourable.

He had better be getting along, he thought to himself, and slinging his sack across his shoulder carried on his journey.

The sun was now beginning to set on the western horizon, and Timius was still on the track to Narnee, which was now following a course through vineyards. He could see the people in the vineyards gathering their baskets and other articles used for their work because their day was now drawing to an end. Suddenly a strange feeling came over him. He did not know whether he wanted to run, walk, or sit down. His mind was in a complete whirl. He knew there was something wrong but knew not what it was. All of a sudden the cause of his sudden disorientation occurred to him. Snap out of it, you silly fool, snap out of it, he repeated to himself. In the change of day there was something drawing him back to the latrines at Larcia, the routine was in his system, but he had to shake it off. Taking control of his senses he was now determined to make his break from the routine. He knew he would find it a little strange, because the routine had been part of his life for over ten years. Quite naturally, now that it was sunset, his thoughts turned to Carpus and his colleagues. The thought also crossed his mind that he should return to Larcia, but naturally he knew that he could not do this. He must go on. Tears welled up in his eyes because loneliness swept over his again. Fortunately he was also hungry and this helped to occupy his mind with the thought of obtaining something for his evening meal.

He still had not reached Narnee, and he was behind schedule. If he did not reach the town before nightfall he would not be able to get a bed for the night, nor would he be on time in the morning to get a passenger cart to take him to Rome. But he felt he must try and find something to eat before going any further as he was beginning to feel weak with hunger. Naturally he had his eye on the many bunches of grapes that were hanging from the vines which were supported by trellises.

He could not help himself to any because there was still too much activity around. At least too much activity for his comfort, and he did not want to get into trouble on his first day away from the college, so he decided to wait until nightfall. When nightfall descended he still had to wait until the opportunity presented itself before helping himself to a bunch of grapes. This he did, by this time being ravenous, and ate his way through two bunches, surrounded by the darkness of the night. While he was eating his grapes his eyes were cast up to the heavens and he was attracted to the constellations in the sky. His mind began to wander, but he was soon jolted back to reality when he realized that he must get to Narnee before it was too late. He had no idea how long it would take him, but he would make his way there as quickly as he could. The road seemed endless because it wound its way through numerous vineyards and the distant lights of Narnee never seemed to be getting any closer.

Timius was beginning to feel quite tired. He thought perhaps if he could rest for an hour or so he could be on his way, refreshed, in time to reach Narnee by dawn. Anyway he could not rest along the road because there was also the possibility of marauding wolves in the district attacking him, so he would press on. His progress seemed to be slow. Just ahead of him he could see a small building lying back from the road and the stonework of this building seemed to glisten in the moonlight. He thought he would investigate and ran up to it as quickly as he could. It was a shrine. He entered through the tiny archway and, in the centre he could discern a small statue—set on a pedestal. Timius immediately thought that it would be the ideal place to rest for a short while. After all it would offer him some shelter for the night and protection from any wolves. The tiny building was in darkness apart from the moonlight that played through its low and narrow portal. Besides, he thought, whichever was the incumbent god for travellers he would place his trust in that god to protect him through the night. The shrine was one that had been erected by the folk who worked in the vineyard, to Saturn in whom they placed their faith and trust for good grape harvests.

It was still dark when Timius left the shrine, after resting and sleeping intermittently for a few hours. He had lain himself on the stone floor and used his sack for a pillow. It had not been very comfortable and from time to time he felt the cold creeping into his bones. But after a few hours rest, he felt much better. He was on his way again in the stillness of the night. After what seemed like ages to him he could see the faint flow of sunrise in the eastern sky. He made his way over to a nearby stream took off his tunic and underclothes and washed himself in the clear, cold water. Feeling refreshed and much better, he continued his journey and eventually entered the town of Narnee just as dawn was breaking and he could hear the crowing of the cocks coming from the various directions around him. Timius rested for a while on the step of a veranda of one of the buildings in the street. There was very little activity and he would have to wait for people to appear from their night's rest before he could make enquiries as from where he could get a passenger cart that would take him to Rome.

He would also try and buy some freshly baked bread to breakfast on. As he looked around, at the variety of buildings which surrounded him, he was quite fascinated with their differing architecture. His only memories of a town or city before he went to Larcia were very distant ones. People began to appear, and although their appearance excited him, he found it difficult to gather the courage to make his enquiries. He soon got control of himself and was encouraged in the knowledge that he would be on time to get himself a seat on the passenger cart bound for Rome. He was happy in the thought that he had saved the expense of his previous day's meals and also the expense of a room, as he enjoyed his piece of bread.

Since Timius had spare time on his hands, as it was pointless for him to be at the staging post for at least another two hours, he found a side road leading away from the high street in Narnee and followed it out of curiosity to see what lay beyond. After travelling two hundred yards the road petered out and the number of buildings on either side of it diminished. He was now in an open grassy field and began to hear the trickle of water. Still chewing pieces of his bread, he made his way to the spot from where the sound came from and was very soon standing on the grassy bank of a brook that wended its way in the direction of Rome and from the knowledge gained in the geography lessons he had attended at the college concluded that the brook could very well be a tributary of the esteemed River Tiber. He sat himself down on a rotting log to digest the scene that was before him. He was now coming to the end of a hunk of bread but decided to share the last remaining piece with birds that chirruped and fluttered from the bottom bough of the few overhanging willows that proudly stood along the banks of the brook. He had brought three loaves of bread, and it was his intention to keep two of the loaves to sustain him for the rest of his journey to Porta Collina at Rome.

He had been informed that the passenger cart terminated its service at the Porta Collina. The birds thoroughly enjoyed the small broken pieces of bread that Timius fed to them, and they seemed to be asking for more, but even though he was a generous young man he refrained from getting the other two loaves out of his sack to feed to them, because he was well aware that in such pleasant surroundings there would be no shortage of food for them. He suddenly spotted a duck being followed by four little ducklings. One of them was trying to jump onto its mother's back, and Timius soon discovered the reason for this. Sitting on the back of the mother duck and looking quite nonchalant, was another little duckling taking a ride on its mother's back. The other little fellow wanted to join him. He tried desperately to lift himself out of the water, but his efforts were to weak, and he kept plopping back into the water, which meant that he had to swim a little harder to catch up with his mother, who was leisurely swimming forward

This little incident Timius found most amusing, and he chuckled aloud. Slinging his sack over his shoulder, he followed the duck family by walking along the path of the brook. He did not go very far because he did not want to be late in his arrival at the staging post, so he stopped, turned round, and walked back. On his way back along the bank his keen interest was focused on the reasonable variety of plants and shrubs through which the path led. He was very attracted to the fresh and lovely primroses, among other things, and thought how wonderful nature was to produce such variety and colour with what seemed so little effort. He had had many opportunities at Larcia to study his natural surroundings more closely, but somehow, in the kind of environment that surrounded him at Larcia, all these things were taken for granted, and he had not paid any attention to the wonders of nature. He began to realize that he was now entering into a phase where every mortal thing would present itself to him as a new and fresh discovery, and he was determined to enjoy every moment.

His thoughts were still on the wonders of nature when he arrived at the staging post and found that he was the first arrival. He even thought of the lizards and the snakes and other weird little reptiles that he clearly remembered seeing as a little boy when he went on his expeditions to his favourite gulley in Velitrae. He planned to go back there and study the creatures and the surrounding vegetation, rock formations, and so on, with an exciting and new interest. He pondered the thought that if he paid attention to and directed his acute interest in everything that surrounded him, a whole new world would present itself to him, and by so doing he felt that his life would be really worth living with plenty of excitement ahead.

During the journey to Rome, every crook and cranny that the horse-drawn cart passed was of immense interest to Timius, especially the variety of formations in the surrounding countryside. His other five companion passengers, all much older than himself, spent the journey disinterestedly. One or two of them nodded off to sleep, and Timius could not understand what to him appeared to be their complete lack of interest in life, and he was very pleased that this was not his attitude. He was now a lone explorer, but there was no one else with whom he could share the excitement and thrill of his explorations.

It was mid-afternoon when they alighted from the horse-drawn cart at Porta Collina and, after paying his respects to the driver of the cart, Timius entered the city of Rome. As our young traveller progressed on foot through the city, the city scene became much busier, with people going and coming in all directions. Many were hurrying along as though they had urgent business to attend to, while others merely strolled leisurely along the streets. The large buildings, statues, and colonnades that he passed fascinated him and he promised that when the opportunity presented itself, some time in the distant future, he would make a point of spending many days in Rome and try to visit every corner of the city. He suddenly thought of that crippled man he had met at Narnee, so many years ago, and wondered if he was still living on the Palatine Hill. However, it was no use him making enquiries at this juncture because he knew that he had to get to Velitrae as soon as he possibly could otherwise he might be persuaded by events that might overtake him to remain in Rome longer and then suddenly find that he had run out of money. He did not want to be destitute because he had some idea of the results of destitution.

He had just passed the rectangle with the Statio and Annonae, which was situated some two or three hundred yards from the southern bank of the River Tiber. He remembered the story he had heard told many times, when he was at the collegiate of the legendary hero of Rome, Horatio, who had single handed held back the might of the enemy army at the northern end of the wooden bridge crossing the Tiber, to enable the vastly out numbered Roman soldiers to withdraw and to hack and demolish the structure to foil the crossing of the enemy into the heart of the city. The task complete, Horatio jumped into the River Tiber with enemy arrows showering all around him to escape and live another day.

There were hardly any wooden bridges now crossing the Tiber. They were all constructed with stone, so an emulation of Horatio would not be possible now but then, he realised, there would not be any need for it as the northern boundary of the city extended far beyond the Tiber.

Looming ahead of him lay the north-western wall surmounted by very big stone parapets of the Circus Maximus. As he approached the wall, he began to detect that the crowds were becoming denser and that the size of the amphitheatre was larger than he had ever imagined. He had heard about the amphitheatre of Rome and other cities, but he never imagined that they would be this big. Dotted along the foot of the walls were men in very gaily coloured robes standing on wooden pedestals and excitedly bargaining with groups of people who were clustered around the pedestals. They were taking bets, and it appeared that enormous sums of money would exchange hands that day. There were gamblers trying to outbid each other but Timius was not to appreciate that the whole façade was a farce.

Bets were being placed on charioteer teams and each team sported and represented the colour green or blue. It had been conveniently arranged for a long time that the greens would automatically win each tournament because the corrupted hierarchy and nobility, including Caesar himself, had heavily backed the green team to win. Newcomers to the city and innocents of this corrupt façade would soon be relieved of their capital having been cunningly induced and encouraged to lay their bets on the blue team. It was also a means of relieving wealthy senators and landowners and other members of the aristocracy who were strong supporters of republicanism of their entire wealth under threat of banishment or total public humiliation. Many of the republican nobility acquiesced in this manner when they knew that their station in life was doomed, as they naturally found it a more respectable way of losing their position and wealth in society to gamble it away at the circus than by public humiliation and trumped up accusations and charges of sedition.

Very soon Timius heard the sound of music approaching and, before very long, from his position in the crowd he could see above the heads of the others the Praetorian Guard brass band with trumpets and horns blaring. He made his way out of the crowd and was able to join a few others at the rear who were stood on a marble bench and from this position he could see the band more clearly. They were now entering the portals of the amphitheatre and following them he could clearly see rolling along, four horse-drawn chariots. A tremendous cheer went up from the crowd, and the response from the charioteers was to wave and gesture to the crowd.

The chariots moved along with two charioteers wearing blue tunics flanked by two charioteers wearing green tunics. The brassware on the chariots glistened brightly in the late afternoon sun, and when they had passed there followed, on foot, a large contingent of gladiators.

These would provide the crowded amphitheatre with early evening entertainment, and it was customary that the gladiators fought each other to the death unless pardoned by Caesar, if he was in attendance, or one of his subordinates, for putting up a good contest. The crowds invariably demanded the death of the loser and the loser's life depended largely on the mood of Caesar that day or his subordinate dignitary who might have been presiding. Bets were also placed on gladiators and the outcome of the match was heavily loaded by the way the bets had been placed. The gladiators were brandishing their various weapons as they passed by; some relied on the sword, other the javelin, others the trident, while there were a few who placed their reliability in a small fisherman-type net.

Each of the gladiators was armed with a dagger to defend himself lest he be denuded during combat of his favourite weapon. Gladiatorial schools were set up and run as efficient organizations in various parts of the city. Their training was severe, but their rewards were untold. Some fortunate gladiators had reached positions in the highest echelons of the nobility merely by their proficiency in combat in the amphitheatre. It was an extremely hard way to be exalted to a position in the higher echelons of society. But for those men of the right physique and temperament, condemned to a certain death for past errors, the gladiatorial school provided them with the only means of cheating death, and their diligence to the art of combat was unquestionable. It was getting dark as Timius entered the vicinity of the Porta Metrovia. Walking along the Vicus Cyclopsis, he began to feel very uneasy. He could still faintly hear the spasmodic roaring of the crowd emanating from the Circus Maximus, but this was not the cause of his uneasiness. The cause was one that was quite natural because at this time of the day, for many years, he would be about his latrine duty had he still been at the college, and it was very difficult for him to accept the fact that he would not be doing that again.

He put such thoughts to the back of his mind as best he could and, as he reached the Porta Morovia, it was quite dark and the torches were now shining over the gates to the city. He passed through the gates beyond where he found slum settlements and—not knowing what to do—he decided to find himself an inconspicuous spot under a few fig trees and settled himself down for the night. He would eat some of his bread but before doing so he would try and get a drink of some sort. This he was able to do quite easily, and as he settled down under the fig tree he began to plan what he would do if any of the militia or municipal workers approached him to ask him his business. He would have to tell an untruth. He would have to tell the enquirer that he was waiting for his father who was a member of the Praetorian Guard on duty this night in the capital. If the enquirer questioned him further he would just have to make a run for it. He was quite confident that with the athletic training he had received he would soon outdistance his pursuer. In the morning, however, he would have to make enquiries as to how he would get to Velitrae. He hoped it would be possible to be able to travel as a paying passenger on a cart that was going in that direction. The excitement of the day had made Timius quite sleepy and it was not long after laying his head upon his sack, which served as a pillow, that he was sound asleep. Throughout the night there was activity around the gates of Porta Morovia; there were groups of Praetorian Guards exchanging shifts; crowds of people were noisily returning from the Circus Maximus and other theatres; groups of drunks went by singing and shouting at the top of their voices. All these noises disturbed the pet dogs kept by the settlement folk. None of these things did our young traveller hear except the crowing of cocks in the early hours of the morning. He felt refreshed after a good night's sleep, with the excitement pounding in his heart with the thought of being in Velitrae soon and meeting up with his dear friend Marcus again.

After spending nearly four hours since daybreak making enquiries and being disappointed in not being able to get himself a seat on a passenger cart travelling to Velitrae, Timius would soon have become disheartened had he not been offered a lift by the driver of a cart who enlisted his help to off-load the cart load of basketry at a small depot just outside Porta Morovia. He then had to help to load some caskets containing molasses for delivery at Fregellae, and the driver informed him that since he would be passing through Velitgrae, he would give Timius a ride in payment for his services. The driver was a grumpy man and not very talkative, and however much Timius tried to make conversation with him, during the journey, the driver only responded with grunts. Timius could never understand why the man was so miserable and was glad when he was finally dropped off at the eastern end of the high street.

Timius realized that he had not spent very much of his money since leaving Larcia, and what little he had left he would be able to give to his sister as payment for his keep for at least two or three days. But the thought occurred to him that since it was many years since he had been in Velitrae, he did not really know the town very well, and, moreover, he had no idea where she lived. He had not got her address and, in addition, the town seemed to have changed a good deal. From the first indications in the high street, new buildings had been erected which he could not recognize. He was in a predicament, and not knowing what to do, he strolled down the high street knowing that he would have to make some enquiries. But whom should he ask and what should he say he had no idea. His plan now was to walk all over the town until he was able to recognise some feature that might remind him of the past and jerk his memory and get back his sense of bearing. He turned left down an adjoining side street towards the bottom of the high street. There were very few people about but sitting at the far end on the steps of the veranda of one of the houses he saw the back of a man who was dressed in what appeared to be drag tunic, and the man appeared to be clutching a stick. "Perhaps he might be able to help me," Timius thought.

"Excuse me, sire, can you help me?"

As he asked the question Timius moved around to face the man and immediately realized that the man he was facing would be the last person on earth to help him. The man was blind, and he gazed out in front of him. Timius noticed underneath the stranger's dishevelled beard, that he was badly pock marked, he said, "I am sorry, sire, I didn't mean to trouble you."

Timius was about to move away when the man called after him, "Wait! Wait! Come back!"

Timius turned back. "Yes, what is it you want?"

"You asked if I could help you," replied the stranger, "and I'll do my best to do so, even though I am afflicted with blindness, I will help you in any way I can."

"That's very kind of you, sire, but I do not think you can help me, because I am looking for two people whose full names I do not know."

"Who are the people?" enquired the blind man.

"Oh, they are only my sister and brother-on-law, and I do not know their married name and in a town of so many people I am sure you will not know them."

"That is so," replied the stranger, "but never mind. Take a seat beside me and tell me what your name is. Tell me who you are," said the stranger with earnestness.

"I am nobody," Timius replied, "and my name is of not consequence."

"Please do tell me your name because my name is Alphonsus, and I have wandered around this town for many, many years relying on the generosity of the townspeople for my livelihood. I can assure you," he continued, "there are an awful lot of generous people in this town, and it must surely be a town looked on with pride by the gods above."

"My name, sire, is Timius Arbutus."

"Arbutus, Arbutus did you say?"

"Yes, sire."

"Do you live in this town?"

"No, I don't now," replied Timius, "I did used to when I was a little boy but that was nearly eleven years ago. Since then I have been away receiving an education at the Augustan Institute at Larcia and today is the first day I have been back here since leaving all those years ago."

CHAPTER XIV

Luvat ire et Dorica castra videre.

VIRGIL

It is pleasant to go and view the Doric camp.

A LPHONSUS WAS ABOUT to ask further questions when he was interrupted by somebody's pet dog that had strayed from its master. The animal came bounding up to Timius, panting heavily, and he immediately pounced onto Timius, almost scratching his bare flesh, as it did so, it also started licking Timius around his face. Timius was astounded with the amity of the creature, and pushed him down and, in turn, commenced stroking the dog furiously Timius momentarily forgot himself and, speaking his thoughts aloud, said, "Isn't he a beautiful creature, Alphonsus?"

Alphonsus knew it was a dog from the noise it made and agreed with Timius, although obviously he could not see the animal.

"Oh, I wish I had a pet dog like this one," expressed Timius.

"Well, replied Alphonsus, there is no reason why you cannot own one, as there is plenty of scope for a young man like yourself to do so.

As Alphonsus spoke these words, the animal turned round and bounded off. Timius collected his thoughts and informed Alphonsus that he had better be on his way.

"No, please don't go yet," pleaded Alphhonsus. "Stay awhile and talk to me," he continued. "You did say your name was Arbutus, did you not?"

"Yes, that is correct," replied Timius.

"Well, as a matter of fact, I did used to know a family by the name of Arbutus. They used to live in the Palsis Chaulus Precinct of the town. The good lady of the household died of a terrible disease some twelve years ago, and her poor husband, who was a frontier legionnaire, was killed in battle so I was told, some years after, while serving in Germania. They had a daughter and son-in-law who lived with them. Do you know what your mother's name was?" asked Alphonsus.

Timius was now quite embarrassed and replied, stuttering as he did so, "No Alphonsus, I'm afraid I do not know, in fact, I cannot really remember."

"Was your father's first name Sejanus?"

"That is correct, yes it was," replied Timius excitedly.

"Well, you will be surprised to know that I had the honour of knowing them both."

Eager to find out more, Timius asked the blind man whether he knew his sister, Mena, and her husband, Silius. The old man informed him that he had known them very well, but what he said next made the bottom drop out of the young lad's world because Alphonsus went on to inform him that Silius and Mena and their two young children had now moved away from Velitrae, and he had no idea where they had gone. Evidently Timius' sister and brother-in-law had had some good fortune come their way, some years ago, and used the money to buy a small holding in another part of the country where land was less expensive.

Neither Timius nor the blind man was to know that the good fortune that had been bestowed on Mena and Silius was the estate left to her by their father, Sejanus, after his tragic death. There was accumulated army salary, his personal savings, and investments, army gratuities, and a posthumous donation from the Emperor. The estate of a fallen soldier was always left to the eldest child in the family if the soldier's wife was deceased.

Timius was dumbfounded to hear that he now had no relatives in Velitrae and apart from a blind man for a friend and his old friend Marcus, whom he had yet to find, he was once again very much alone and it seemed to him that his hasty journey to Velitrae had all been in vain when he could, quite easily, have stayed in either Narnia or Rome and found himself a job. However, the blind man went on to reminisce about the old times. He told Timius how well he knew his mother and described her as being a very generous and good woman. He told Timius that he had visited her at least one a week, and he was always sure of receiving either a morsel of bread, or the luxury of two or three fresh eggs. He told him that in addition to this he enjoyed the company of the young man's mother. He went on: "each time I went to see your mother, I would always strum my lire, and we would sing a song in praise of the gods, and there was a favourite one which we both loved to sing together."

As he said this he removed a five string lire, which looked rather decrepit with constant use, from around his neck where it hung on a cord, held it to his chest with his left hand and began strumming it softly with the fingers of his right hand. After a moment, he gently broke into song. The lyrics of the chorus made Timius feel rather confused because they were:

'As the morning sun rises in the sky
The gods be praised above on high
And gracious thanks from all us mortals
With sacrificial offerings at their portals
For all the wondrous gifts bestowed
To us in our, earthly, abode'

Timius was also quite bemused with this chorus because he now began to remember the blind man visiting their home and sitting on the veranda with his mother singing songs of praise to the gods. Timius, even at an early age, realized that his family were not well off and moreover the blind man was a beggar and even to this day he could not understand why two people in the world who had very little, and indeed nothing in the case of the blind beggar, should be praising the gods for their generous gifts. He felt that the reverse was true and after the old man had finished singing Timius turned to him and said, "I enjoyed that very much, Alphonsus," to which Alphonsus replied.

"You are only being kind to me because at my age my voice isn't as good any more, and my playing of the lire is atrocious. However, what do you plan to do now young man?"

Timius pondered the question a while and then replied, "I don't know, I shall just have to stay quiet and think my way out of my predicament. Perhaps I could stay with you for the night?"

"No, no, you must not do that," insisted Alphonsus.

"Well, why not?" enquired Timius. "After all, I consider you to be my friend. You were a good friend of my mother's and as far as I am concerned, you are a good friend of mine now."

"That's very noble of you," replied Alphonsus, "but that is not the reason why you must not stay with me. You see, young man," he continued, "I am well known in these parts as the blind beggar, and I have to rely on the pity and generosity from the townspeople for my livelihood. But if you are seen in my company by any of the town officials, you will be arrested as a vagrant and taken away, perhaps into slavery, and that is something you do not deserve. You have not committed any offence. You are just an innocent traveller passing through the town, and you have your whole life ahead of you, so you must not jeopardize your future by spending even a few days in my company."

"I understand," replied Timius, "but what am I to do now, have you any suggestions?"

"Not really," replied the blind man. "It all depends on what your plans are for the future. All I can suggest for you, over the next few days, until you have made up your mind what you are going to do, is for me to take you to an old innkeeper friend of mine and ask him to give you accommodation, however meagre, for a few nights, and you can repay the man by doing household chores for him during the day. This will give you time to think. And having done so, you can then pursue your plans. So come along with me now because it will soon be sunset."

"Please don't bother," said Timius. "I don't want you to trouble yourself on my account, although it is extremely kind of you to offer."

"Come, young man, think nothing of it. It is the least I can do for you, and perhaps the only way I can repay your mother for all her kindness towards me before she left us to join the gods."

Timius followed the man and was soon guiding him along the road by the arm. He was beginning to feel the usual uneasiness because it was the time of the day that the latrines were cleaned out at Larcia, but his immediate thoughts were on getting himself settled for the next few days. It would also give him a chance to try and seek out Marcus that was of course if Marcus was still in Velitrae. However, he would try and find out at the earliest opportunity.

As they made their way to the inn, Timius was able to relate to Alphonsus his past and Alphonsus listened intently. Alphonsus also expressed his opinion that he thought Timius had been very fortunate to have had a good education and strict disciplinary training over quite a lengthy period. Timius asked Alphonsus whether he followed a regular routine or a routine of any description, which would enable Timius to spend some moments in his company when the opportunity arose.

"You will always find me in the same spot where we met late this afternoon. It seems to be habit with me," continued Alphonsus, "to sit on the step before sunset and contemplate the mercy of the gods. They're most gracious and merciful, you know, young man, and you must never deny them their due regard."

Timius mumbled in agreement. They arrived at the inn, and our young traveller observed quite a lot of coming and going of guests who appeared to be people who held high positions. Certainly much higher than the position he held, he thought. Alphonssus directed the young man to lead him to the rear of the inn. This Timius did and when they arrived at a wooden door, which appeared to be locked. Alphonsus stopped, through instinct as he had been to this part of the inn several times before, and with his stick knocked on the door. After a while, the door opened, and a young slave stood in the doorway. There was an enquiring expression on the young slave's face as he said, "Ah, it is you Alphonsus, but you have a companion with you today."

"That's quite right," replied Alphonsus. "Would you be so good as to ask your master if he could spare a few minutes to see me. I'll not take up much of his time."

"I don't know whether it will be possible," replied the young slave, "but I will try. Wait here a while," With this he disappeared.

After some time had passed, a well-dressed man, in a flowing toga with his hair well groomed, came to the door. He looked a trifle annoyed at being disturbed but anyone could see that on seeing Alphonsus the expression on his face softened.

"What can I do for you my dear friend Alphonsus," asked the innkeeper. "You only seem to come here when your beneficiaries exhaust their benevolence, but no matter, I am pleased to see you. Pray tell me in what way may I help you?" he asked again.

Alphonsus then explained to the innkeeper his purpose, and after the innkeeper had listened and looked over Timius, he merely said to the young man, "Come with me."

Before following the innkeeper, Timius thanked Alphonsus for all his help and promised him that he would see him again. Very quickly he tried to offer Alphonsus a few coins, but Alphonsus refused to accept them. They shook hands and parted. Timius followed the innkeeper along the corridor and into the kitchens. Timius was then introduced to a burly man whom he estimated to be in his early fifties and whose name was Thengus. The innkeeper than made off to attend to other business. Thengus rather sourly ushered Timius out of the building and into another building across a small courtyard. Thengus opened one of the doors of the storehouse and told Timius that he could sleep in the small store house for the duration of his stay at the inn. There were empty sacks and there was also a small oil lamp on one of the window sills. Timius placed his own sack of belongings behind the door and on instructions from Thengus, who was the master slave in the kitchens, followed him back into the main building where Timius was promptly put to work washing out the containers in which the evening meal had just been cooked. On Timius' arrival, a very old slave who was doing the work was relieved of it and given instructions to do something elsewhere in the building. Timius worked very hard that evening and was most grateful at the end of it to receive a bowl of broth and a dried lump of bread. This was thrust at him by Thengus who then dismissed Timius and at the same time gave him instructions to return to the kitchens at dawn the following day.

When Timius returned to the little storehouse the oil lamp had been lighted. He expected to find it so because Thengus told him that he was not to extinguish it during the night because the light from the lamp helped keep away prowling rats. Timius made a bed of the empty sacks which were stacked in neat bundles, went out to the tap in the corner of the courtyard and washed his body. He then returned to the storehouse and, as he closed the door and glanced down at his makeshift bed, was startled to see standing quite still on the bed a large reddish grey scorpion with its tail curved well over its body ready to strike at anything that might approach it. Timius very quickly collected his thoughts, removed his sandal and threw it at the creature. He missed and the scorpion ran towards the door. Timius recovered his sandal, ran over to where the scorpion was, and stamped on it.

"That's got you," he said to himself. "You will not come in this place again!"

He opened the door and kicked the remains of the scorpion outside. He was now very tired and lay on his makeshift bed. Before he went to sleep, his thoughts were on the day's events and, in particular, the disappointment of finding out that here in Velitrae there was no longer any member of his family. He was grateful for Alphonsus' kindness, and his thoughts then again turned to Larcia. How happy he thought he had been there, on reflection, and he now knew why people like Praetorian officers Paulo, Carpus, and Lictus had continued to serve at Larcia even after their five years secondment had come to an end. Not long after this, he dropped to sleep.

*

Some eight days had passed since his arrival at the inn, and he had never been beyond its confines. The realization soon came to him that he was not obliged to remain here, nor was he under any contract to stay, but nevertheless he did not feel aggrieved at being given one of the most menial tasks to perform, and did not feel humiliated by being treated no better than a slave. Some of the slaves at the inn had much less menial tasks to perform than that which he was given, so he decided to pluck up the courage and ask Thengus for leave of absence for one day. He did so want to seek out Marcus, and he needed a day in which to do this. Thengus was rather reluctant to let him go until Timius pointed out to him that he was under no obligation to stay. After all, as Timius explained, he was a freeborn Roman and had not committed any offence or indiscretion and that he had only agreed to do the most menial job in order that he could earn his nightly accommodation and the scraps of food during the day. He made it known to Thengus that he was not complaining but was in fact grateful for what he was given. Even so he felt that it was a bit hard that he could not even be allowed a day of respite. Thengus brooded over the question throughout the day and before Timius left the kitchens that night, Thengus approached him and informed him that he would not be required in the kitchens tomorrow, but that he would expect him back the following day, that is, of course, if he still required food and accommodation. Timius was very happy to hear this and thanked him. He also asked Thengus if he would be so kind as to tell him the directions to the pottery because, as Timius explained, he was a complete stranger to the town. Thengus softened in his attitude and did as requested.

Eventually Timius found his way and at the pottery gates asked the gatekeeper if he could see Marcus Piritus. The gatekeeper asked him to wait, as he would have to seek permission from the pottery manager, Dodimus. Timius expressed his thanks and agreed to wait. It was not long before he saw Marcus come running out of the building straight towards him. Marcus threw his arms around Timius, and they embraced and shook hands.

"What are you doing here, you old rascal?" asked Marcus.

Very excitedly Timius explained that he once lived here when he was a little boy and that he had now returned to find that his sister and brother-in-law had moved out of Velitrae. Marcus was sorry to hear this but quickly explained to Timius that he ought to really go along and approach Dodimus to ask him if he could have a couple of hours off from work so that he and Timius could have a good long talk together. Timius agreed, and Marcus hurried off to seek permission from Dodimus. After what seemed like nearly an hour Marcus returned looking very crestfallen.

"What's the matter?" Timius asked Marcus, "I hope I have not been the cause of you getting into trouble?"

"No, no, certainly not," replied Marcus, "but that old so and so Dodimus is a most difficult man to work for, and I'm afraid I have had enough. I have told him that I am leaving in three days time," said Marcus dejectedly.

"Don't go and do that, Marcus," said Timius, "you've got a decent job here, and you are earning some money and you will be making a foolish mistake."

Both young men made their way towards the pottery fence and seated themselves on the grass verge. They then related each other's situation and discovered that neither of them was really happy in what they were doing. It was beginning to come clear to both young men that they were virtually ducks out of water. Neither of them was suited to this kind of life, although Timius had experienced only eight days of it. Timius informed Marcus that he had had the good fortune to be visited by Cyrus at Larcia. Marcus informed him that Cyrus had also visited him here at the pottery, and Cyrus seemed quite happy and proud to be in the army. Both young men looked at each other for a while as though they could read each others thoughts. Marcus broke the silence by saying, "Why don't we go and join Cyrus?"

"Oh, I can't do that," said Timius, "because I am not yet eighteen years old, but you can certainly join the army."

"Of course you can," explained Marcus, "You can tell them you are eighteen and they won't know. Besides I wouldn't join without you."

Timius immediately thought of that day back in Larcia, some years ago, when Marcus had told him to tell the woodsman that he was merely trying to see if he could use the axe when he was caught stealing it. Marcus had encouraged him to do that and had put the words into his mouth. Here he was trying to do it again.

"Oh, Marcus," Timius said, "you will never change. You were always trying to influence me when we were at school, and it always got me into trouble, but I still think a lot of you, you old rogue. Suppose the army was to find out?" continued Timius, "I would be in very serious trouble, wouldn't I? What would they do to me?"

"Not much," replied Marcus, "except make you a galley slave I suppose."

"That would be great," replied Timius, "and the laugh would be on me, wouldn't it?"

"Don't worry old boy," said Marcus, "I would then volunteer to be the captain of the galley, and then you would have an easy time of it."

Timius was quite bemused by Marcus' latest remark and began to be more serious and administered a gentle reproof to Marcus that in his opinion he had acted rather petulantly with Dodimus and, moreover, he felt that it was rather ungracious of Marcus, especially since Dodimus had not only offered him a job with security but also reasonable accommodation. Marcus relented and agreed that his attitude and petulance had been somewhat hasty. However, he was quick to point out to Timius that this was caused, primarily, through his restlessness of the kind of environment in which he was now living, after all the years at the Augustan Institute at Larcia, with its strict discipline and routine not to mention the comradeship that abounded there. Both young men realized their predicament and knew that it would not just go away.

They would have to do something about it and, after a lengthy discussion on the subject, they finally agreed to meet outside the pottery gate, complete with their meagre baggage and make their way to Rome to join the army. Timius felt that the only thing he could do was to bluff his age, and he was sure that a matter of months under age would make little difference to whether they accepted him or rejected him. They were both certain that, armed with each of their papyrus documents and attestation given to each graduate by the institution, they would have little trouble in being accepted for military service. Both the young men shook hands and promised each other faithfully that they would keep their respective appointments.

It was still quite early in the afternoon, so Timius had planned not to return directly to the inn, but to make his way through the town and beyond it towards his favourite childhood playground. As he reached the outskirts of the town he was in the vicinity of the little house in which he used to live with his mother, sister, and brother-in-law. He was drawn towards it out of curiosity and when he stood opposite it, childhood memories came rushing back to him. He could picture the egg men from the village proffering samples of their produce to his mother and he could remember the occasions when the blind beggar would sit on the step of the veranda beside his mother and sing to their hearts content. It was all changed now. The little compound was silent although the house did appear to be inhabited. However, he knew that he was only a short way from the gulley; perhaps half a mile. With a spring in his step, he walked off in the direction of the gulley. He was quite surprised to see that an awful lot of construction work had taken place during his years of absence. There were little villas and tiny gardens dotted all over the area that was once barren, and for a moment he felt quite sad that even his gulley had changed beyond recognition. At the perimeter of the newly constructed housing estate, he came upon a landscaped park through which ran the tiny road that was arterial to the main road to Rome.

This was the road on which the old man in the litter had tossed both him and his childhood friend Ciatus a gold coin each. He crossed over the road on the other side of which was the continuation of the park. It was very beautifully laid out with an abundant variety of shrubs, small trees, beds of flowers, with stone statues of the gods dotted here and there. A tinge of sadness affected Timius again because he much preferred it when it was quite barren. But, however, he continued through the park which came to an abrupt end and there before him, rolling down the slope, was his rough scraggy gulley. It was still full of thorn bushes, rocks, and other wild vegetation and his old surroundings made him feel as though he was home again. He spent over two hours wandering around trying to identify the many little crags in which he had played and mucked about when he was a little boy. He now decided that he should return to the inn before sunset, because he felt that he had to find Alphonsus and tell him about his plans to join the army. He felt sure that Alphonsus would endorse his decision. So he decided to make his way back.

It was late afternoon when he arrived at the perimeter of the park and thought he would rest a while before proceeding further. He perched on a rock and quietly began to think of all the statements of greetings he could have made to those lizards and other little reptiles when he was down in the gulley. Unfortunately, he was so absorbed with the past that he had forgotten to even say hello to them. Anyway he would come back here again, and perhaps next time he would bring them a handful of dead flies to feed on. Timius looked around to his right slowly in the direction from where he could hear the sound of voices and approaching along the pathway were three people. There was a woman walking between two young girls, and as she did so she held hands with them. One of the girls appeared to be aged about ten or eleven, whereas the girl walking on the left of the woman seemed to be about fifteen or sixteen. All three of them were very simply dressed but there was a kind of freshness about their whole appearance. The fifteen-year-old girl, Timius noticed, had dark, flowing hair, and from where he was sitting he could discern that her eyes were very dark.

As they approached him, they stopped their talking and in silence passed by. When they had gone about ten yards beyond where he was sitting the very dark haired girl turned her head around and looked at Timius with what seemed to be an expression of curiosity. They walked on further, and again she turned around to look at him and a lovely smile crossed her face. Timius very bashfully returned the smile, and he did not know whether to run after her and speak to her. He decided to do nothing because, after all,

all three may have belonged to one of the noble families of Velitrae. Before the party turned to take another pathway the dark-haired girl looked around again and smiled at Timius and lifted her left hand gently and waived. Timius stood up and responded with both arms high above his head. He was quite touched by this and a little excited but took immediate control of himself and made his way back through the park and into the high street area of Velitrae.

Timius' attention was distracted when he was in high street vicinity by two municipality men who were carrying a large sack suspended on a pole which each man supported on their left shoulders. He knew not what the sack contained but it seemed to him that they were carrying a body of some description, perhaps that of a dead dog or boar. He watched them pass by and into the distance and thought no more of it. Because his mind was now on getting to the spot at the end of the side street where Alphonsus had told Timius he could always find him at that time of day. He arrived at the step of the veranda, but there was no Alphonsus in sight. Perhaps the old man had been surrounded by rather an abundance of beneficiaries and would be a little late, so Timius thought he would wait for him. After over an hour had elapsed, there was still no sign of Alphonsus. Timius was very disappointed but thought he had better return to his storehouse accommodation at the rear of the inn.

Timius was about to collect his homespun towelling from his sack of belongings to go and get refreshed under the tap in the courtyard, when the door of the house burst open and in walked a young slave to light the lamp. He cupped a lighted taper in his hand as he did so, so that the draft would not blow the flame out.

"I am sorry for not knocking before entering," said the slave, "but I thought the store house was empty."

"Think nothing of it," said Timius, and, after lighting the lamp, the slave walked out.

Timius was returning from his wash when he met the young slave, who had come to fetch him, again in the courtyard.

"Master Thengus would like to see you, Arbutus, right away."

"What for?" asked Timius.

"He did not say," replied the slave, and he abruptly turned round and returned to the main building.

Timius left his towel in the storehouse, tidied his tunic, and reported to Thengus.

"Ah, your back I see. We didn't expect you back at all, but the innkeeper Gaius Apuleius would like to see you right away. Come with me," instructed Thengus.

He led the young man along the corridor to the innkeeper's office, and on his way there, Timius decided that this would be an ideal opportunity to inform the innkeeper of his plan to leave in three days. He would also tell him his purpose for leaving and must make sure to thank him for his generosity in allowing him to stay in the storehouse. Thengus ushered Timius into the innkeeper's study and left the two to discuss whatever business the innkeeper had in mind.

I'm glad you have come back," said Gaius Apuleius, "because something has occurred in your absence which you may or may not know about."

Reaching over to a shelf, he picked up a small lire, a very roughly caste bowl and a small leather pouch. As he did so, the innkeeper gave the appearance that he did not want to be contaminated by the articles, especially in the way in which he handled them. He placed the items on the corner of the desk and, as he did so, said to Timius. "These are for you".

Timius was astounded and remarked, "For me, but from whom?"

The innkeeper was quite surprised and asked, "Didn't you know?"

"Know what, sire?" asked Timius.

"Didn't you know that your friend Susta Alphonsus died this afternoon?"

"No, I didn't, sire," he replied, choking back the lump in his throat.

"Well, it is so," said the innkeeper very sombrely, and the woman who brought these to me said that Alphonsus was sitting at the side of the road begging, when he suddenly yelled out and this same woman ran to his assistance and in his dying breath he asked that his belongings be brought here to me to be handed to you."

Timius had no idea what to say, but asked, "Where have they taken his body, sire, because I should like to go along and pay my last respects to him before it gets too dark."

"Goodness knows," replied Gaius. "Usually with these sort of cases the *municeps* merely put them in sacks and take the bodies away to one of the clearings near the rubbish dump and bury them post haste, so unless you can seek out the municipal workers who buried Alphonsus, I should think your chances of finding his last resting place very remote."

Timius was speechless for a while, until the innkeeper advised him that he had work to get on with. However, Timius thought that it was now appropriate to broach the subject of his departure. The innkeeper took it very calmly and remarked that he was not surprised to hear of this because he was fully aware that Timius' stay would be of only a short duration. He was most understanding of the young man's situation and wished him well in his career. He also asked Timius to return to the inn from time to time, where he would be welcome as a guest, and not as an assistant in the kitchens. Timius was thrilled to hear this and asked the innkeeper if, since he had nowhere to keep some of his belongings that he would not be able to take with him into the army, perhaps the innkeeper would allow him to leave them in his care.

"Certainly, I don't mind at all. You will be welcome to do just that," responded the innkeeper. "Anything you leave behind will be in safe custody here, but make sure to say farewell before you leave."

Timius picked up the total estate of the blind beggar Alphonsus, which had been willed to him in the old man's dying breath and returned to the storehouse. He sat himself on the makeshift bed and opened the leather pouch. It contained money. Timius counted it and felt awful when he contemplated spending it. He thought it was very kind of Alphonsus, but he wished he could have seen him before he died. Anyway, he thought, the old man would not have left him the money if he had not intended Timius to spend it, and it would come in useful to pay for his fare on the passenger cart to Rome.

He had arranged with Marcus to borrow the money from him with a view to repaying Marcus in due course. Marcus had offered to give him the money, but Timius insisted on borrowing, with a view to paying the sum back, because he was most averse to abusing friendship. Thanks to Alphonsus, bless him, he would not now have to borrow. His last thoughts of the day were that, although Alphonsus had now passed on, it was obviously a happy release for the poor man because he must have led an extremely lonely life and, moreover, in a world of complete darkness. He would never forget his benevolence, and promised that the next time he passed the temple he would pray that the great god Augustus would take him into his care.

CHAPTER XV

Quamquam festinas, non est mora longa.

HORACE

Although you are in haste, the delay is not long.

M ARCUS PIRITUS AND Timius Arbutus were now in Rome. They
had arrived in the city in the early afternoon and had spent some two
hours making enquiries as to the whereabouts of the nearest cantonment
to which they could proceed and enlist for military service. They had been
told that the appropriate establishment to which they should apply was the
Campus Tarquinius. They were very near the Campus Tarquinius, which
was situated near to the northern boundary of the city, beyond which was a
large expanse of heath land. The weather had been changeable throughout
the day with periods of sunshine and showers.

It had begun to rain again and both young men took shelter in a shop
doorway. From this vantage point they could see gradually forming in the
sky, ahead of them, a beautiful rainbow. Both young men immediately
tested each others wits by enquiring of each other to name the colours of
the rainbow. They were aware that there were seven primary colours, and
Marcus guessed five of them: **red, orange, yellow, green,** and **blue**. The list
was completed by Timius, interjecting that the remaining two colours were
indigo and **violet**. It was some time before the shower ceased and they were
on their way again, and when they arrived at the gatehouse of the campus
both young men looked at each other apprehensively, knowing that the hour
of reckoning had now arrived. There was still time for them to change their
minds, but both were aware that if they did there was little else in store for
them, as the prospects of beginning a life like that, which they had become

used to at Larcia could not really be found outside the life of a legionnaire as described to them by their old faithful friend Cyrus.

Both young men had kept their appointment—at dawn that day—as previously arranged and were able to get to Rome by way of a passenger cart drawn by a team of six sturdy horses. It was a non-stop journey from Velitrae because the owner of the passenger cart had been an enterprising type who tried to provide an express service to those passengers requiring it. Marcus had left the pottery the previous day and the accommodation provided for him by the pottery manager, Dodimus, was relinquished in gratitude. Both parties severed their relations on most amiable terms. The pottery manager had extended an open invitation to Marcus to visit him and his family at any time he was in the vicinity of the pottery, making the young man feel that he would always be welcome in the household. Dodimus had realised months ago that the kind of work Marcus had been performing was really not the type to which he could devote unbounded interest and enthusiasm. Dodimus also knew that the work he had performed was of a good and proficient standard, but deduced that this was purely because the young man was disciplined. He could see from time to time the frustrations the young man was feeling and he therefore did not feel disappointed when Marcus had expressed to him his desire to leave in order that he could join the army. Dodimus knew that life in a legion would be more suited to a young man with the outlook, attitude and discipline of Marcus. They had had several minor differences of opinion over issues of little consequence, but this was not unnatural between a spirited young man and an enterprising overseer.

Timius had said his farewells the previous night to the innkeeper and, at the same time, had deposited a few of his belongings in his care. These comprised the lire and pewter begging bowl that Alphonsus had bequeathed to him and also his broken musical pipe and the small bag of gum Arabic. Apulaius reminded him that he would always be welcome to stay at the inn whenever he came back to Velitrae. Before saying farewell to Thengus, Timius thanked him for the concession to cease his work in the kitchens at midday that afternoon. The sombre and not very talkative Thengus also expressed his gratitude to the young man for the diligent manner in which he had performed his work and assured him that on his return to the inn as a guest, he would see to it that he was served a stout portion of the delicacy of the day. Timius had spent the afternoon wandering around Velitrae and was attracted, as though by a magnate, towards the sector of the town where he once lived. Again, as he passed the house, he stopped and surveyed it subconsciously. The attraction led him back through the newly set out municipal park and towards his childhood playing ground, the gorge. When he arrived at the approach to the gorge he felt that since the afternoon was wearing on, he would not have the time to wander through the many well-known crags and crannies that were stamped deep in his memory, so he decided to sit on the rock. It was the same rock that he had perched on when he visited the area on the earlier occasion. From this position, he had the added advantage of looking down into the gorge and, because of the solitude of the spot, he was able to relax and lose himself in his own thoughts and memories. After sitting there a while, he again heard footsteps and voices from somewhere along the pathway that ran along the boundary of the park. He looked around towards the direction from where the voices appeared to be coming, and again he saw the woman with the two young girls who had passed that way when last he was there. Timius remembered the elder of the two girls smiling and waving to him on that occasion, but he thought that it was only a trifling incident that had taken place previously, so he paid no more attention to them until they were about to pass by close to him. He noticed that they had stopped talking again, and when he looked at them the dark-haired, dark-eyed, elder girl gently smiled at him again, and very bashfully he returned the smile. She continued to keep smiling and, looking at him as they walked up the path and again before the party disappeared from sight, she waved to him, but appeared to have been admonished for doing so by the woman who seemed to be acting as the two girls' chaperone.

Timius responded, albeit bashfully, by waving back. He now wished that he had not made up his mind to join the army because he had a feeling that the elder girl was trying, in her very naive way, to communicate with him, and he thought that if he could make a friend of her, it would give him an absolute thrill to introduce her to his make believe world that lay in the gorge and, with tremendous enthusiasm, he would be able to give her a conducted tour of the area. But he wondered if she would like that because from her appearance it seemed almost certain that she was a member of the nobility of the district. He had decided to join the army and there was no way he could retract from it, and he would go through with it. However, at the first opportunity he was given he would return to the place, and if there was ever a chance meeting again he might be able to pluck up the courage to speak to the girl. This was a hopeless plan that he could look forward to, but he had a feeling also that indeed the hope was not so forlorn.

Marcus and Timius arrived at the gates of the Tarquinius Camp and enquired of the guard on duty as to where they could apply to register their names for military service. He directed them to the central building, which lay about seventy yards from the gate outpost across a stone quadrangle. They apprehensively entered the main building and made enquiries of other soldiers, very smartly dressed in their uniforms, and finally found themselves in what was the main recruiting office. It was empty, so they seated themselves on a wooden bench in the spacious and sparsely furnished recruiting office and awaited the attention of the officer in charge of recruiting.

They waited a very long time, and when he finally arrived, it had crossed their minds that perhaps he had been taking an afternoon rest, before attending to any duties. He was a big man, chubby faced, and balding. He sat down behind his desk and helped himself to a glass of red wine as a refresher and, having taken a few sips, looked up at the two potential recruits and called them over to his desk. Marcus and Timius obeyed and were now standing before him. Another soldier approached and took his place standing behind the recruiting officer.

"I take it you want to join the army," said the recruiting officer.

"Yes, we do, sire," replied the young men in unison.

The recruiting officer then looked over both the young men in what appeared to them to be a very strange manner and, turning to Marcus, said, "I expect we will make something of you, but, as for your friend, I am no so sure! The Emperor needs sturdy, strong resilient men in his legion, and your friend doesn't appear to look very strong and robust enough to withstand the rigours of a legionnaire. But, however, we might give him a try."

The recruiting officer enquired into their backgrounds, and as the brief interview proceeded, he became more reassured that the two young men before him would be suitable material for the army. Each produced their attestation documents given to them at Larcia and after the recruiting officer studied the contents, he asked Marcus his age. Marcus' reply was confirmed by his date of birth on his attestation documents. But when he asked Timius the same question, Timius burst out the untruth that he was also eighteen. The recruiting officer frowned slightly and rubbed his chin with his right hand while still gazing at Timius' attestation documents. He then looked up at Timius and, in a very serious tone asked, "You are not related to the god Mercury, are you?"

"No, sire," replied Timius, not knowing what the recruiting officer meant.

"Your father wasn't the marathon runner, Pheidippides?"

"No, sire," replied Timius.

"I see," said the recruiting officer and, with a twinkle in his eye, went on to say facetiously, "Well, young man, you must have been on poor terms with your mother. She must have discovered very early in her pregnancy that you were unwanted and disposed of you from her womb very prematurely. Either that or this document is false."

"I don't understand, sire," said Timius, wondering what all this was about.

"Well, let me tell you," said the recruiting officer, "because it may never have occurred to you. You have told me you are eighteen, but from this document I have here, you are only seventeen years and five months, and I am at a loss to know what is correct.

Timius realized that he was beaten and admitted the truth. At this moment his spirit felt dashed, until the recruiting officer advised him that they would ignore the discrepancy and that they would accept him. Marcus had no problems at all, and there were no doubts cast with regard to his age or his suitability. Marcus was a sturdily built youth, nearly six feet tall, with dark brown hair and brown eyes, whereas Timius was a very lean youth of about the same height as his friend, with dark hair and dark eyes. He gave one the impression that he was always in need of a good meal, but his appearance hid his agility and athletic prowess. It also hid a very sensitive nature.

The recruiting officer went on to describe the seriousness of their venture. He told them, quite plainly and firmly, that it was not the habit of the army authorities to accept recruits *ad lib* for regular service or for career service in the legions. Both young men would be required to take an oath of service, and after this oath had been taken, they would then be required to undergo four months of arduous training here at the Tarquinius Camp before being posted to one of the legions that were at that time within the provinces of Italy. There were three legions in service presently on the Italian peninsula. This was the seventh legion, which was based in the southern part of the peninsula, the fourteenth legion based in the southern province of Rome and the fourth legion on service in Transalpine Gaul. They would be given a choice of which legion they wished to join and were immediately asked what their choice would be.

Unhesitatingly, Marcus chose the fourth legion and Timius wondered why this was so, until it occurred to him that it was in the fourth legion that their old friend Cyrus would be found, and Timius agreed whole heartedly that this would be his choice also. They were discreet enough not to tell the recruiting officer the reason behind their choice, but merely informed him that, since Transalpine Gaul was a northerly province of the Italian peninsula, it might hold some attractions to them from the point of view of travel and a change of scenery. This plausible explanation was accepted by the recruiting officer. However, he went on to inform them that if they did not make the grade, or reach the required standard after four months training they would not only forego their donative, but would also lose acceptance as legionnaires. The only alternative in that kind of situation would be for them to try and gain acceptance to one of the auxiliary centuries that accompanied the legion, or the supporting camp followers and servants of the legion. They would receive no money during training, which they felt was a little bit harsh, but they were soon to discover that they would have no purpose of money, during four months training period, because they would have little time or opportunity to spend it.

The recruiting officer explained to the potential recruits that their oath of allegiance and service would be strictly adhered to. Any breach of discipline would be severely punished. Even the most minor breach had its appropriate punishment and the most severe resulted in execution. They were told that their officers and senior ranks would be obeyed without question, irrespective of what the order was. The legions had a way of dealing with disobedience from whatever quarter. Each legion had its own eagle, and the loyalty and defence of the eagle was the paramount duty of the Roman soldier. The Roman soldier was the ambassador and pillar of Rome and Roman civilization, and their standing would on no account be trivialized. He warned them severely that there would be numerous occasions in the future when they would wish that they had never taken the oath of allegiance.

Summing up, the recruiting officer said to them both, "Well, I have told you both the absolute truth, and I have not in any way tried to give you the impression that the life of a legionnaire would be carefree and one of ease. I shall give you a few minutes to contemplate what I have just said and to change your minds if you so wish."

He then departed from the room with the other soldier, leaving Marcus and Timius alone. Marcus had a tingling of apprehensiveness about going through with it, but Timius reminded him that after the hardships and discipline of Larcia, they could soon both adjust and adapt to the life without too much trouble, and with this slight word of encouragement, Marcus agreed to go through with it.

The recruiting officer returned, followed this time by two soldiers who appeared to be his assistants. Timius and Marcus indicated to him that they had made up their minds to go through with their desire to join up at which point the recruiting officer ushered them into a smaller room. In this smaller room was a marble bust of Emperor Tiberius, behind which were stood three replica emblem eagles of the seventh, fourteenth, and fourth legions. Grasping the eagle emblem of the fourth legion, and standing it in front of him, the recruiting officer asked the boys to kneel on both knees, to bow their heads, and to raise their right arms out in front of them. He then asked them to repeat the oath after him, which they did. After they had taken the oath, a parchment scroll was handed to the recruiting officer by one of the assistant soldiers, and the two young men's names were recorded. They were then asked to give their signatures alongside their names, alongside which was appended the signatures of the two assistant soldiers as witnesses to the act. The recruiting officer wished them every success and asked one of the assistant soldiers to take the young men to be placed in the care of Centurion Hiero.

*

Three months had now elapsed since their joining the army, and both young men had regretted every moment of it. The training was so rigorous and hard that each blamed the other for influencing their hasty decision. They wished they had delayed their decision longer in order to find out more about army life, but to their regret this was no longer possible. The only consolation was their hope that when they joined the legion proper the life would become rather more interesting and a little less arduous. The training began in the early hours of the morning and did not cease until well after sunset. The care of their equipment and the attention paid to the treatment of their weapons was considered to be foolish at times by both of them. It was impressed on them that their weapons and equipment were to be cherished and cared for much more passionately than anything else they possessed. Certainly at Larcia some of their training included the use of weapons such as the sword and the javelin, but their training at Larcia was child's play compared to the training at Camp Tarquinius. Many raw recruits were expelled before even their first month's service had elapsed, and it was only the obstinate and determined recruits that ever got to the end of their training. Marcus and Timius had only one month in which to survive their ordeal at the Tarquinius Camp, and they now counted the days to their release and posting to the fourth legion.

Their food was of the most unappetizing and rawest form out of intent rather than through shortage, and the wines served to the recruits were akin to vinegar. Only the coarsest wines were considered suitable for recruits. Throughout their training, they were confined within the camp's perimeter. Aside from the training in weaponry and combat formation their training also included that of personal hygiene, community hygiene, and the many other varied tasks that they would experience as fully fledged legionnaires. The discipline was of the highest standard, far surpassing any standard required of a common slave. They now began to fear their seniors to a point of agreeing, without any opposition, to all the personal insults that were levelled at them. They began to feel that they were merely machines and that these smaller machines would one day form part of a disciplined military machine that was the fear of the rest of the civilized world. The valour of the Roman soldier was of the highest order, and the word retreat would never enter into his vocabulary. To retreat was considered the lowest form of cowardice, and no roman soldier could be accused of cowardice, no matter what the obstacle.

The Roman soldier was issued with practical uniforms and accoutrements. These had to be serviceable in all dispositions and in various geographic and climatic conditions. He was issued a helmet, which differed from the Greek helmet in that it lacked a visor. It was carefully designed in bronze and had a projecting piece at the back which shielded the neck and a ridge on the front which protected the face. The breast plate was made from about five to seven stripes of beaten bronze and each of these stripes were equal in lengths of about two inches to which were attached leather straps. The breast plate was then fastened around the body from the waist up to the armpit with hooks. Similar stripes were placed across the shoulder, and these were fastened by hooks to the upper stripes of the breast plate. The breast plate was worn over a heavy cotton tunic and the bottom edge of the cotton tunic ended just above the knees. Around the waist of each soldier, especially when in combat or on official duty, was worn a leather apron fastened at the waist and dropping over the skirt of the tunic to meet it at the edge.

This leather apron was cut into strips in widths of about three inches. Metal greaves were not worn extensively but were often replaced by stockings made of wool or leather. The leather used for the stockings was of a fine leather and much more pliable to the leather used in the aprons. Heavy sandals formed an essential part of the uniform. Depending on the kind of activity that was required of the soldier, the feathered plume of the helmet was dyed an indicative colour. Red, green, blue, and yellow were the dyes mainly used, but were not worn on the helmets of all cavalry troops, only on the helmets of swordsmen or the foot soldiers.

Bowmen did not wear coloured plumes on their helmets. The infantrymen's arms were uniform and were adapted to the nature of the service. Each legionnaire carried a javelin which was ponderous with a length of about six feet. This was terminated by a triangular point of steel of about eighteen inches. In addition, the legionary also carried a smaller spear. To this was added a rectangular shield or buckler. This was oblong and concave, about four feet in length by about two and a half feet in width, and was made of a light wood which gave the impression of thin sheets of wood glued together, the grain of each being at right angles to the grain of the other. The edges of the shield were bound by iron and the whole of it was sometimes covered by bull's hide. It was gripped by means of a hand grip protected by a metal boss. Each legionary also carried a sword. The sword was about two feet in length and had a double-edged blade. The hilt was of a corrugated bone. The scabbard was made from heavy leather on which was engraved the emblem or symbol of the legion. Besides their arms, which were not considered an encumbrance by the legionnaires, they were laden with their kitchen furniture, instruments of fortification, also a bedroll and the provision of food and water for many days.

The new recruits at Camp Tarquinius were diligently instructed to march and run, to leap, and to swim. They were also instructed to carry heavy burdens and were trained to handle every type of arm that was to be used, either for offence or defence, in either in distant engagement or close combat. Timius and Marcus were able to do all these things before they joined the army. The basic training and discipline that they received at Larcia prepared them well. But here at Camp Tarquinius the training was much more serious and intense. They were trained to form a variety of evolutions and to move to the sounds of military trumpets and flutes in a martial dance.

The heath land to the north of the camp was used for military type exercises. Included in these exercises was training in field duty. Each recruit was trained in spending weeks on end in rough outdoor camp situations and, in between, they were trained to march around and around the heath land, covering a number of miles in one operation. During the marches that were simulated, each trainee carried his full equipment and the weapons were of a much heavier variety than was normally used in combat training. It was during these long marches that Timius and Marcus had doubts about their wisdom of joining. The march seemed endless with only nightfall to break the monotony. Sometimes the monotony was broken by the introduction of the Tarquinius training camp military band which headed the small cohort of trainees, but this light relief from the monotony lasted for under an hour at a time. Other forms of relief included pyrrhic dances and brief stops when the recruits were instructed to take up formations against the imaginary enemy. In one of these formations it meant that the recruits would form in a tight rectangle, kneel on one knee and raise their shields above their heads presenting a massive shield above them comprising of each shield in the cohort against imaginary showers of arrows directed at them from imaginary enemy bowmen. In addition, after marching for long hours they were suddenly halted, separated in two groups, and in their fatigued state, commenced sword fencing between individual members of the sections. The swords they used were much heavier than those actually used in combat, and it took great effort for each individual to raise the implement, let alone manipulate it for defence or offence. Javelins were thrown at objects which represented the enemy, and it was during these exercises that many of the recruits collapsed. A few even died through their efforts, but the persistent training urged on and demanded by Centurion Hiero, continued relentlessly.

Centurion Hiero was an extremely hard-hearted man and treated all the trainees with an unrelenting harshness. There was no mercy shown towards any stragglers, and the weak among the recruits were merely dismissed contemptuously. Experience had shown him that it was only the relentless and well-trained legionary that would be able to withstand the rigours of extremes of climate from the very cold climate of the northernmost province of Germania and the hot dry, and arid, climate of the desert in Syria.

He also knew the variety of enemies. The attitude and cunning of the barbarian German differed from the disciplined and climatically accustomed Parthian. He also realized that between these two extremes lays the rebellious nature of zealous bandits and political opponents with a varying spectrum of intelligence and military aptitude that the legionary would be confronted with in the settled parts of the Empire. Therefore, the main aim of the training of a legionary was to ensure that he could adapt himself and bravely face any type of enemy that might confront him. He knew that if he was to show mercy towards trainees of a lesser stature than the highest that was demanded, he would probably be sentencing them to their own death, because he was fully aware that, at some time or another, in the not too distant future, these young men in the trainee cohort, who were entrusted to his care for training purposes, would be grateful for the harshness and mercilessness it had been his pleasure to inflict upon them.

It was customary for the legionaries to take care of their own personal needs as and when the occasion arose and to meet this they were taught basic preparation of their basic rations and they were also taught the art of fasting for days on end. The Roman soldier was not only a fighting machine but a military machine in every sense of the word. He could be relied on to either perform or attempt any task. He was indoctrinated to believe that the focal centre of his honour and devotion was the eagle standard, which was the emblem of the legion in which he served. All other considerations were of no consequence. Their families and friends were only important after the Emperor, the eagle standard, and his superior officers. Many could not accept the rigidity of this doctrine, which undoubtedly resulted in disciplined valour and either perished to their own depression or through the lack of that extra courage that was needed to overcome enemy adversity.

Timius and Marcus were two of a total of thirty recruits that had successfully completed the four months of training. The cohort began with a possible eight legionnaires, but the harshness and fatigue of the training had caused the largest percentage to relinquish their ambition. It was noticeable that of the thirty remaining the vast majority were those who had no other life to turn to if they failed in this enterprise, and therefore their whole effort and dedication was devoted to success, even at the expense of denying themselves of personal happiness, and when the general in charge of the training establishment had congratulated them on their success, his words were meaningful and not merely a platitude of satisfaction.

CHAPTER XVI

Fit ut nemo esse posit beatus.

CICERO

It is the case that no one can be happy.

FOR EACH MONTH of basic training completed, each recruit was granted one day's leave. They were also given a donative as their first salary for the period of training. Many of those recruits that did not make the grade within the stipulated four months period, if they showed promise were granted an extension of one or two months additional training. It was only the unpromising recruits who were rejected. The legions were never short of volunteers, and the vast majority of recruits were men in their early and mid-twenties. The attraction to the legion was very mundane in that legion life offered them the basic essentials of life, comradeship, security, and ample rewards in the way of salaries and gratuities; not least of all it offered the freedman Roman citizenship. Naturally, the life of a legionary was arduous and demanding to an extreme, but the respect shown for the legionnaire by the populace in general was very often a reward in itself. The citizens of the Empire were fully aware that without the existence of the legions their own humble security would be non-existent. This attitude induced a sense of pride, self-respect and self-discipline into each legionary, and he took his vocation seriously.

Marcus and Timius were busily discussing what their plans should be for the four days of respite that they had been granted. Marcus suggested stolidly that they should spend the four days in Rome and enjoy themselves as much as possible, because from what they had heard, the opportunity of doing so would not occur again for many months. Timius, of course, was most reluctant to do this. He felt that he would like to spend the four days revisiting Velitrae. He somehow had a strange feeling that it was only at Velitrae that he would be able to gain a well earned rest. There was a gnawing sense of urgency to return, but he knew not the reason for this urge. After arguing for some time they reached an equitable solution. Marcus decided to remain in Rome, and Timius to go to Velitrae.

The inn keeper Apuleius was very pleased to see Timius again and offered him a small room in the inn for the two nights he was to stay there at a greatly reduced cost. Thengus kept his word also and, at the evening meal, served him the largest portion of the delicacy of the day. Timius was quite thrilled with the reception he received and he had never tasted grilled nightingale tongues before. The wine that was served him that night was also of a delicate bouquet, but its potency was a little too much for the young man. It drove him to an early bed, and as he staggered along the corridor to his room he met Thengus on the way and very gaily slapped the burly man on the back and started relating to him the idiosyncrasies of that disciplinarian, Centurion Hiero. Thengus merely played along with the young man, gradually ushering him into his room.

He knew the wine had gone to his head and that a good night's sleep would soon get rid of any illusions of him becoming an officer in the fourth legion. The following day Timius awoke late and had to wait some two hours before being served his midday meal. He enjoyed every morsel of it and planned to spend the afternoon in the shopping precinct of Velitrae. It was while he was in the shopping precinct of Velitrae that he met, quite accidentally, an old sage who on meeting the young man began to philosophize. After a while, Timius brushed aside his philosophical renditions to continue on his way, but the sage then began to question him about his knowledge of the history of this town in which he was born. Timius knew not the history of Velitrae.

The sage, very imposingly, began to tell him that the town which was situated in the Alban Hills, on the borders of Latium, occupied a strategic position dominating the approaches to the Alban Hills from the south, and that the town had had a complicated early history. He told him that the town itself had an Etruscan name and that there was a large cemetery of Villanovan culture situated there. The early inhabitants had been a community of Latin stock. He told him that when the Volsci pushed northwards into Latium, the town changed hands many times, and after the revolt of the Latin community the town was severely punished. The walls of the town were demolished and the local Senate was deported to live on the other side of the River Tiber. The new colonialists were sent to occupy lands confiscated from the exiled Senators and this practice thereafter became Rome's customary method of dealing with revolts in refractory states.

Timius did not want to hear any more, as the afternoon was getting on, and he thought that the best thing for him to do would be to get away from the vicinity of the market place. He then wandered aimlessly through the town and was again attracted to the newly laid our parkland near to his favourite childhood playing ground. It was not very long before he was at the approaches to the gorge, but this time instead of making his way towards its entry, he decided to sit on a marble bench alongside the perimeter pathway. Behind him was a fully developed Acacia tree, the spreading branches of which provided him shade from the late afternoon sun.

Timius sat awhile thinking of the trials, tribulations, and the fun he had experienced over the last four months, and he thought to himself that, if he could withstand the kind of punishing life he had just inflicted upon himself, the lesser inflictions of life in a service legion could be easily tolerated. As he sat under the tree, something wet landed on his shoulder. Quite startled he looked to see what it was and, cursing to himself, started to brush off the bird dropping from the upper sleeve of his tunic. He looked into the branches to see if he could see the culprit, but it was not there. Instead, he saw a little speck coming down towards him very gently. He did not take a lot of notice of this until it came nearer to him when he discovered that it was a small spider floating itself down to earth on a gossamer thread. He watched the little creature float down, and when it was about a foot above his head, the gentle breeze blew it and its gossamer thread over to the left. It then blew back over to the right and wafted back over to the left, and it gave Timius the impression that it was flying. When the gentle breeze dropped for a moment, the little creature continued down its thread until it landed safely on the path in front of him.

It immediately scurried off into the neatly cut grass. How fascinating nature is, thought Timius, and before he could concentrate his thoughts on seeing nature at work in other aspects, he heard voices which were familiar to him. The dark haired elder girl, on spotting him, as they came around the bend in the pathway which lay about fifteen yards from where he was sitting left her chaperone and ran towards him. She was called back by her chaperone, but took no notice. As she approached Timius, he stood up. She took a few gentle steps and was now standing in front of him and in between regaining her breath, she asked him,

"Where have you been? We haven't seen you for ages?"

Timius replied very bashfully, "I haven't been here for ages because I have been away."

Just at that moment her chaperone and the other younger girl came alongside them, and her chaperone instructed the dark-haired girl to come away. She pleaded with her chaperone to stay and talk awhile with the stranger, and after the chaperone reluctantly agreed seated herself with the other young girl on another wooden bench further along the pathway. The dark-haired girl then, being rather lost for words, asked Timius, "Where have you been? Don't you live here in Velitrae?"

Timius replied briefly that he once did but had only returned for a couple of days and was now staying at the inn belonging to Apuleius. Timius asked her to sit on the bench beside him, which she did, and as she did so she asked him what his name was. He then asked her for her name and she replied, "Tricia, Tricia Roussus."

"That's a nice name," said Timius. "Do you live here?"

"Yes, I do," she replied, "not very far from here, and each day," she went on, "my chaperone, Lygia, brings both our neighbour's daughter, Marina, and me for a walk along this pathway through the park, but not if the weather is inclement."

"I can understand that," said Timius.

Tricia then asked, "Why have we always seen you sitting here on your own?"

"Because I haven't anything better to do," he replied, "and I am only really happy and contented when I am here in the company of nature. When I was a little boy and lived in Velitrae I used to spend hours on my own rummaging around these parts, particularly those crags and crannies in that gorge."

Before he could finish, Tricia was again being called by Lygia and Timius quickly asked her if he could see her again tomorrow afternoon. She excitedly agreed and informed him that she would ask Lygia if she could cut short her walk to come and meet him and talk to him for a longer period. Both parties, bursting with excitement what the 'morrow held for them, said their farewells and parted.

The following day Timius started out before noon to keep his appointment with Tricia. He had looked forward to it because he thought it would be an exciting change to take to someone who appeared to have an attitude of freshness to life in general. It would be different and this was all important to him. He had some time on his hands which he had to kill, and since this was his last day in Velitrae, before returning to Rome and thence to join his legion stationed somewhere in Cisalpine Gaul, he decided to do a detour of the town and perhaps spend an hour or so of his last day wandering through the gorge.

His detour brought him to the cemetery, which he now clearly remembered as a play ground of his when he was a little boy. He found an opening in the hedgerow and wandered around the graves towards the spot where his mother was buried. He remembered the spot quite clearly. He only vaguely remembered other parts of the cemetery. Unlike the majority of graves his mother's grave did not have a headstone or indication of the name of the person buried there. Sunken into the burial place was a simple roughly hewn granite slab. He spent a few moments at the foot of the grave, and it occurred to him that as a gesture of affection and remembrance he ought to collect a small bunch of flowers from some of the many shrubs that were dotted around the cemetery, to place on the grave, but he could not see any in bloom. However, on top of a tombstone of a grave some few yards from where his mother lay, he noticed a large bouquet of flowers which were now beginning to wither. He crept over to the stranger's grave and helped himself to a few of the withered flowers. There were plenty of withered blooms in the bunch, so he thought a few would not be missed. He laid them on his mother's grave and wandered off in the direction of the parkland.

As Timius came out of the approaches to the gorge he was surprised to see Lygia and Tricia already seated on the marble bench awaiting his arrival in anticipation. Her face lit up as soon as she saw him, and she excitedly asked him where he had been.

"Oh, just down in the gorge," replied Timius. As he spoke, Lygia made a move to sit down on the other nearby wooden bench, but Tricia asked her not to do so, but to remain with them. The neighbour's daughter was not with them on this occasion and when Timius asked after her whereabouts, he was politely told that she had refrained from coming with them. Tricia went on to ask him, "What did you go down to the gorge for?" as Timius sat down beside her.

"Nothing much really," Timius replied, "I just went to see some old friends."

Quite amazed, Tricia asked him if people lived down in the gorge and if so, were they outcasts.

"By Jupiter, no." responded Timius. "Nobody lives down there. the friends I am referring to, and you will probably think it silly of me, are the lizards, the wild rabbits, squirrels, and now and then a viper that abound down there. There are also other little creatures, too numerous to name."

Tricia was quite perplexed to hear this and revealed her perplexity in her expression. Timius explained that it was one of his favourite childhood haunts, which he would often like to return to, unless of course the construction team of the developers turned their hands to using the gorge in some sort of development scheme of theirs. He also told her that he would like to take both her and Lygia on a conducted tour sometime, to point out to them the wonders of the place. Neither Tricia, nor Lygia, seemed too enthusiastic about the idea, so he let the matter rest. Tricia then went on to ask Timius, "When will you come here again, Timius? Will it be within the next few days?"

"Unfortunately, no," he replied, "I don't think I shall be returning here for a very long time."

"Why is that," she asked. "I thought you liked it here?"

"I do, indeed, but my work will take me far away for lengthy spells."

"What is your work? What do you do?"

"I am a legionary." Hesitatingly, he added that he had only just undergone four months training and that he was returning to the Campus Tarquinius in Rome, and from thence to join the Fourth Legion in Cisalpine Gaul. An expression of disappointment and sullenness crossed Tricia's face, and after a while he broke the silence by asking her what kind of work or life she would hope to take up. She did not know how to answer this because she was not sure. She informed him that she was receiving tuition in, among other things, singing and playing the lyre. He excitedly told her that he had among his possessions a lyre, and although it was old he offered to lend it to her if ever she wanted to borrow it. He also discovered from the conversation that she belonged to a Patrician family and that her father was the assistant administrator of the library under the auspices of the temple of Appollo here in Velitrae. She asked him, "Are you from a Patrician family?"

"Me?" he replied astonished, "by Jove, no, "my family were Plebians, I think." He then informed her of his family background, which she found very interesting but was, nevertheless, sad to hear from him of the loss of both his parents. Lygia then suggested that the next time he was in Velitrae, he call at the house in order to become acquainted with Tricia's mother, father and elder sister. Tricia thought this was an excellent idea and wholeheartedly endorsed the invitation. Timius shook his head and declined because, as he pointed out to both of them, while he accepted their kind invitation, it would not really be possible for him to do so because if the pattern of the service of a legion continued as it had done over the past decades, it would probably be years before he would be able to return to Velitrae.

"He told them that he was quite sure that by that time Tricia would have grown into a most attractive young woman and that she would either have entered a vocation that demanded all her time and attention, or she would have been married off to some worthy young Patrician. He would hate to have to trespass on her happiness, even as just an old friend from the past. Both of them brushed this aside and insisted that this would not transpire, and Tricia seemed quite adamant that even though she might have undertaken a vocation of some sort, she would certainly not be married, and that he would be welcome to pay them a visit, as she would be absolutely delighted to see him again.

"You will be able to tell me all about your exploits as a legionary, and I promise to listen intently to all the exciting things that you will have to tell me when you return. I am sure Lygia would also like to hear all about them too," she said.

Timius detected a note of sincerity and trustworthiness in her reply and somehow felt that his intuition could be relied upon. However, he still did not feel that he could merely call on her at home—out of the blue—but said that if ever he was granted a vacation from the legion, as he was sure he would, some time in the future, he would return here to this spot each day of his vacation in the hope of seeing her. Tricia did not think this was a very good idea, but reluctantly promised to always look out for him when she visited the park.

Lygia reminded them that it was time they should be on their way. Tricia asked if they could remain a little longer but Lygia quickly drew Tricia's attention to the fact that any delay of theirs could be the cause of some anxiety to her parents and bring about a reprimand upon her. Before Tricia stood up, she bent over with her head nearly level to the seat of the marble bench and plucked a small wild daisy from a clump that was growing under the bench. She handed this to Timius saying, "Here is a little parting present for you, Timius. I shall always look forward to the day when you return, on vacation from the legion. Until then farewell and might the great god, Jupiter, be by your side."

Timius was sorry to see them go because he had spent a most pleasant hour in their company and promised to himself that he would return at all costs, but he could not hide the gnawing feeling that if and when he did return, it would only be to face disappointment. He half accepted the fact that he would never see her again. He was about to throw away the little daisy, as he wandered back through the parkland, but stopped himself from doing so as a thought occurred to him: he should keep it as a little memento of their meeting.

He thought he would place the daisy between the papyrus folds of the two letters written to him by his father, which he kept among his humble prized possessions. He was naturally dejected, but consoled himself with the thought that the life he was going to lead in the legion would have its many rewarding moments.

Marcus was not very excited when he related the manner in which he had spent his four days in Rome. Any excitement that came through in his explanations to Timius appeared to be a trifle false. He had spent the four days seeing some of the sights of the city and spending hours in the market places and the forums. After getting himself partly drunk on the first night in one of the wine houses, one of his fellow revellers had suggested that they should spend the night in a brothel. Marcus was fully in agreement with this in his half drunken stupor, and when he arrived at the brothel, he took fright of the situation and beat a hasty retreat. He could not go through with it and came to the conclusion that this sort of event could only be followed through if his two friends Cyrus and Timius were here with him. He always had plenty of confidence in their company. Marcus realized that his four-day vacation was a disappointment and the more both young men repeated their experiences of the past four days, the more obvious it became the vacation was an anticlimax. They found that they were only really happy to be in each other's company and in the company of other legionnaires. They also felt that they were able to melt into their military surroundings and lend themselves to military attitudes with ease, and any other distraction was not welcome. That night they talked excitedly of what lay ahead of them and, in particular, of meeting their old friend Cyrus. The fun and games of Larcia could be relived.

It was a misty Friday morning when the replacement contingent and fully trained recruits formed themselves into a smart body of a cohort, under the command of a Centurion, to march to Cisalpine Gaul. Each soldier was fully equipped with his weapons and military accoutrements. Timius was proud to be marching through the streets of the capital, where now and then small groups of people cheered them and wished them well, as somehow they knew these were the men in whose hands the security of the Empire, and the security of them and the families, rested. He was awe-inspired as a little boy when walking behind his father through the streets of Rome, when he saw a group of legionnaires smartly march by, and he could not believe that he was now part of the Roman scene. He felt on this occasion that it would be a wonderful thing if the Emperor, Tiberius, could be leading them out of the gates of the city. Because after all, Emperor Tiberius was their supreme general, but on reflection he thought that Tiberius could not possibly be at the head of every cohort that marched through the City of Rome at the start of their journey to take up their duties in distant frontiers. The Emperor was shouldering the affairs of state, and the event of a cohort of legionnaires in despatch to distant frontiers was of little importance. They were not allowed to talk while on the march, and Timius' thoughts turned to his meeting with Tricia. He thought how wonderful it would be if she could only see him marching proudly in the cohort through the City of Rome. He felt she would be proud of him, but he was not very sure of this because she did look rather disappointed when he informed her that he was a legionary. Perhaps a legionary was not held with much respect in her family circle. Many people in the provinces, who led lives that were fairly routine and of a secluded nature could not be expected to fully appreciate the importance of the legion towards their own well-being.

It was only in the City of Rome where the presence of members of the legions made any noticeable difference to the attitudes of the populace. This was simply because the vast majority of the populace had come here to Rome from far off lands, where they had seen the protective arm of the legion at work, or travellers who had travelled away from Rome and now returned, and could appreciate the important part the legions played in securing Roman civilization.

The cohort had left the city of Rome some four hours earlier before they stopped for the first time on what was to be a very long march to the township of Mediolanum in Cisalpine Gaul, where the Fourth Legion was encamped. The centurion in command had informed them at the start of the march that the distance had to be covered within two weeks because a message had come through that the Fourth Legion were to break camp and march further north into the region of the River Danuvius, in the province of Noricum. This was to occur on the first day of the week during the Calens of September, so the centurion had told them that there would be very few breaks during their march and the pace that would be set would be steady and trying. They would not be expected to do any road maintenance on route because there would not be any time for it. But he was quick to point out to them that they would have plenty of opportunity to carry out road maintenance during the Fourth Legion's march between Mediolanum and the banks of the Danube

CHAPTER XVII

Reliquae legions magnum spatium aberrant.

CAESAR

The rest of the legions were at a long distance.

THE TWO-WEEK'S MARCH from Rome had been arduous labour for all the men in the cohort, even though their recent strict and tough training had prepared them for this sort of event and without the training the cohort would have been depleted by large numbers of men who would have quit due to lack of stamina and resilience. At the start of the march, the pride of Timius Arbutus being now a fully fledged Roman soldier was at its height, but now that they had approached the encampment of the Fourth Legion at Mediolanum, much of it had been sacked. However, he was endowed with the kind of nature that would enable him to bounce back in a very short time and his life long ambition and recent pride of being a legionary would soon return.

All the replacement troops in the cohort were quite amazed at the organized and disciplined layout of the camp of the Fourth Legion. Before they were to be dismissed to join the permanent cohort of the legion they were all marched to the central tent which was set up in the centre of the camp and in which, under strong guard, stood the legion's revered golden emblem of the legion. On their arrival at the tent the officer in charge of the legion raised it in front of him after which they all had to pledge an oath of loyalty to the legion. To desert the revered emblem or to refuse a task given to them under the auspices of the emblem was a heinous crime deserving maximum penalties, even execution. After taking their oaths of allegiance the cohort were then marked to another store tent and each man was issued with a red cloak bearing a small crest in replica of the emblem and this cloak was considered to be the one garment of the legionnaire that he was most proud to wear.

After the issue of the cloaks the officers from the headquarters maniple made their appearance in front of the newly arrived cohort and placed their bids for replacement men. Timius and Marcus were selected to join the Fifth Cohort, as it had been notified to the officer of the Fifth Cohort that these two young men would be worthwhile additions to his troop. Their arrival into the camp did not go unnoticed by Cyrus Vinicius, who was busily engaged in loading the store vehicles with provisions for the legion's move to Noricum. Immediately, he spotted his two childhood compatriots. His persuasive powers began to work, and he let it be known to the officer in charge of the loading party, who was also a junior officer in his own cohort, that among the new arrivals were two exceptionally able young men whom the Fifth Cohort would find useful additions to their ranks. He was most praiseworthy of Marcus' strength and tenacity, and he was equally praiseworthy of Timius' athletic prowess; therefore, it was not long after his selection to the Fifth Cohort, that Timius Arbutus was detailed as one of the two foot messengers that would be required. Messages between the cohorts were usually sent by horsemen, but the Romans were prudent enough to recognize that there might be occasions when the use of a horse, or indeed the availability of an animal, for use by a rider, for the purpose of carrying messages would not always be forthcoming, and it was the second-line eventuality each cohort had within its ranks two young athletic legionnaires trained and kept in constant training to carry messages by foot over long distances. Naturally, Timius was very proud to be selected for this job, but he was also soon to discover that it was an additional job to all the other jobs he was required to do as a legionnaire. It was instilled in him that he ought to be proud to be a messenger for the cohort and should be able to take the added task in his stride.

Cyrus was absolutely delighted to meet them again and immediately started planning games of dice and knuckle bones with his two companions. Cyrus also introduced his two companions to another newfound companion of his, in the cohort, whose name was Lipsius Vegitus. He was referred to as Veg by all the others in the cohort simply because this young man gave the impression of a vegetable. He was a brawny young man with a head of dark tight curls and a very broad square shaped head. He tended to lack basic intelligence, but for tasks that required manual strength old Veg was a most worthwhile member of any team. He was a stolid character with not much sense of humour. The jokes and amiable insults from his companions merely bounced off him, simply because he did not understand their subtlety. Veg had been a very loyal friend to Cyrus as they had both joined the legion together. Cyrus had gone to his defence in many a verbal battle, because Cyrus was adept at striking the appropriate remark at his opponents just when it was most needed to put an end to any argument. There had also been occasions when Lipsius Vegitus had gone to his assistance in a physical fracas.

Cyrus was able to conduct his newly arrived companions around the camp at Mediolanum and to explain to them, as he did so, the consistency of a Roman encampment wherever it might be situated. The camp of the legion gave the appearance of a fortified city. As soon as a legion arrived at a suitable camping site, a space was marked out, and troops that had been trained in the art of clearing away rubble, boulders, and other obstacles, and who were commonly referred to as pioneers, very carefully levelled the ground and then began to remove every impediment that might interrupt perfect regularity. The encampment formed a quadrangle. In the midst of the camp rose the Praetorium, and it was in the Praetorium that the general of the legion had his quarters. The cavalry the infantry and the auxiliaries occupied their respective stations. The streets of the camp were broad and straight and there was a space of about three hundred feet left on all sides between the tents and the rampart. The rampart was about twelve to fifteen feet high and was armed with a line of strong and intricate fencing made from branches of trees which were hewn and gathered from nearby woods. It was defended by a ditch of twelve feet in depth, as well as in width. The construction of the rampart was considered to be important labour and was performed by the hands of the legionnaires themselves. The legionnaires were fully trained in the use of the spade and the pickaxe, which were no less familiar to them than that of the sword or the pilum. The construction of the rampart and ditch required patient diligence, and this was the fruit of habit and strict discipline. The legionnaire was noted for his construction ability, as much as he was noted for his valour.

"Tell me, Cyrus, what it is like along the Danube frontier?" asked Marcus.

"Plenty of water to wet your whistle," casually replied Lipsius, and immediately he said this, so all three young men began to laugh.

It was not what he had said but the manner in which Lipsius always replied to the important question. He was very dry in his weird sense of humour, if one could call it that, and this often caused his companions to be genuinely amused by his remarks.

The four young men were merely discussing things in general while they were busily preparing their equipment and packing their packs for the commencement of the long march to the Danube frontier on the morrow. Cyrus replied that he did not know what it was like on the frontier because he obviously had never been there. Marcus was aware of this, but he asked the question hoping that Cyrus had been able to pick up information from some of the veteran legionnaires. This Cyrus had done and was able to relate to them what he had heard.

"I understand that the winters on the frontier are fearsome, and the howling winds that blow from the northeast are said to be directed at Rome and her legions by the barbarian gods, Thor and Woden. I am told they have an obvious dislike for Rome and everything Rome stands for and, by the time we arrive there, winter will be approaching, and it will not be very long before we experience it for ourselves."

"I also understand," continued Cyrus, "that the area experiences heavy falls of snow followed by days on end of severe frost, and frostbite is one of the main complaints of the troops. However, some of the veterans don't dislike the area because there is plenty hunting of the deer to be had, and venison is always available in large quantities. I believe venison is a delicious meat, and I am looking forward to trying some of it."

"What are the barbarians like though?" queried Timius.

"What do you mean, what are they like?" responded Cyrus.

"Well, are they very troublesome?"

"Yes, I believe they are constantly troublesome, but the troops of the legion, I am told, cope with them quite easily and soon put them to flight without much trouble."

Their conversations continued in a general manner until nightfall, and early the following morning the whole legion broke camp, as they had previously been instructed to do.

The trumpet gave the signal of departure and the camp was instantly broken up in a highly organized manner. The legion assembled in its prearranged and organized manner, ready for the march with the general and his bodyguard at the head of the column. General Flavius Julianus had commanded the Fourth Legion for the past six years and was a member of the noble Julianus family, a well-known Patrician family. He was an extremely intelligent man, well versed in the arts of battle and the strategy of successful campaigns. In addition he was also well versed in the arts of literature and oratory, but he presented to the troops in his command an impression of efficiency and stern discipline.

There had been many occasions when he unhesitatingly had approached the procurator of the province in which his beloved legion had the honour of serving to demand permission for the execution of a legionary who had committed the offence of cowardice or extreme idleness. His reputation for harshness was feared throughout the legion, but he was also respected for his good judgement and fairness. The vast majority of the men who commanded the legions were of a very high calibre, and the legionnaires feared their generals far more than they ever feared their adversaries. To be summoned to the presence of a Roman general in command of a legion was a more fearsome ordeal to the legionnaire than it was to face, unarmed, a cruel barbarian. Their military powers over their troops were often considered tyrannical to an extreme, but in the conditions and the circumstances in which the legionnaire was called to serve and fight, the imposition of strict discipline through absolute fear of their superiors was an essential element in the conduct of maintaining the fortifications along the frontier and in pursuit of the enemy.

The methods they employed in maintaining the strong trained attitude of their troops were of the severest nature. They conducted constant exercises in which battles would be simulated. Every aspect of reality was introduced into such a situation and the only difference between a simulated battle and a real one was the absence of blood and dead bodies strewn across the battlefield after the event. It is remarkable that there was a lack of large-scale mutiny and desertion, but such adversities in the life of a legionnaire only made the bonds between himself and his comrades—and between himself and his beloved Rome—much stronger. Their reliance on each other was of the highest order. Their loyalty to the legion and their revered eagle was without question and woe-betide any enemy force that tried to break down their formidable valour although there had been occasions in the past when the enemy had succeeded. On these occasions it was neither the valour of the troops, nor their lack of discipline or training which caused them to succumb but the mere fact that they had been grossly outnumbered.

The trumpet sounded again, signalling the commencement of the march. Following the general in command of the legion and his bodyguard, was a band of musicians. The musicians consisted of trumpeters with instruments fashioned from beaten brass, with pipers. Following these was a row of musicians who played musical bells and clashed brass symbols. These were supported by drummers, a cylindrical brass shell over the opening of which was tightly drawn the cured skin of a calf. The regular and constant rhythm, drummed out on the instruments, provide the troops that were following with a regular beat and pace. The musicians' uniforms were enhanced by various regalia. Very close behind the musicians followed the standard party which proudly bore the eagle and as the sunlight caught the golden emblem it sparkled brilliantly to inspire its followers in their every step forward. Next in line were the archers. There were three cohorts of bowmen who, in addition to their specialised weapons, were also equipped with the sword, a dagger, and a pilum. Their training in the use of the pilum and the sword was secondary to that of the bow. Their accuracy in launching their arrows was of the highest standard. The bowmen did not carry the shield because of its encumbrance when engaged in their specialised activity in the course of battle. But when in extreme difficulty they relied wholly on the protection afforded to them by the swordsmen who were following in the line of the march. The swordsmen's shields also glistened in the sunlight, and with every step of its bearer the shield would naturally evolve gently from side to side and, as it did so, the sun's reflections gave the onlooker the impression of formidable strength. The sight of a legion on the march caused many of the citizens of the provinces to fearfully admire their protectors. To witness a formidable fighting machine, such as this, tempered their ambitions of opposition to Rome but, at the same time, it was to breed in them their acceptance of subjugated protection.

Following the swordsmen were the cavalry and because they were mounted on horseback their main weapon was the pilum. Each of the troops on the march was armed with both the sword and the pilum and they all specialised in the use of the latter with an onward thrust towards the enemy with that weapon held horizontally to the ground. The onward advance of the troops presenting their weapons in that fashion were in regular straight lines where each soldier strode forward relentlessly shoulder to shoulder with his neighbour. The front line was separated from the second line by about ten feet and so on. If disciplined arrangement was broken, they were each trained to move into different evolutions and, by so doing, confuse the enemy. If and when the enemy tried to outmanoeuvre the pilum bearing cohorts and did not confront them face to face, the pilums were then launched most accurately at the enemy, but this stage was invariably reached only after the bowmen had expended their missiles. A sudden renewed offensive by the enemy would then be faced by the wielding of the sword, whereas, meanwhile, the cavalry would have approached the enemy on its flanks in the endeavour to drive them into a congested centre to be showered on by arrows, followed by showers of pilums.

Trailing behind the cavalry were the military machines which were known as *tormenta*. The tormenta consisted of arcs, which bore battering rams and *catapulta* which were machines used for discharging large arrows and the heavier javelins. There was also *ballista* machines designed to hurl large rocks or other solid objects at the enemy. The machines were drawn by teams of horses alongside which marched legionnaires specially trained in the manning of these engines. Those men selected for this specialised job were usually those having tremendous physical strength, which was required to manhandle the machines when being brought into use and also the manhandling of the heavy missiles that were hurled from these launchers. In the rear of the legion was a large group of ordinance vehicles drawn by stout horses.

These vehicles contained the essential supplies, tents and equipment for the legion. There were no auxiliary troops following the Fourth Legion, because on their arrival at the Danube frontier they would take over a detachment of some four thousand auxiliaries who were at present attached and under command of the Seventh Legion, whom they were on their way to relieve. The auxiliary detachment of the Seventh Legion would not be returning to Italy with that legion because they were all locally recruited provincial troops and therefore, remained for the bulk of their service in the fortifications in and around their local province.

The Fourth Legion column on the march, as in the case of the other legions throughout the Empire, consisted of a body of about seven thousands men the majority of whom were Romans or freedmen who had now acquired Roman citizenship. During the course of their march the legion encamped temporarily on several occasions. Sometimes the temporary encampment was for several days, and the length of the respite was determined by the state of repair of the roads.

The roads between strategic points and townships of settlements were straight and the repairs to these highways were the responsibility of the legion en route to the frontier fortifications. During each of the stops cohorts were sent out in both directions to undertake running repairs of the road. The legionary then put his spade and pickaxe to use. Stones were hewn out from the nearest quarry and carried down to the highways to be properly laid by maniples detailed to undertake this task. Thus the highways were constantly maintained in order that essential supplies and reinforcements could be easily sent from headquarter encampments based in Italy. These roads were never allowed to fall into the hands of wandering barbarian excursions.

Road maintenance continued to be a prime function of the legionary and was an integral part of his training and exercise. When there were no roads to maintain, the legionary was nevertheless exercised in the use of the pickaxe and spade, and the other implements required for the function. In fact the word army was merely a military term for the word exercise and embraces weaponry and civil engineering. The military spirit of the legions stayed preserved, and this at a time when every other virtue was being oppressed by luxury and despotism under Emperor Tiberius at Rome.

He gradually succumbed to the tribune powers and influence of the Praetorian general, Sejanus. It is fortunate that the troops in his service were ignorant of the events taking place and were in allegiance to him mainly out of blind respect for hhis predecessor, Augustus. It was their humble belief that the successor of the great Augustus would continue to rule in the manner fashioned by this august prince. They were not aware of the politics at the heart of the Empire, because the legions were not accustomed to being confined within the walls of fortified cities. Their fortifications lay on the banks of the great rivers which formed the boundaries of the Empire. To remain in city fortifications was considered by the Romans to be a sign of weakness or pusillanimity.

Timius Arbutus was a proud member of the Fifth Cohort under the command of Tribune Tetricus. Tetricus was ably assisted by his second in command Centurion Crassus. Crassus was an extremely likeable commander, but severe and just in the discharge of his duties. He was a veteran who served under General Germanicus when the German barbarian, chief Herrmann Armenius, was defeated and slain. Timius was happy and proud to be in the Fifth Cohort, but for a moment, when he saw the charioteers at the head of the column acting as mobile bodyguard to the standard, he wished that he was able to be a charioteer instead of a foot swordsman. He would have loved to have driven a chariot, especially into battle, as he had often imagined he had done in his childhood dreams. Notwithstanding, he was happy to be in the company as a foot soldier with his friends Cyrus, Marcus and now Lipsius, who were marching alongside him on the outside rank. The pace that was being set had no effect on him, and he quite enjoyed the march. It was the endeavour of the legion to march a distance of six miles an hour. They hoped to reach the Danube frontier within six weeks, which would allow for temporary encampments to carry out road repairs. He had been instructed by Centurion Crasssus that when these occasions arose, he would not be required to undertake any of the tasks. Instead, as designated foot messenger of the cohort, he would be required to run as swiftly as he could to the last camping site and back within the shortest space of time possible. Bearing these instructions in mind, he was fully aware with each stride that he took that he would only have to return by the same route again, no once but twice over, and felt the utter futility of having to march onward. He was now a fully fledged legionary and proud of it.

His thoughts strayed to the girl with whom he had the pleasure of being acquainted back at Velitrae. He wondered whether she would be proud to see him marching along as a fully fledged member of the Fourth Legion. He was almost certain she would. He decided to make a mental note of all the places of interest they marched through on their journey to the Danube frontier. He would do this in order to relate to her in some detail all the places of interest that would make their conversation much more interesting. On second thought, he concluded that, in the event of their meeting again, he would probably be lost for words and would forget everything he had seen. Anyway, he would still continue to do so because it would make the march much more interesting. After all, he was being paid for it, and with his salary he would make sure that he was able to buy her some token to consolidate their friendship. He would make sure that it was something worthwhile and valuable. He knew not what it would be, but he would solve that problem in due course.

It was customary at noon for the legion to halt and take a break. At that time they would refresh themselves from their ration of food washed down with a good gulp of water from their water skins. Timius Arbutus, like all the other men in the legion, welcomed the noonday break because they were also able to relax along the side of the road. Not much conversation passed between them during these breaks, because their commanders had advised them to make the most of the hour of relaxation. They were not allowed to talk to each other during the march, and only the sound prevalent was the constant tread of their footsteps. Vegitus sat down beside Timius and mentioned to him that he had been instructed that morning to report to the officer in charge of the tormenta cohort, to drive one of the catapulta engines, because its regular driver had fallen ill at Mediolanum and was unlikely to improve for a few days. Vegitus explained that he had had some experience of driving a tormenta vehicle, which was why he had been selected. Timius was very pleased for him because Timius realised that Vegitus, would not have to march for a few days, and would be fortunate because the tormenta was horse drawn. Vegitas was also happy about the arrangement and promised that if an opportunity arose whereby he could, by some means, introduce Timius to the art of driving this type of equipment, he would do so in order to give him a little more excitement. Timius was quite excited about the prospect and felt that if this ever materialised, it would give him the opportunity of being a stage nearer to becoming a charioteer. He would do his best to handle the horse-towed machine to impress his superiors of his ability for such a task. This may even relieve him of his messenger duties, which he was not at all keen to do.

The following morning, when the legion broke camp, Vegitus took his place seated comfortably on the catapulta. The legion had encamped during the night on the southern bank of a fairly steep hill. The road ahead dropped away sharply on its left bank. When the march resumed, the other tormenta engines proceeded gradually into line and wended along the road up the hill. Vegitus, who was not fully practiced in handling the catapulta, found himself in dire straights. The wheels of the machine veered to the left of the road, and before he knew where he was and what was happening, the horse was rearing up in front of him, neighing loudly as it did so. Footmen accompanying the machines ran back to him and, after a tremendous effort on their part, were able to recover the machine and guide it safely back onto the road. The officer of the cohort directed that Vegitus was to report to his tent that night, where he would be questioned most severely about his inefficient handling of the machine. A severe punishment for his neglect was bound to ensue.

At sundown Vegitus stood before the officer in charge of the tormenta cohort. He appeared very angry at the way in which the young legionary before him had neglected his duty that morning by his mishandling of the catapulta. He reminded Vegitus of the value of such a machine and also reminded him that through his neglect he had very nearly been the cause of injuries to the foot soldiers who had gone to his assistance.

"Did you not check the braking device when you mounted the vehicle?" the officer enquired sternly.

"No, sire, I must admit I did not."

"Did it not occur to you what you would do if the braking device failed?"

"Yes, sire," replied Vegitus, "I would have had to rely on the horse to provide a brake."

"I see, and what if the horse couldn't provide you with a brake?"

"I would then have to rely on a rut in the road into which one of the wheels would become trapped, and thus provide a brake," explained Vegitus.

"There was no rut, was there?" asked the officer, again very sternly, and continued, "If there was no rut to rely on as a brake, what would you have had to do then?"

Vegitus paused for a while and then answered very pensively. "Well, sire, in that event I suppose I would have had to rely on my noonday break

The officer was livid at this last and insolent utterance although it somewhat amused his assistants. In his ferocity, he ordered the centurion of the cohort, who was also present in the officer's tent, to take the man out and see to it that he received twelve strokes of the lash across his back.

When Vegitus related the day's mishap and resultant penalty to Timius, the latter knew that his hopes were dashed for a long time to come of ever becoming a charioteer. He would have to content himself with being a foot soldier and messenger for the Fifth Cohort.

CHAPTER XVIII

Fortuna nunc mihi, nunc alii benigna.

HORACE

Fortune kind now to me—now to another.

CENTURION CRASSUS HAD called the men in the Fifth Cohort to assemble. He was stood at his appointed place on the edge of the assembly area, near to where the Fifth Cohort was stationed in the encampment with hands placed on top of the *vinestaff* that was his wand of office, while the men hurriedly took up their positions in front of him. The Fifth Cohort officer was soon to join them to take charge of the assembled troops who were now in readiness to march out on their patrols some ten miles northwards along the banks of the River Danube.

Three years had elapsed since the Fourth Legion had arrived at the Danube encampment. They had marched from Mediolanum to the township of Juvavum and from there to Lentia. Lentia was the largest township in this section of the Danube frontier, and the garrison of the fourth Legion was encamped along the Danube between Lentia and the much smaller township of Passau. This was rather a lonely, dreary area of the Noricum boundary, and there was little to relieve the tensions of duty in this part of the world. Many legionnaires spent a lot of their off-duty days in either the townships of Lentia or Passau, during which time they would indulge themselves drinking at the local wine houses or visiting the brothels. Timius and Cyrus had only been to Lentia and Passau on the one occasion because off-duty days were a most rare luxury to them. Their boyhood mischievousness had continued even into early manhood, and this had resulted in days and months of confinement to the encampment involving fatigue duty or additional patrol duties. Also, they had both experienced the penalty of the lash across their backs for some indiscretion of insubordination and also the penalty of starvation over given periods. Marcus, on the other hand, had sobered up somewhat, probably because during the first year of their arrival here on the encampment, he had met and become very attracted to a local girl in the township of Passau. Since then he had fallen in and out of love with his girl friend Sonita, but at this moment he was going through about the sixth cycle of being in love with her. His companions often teased him about this, but they were the first to agree that his emotional life had kept him out of trouble and its resultant penalties. Lipsius Vegitus, on the other hand, would not venture into either of the towns without the company of Cyrus or Timius. Being a very reluctant young man he was not easily persuaded into joining in mischievous acts or questioning authority. His parents, who were still living in the suburbs of Rome, had given him a severely disciplined upbringing, and it was abhorrent to question authority or disobey orders. His attitude, try though he may, could not influence Cyrus or Timius. So far as Cyrus was concerned, orders were given and rules were made only to be disobeyed, and authority must be questioned. His attitude had a tremendous influence on Timius, although neither young man would disobey, nor contravene, regulations of substance and of real importance.

They had spent three winters here along the Danube and they had experienced the harshest vagaries in the weather and were now quite hardened to it. During their first winter here there were many moments where not only these young men but many others yearned to be back in civilization and the extreme temperatures even drove them to tears. However, they had now fully adapted themselves to the very harsh life of a legionary and despite their attitude to military discipline in some instances they were now worthy members of their cohort. They had also faced the enemy on several occasions in minor skirmishes, and apart from minor superficial wounds they had come through their tour of duty at that point in time unscathed. The ordeal of the past three years had strengthened the bonds between them, as it had done among members of the rest of the legion. Each one knew that, whatever the future might hold, if they could maintain their bond of friendship, they had very little of which to be fearful. The spirit and morale of the legion was extremely high, and the respect of their general and other officers had grown accordingly.

It was routine for a cohort to make their way to a point between ten and twenty miles northward along the banks of the Danube and then set up cohort headquarters at the outermost position. One cohort also travelled southeast and set up headquarters similarly between ten and twenty miles away. From these headquarters, patrols would be despatched at varying intervals and on a rota basis to carry out the actual task of the patrol. Each cohort remained in the field for a period of a month, and the cohort would then be relieved by another. During their retreat back at the encampment, they would be given time to relax and also their military training would be maintained. Wherever cohort headquarters were set up so they would at the same time set up suitable fortifications. The auxiliary troops maintained much more permanent fortifications all along the frontier. But the extent of their patrols from their own fortifications went much further along the frontier.

The auxiliary troop had periods of active patrolling, followed by periods of training and relaxation within the garrison. This varied with that of the Roman element. The auxiliaries were mainly local troops recruited from the province in which they served, and it was therefore prudent that the time they spent on patrol was of longer duration so that their time for relaxation and leave from duty could be longer, to enable them to visit their families and friends in the small townships dotted around the province. It was not feasible for the large Roman element of the legion to be treated in this manner because their periods of relaxation and leave of duty would have to be enormously long and, correspondingly, unfair, if they were to be given the facility of returning to their homesteads in Italy. Therefore, the Roman element of the legion was the dedicated professionals who remained abroad from the provinces of Italy for years at a stretch.

Centurion Crassus was the senior centurion of the six centurions in the cohort. Each centurion was responsible for eighty men and six centuries comprised a cohort. The cavalry cohort sent out daily patrols northwards and southwards from the encampment and each of these patrols consisted of half a century. The horsemen of the cavalry were able to augment the foot patrols and report back to encampment headquarters the daily situation that existed on the frontier. Riding on horseback, these patrols were able to undertake complex evolutions in their watchfulness of the frontier boundaries.

The Fifth Cohort was marching at a steady pace northwards along a well-worn track beside the Danube. It was a very wet morning with the sky heavily overcast. The rain was falling at a steady drizzle and none of the troops were comfortable during the march, but because they had become hardened and used to the climate of this region apart from the grumbling under the breath, there was no major complaint about the conditions in which they found themselves. It was mid-afternoon and the rain had eased off slightly. None had enjoyed the midday break because their ration of bread carried in their lambskin pouches had become soaked by the rain, but they relished each portion they ate because the cold and damp of the morning march had driven them to a ravenous appetite.

Timius felt that there was something that made him rather uneasy about this particular cohort in its march of relief. He could not pinpoint what it was, but he could sense something was wrong. During the march, they could hear wolves baying in the distance but he was sure that was not the reason, because wolves prowling the area occurred regularly in this part of the world. The cohort was now approaching a slight bend in the river. On the western side of the track lay an embankment covered with overgrown thickets and as the cohort entered this part of the track an eerie silence seemed to descend all round. Then suddenly it happened.

The cohort was completely ambushed. This part of the boundary had never experienced an attack by the barbarians in the past, because it would have meant crossing the river by boat and thereby giving away their presence with the numbers of boats they would have to moor along the banks of the river, and this part of the river did not provide the facility for concealment of their craft. The barbarian masses had in fact crossed the river and moored their boats some five miles north along the bank, but these boats had not been noticed by the Roman patrols from the northernmost fortification because soon after they had disembarked, their warrior passengers, the boats had been taken back to the barbarian side of the river, where concealment facilities were plentiful. Thickets and hedges and river reeds were not cleared by the barbarians on their side of the river for obvious reasons, whereas on the Roman side, large stretches of the bank had been cleared to denude the enemy any form of concealment. The barbarians attacked ferociously, and as they launched their spears and arrows into the Roman cohort, they yelled and screamed like savages. The Romans were astonished to see the large numbers that had descended upon them but their discipline and training helped them to stand fast and face the enemy.

This tactic did not work for long because many of the men of the cohort were falling like flies because of the missiles launched at them. Those remaining immediately evolved other tactics and broke away into other groups. The Romans had in the early part of the fracas launched their pilums as effectively as they could, felling many of the enemy, but now they had to resort to their skill with the sword, which they did with the utmost valour. Timius dropped his shield and started making tracks towards the direction from which they had come, because it was his intention as messenger of the cohort, to get away from the fighting and run as swift as a fox back to the legion headquarters in order that reinforcements could be mustered and sent to their rescue.

He was not able to do this because very soon an angry looking barbarian smashed at him with a javelin. He tried to parry the blow with his sword but failed and rolled down the slight incline, still clutching his sword until his body came to rest beside that of a legionnaire. The legionnaire was lying on his back, and his helmet had rolled away. Timius was in the process of getting back on his feet when he suddenly realised that the man lying beside him was the officer in charge of the Fifth Cohort, Tetricus. He had the presence of mind to roll Tetricus further down the bank and quickly lay him in a face downwards position. As he was doing this the officer looked up and recognised Timius. He was very badly wounded, and all Timius could say to the officer was,

"Keep still, sire, pretend you are dead, I will try and get help."

He was on his feet again in a second attempt to get help, but again he had not gone far when he was again confronted by four barbarians who had now acquired the swords of dead Romans, and who came lumbering at him with full force. Timius produced his most masterly skill in the use of the sword and fought them off and was able to kill all four assailants, but again he was knocked over by the glancing blow of the javelin. This time his body fell right across the badly wounded body of Centurion Crassus.

Again he did the same thing for Crassus as he had done for officer Tetricus. He rolled him over onto his face and told him to lie still, as though he were dead. When he regained his strength slightly, he could see, in the distance, along the track, a Roman colleague fleeing down the track as fast as he could run towards encampment headquarters.

He was astonished to recognise Cyrus. He felt that if he was able to get away now, he would be able to not only catch up with Cyrus but get to headquarters much quicker because he was a trained long-distance runner whereas Cyrus was not. In those few fleeting moments he was dumbfounded to realize that Cyrus could run so fast, and for a moment he was tremendously proud of him. Timius was not able to catch up with Cyrus because he was very soon surrounded by barbarians, each with a sword in his hand, and each sword was pointed directly at him. He knew now that the fracas was all over. There were no Romans to be seen (alive, anyway) until the circle that surrounded him was suddenly broken and a badly wounded Roman thrown into it with the body landing near Timius' feet.

He glanced down to see a deep gash in the lower part of the soldier's stomach, and when he looked at the wounded man's face, underneath the sweat, the pain and dirt he was absolutely shocked to see that the legionary was Marcus. Timius was too terrified by the events which were taking place for the sight of Marcus to have any effect on his emotions. He was dirty, wet, tired and frightened. There was a gash on his left arm and one on his left shoulder; both were sword wounds. The Sythian barbarians surrounding him and Marcus were now jeering at them and were contemplating thrusting swords into the two captives and were about to do so when they were suddenly stopped by a burly man who was heavily clad in animal furs, who came striding up to them pushing his way into the circle.

"Wait, he yelled. Don't kill them yet. This one who is about the only one on his feet will be useful to us. We might be able to get some information out of him, and it would be a good idea if we dragged the other evil Roman along with us, because when he sees this other one suffering—pointing to Marcus as he spoke—he will be keen to talk. So tie them up and bring them along."

Marcus was dragged to his feet, and although he was in excruciating pain, when his eyes met Timius', there was a slight sign of relief in his countenance. He knew he was not alone and that Timius was with him. The two young soldiers were not tied up because there was no means of them being able to escape now. Also, Timius, the barbarians knew, would be able to assist his wounded colleague on the trek back to the barbarian encampment. The two captives assumed they would be taken further upstream and then taken across the river by boat, but this was not so. Instead they were marched by the barbarians in a north-westerly direction and away from the river banks. After about an hour they arrived in the midst of the Sythian encampment, and Timius immediately realized that the situation was now ominous.

The encampment seemed to contain thousands of barbarians. The horde had clandestinely crossed the river, out of sight of the Roman patrols, and they must have timed their crossing very cleverly over the previous few days, and had massed for a sudden attack on the Fourth Legion's encampment. They had also been joined by a horde from the north-west regions of the province, which had made its way in dribs and drabs undetected. It was early evening when they were finally dragged into a small animal skin tent, hurriedly erected for the purpose of the massing Sythians, for the chief of the Sythhian horde, Dorian Quingenta. Marcus and Timius were hobbled by their feet but their arms were free. This was allowed so that Timius could support his wounded colleague.

Quingenta's two associates commenced questioning Timius about whether the arrival of another legion to support the Fourth Legion was expected. Timius replied that he did not know. They accused him of lying, but he reminded them firmly that he was only an ordinary Roman soldier, and military matters of a strategic nature were never communicated to the ordinary soldier. The Sythian chief would not accept this, and he accused Timius of lying. Timius retorted, "I am not lying, and you know it."

The Sythian chief very coldly replied, "I will not have you raise your voice to me," and turning to one of his men said, "Perhaps a little persuasion is called for."

At that moment Marcus slumped to the floor, and quite unconcerned about Marcus, the man to whom the chief had spoken picked up a stick of willows, about five feet long and laid it fiercely on the back of Timius. He was struck several times until he too eventually slumped, in agony, to the floor. He was dragged back onto his feet by the scruff of his neck, and Quingenta looked at him very coldly and again asked, "Is there another legion on its way to give support to the Fourth Legion? I ask you this," he continued, "because I am sure you Roman scoundrels have your spies all over the place and know all about the congregation of our free tribes to see to it that you Romans are driven out of the region once and for all. Now are you going to tell me?"

Timius paused for a while, not knowing what to say and felt that he could only tell the truth and equally sharply retorted, "I do not know, we are never told such things."

Quingenta's associate was livid with the way in which Timius, the young Roman upstart, had replied to his chief, and struck him twice across the face with the stick, causing Timius excruciating pain and sickness. Quingenta knew that to question the Roman further would be hopeless, so he instructed that they both be taken out and killed.

Marcus and Timius were about to be dragged out to face their fate when Quingenta called to his man to stop. "I have changed my mind," he said. "It would be rather better if we were able to sacrifice them to the gods at dawn tomorrow, so that the gods may bestow good fortune on us. Take them away and stake them out for the night."

The two captives were dragged to the perimeter of the encampment, where their hands and feet were tied. They were then both made to lie flat on their stomachs on the damp ground. Stakes were driven into the ground at the head and at the feet of each captive. The ties on their hands and legs were in turn tied to the stakes. Although Timius was suffering terrible

pain from the lashing he had received, he was still conscious of what was
going on. Marcus, on the other hand, was semi-conscious, and when Timius
called to him in a whisper, there was no reply. Timius half believed that his
dear friend Marcus was now dead, but he hoped that his worst fears were
unfounded.

Darkness was falling rapidly while Timius was lying on the ground in
agony from the merciless beating he had taken earlier. As the hour moved
on, he raised his head painfully from the ground to try and survey his
surroundings in the darkness. He could see very little because there was
a complete absence of light or campfires outside the makeshift shelters of
the barbarians. Quingenta had obviously instructed his men not to give
their situation away by lighting fires that would attract the watchful eye
of Roman patrols that might pass by during their night duty. There was
also a complete silence overhanging the vast encampment. Timius lay his
head on his right outstretched arm, which afforded him some measure of
comfort. He was now trembling, not from the cold and damp, but out of
fright because he knew not precisely what the dawn would bring. He knew
that he was to be murdered along with Marcus the following morning and
he now began to wish that he was as unconscious as Marcus. He decided to
alleviate his fears by thinking about other things, but the only things that
passed through his mind were the memories of the past.

He thought about Tricia and wondered if she were now married to
some young handsome career nobleman. She had written two letters to him
since his arrival here in the province of Noricum, and he had duly replied.
Her last letter to him was some eight months ago, but he remembered that
in each of her letters she had emphasized the fact that she was looking
forward to seeing him again. He could not believe this to be wholly truthful
and concluded that she was probably only trying to be reassuring for the
duration of his lengthy absence. He wondered whether Cyrus was able
to reach the Roman encampment and whether assistance had been sent,
although he realized the futility of it because, as far as he could tell, the
majority of his colleagues in the cohort had been slain. Nevertheless, it was
possible that they were able to save the lives of many of the wounded that
were left to die. Yes, he was sure Cyrus would have reached his destination
because Cyrus did not lack stamina.

He wondered if Carpus was still at Larcia, and when he thought about
Carpus, his eyes welled with tears, because the bulla Carpus had given to
him as a parting present, and which he had treasured so much, had been

confiscated from him by the barbarians when they captured him. He remembered some of the inspiring and noble speeches of Artimeses and he particularly remembered Artimeses most cherished philosophy: *a good Roman must never give in to any adversity, or to anything dishonourable.*

This philosophy had a rather thin meaning now because he had no alternative but to submit to the wishes of the Sythians. From what he had heard from veterans in the legion, the Sythians usually offered sacrifices of their human victims to the gods by burning them alive. Gritting his teeth in determination, Timius decided that he would not submit to such a humiliating death. When the time came, with every ounce of strength of his body, he would frustrate and act in the best way he could, in the circumstances, both physically and verbally to arouse the barbarians' fury so that in morbid anger they would thrust a sword or javelin through him and kill him before burning his body. He would also make sure that if his dear friend Marcus was alive, he would do something equally rash to ensure that Marcus received the same fate. He was determined not to be burnt alive.

Moments passed when he began to feel sorry for himself. The trials and tribulations, disappointments, and sorrows of his life flooded into his mind. Without hesitation, he rejected such thoughts and began to conclude the fortunes of his life. He was lucky to have had a loving and understanding mother and father. Although his father had put him into a boarding institution, he realised that his motives were not selfish. Indeed, they were most unselfish because, by virtue of going to Larcia, he had had the privilege not only of a good education but also of associating with worthy and noble colleagues. He was grateful of the gift of being able to appreciate life for what it was, and not what it should be: he was grateful for the gift of being able to appreciate the very ordinary, and often taken for granted, things that surrounded one's life; he knew nature was full of wondrous things and even now, while he was all alone, he was not really lonely because growing just a few inches away from his eyes was a small clump of daisies which he could just about distinguish in the darkness.

The daisies would keep him company for the rest of the night and he talked to them as though they were his friends. He had enjoyed his few years in the legion and felt privileged to be associated with all the many comrades in his cohort, who were now either dead or severely wounded. He was grateful to have enjoyed the close companionship of dear Marcus, Cyrus, and, of course, Veg. The night was wearing on, and in the distance Timius could hear the baying of wolves. It was not long before the baying and howling drew nearer and it seemed as though they were coming in his direction. Ah, perhaps, he thought, both Marcus and I would be happily relieved if the approaching pack of wolves mauled us to death. It would be a terrible death but, at least, it would be more honourable than being burnt alive.

CHAPTER XIX

Canis nonne similes lupo est?

CICERO

Is not a dog like a wolf?

IT WAS NOT long before the pack of wolves was close enough for Timius to hear the loud snorting and howling of the beasts. He could hear them scratching and prowling around quite nearby. He was terrified. There appeared to be no barbarian sentry guard in the vicinity where he and Marcus lay, because none had passed by or checked that they were still secure for the past two hours. In desperation, Timius tried to loosen the bond round his wrists, but all his present and previous efforts only stretched the rope slightly, so that his two wrists were now about six inches apart. The tie attached to the middle of the lopped bond, which in turn was held fast by the stake, had also only stretched a fraction. It was now inevitable that unless the wolf pack was driven off quickly and soon, both he and Marcus would be prey for the creatures. He called to Marcus vainly and was surprised when Marcus replied in a feeble agonised mumble. Before he could say any more one of the wolves, which he could see fairly clearly, was but a few feet from him.

At the moment he heard a swishing sound just above his head which very nearly parted his hair, followed immediately by the thud of an implement as it struck the ground only inches away from him. It landed between the palms of his hands. The beast lurched back and yelled, but it was only seconds later before it regained itself to make another attempt to attack the two captives. The pack of wolves had been attracted to this corner of the camp by the scent of the blood from Marcus' wound and from the fresh drawn blood on Timius' back and neck. Again he heard a swishing noise above his head, but this time the noise seemed higher above his head. Immediately the leading beast gave out a terrible yell and fell to the ground.

The remainder of the pack turned tail and ran off. The beast that had tried to attack them was now pinned to the ground, in front of the captives, with a spear launched by what must have been one of the Sythian night sentries. Very soon after, Timius heard footsteps just beside him, and it was the sentry who had come to retrieve the spear. He yanked at it and freed it from the body of the dead beast, after which he collected the axe that he had hurled in the first attempt to fell the creature. As he walked away to take up his position, again, in the darkness he remarked, "I should have let the wolves devour you pair of Roman bastards, but Quingenta has given orders that you are to be the object of our sacrifice come the morning."

Timius winced when he heard this and hearing him do so, the Sythian sentry kicked him in the ribs before striding off to his post, which was some sixty yards away. The kick from the Sythian forced Timius to turn over onto his right side. This movement caused tension in his arms. To his utter amazement he could now part the palms and wrists. He realized that the axe had severed the rope as it landed in front of him. He was quick to take advantage of this fortunate quirk of fate, and was most thankful to the gods for their mercy. He immediately freed his wrists from the rope and then untied his feet and slithered over to Marcus and freed him, also. He then gently patted Marcus' cheeks to arouse him sufficiently to get him on his feet. Marcus responded favourably, but before the two young Romans were to steal away from their captives, Timius crawled back to the spot where he had been lying and helped himself to one of the little daisies from the cluster. He quickly put this into his tunic pocket and, as stealthily as possible, he half crawled, half slithered, dragging Marcus most of the time until they were free of the Sythian camp.

The moon that had shone, since darkness had fallen, intermittently through the broken clouds disappeared again behind them. The two young Romans were surrounded by the darkness of the night, and Timius did not know which way to go. He knew that the Sythian encampment was quite near to the village of Garnentum, which was to the east of the Danube. He decided to proceed in the southerly direction. Their progress was very slow because it was hampered by Marcus' inability to walk unaided. The wound in Marcus' stomach was causing him agony, and every step he took caused him to groan with pain. Timius did his best to support him, although he was also in pain from the whipping he had received and from the fact that his limbs had been shackled for several hours.

He could again hear the wolves baying in the distance but realized that he could not, under the circumstances, quicken the pace. Marcus was becoming heavier to support and slower with each step they took. There was only one thing for it, Timius crouched down and lifted Marcus over his shoulders, grasping one leg of Marcus' with one hand, and the arm of Marcus with his other hand. It was as though he were carrying a sack of vegetables. Weighed down with Marcus' weight, Timius endeavoured to progress slightly quicker than previously. He was becoming desperate because there was no means of him telling where on earth they were until he began to hear the distant trickle of a stream. He followed the direction of the sound and eventually found that he was standing at the edge of a stream. He felt certain that the stream would be flowing as a tributary to the Danube, but could not tell in which direction it flowed because he could not see the water clearly in the darkness. He lowered Marcus to the ground, knelt down beside the stream and placed his hand in its cool waters to ascertain the direction of its flow. He then swilled his face with water to freshen up and did the same for Marcus. With Marcus back over his shoulders, Timius followed the direction in which the stream was flowing.

It was over one hour before they reached the banks of the Danube. It was a torturous hour for him because there were several occasions when he himself felt that he was about to collapse with exhaustion. He concluded that he could not go any further under these circumstances. The distance to the legion encampment was far too great for him to cover during the remaining hours of darkness, with Marcus on his shoulders. He knew that there was no alternative for him but to leave Marcus if he was to reach the encampment in time to warn them of the impending danger of the Sythian hordes. He was absolutely loath to leave his dear friend Marcus as though he was deserting him, but Timius planned to hide him in the bulrushes that grew on the lower banks of the river. He spent a few moments trying to find a suitable spot that was dry and away from the lapping water. He put Marcus among the rushes and, as he did so, he discovered that the wounds his friend had sustained were now bleeding again. His own tunic was covered with blood. Although he could not discern it clearly in the darkness his tunic felt damp and sticky. He was desperate to know what to do to stop the bleeding when a remedy occurred to him. He made his way near to the water and grabbed with both hands some of the black alluvium clay and returned to where he had placed his friend and slapped the clay on the wound as a poultice. Marcus was only semi-conscious when Timius decided to tell him that he would return for him. He slapped Marcus' face to rouse him and explained to his friend what he planned to do. He told Marcus that he would endeavour to reach their encampment as quickly as possible in order to bring help.

He also instructed Marcus not to move because he was still in danger from Sythian search parties who would be hot on their trail as soon as it was discovered that they had escaped. Marcus agreed, although Timius did not really believe that he fully understood what he had been saying. He was too ill by now to care, but Timius said to him, "Don't give in, Marcus, try and cling on. I promise I will be back as quickly as I possibly can with help."

He could saw a fleeting smile cross Marcus' face as he replied weakly, "Don't worry about me, old friend. Get yourself to safety as quick as you can. I may not be alive when you return, and should this be the case, will you do me a favour if you return and find me dead?"

"Of course, but don't talk like that. What is the favour?"

"Will you go to the township of Passau and call on my girl friend, Sonita, and tell her what has happened? Do you know, Timius, that the last time I saw her she assured me that she would accompany me on patrol of this frontier in spirit, of course. I didn't know whether to believe her because she, like a lot of other people outside the legion service, say these things, but they haven't the slightest idea what we have to put up with so that they can remain safe and secure. Don't you agree, old friend?"

"Of course I don't, Timius reassured him. "They must know what we have to go through, otherwise the locals wouldn't cheer us each time a legion or a cohort marches through a township or village."

"I'm afraid you are very naïve," Marcus replied cynically.

"I suppose I am, but I had better be getting along otherwise I will be unable to bring help back to you. I'll be seeing you old friend," said Timius as he turned and ran up the bank.

Timius was on the track that followed the river and was heading southwards. He was weak and terribly hungry, aching from limb to limb. The wounds on his back and neck were now causing him to feel feverish and ill, but he grit his teeth in determination to reach the encampment. He had the presence of mind to decide that he ought to make a mental note of the number of tributary streams that crossed the track before he reached the river proper. This was to enable him to find Marcus because there was no other landmark that he could see in the darkness that would point to the spot where Marcus was hidden, if and when he was able to return. Timius continued half-running, half-hobbling, and there were several times when he fell over through utter weakness. It was only grim determination and his fear for his friend's life that kept him going.

Dawn was breaking, and peering into the distance in the hazy light, he could faintly see the watchtowers of the encampment fortification in the distance. The sight of the encampment spurred him on to summon every ounce of strength left in his body to reach his goal. It was nearly an hour later before he slumped absolutely exhausted at the gateway of the encampment. The guards at the gate quickly ran to him and carried him into the guardhouse. They revived him with a tankard of the local wine, after which they dipped his head into a cauldron of cold water.

Revived, but still exhausted, Timius implored the two guards that they must take him, without any delay, to the headquarters office of the general. He told them that he had a matter of the utmost urgency to convey to the commanding officer. The guards could not believe him and hesitated, thinking that his demands were a result of his delirium. Not knowing what to do, one of the guards quickly summoned the duty officer. On his arrival, with as much respect as he could muster, Timius implored the duty officer that he must be taken to General Julianus. He was able to convince the duty officer of the importance and severity of his demand. Unfortunately, Timius was unable to walk another step and collapsed immediately. They helped him to his feet. The duty officer summoned two other guards to carry him to the headquarters building, while he led the way. Many moments passed before the duty officer emerged from the headquarters building to summon the guards to carry Timius into the presence of General Julianus.

The general gave the impression to his audience that he was extremely annoyed to be disturbed at that hour of the morning and firmly reminded Timius that his mission had better be worthy of his immediate attention.

Timius then explained to the general, as respectfully as he could and indeed as briefly as he could, because he realized that time was not on their side; of his escapade that night and the plans of the Sythian chieftain, Quingenta. Very convincingly he told the general of the vast numbers of barbarians he had seen present in the clandestine encampment. The general realized the urgency of the matter and associated it with the massacre of the Fifth Cohort the day before. After pondering awhile, General Julianus instructed the duty officer to summon all the officers of the legion to his presence immediately and, also, ordered him to instruct all centurions to assemble the legion on a war alert. The duty officer turned smartly and proceeded to carry out his orders.

Turning to Timius, Julianus then said, "Thank you, young man, for your loyalty and honour to you duty. I will see to it that this deed of yours will be communicated to the highest authorities in the Empire. You can now take the young man to the sick bay for treatment," he instructed the guards.

But as he was about to return to his private quarters, Timius interrupted him, "Pardon me, sire, but my wounded colleague, Marcus Piritus, is desperately in need of help, as he was severely wounded yesterday. Could you please arrange for somebody to go back with me to bring him back to safety from where I left him hidden?"

Timius briefly explained to the general, Marcus' part in the episode. The general indicated that Marcus Piritus would probably be dead and that it would not be worthwhile sending any help. Timius was distressed to hear this remark and pleaded with the general that after all they had gone through that something must be done to try and help Marcus, as there was a possibility that he was still alive. Timius pertinently pointed out that it would add to the honour of the legion if it became known among the troops that one of their wounded colleagues was not abandoned by their illustrious general, but that he himself had taken steps to bring a wounded, and near to dying, soldier back to safety. The general was convinced with the ethic of the young legionary's argument and acceded to his wish.

"How will the legionaries I send out to young Piritus find him?" asked the general.

"Well, sire," replied Timius," after I left him at the mouth of the stream where it entered the great river, I counted four other streams that crossed the path of the track from that spot to the gates of this encampment. If they search the area at the mouth of the fifth stream from this encampment, they will find him hidden in the rushes."

"Are you absolutely sure it is five?"

"No, sire, I am not absolutely sure but I believe I counted five. I'll go with the rescuers, sire, if I may?"

"But you are too ill and too much of a wreck to even walk, let alone ride on horseback."

"That is true, sire, and, moreover, I cannot ride a horse."

The general paused awhile and then instructed one of his assistant officers to bring to him five chariots from the cavalry troop with the best charioteers at once. He also instructed another assistant officer to bring the young soldier some food and wine from his own personal kitchen. Timius was given a bowl of hot milk and some whole wheat bread to eat and drink. After he had ravenously devoured the food and gulped down the tankard full of wine he began to feel a little stronger. He tried to get up off the floor on which he was slouched throughout the interview with the general, but was too weak to stand unassisted. The sound of chariots soon could be heard draw up outside the headquarters building, and in marched a charioteer officer. He halted in front of General Julianus and very smartly saluted him by slapping his clenched fist across his chest. The general then instructed him about the purpose of his mission. A blanket was wrapped around Timius because he had begun shivering, which was a natural reaction to his ordeal.

He was carried out and placed on the floor of the chariot of the officer in charge of the troop. The five chariots proceeded with haste through the gates of the encampment and up the track by which Timius had travelled a short while earlier. The troop soon arrived at the mouth of the fifth stream from the encampment gate and Timius felt some strength return to his body, mainly through the anxiety he felt for Marcus. He was helped out of the chariot and, desperately stumbling and crawling, searched for his friend. He finally found Marcus where he had hidden him. He called to the others and they ran to his side.

Poor Marcus looked in a terrible state and, although alive, he was unconscious. Timius broke down with relief to find that his friend had hung on to life. Marcus was picked up and carried and placed on the floor of one of the chariots and Timius was helped to another. The rescuers tried to revive Marcus with water, but were unable to do so. In their haste to reach him, they had not taken any medicines with them. Very soon, the five chariots approached the head of the column of the Fourth Legion. The officer in charge stopped the chariots to report the success of their mission to General Julianus, who was resplendent on horseback, leading the Fifth Legion against the Sythian chief, Quingenta, and his barbarian horde.

Timius had learnt from the two guards that had assisted him to the presence of Julianus—while he ate his bread and drank his milk earlier—that a young soldier by the name of Cyrus Vinicius had returned yesterday in a state of exhaustion to report that the Fifth Cohort had been massacred by a barbarian ambush patrol. Relief had immediately been sent to the area of the ambush, but they had arrived too late. They were only able to bury the dead and bring back the wounded. He was told that many of the wounded had since died. Timius was delighted to hear that Cyrus, too, was safe, but he was desperately anxious to know what had become of Vegitus.

On their arrival at the encampment, Timius and Marcus were delivered by the charioteers to the medical quarters. The *medici* quickly carried them into the hospital bay, where they were very soon attended to. Before dropping to sleep, in a bed allocated to him, in one of the long medical halls, he asked one of the medical assistants if a legionary by the name of Lipsius Vegitus had been brought into the medical quarters the previous day. The medical assistant answered in the affirmative, adding that he was one of only eighteen surviving wounded, from the previous day's debacle, still alive. Timius was very much relieved to hear this and dropped into a semi-coma with grateful thanks to Jove and the other gods still on his lips.

CHAPTER XX

Avida est periculi virtus.

SENECA

Valour is greedy of danger.

AFTER JUST TWO days, Timius was released from the hospital quarters. He had not fully recovered from his ordeal but the situation existing in the encampment left the hospital officers no choice but to discharge him and two other patients long before they were due for release. The Fourth Legion, under General Julianus, had inflicted a terrible defeat on Quingenta and his followers when they had confronted them unexpectedly on the day after the Fifth Cohort had been massacred. Every space in the hospital quarters was occupied by severely wounded legionnaires, and space had to be found in other parts of the encampment to serve as an extension to the medical facility.

Timius and Cyrus were overjoyed that both they and their two other companions had survived the onslaught in which they had been active participants. Timius was full of praise for Cyrus' courage and intelligence when he broke away from the affray to seek assistance. Cyrus on his part was most surprised and astonished to hear of the good fortune that had presented itself to Timius, enabling him to escape from his captors. The story Timius had related to Cyrus was unbelievable, as far as Cyrus was concerned, but nevertheless he was extremely pleased to know that his two friends, upon whom fortune had smiled, were back with him again.

Cyrus advised Timius that it would be wise never to hunt wolves again for the mere sake of doing so. After all, he reminded him that it was the wolves that had saved him and Marcus and, like Romulus and Remus, they must always remember that they owed their lives to a hungry wolf. Had they not escaped, they undoubtedly would have been placed in wicker baskets and burned alive. The thought of this kind of death made both the young men shudder.

General Julianus was a reputable strategist. He did not wait, as some might have expected, for the barbarian horde to attack the encampment, with a view to repelling the attack from the solid fortifications of the fortress as any other general might have done. Instead, his strategy was consistent. He preferred to confront the enemy head-on, but on this occasion there was an element of surprise in his approach. Quingenta had misjudged the speed at which the Fourth Legion could be mustered and marched to the attack and when the attack came, Quingenta's barbarian forces were sufficiently alert to repel it. They fought bravely, but the valour and discipline of the Romans gave them the supremacy after a whole day of bloody battle. By the end of the day, although the legion was outnumbered, Quingenta's forces had been routed. The loss of life among the barbarians was enormous. Roman losses were also great, but a larger part of the casualties were not fatal. The remaining followers of the Sythian chief endeavoured to escape to the boats that had been anchored and drawn up on the western banks of the river, but Roman cavalry was quick not only to intercept them, but also to set a large number of their craft on fire. This meant that the remaining barbarians had no choice but to scatter in all directions. General Julianus, late that night, led the Fourth Legion triumphantly back to their encampment.

Nearly four hundred barbarian prisoners were taken and were put to work on extending and strengthening the fortifications of the encampment. They were used as slave labour to do the tasks that required the most effort.

Timius looked up at the clouds above him, which were edged with a silver lining. He had always appreciated the changing patterns of nature viewing each change, whatever it was, as though it was a new experience, but this time his appreciation went much deeper. The realization that he was lucky to be alive made even the changing cloud pattern even more wondrous to him. He had had sleepless nights since that fateful day when he had been taken captive out of fear for what was certainly in store for him.

He was now engaged in light duties and had been for the past few days. This meant that the best part of the day was spent in the herb gardens that were under cultivation at the northern extremity of the encampment fortification. As he looked at the clouds, he was so grateful to the merciful gods of the Empire for sparing the lives of his companions—least of all himself. The gardens that surrounded him, in which he was at work, fascinated him.

Before he came to work in the herb garden, because of his reduced capacity for normal duties, he had no idea of the purpose for such horticultural activity within the boundary. The gardens were normally tended by local servants hired for this particular task alone. They were supervised by a head gardener, who was a most able horticulturist. The organization of Roman military medicine was an important responsibility placed on the general in charge of a legion. Medical care in the legions was not a matter treated casually. There were usually Greek physicians attached to the legion, and these physicians were ably assisted by legionary volunteers who had a bent for the profession. The Roman army was a frighteningly efficient organization, and the medical attention of the troops was no mean function. In addition to the physicians and their assistants, there were also some Greek doctors who, because of their lack of citizenship, would be civilian employees not actually on the strength of the legion. These medical functionaries come under the umbrella of the term *medici*. Medical orderlies combined their duties with those of ordinary soldiers, whereas the *medici* were known as immunes and were free from any other military duties. Some of the medical orderlies were known as *capsari*, getting their title from a round box called a *capsa*, which they carried with them on the march or on patrol while undertaking military duties. The *capsa* contained bandages and other medicines providing first aid.

The herbs grown were useful to the *medici*, as many were used as remedies for various complaint and the healing of wounds. Therefore, it was only the plants that had remedial qualities that were selected to be grown in the allotments set aside for them. Some of these included common herbs, such as thyme, sage, garlic, onions, and so on. But other remedial plants grown for their curative properties were: century, henbane, plantain (genus Plantago), and Saturn's wort (St. John's wort). Nightshade for atropine, poppy for opium, linseed for poultices, and flax for dressings were grown extensively. Pyrethrum and mandrake root was also under cultivation. The mandrake was cultivated mainly for its narcotic properties and was used extensively as an anaesthetic, together with opium. The *medici* numbered chemicals like arsenic, salicylic, thymol, among their medicines. Pyrethram and tannin were used extensively for cleaning wounds. The *medici* relied to a very large degree on cleanliness, as part of the curative functions. Special baths were provided for the sick, and the hospital quarters were maintained to the highest degree of cleanliness possible. The implements used for surgery were kept constantly immaculate, but this does not mean to say that they were not selective in choosing the casualties that they were prepared to treat. Soldiers who sustained combat injuries were either left to die or received medical treatment, after which, if they were incapable of continuing their career as active soldiers they were returned to Rome for normal discharge.

Those casualties that the *medici* felt were incurable were very often quickly put out of their misery. Orthopaedic footwear was provided for those who needed it. Invariably, after sustaining an injury in combat, those who recovered found themselves left with a slight lameness. The *medici* formed part of the First Cohort. The First Cohort had an extraordinary spectrum of headquarters staff, among who were found a variety of specialist and technicians, such as builders, shipwrights, clerks, ballistic experts, surveyors, glaziers, hydraulic engineers, farriers, veterinary surgeons, signallers, and, of course, priests. The priests were necessary for the spiritual needs of the legionary.

From time to time a detail of soldiers were instructed to collect and bury chests filled with scrap bronze and iron, and the burial of these chests and the date on which they were buried were properly recorded. Periodically, after some two or three years had elapsed, the chests were dug up on a rotation system. The motive for this burial and exhumation was to obtain rust and verdigris from the metals which the *medici* used as astringents and for the purpose of cleansing wounds. It had only been some two weeks earlier when Marcus was instructed to form such a detail, but he could not imagine at the time that the product of one of these expeditions, which had taken place two to three years earlier, would be used to cleanse his own wound. The importance of such an exercise did not register with him at the time, as it did not with many, many others.

Timius had not been able to visit Marcus or Lipsius Vegitus yet. The *medici* told him that they were too ill and too soon to receive visitors. Lipsius sustained an appalling wound when a barbarian's spear lodged itself between his shoulder blades. Fortunately, his lungs were not penetrated. Timius planned to visit them together with Cyrus on the first opportunity.

Many days elapsed before Timius was able to return to his normal duties, but his nightmares continued causing alarm and concern among his colleagues and immediate superiors. However, he was able to take the opportunity of carrying out his promise to Marcus by paying a visit to the household of Marcus' girlfriend, Sonita, in the village of Passau. He now regretted having been there and, although he looked forward very much to seeing Marcus and Vegitus again, he was apprehensive about telling Marcus the result of his visit. He had discussed it at length with Cyrus, who advised him not to disclose his findings to Marcus, but Timius felt that since he had given his friend a promise, he had kept his promise and he must tell him the outcome. Both Cyrus and Timius were eventually permitted to visit their two friends in the hospital quarters, and they were both full of joy to see that their companions Marcus and Vegitus were now well on the way to recovery.

Both young soldiers were now back on their feet and convalescing, but poor Marcus was left slightly lame as a result of his injury. He was therefore required to wear an orthopaedic sandal on his left foot to reduce the accentuation of his limp. The wound sustained by Vegitus would leave him considerably weaker too. Where he had been a tower of strength, his strength would now be that of the average soldier. Neither of them felt any regrets about what had happened because as they pragmatically viewed their slight misfortune, they consoled themselves with the fact that this was what they were paid for, and this was the sort of life they had chosen freely for themselves. Cyrus was able to inform them that he had heard about a list being drawn up, at legion headquarters, of those who were due for repatriation to Rome, either because of their slight incapacity to continue service or because of their length of service in the province. Three years in such a highly active frontier posting was considered the norm, and Cyrus had also heard, although he was not absolutely certain of it, that all four of them were listed for repatriation.

Marcus' expression turned rather sombre, although he was pleased to hear the news—or rumour, as he was corrected by Cyrus.

Very bashfully he said to Timius, "Thank you, old friend, I owe my life to you. If it were not for you, I would have been burned alive caged up in a wicker basket."

"Don't talk nonsense," replied Timius. "You would have done the same thing for me or anybody else for that matter, so don't mention it again."

Timius' expression now took on a look of anxiety because he had something to tell Marcus, and he didn't know how to broach the subject.

Marcus detected there was something wrong and asked Timius, "Is there something wrong, Timius?"

"No, nothing," replied Timius.

"Are you sure there is nothing bothering you?"

"Well, there is, really."

"Ah, I know what is bothering you," said Marcus with a slight smile on his face. "I bet you think that if we are to be repatriated soon, that I shall hastily have to arrange my marriage with Sonita so that I can take her back to Rome with me. And what really bothers you is that once I am married, I will probably ignore and forget you all. Let me put your minds at rest. When I get married, I will continue to hold the friendship of my three companions very dearly, and you will all be most welcome in my humble household if I am lucky enough to get one."

"Thank you very much," replied Cyrus. "That is very noble of you. But I don't think marriage will suit you and you should put the idea out of your mind completely."

"Stop teasing, Cyrus. You don't want me to get married because you will not have anybody to cheat at dice and knuckle bones."

"Timius and Vegitus were not cunning enough to provide you with the interesting opposition you require. That is really what is behind your thinking."

"Of course it isn't," replied Cyrus.

But Marcus brushed this aside and, quickly turning to Timius, he asked, "Were you able to go and see Sonita, Timius? I don't suppose you bothered because I only suggested that you go in the event of my death."

"As a matter of fact," Timius responded, "I did go, and that is what is bothering me."

"Well, then tell me about it," said Marcus impatiently.

"It took me some time to seek out her household, but when I did, I was most disappointed with her reaction. She appeared most disinterested to learn that you had been severely injured and, in fact, at the time she seemed more concerned and interested to be in the company of another young man who was also present. Sonita said nothing about seeing you again, and from her manner and the tone in her voice, I detected that she wasn't even bothered whether she ever saw you again. I am sorry, old friend, but this is the absolute truth I am telling you, and I am not fabricating any of it. Had it been otherwise, I would not have felt so apprehensive in broaching the subject."

Marcus seemed shocked for the moment and said nothing, but after a while he replied very matter of fact. "Never mind, I suppose it was expecting too much of her to continue her friendship with a mere Roman, and I don't think she would have ever married me. I suppose everything happens for the best. But thank you anyway for going along and seeing her and for reporting the truth to me."

Marcus had accepted the situation philosophically.

A month had gone by since the Fourth Legion's victory over the Sythian horde. Since then many small groups of Sythians had been seen along the frontier for the purpose of harassing the Roman commanders and their troops, but these were soon driven out of the area by General Julianus's policy of hot pursuit immediately they were spotted by the Roman patrols, more diligent now in their role of guardians of the frontier. Cyrus and Timius had also been on the receiving end of the hot pursuit policy. Both young men had fully recovered and were back to their normal selves again. They had been pursued through the encampment by sentries while trying to steal the sacrificial sheep and deer from the Temple of Mars, which had earlier on that occasion been offered to the god by General Julianus and the officers of the legion, in gratitude for their victory over their adversary. Cyrus and Timius thought it would be a good idea if these offerings could be put to better use than merely left to the priesthood to devour the roasted animals to conclude the religious rite. Cyrus felt this was most unfair and persuaded Timius that the god Mars, would be much more satisfied if the sacrificial animals were to be eventually consumed by the warriors of the Fifth Cohort. The result of this escapade meant the two young culprits serving out severe penalties. They were sentenced to one week solitary confinement, which neither took to kindly to, and they were now nearing the end of the second part of their sentence, which was two weeks fatigues, in the encampment cookhouse. The cookhouse fatigues, to which they were sentenced, they undertook in good spirit, mainly because it had given them the chance of acquiring additional food at each meal, primarily in the form of leftovers, which compensated for the dirty menial task of cleaning out the large and sometimes greasy cooking vessels.

The wound sustained by Vegitus left him rather shaken up and sullen, but Marcus tried to keep up the spirit of Veg by reciting to him comical poems that he had composed. Many poems referred to his own slight affliction, as he grew accustomed to his orthopaedic sandal that had become part of his attire. Without the sandal built up with extra layers of leather, with a difference of about three inches in height, to his left sandal, his limp would have been very pronounced. In addition to our four friends, there were many other legionaries, either fully recovered or very nearly fully recovered who also were casualties of the battle against Quingenta. However there was a slight apprehension among many of the veterans of the legion that this battle would be the first among many more in which they would be called upon to fight. The Sythians, they felt, were becoming more daring and less respectful of the Roman military machine. Many felt that the interpretation by the auguries of the past portending that the twelve vultures seen by Romulus represented the twelve centuries that the city he had founded would last. The veterans felt that the auguries could possibly be wrong and that the twelve vultures need not necessarily have represented twelve centuries, but indeed either twelve half centuries, or twelve quarter centuries, which meant that the city, and now city state, was almost nearing its doom. News had come to them that legions in other parts of the Empire were also experiencing increasing harassment from the barbarians beyond the frontiers and something that was more ominous was the news of the discontent that existed in Rome under Tiberius and in a few other provinces, much as Judea. The veteran legionaries were not comforted in the fact that the present generals of the army were not of the same calibre as men such as Germanicus and, in the past, Pompei, Sulla, and the great admiral Marcus Agrippa. They felt that unless the much needed leadership was given to Rome and her legions, the gradual decline of the once proud and invincible empire would begin. Certainly they all stood shoulder to shoulder and with the utmost loyalty to defend their respective eagle, but they felt that this alone was not enough. Things were getting a little out of control in Rome, and the eagle that symbolized their loyalty, which was, in fact a symbol adopted from the twelve vultures that Romulus had seen, were perhaps now coming home to roost. They trusted that their apprehensions would be found to be totally wrong.

The list of those selected for repatriation was finally published, and it contained two hundred and fifteen names of legionnaires. The list included the majority of those who had sustained severe wounds, injuries during the battle, and those who had contracted curable and incurable diseases while at Noricum. The list also included a few legionaries who had served over and above the three year python away from Rome and the Italian provinces. Cyrus, Marcus, Vegitus, Timius, and a newly acquired friend of theirs by the name of Protius Geminus were excited to see their names on the list. Cyrus had paradoxically asked Timius to vow to him that he, Timius, would not lead him into any more trouble before they arrived in Rome.

"You're a cheeky swine," said Timius. "You're the blighter who keeps getting me into trouble."

"Come off it," retorted Cyrus, "nothing of the sort. I only come up with the ideas, and you only tell me my ideas are good and then we follow them through. But if you rejected some of my ideas, then we would never get into trouble."

Before Timius could reply, Centurion Crassus came into the dormitory and called for legionary Timius Arbutus. Timius lost all colour from his face. He gazed at Cyrus, wondering what this was all about. For a moment he wondered if Cyrus had dropped him in trouble again without him knowing about it, and when Timius reported to Centurion Crassus, he was trembling slightly because it had also occurred to him that the centurion may have come to inform him that his name had been struck off the list of troops for repatriation. This was not so.

Centurion Crassus instructed him that he was to report to the headquarters officer after breakfast the following morning and that he would be properly dressed in full battle order. Centurion Crassus also instructed the rest of the cohort that they would similarly assemble on the Fifth Cohort square. All of the men in the cohort now began to wonder what was in store for them. They started mumbling and exchanging speculations among themselves. Perhaps they were to be sent out on a patrol, their first, since the vast majority of their colleagues had perished. The Fifth Cohort was now back to full strength made up of new arrivals sent from Rome. There were more relief troops on the way, and those listed for repatriation would not be able to leave until the relief arrived.

Timius reported to the officer of the day, punctually as instructed, and he was told to take up his position in front of the headquarters building, facing its central doorway. He was the only legionnaire standing in the small quadrangle in front of the building; there were two sentries on duty on the veranda. He was an absolute bag of nerves as he stood there, His stomach was uneasy and his legs were trembling. He had never been placed in such a situation before. It was not very long before he heard the regular rhythm of a drum beat approaching from his left. He gently turned his head in the direction of the sound and saw a drummer leading a cohort of troops. The small column was headed by the four cohort officers who were on horseback. As the cohort approached nearer, he recognised Centurion Crassus, vine staff in hand, marching on the left flank of the column. He also recognised many of his comrades among the ranks. The cohort marched up behind Timius. Then they were abruptly halted. Orders were given for them to turn left so that they faced the veranda. Timius was now right in front of them. He dared not turn around to survey the assembled troops lest he find himself in more trouble. The way he was feeling he did not particularly want to anyway because he was trembling so much that he very nearly urinated his pants.

The officer in charge of the cohort was a new arrival because officer Tetricus was still convalescing. The officer disappeared into the headquarters building and after some twenty minutes re-emerged followed by General Julianus and four other assistant senior officers. Timius felt his pants becoming wet through terror. The officer in charge of the cohort ordered the assembled troops, including legionary Arbutus, to attention, and after a moment General Julianus began to speak. Timius was shaking like a leaf to the point of sheer embarrassment because he could feel a slight trickle of urine running down the inside of his leg. He wondered if his comrades, smartly at attention behind him, had noticed this. They must have noticed that he was trembling. He could not give them the excuse later that it was cold because it was a bright fine morning; the air was still and warm.

"Noble Roman legionnaires you have been ordered to assemble here today to be present at, and to witness, the honour which is about to be bestowed on one of your loyal and courageous comrades. This honour of a citation has been passed to me to bestow on your comrade Legionnaire Timius Arbutus by command of the Senate and the First Consul of the Roman Empire. It gives me the greatest honour and pleasure to read out to you all the citation, after which I shall be equally honoured to give it to Legionnaire Arbutus."

General Julianus was then handed a scroll of paper, which he gently unravelled and read aloud for all to hear.

> 'I, Tiberius, Claudius Nero, First Consul of the Roman Senate and people, hereby register our appreciation and gratitude to Legionary Timius Arbutus of the Fourth Imperial Legion who on the sixth day of the sixth calends of July did act with valour above and beyond the call of duty, in that he was instrumental in alerting the commander of the Fourth Imperial Legion and its superior officers to the danger impending on the illustrious legion.
>
> It is our pleasure to also register that if on any future occasion the said legionary requires recourse to the highest authority in the Republic and Empire for whatever reason, unless considered trivial by his superiors, we decree that it shall be granted to him.
>
> Signed and sealed TIBERIUS CLAUDIUS NERO
> First Consul

Young Timius was speechless from what he had just heard, and he hesitated a moment when he was ordered to receive the citation from the general. However he did so, halted, smartly saluted, and accepted the honour. An expression of appreciation crossed the face of the general, as he said to Timius, "Soldier, you deserve this award with the utmost worthiness.

You did a tremendous service to all of us and have set an example to all your comrades. I wish you a happy and successful career in the army."

"Thank you, sire," replied Timius hesitatingly. He saluted and marched back to take up his position behind the officers of the Fifth Cohort.

During the remainder of the day, at least when he had the opportunity to do so, Timius read and re-read the citation. Also, throughout the day and for many days that followed, his companions wise-cracked and had fun with him over the event. It was all in good spirit. His comrades in the cohort, and indeed many of those he had occasion to meet or pass when going about his duties in the legion, offered their congratulations to him. He was extremely modest in accepting their good wishes and was bashful at the witticisms of his companions.

Marcus teased him by saying, jokingly of course, "Hey, Timius, that citation will be the first step to you becoming Caesar."

"Don't be silly," exclaimed Veg. "He is not a member of the aristocracy. His veins lack the essential royal blood. In fact he isn't even a Patrician like us, he is a mere Plebeian."

"What difference does that make?" asked Marcus.

"It makes a lot of difference," answered Veg. "To become Caesar, noble blood must flow through his veins."

"We'll soon fix that," said Cyrus.

"How can you do that?" asked Marcus.

"Well, the next time we are in Rome we'll sneak up to the royal household on Palatine Hill and then sneak into their wine cellars."

"What will you find in the wine cellars?" queried an amazed Marcus.

"Well, think man, think. If we can steal a few jars of that rich royal wine, we could forcibly make our friend here drink it and, after a few jars of it, his blood would soon be royal and noble; sufficient enough anyway to be considered Caesar's heir apparent! What do you think of that idea, Timius?" asked Cyrus.

"Not much, and this time I am not agreeing with your idea!" he said pointedly.

"Don't you want to become Caesar?" asked Cyrus.

"No, and if I did I would make you all my slaves."

"Oh, I'd love that," said Veg.

"So would I," exclaimed Marcus. "Think of all the orgies and the banquets we could all partake in."

"You'll do nothing of the sort," responded Timius. "In fact, I would have you working your fingers to the bone if I ever became Caesar," he joked.

The witty conversation made Timius remember some of the things his mother used to say to him. She always implored him when he was a little boy to try and keep always clean and tidy, and when he asked the purpose of it she would say, "Well, if you are clean, tidy, and well behaved, you might grow up to become Caesar."

He never believed this because he knew he could never really keep himself clean, tidy, and well behaved like other boys of his age. So there was no likelihood of him ever becoming Caesar, either through his past actions or to any present or future acts.

CHAPTER XXI

Labitur aetas.

OVID

Time glides away.

THE COHORT WAS by this time three weeks' march from Rome. They had left the Danube frontier nearly five months ago, but the pace of the return march was of a slow measure. There was no urgency for the return to Rome, and in these circumstances, it was necessary that several minor repairs be carried out on the highway. The maintenance work, although of a minor nature required frequent short stops and since many of the troops of the cohort, including the senior officer and senior centurion, were those who had recently been wounded in skirmishes and head-on clashes with the barbarian enemy. The senior officer was Tetricus, and the senior centurion was Crassus. They had both discreetly chosen the right moment, after the cohort commenced the march from Mediolanum to approach Timius, to express their heartfelt thanks for helping to save their lives. But the subject was never referred to again because it was an accepted duty of a legionnaire to go to the aid of a comrade of whatever rank and fight for his comrades' life even though his own life may be in danger. Therefore, the gratitude expressed by the two senior ranks of the cohort was of a very personal nature, and young Timius understood completely.

For most of the march, Timius took his place alongside Protius Geminus, and during the many weeks that passed, his friendship with Protius grew to the point where it equalled his friendship with Cyrus, Marcus, and Lipsius. He discovered that Protius Geminus was the offspring of an aristocratic family. His father was a senior tax collector in Roman suburbia and was a patrician. He learnt that Protius' father had planned for his eldest son to enter an administrative vocation, but Protius agreed to the plan on the condition that he could spend the first few years of his early life as a legionnaire. His father was not at all enthusiastic with this idea, and argued that the years spent in an administrative training institution, or even in a situation where he could receive private tuition, would be of more value to the young man. But Protius insisted that experience as a legionnaire would make him a much shrewder and able administrator, although his father recognised that the real reason that attracted him to the legion was the young man's spirit of adventure, to which he finally succumbed. He also recognised that there was the possibility that once his spirit of adventure had been satiated he would apply himself to an administrative job far more diligently. Protius was therefore not a legionnaire as a means of earning a living. He had the opportunity of entering the army as an officer cadet, but rejected this. After all, his whole childhood had been spent in the company of members of the patrician class, and the young man was keen to know how the other half lived.

He was intelligent enough to realize that the attitudes of the patricians and the plebeians differed, and it was important to him to acquire an insight into the attitudes that were extant across the class spectrum. The role of a common legionary, he felt, would provide him with such an experience. His family were landowners also, and like all newborn children in the family, he was presented with a symbolic silver spoon, very soon after his birth. It was customary among the wealthy classes that this presentation take place, because it was a belief among them, and one very strongly held, that the presentation of a silver spoon to a newly born child would perpetuate a life of wealth and well-being. This certainly did happen, because it could be argued that it was only the wealthy that were able to continue life at the level to which they were accustomed. On the other hand, the presentation of a silver spoon to a plebeian child or to one of a much lower class was pointless because it would have eventually meant the total disappearance of the plebeians and the lower classes.

The silver spoon would guarantee the acquisition of wealth, either through personal accomplishment or otherwise, and it had no real significance. Protius Geminus had very kindly invited his comrades to his father's villa, if and when they were given some leave on their arrival at Rome. Lipsius Vegitus declined the invitation because he was naturally keen to call on and stay with his own family. But Cyrus and Marcus accepted the invitation most enthusiastically. Timius declined for other reasons. He wanted to return to Velitrae and pay a visit to his benefactor, the inn keeper, Gaius Apuleius.

His companions tried desperately to persuade him to change his mind, but this he would not do because he was eager to return to his old childhood hunting grounds on the outskirts of Velitrae. He was very nearly tempted to accept the invitation, but refrained from doing so because he had convinced himself that a few days spent with the inn keeper, with the opportunity to walk around his old haunts he frequented as a child, would be more satisfying to him. He convinced himself there was no other underlying reason, but deep down he knew there was, as the last letter he had received from her was nearly a year old and he wondered if Tricia would still be around. If so, she would be one person he would very much like to see. Throughout the march he had made up his mind to call on her and then changed it again almost immediately. He was completely undecided, because he knew not what kind of reception he would receive and indeed whether it would be convenient. He even thought that it could be a case of him being the absolute intruder. All kinds of thoughts went through his mind when he thought about her, and even now he was totally undecided, but he had made up his mind to return to Velitrae if the opportunity arose, and this he would do at all costs. After all, it would be worthwhile to return even if it meant that he would be able to place a handful of flowers on his mother's grave.

The arrival of the cohort at Campus Martinus, a cantonment on the southern outskirts of the city, was uneventful. Their first few days in the campus were spent in personal selection and reorganization. This entailed medical examination by Greek physicians and orthopaedic experts in order that the fittest could be selected for continued service in other parts of the Empire. Those that required some further measure of rehabilitation were selected for posting to a legion, or smaller military establishment within the more peaceful provinces of Italy.

Many were discharged on health grounds and offered large gratuities for their resettlement. Timius, Cyrus, Marcus, Vegitus, and Geminus were selected for further service abroad. They were listed, together with many others, to join the Ninth Legion in the African province of Cyrenaica.

The province of Cyrenaica was one of the more peaceful provinces of the Empire, and troops that had spent a period the length of a three year python, or more, guarding the more troublesome frontier provinces were given postings to those more peaceful provinces as a means of relief and rehabilitation. It must be said, though, that even in these provinces, military discipline and training was maintained at the highest level. There were moments when his companions were anxious about Marcus, because although he walked with a limp without an orthopaedic sandal, the limp was hardly noticeable when it was worn.

But it was some while before the orthopaedic experts decided that his slight affliction would not be detrimental to continued service in the North Africa province. Naturally, they were overjoyed that their companionship could remain in tact, and when they received their accumulated salary, three quarters of which was compulsorily withheld by the authorities to be later added to their terminal payment on termination of their service, they excitedly planned the easy expenditure of their reward. They were even more excited when they had been advised that the authority had granted them leave of absence from military duties for the period of one month. Cyrus and Marcus considered that it would be an impolite intrusion for them to accept the invitation of Protius to spend the whole of their leave with him and his family and after a lengthy discussion they amiably agreed that three weeks would be more acceptable. Cyrus came up with an idea for the fourth week.

"Hey, Timius, are you going to spend the whole month at Velitrae?"

After contemplating the question awhile, Timius replied, "Well I have not thought about it very seriously, and after all a month is a long time, but on second thoughts not long enough to be away from the company of you rogues. What did you have in mind?"

"Well, if you don't want our company, you can stay away, we don't want your company either." Cyrus joked.

"That's right," retorted Marcus, "you can keep right away from us. We'll probably be better off without you anyway."

"Come along, now, I was only joking." Not knowing whether Cyrus and Marcus were joking. "But what were you going to suggest we should do?"

After studying their expressions, Cyrus replied, "Well, a thought did occur to me. It would be rather nice if we three were able to meet up here in Rome and then go up to the old school at Larcia and see how some of our old masters and Praetorian officers are getting on. That is, if any of them are still there now. After all, we each promised them that we would return to see them one day, and god alone knows how long we will be in Cyrenaica, and by that time who knows they might be dead or retired."

"I think your idea is marvellous," Marcus said excitedly.

"So do I" added Timius. "Let's do that."

They all agreed and immediately arranged to meet on an appointed day at mid-morning in the courtyard of the Pantheon.

No sooner had Cyrus, Marcus, and Timius agreed on their arrangements to visit Larcia than Protius very apprehensively came up with a suggestion that was to alter their plans.

"If you fellows do not mind," suggested Protius, stuttering slightly, "I have given the matter a little thought, and please don't feel that I am going back on my word to you Cyrus and Marcus, but I think it would be only good manners for me to go to my home and family on my own for the first week and arrange with my parents, after seeking their permission, of course, for both of you to come and stay. I could then meet the pair of you in a week from now, at the same appointed place that you have discussed with Timius."

He looked at both Cyrus and Marcus enquiringly, wondering what reaction he would receive. They did not reply immediately and Protius again hesitantly tried to quality his earlier statement: "I am sorry to upset the plans, but I have been away from home for over three years, and I am sure you fellows will understand that I should at least be on my own with my family for the first week, where we could enjoy a few days of privacy. My mother and father are very generous and hospitable, and I don't really want to abuse their kindness by arriving with my two army friends, especially after a lengthy absence.

Cyrus and Marcus were quick to respond this time, and in unison they replied. "Of course we understand." Cyrus went on to say, confident that he was speaking for Marcus as well, "It would be selfish for us to impose on you and your family from the very first day of our vacation, so don't worry about it, old boy, if you would still like us to come and meet your family and stay a while with you, we would love to and, as you have already suggested, we could meet you at the Parthion in a week's time."

"I am glad you agree," said Protius, a smile and an expression of relief crossed his face.

Cyrus then suggested—and the suggestion was directed at Timius—that the three of them should make their way directly to Larcia and try to spend their first week in the company of their old tutors and officers. Timius had not made any hard and fast plans with anyone so he amicably agreed, stood up, and smartly pointed in the direction of Larcia. As he did so, he hailed, Larcia, here we come." The call was repeated by Marcus and Cyrus.

With the permission of the assistant on duty in the foyer of the main building of the institution, our three companions were now standing in front of the closed door of the principal's office. Cyrus hesitantly knocked on the door. There was no immediate reply, and each young man looked at the other wondering what changes had occurred, not only in the routine of the past, but also in the staff. Cyrus knocked again, and they now heard a weak voice summoning them to enter. Marcus opened the door and entered the office, followed by Cyrus and Timius. Standing behind the desk, as though he was expecting them, was the principal, Artimeses, but as he recognised his visitors he remained breathless for a while. When he regained control of himself after the astonishment of the moment, with both hands he beckoned them forward.

"Come in, come in," he joyfully cried out in a slightly uncontrolled voice. "I am so very happy to see you."

As they approached his wooden desk, he held out his frail hand to shake theirs in turn. They noticed he was still upright in his stature, although he had grown very grey. Lines of old age were beginning to show on his face, and his once strong handshake was weaker.

"He remembered them clearly, and as he shook each young man's hand he said, "I am very pleased to meet you Venicius, Piritus, and Arbutus. I am absolutely thrilled that you have been able to return. How have you three been keeping? What are you doing now? Where have you been?"

The questions seemed to be rapid and endless until Cyrus was able to explain, helped by his two companions, the details of their vocation. But Cyrus was quick to add that none of them had received any promotion from the ranks since they joined the legion.

"Ah!" exclaimed Artimeses, "That's because your superior officers have obviously found you out just the same way as we found you out, here. You are too mischievous, and a mischievous nature rarely gains the attention of one's superiors when they are looking for people to accept responsibility."

The three young men laughed at this remark. Marcus then enquired. "Is Paulo still here?"

Timius added, "What about Carpus and Lictus, are they still here?"

"Now, young men," said Artimeses, in a slightly admonishing tone, which was underlined with a modicum of humour. "They are still Praetorian Officers, you know, and they would still like you to refer to them as such and address them accordingly."

"Allright, sire," replied Marcus, "We didn't mean to be disrespectful, but are they still here?"

"Yes, indeed,", replied Artimeses and continued, "with the exception of poor Praetorian Officer Lictus who died from a severe lung complaint last year—may his soul rest with the gods. If you young men will seat yourselves for a moment, I will ask one of the assistants to go along and fetch Praetorian Officers Paulo and Carpus."

The three young men sat down, and in answer to an enquiry by Cyrus, Artimeses explained that the military authorities had now become more flexible in their attitude to staffing such institutions as this one at Larcia Praetorian officers seconded for service with the institution were permitted, if they so elected, to remain on the staff until such time as they chose to retire, on the condition that by doing so, while they retained their Praetorian officer rank, they would have to accept a substantial reduction in salary Some officers, namely Paulo, Carpus, and Lictus, had opted to remain at Larcia primarily because it provided them with a much more settled life than that which they would experience actively serving with the Praetorian Guard in Rome.

It was worthwhile for them to take a reduction in salary in order to gain a settled and routine life. It was also policy now that selection to the staff was not wholly made from senior members of the Praetorian Guard, but experienced men from legions in general could also be selected, or directed, into such posts, depending on many circumstances that surrounded the individual's qualifications. Many had been selected on disciplinary grounds, in that it afforded the authorities with a form of exile from the legion for those that had committed acts warranting this penalty.

They did not have to wait long before there was a knock on the door, followed by Artimeses invitation to enter. The assistant opened the door and ushered in Praetorian officers Paulo and Carpus. An expression of complete astonishment crossed the faces of the two officers as they saw seated in front of them Cyrus, Marcus, and Timius. The three young men were quick on their feet to shake the hands of their former officers. Paulo and Carpus seemed to have become slightly shorter in stature, and both men were now greying rapidly. Carpus had developed a slight stoop, which was very noticeable to Timius as they all exchanged greetings.

Again the questions from the two officers were thrust at the young visitors, fast and furiously. Their answers were also brief and incomplete in the excitement. Artimeses intercepted the excited conversation by placing on his desk an earthenware jug filled with red wine. "If I may say so, friends, I do believe that this is an occasion for a minor celebration. Please take a beaker each and let us all have a drink for old time's sake."

Joyfully, they toasted each other and drank a toast to the future, and the conversation that followed became rapid. Artimeses again interjected and said, "I was only saying a few moments ago to our three visitors that it is strange, is it not, that the only ex-members of this institution that ever seem to visit us are those who had gained a reputation for mischievousness while they were here with us. What I am trying to say, friends, is that it is only the rascals that ever return."

He paused for a while and then, directing the question to Carpus and Paulo, he asked. "Why is this so? Have you any idea?"

"Ah, well," replied Paulo, and continued, "I think it is only the rascals that only come along here to see us because they are trying to escape from the penalties, for something or other, they have been up to. Am I right?" he asked the visitors.

The three young men laughed and assured him that it certainly was not true in their case. They had not been up to any tricks from which they were escaping punishment.

"Well, then you surprise me," said Paulo, good humouredly.

"My theory is much more mundane," interrupted Carpus.

"What is it then?" chipped in Artimeses.

"Well, principal, there is an old, old, saying that a villain always returns to the scene of his crime and, as I see it, these fellows are the said villains who have returned here to the scene of their past crimes." With this last statement, uttered by Carpus, they all burst out laughing.

"What a logical explanation you have put forward," proclaimed Artimeses, nodding his head in approval as he spoke.

The next hour or so was spent reciting their past experiences to their hosts, and the principal and his two subordinate officers were proud to hear of the citation awarded to Timius, but were very sorry to hear of Marcus's slight disability. The three young men asked their host if they could remain at Larcia for one week, and if he could give them permission to find bed spaces in the dormitories in order to accommodate them during their stay. The old principal would not hear of this, nor would his officers. After discussing the matter farther they decided Praetorian Officer Carpus should have the pleasure of accommodating them because he had two spare rooms in his quarters, which they could use. Praetorian Officer Paulo would have obligingly put them up after some rearrangement in his household, because he had his in-laws living with him, but Carpus insisted on playing host to the young men as he was better placed to do so; he had a wife and two grown up daughters whom he was sure would be pleased to help in the preparation of meals and to make the visitors generally comfortable.

At the Carpus household, the three young men were introduced to his gracious wife and to young daughters, Lygia and Julia. The two daughters were excited that they were to have three young noble legionnaires as guests for a whole week, and there was an immediate rapport when they all met. Lygia, the elder daughter, aged nineteen, was a very slim and dainty young woman with long dark flowing hair. Cyrus thought she was perfectly beautiful, whereas her younger sister was better developed, although of about the same height as her sister. Julia was very attracted to Marcus from the outset of their meeting. The younger daughter had dark hair also, but styled and somewhat shorter. After the first evening's meal, Lygia and Julia wandered off to the veranda with Marcus and Cyrus, ostensibly to describe to them the horticultural properties of the little plants that hung in baskets above the balustrades.

Timius wondered how they could really study the plants by the light of the oil lamps but, never mind perhaps their hosts were only trying to be hospitable. He remained seated opposite Carpus at the table, and after a little while Timius despondently revealed to Carpus that the treasured bulla Carpus had given him when he left Larcia was now in the hands of the barbarians. He apologized profusely for loosing it because it was something he treasured, and he went on to assure Carpus that he had no means of avoiding its confiscation.

"Do you know, old friend, I treasured it more and revered it much more than the eagle of the fourth under which I served, and I hope one day, if I ever become a general, I will have the opportunity of marching my legion against those Sythian scoundrels, if only to recover my bulla."

Carpus laughed. "Don't worry about it, Timius; don't worry about it, I understand. It was not your fault, and you could not help it." He sat with his chin on his chest for a moment, and when he raised his head, he burst out excitedly, "How would you like to come down to the latrines with me tomorrow evening?"

Timius burst out laughing, and Carpus laughed too, after which Timius replied, "I would love to. Have the flies in the lime pit grown any bigger? They should be the size of flying elephants now."

Again they laughed. "Yes, said Timius, "I'll come with you; in fact, I'll come every evening."

"Good, that's settled then, it will be good to have you among my team again."

As an afterthought, Timius added, "But what will Cyrus and Marcus do while I am with you at the latrines?"

"Don't worry about them, young friend," Carpus assured him. "You take it from me, from the look in their eyes, and from the look in my daughters' eyes, both will be too wrapped in one another's company to worry about us. Didn't you detect there was something going on among the four of them during the meal. They seemed to pay no attention to what my dear wife and you and I were talking about."

The following day, and for the rest of the week, Timius attended the latrines with Carpus, as arranged, and the routine had not changed nor had the appointed hour for cleaning changed. Memories of the past came flooding back into Timius's mind and as they did so, he felt how silly he had been, crying over a broken music pipe. Timius had insisted that he would not stand alongside Carpus to assist him in his supervisory task, but that he would actually assist the young boys in emptying the buckets. The young boys were amazed to learn from Carpus that his companion had spent over ten years doing this routine chore in all weathers.

Cyrus, Marcus, and Timius spent the week visiting the library attending two evening meals in the assembly hall and also attending physical exercise and military exercise sessions. They were able to add advice to the officers and pupils of their first—hand experience in military tactics and physical activities. Needless to say, they also visited many of their boyhood hide-outs, namely the lake and the orchard at 'Pastimes'. Cyrus and Marcus spent most evenings in the company of Lygia and Julia, their new found girl friends, while Timius was happy to enter into discussions and relate some of his experiences to Carpus and his wife Lucia as she busily engaged herself doing needlework placed on her lap.

When the week came to an end, all three visitors were reluctant to leave. Marcus and Cyrus were downright miserable about leaving and had arranged, with much persuasion from Lygia and Julia, to return for the last week of their vacation before returning to the legion. Carpus agreed to this, although they both realized that this would mean a slight disappointment to Protius, in that they would limit their visit to his parents' household for a maximum of two weeks. Timius felt that it was prudent to decline the invitation from Carpus to also return for another week, and made the excuse that he had other business to attend to. He felt left out of it a little, and although they were still the greatest of friends, after all, he had his private life to lead and so did they, and in order that their friendship could continue to survive, it was essential that each respected the other's wishes.

CHAPTER XXII

Et tua et mea interest te valere.

CICERO

It is of importance to you and to me that you should be well.

THE CLOUDS WERE scudding across the sky as Timius walked across to the courtyard of the inn known as the *Latium Rest*, which was owned by his friend Gaius Apuleius. He was not sure whether Gaius was still the proprietor, but if the business had changed hands, he might have the problem of claiming his few meagre belongings that he had left in the care of his friend. He had said farewell to his two friends, in Rome early that day, although he had waited in their company on the stone steps of the Parthenon until the arrival of their mutual friend Protius Geminus.

Each vowed to the other to keep out of mischief, and Marcus asked Timius whether, if the opportunity arose, he would go along and pay his respects to the pottery manager, Dodimus, and his family during his stay in Velitrae. Timius promised to do that. Cyrus was a little anxious about his young friend because Timius was unable to assure them that he would have somewhere to stay when he arrived in Velitrae. Protius too picked upon Cyrus' anxiety. He very generously gave Timius the address of his family, telling him that if he was unable to find accommodation, rather than return to the severe surroundings of the Campus Martinus, he would be welcome to come and join them all for the rest of his vacation. Timius thought this offer most kind and unashamedly thanked Protius, assuring him that he would never forget this generous offer.

When Timius entered the inn it was busy with many customers eating and drinking contentedly. He was approached by a manservant, and when he asked the manservant if he could take him to the proprietor, Gaius Apuleius, the servant's response was indicative to Timius that the proprietorship of the *Latium Rest* had not changed hands. This was a tremendous relief to the young man. Gaius was astonished, but needless to say, overwhelmingly delighted to see his young friend again. They very hurriedly exchanged pleasantries before Gaius took Timius down to the kitchens to see Thengus. Thengus was also very pleased to see him and was quite amused when Timius offered to assist in the kitchen scullery.

"It is very kind of you to offer, but, young man, you are here as a guest, and I am sure the noble proprietor would not wish his guest to undertake menial tasks in the kitchens."

"That's quite all right," replied Timius, "I have plenty of practice doing this sort of thing in the army, and besides it will keep me in trim for when I return to the legion. Indeed, if I insist, I am sure Gaius will not mind."

Both men looked at Timius rather quizzically but understood the simple logic of his suggestion, and Gaius, after a moment, hastened to ask him, "How long will you be staying, young fellow?"

"Well, Gaius, with your permission, may I rent a room here for three weeks, because I have a further three weeks vacation ahead of me?"

"Three weeks," replied Gaius, rubbing his chin with his right hand. "I am sorry but I don't think I can afford you accommodation for the full three week period, as much as I would love you to stay, and I do not have to tell you how very much we all would welcome your company. Unfortunately the busy week is approaching. Members of the various guilds will be arriving and staying in the township while they attend their annual meeting. During the third week, there will be no room at all because we are absolutely fully booked up. Even now, I can only offer you one very small, extremely sparsely furnished, room. I have only two such rooms vacant. Anyway, don't worry about it, because we might be able to think up something during the next two weeks."

Timius thought about it for a little while and then replied, "Gaius, I shall be most grateful to stay even just two weeks here, and please think nothing of the state of the room. As long as I have somewhere to sleep, that will satisfy me enormously, because it will give me the opportunity to spend some moments both in your company and that of Thengus. Please don't worry about the third week. Two weeks will be quite sufficient, because I feel it would be the height of ingratitude if I imposed on your kind hospitality further."

"Fine, that's settled," said Gaius in agreement. "Come along, let me personally take you to your room."

By the time Timius seated himself at a small table in the dining room of the inn, the evening was drawing to a close. It had taken him some time to unpack his bags and to complete his ablutions after his long journey. He had also nearly dropped to sleep when he lay awhile on his bed to rest before taking the meal. He sat alone at the table while he had his bread and broth. He studied the flickering flame of the oil lamp that was burning brightly in the middle of the table. The seat opposite him was vacant, and he felt a trifle lonely because the snatches of conversation he could hear from the other customers, at the tables around him, made him feel lost, because he had no idea of the subjects they were discussing.

He finished his broth and leaned back slightly in his chair to enjoy the remains of the wine. As he did so, a man appeared at the doorway to the restaurant and looked around as though he were surveying some kind of strange scene. He was a tall man and well groomed, wearing a white robe with a broad red stripe down one side. Across his shoulders was a small green cape. He was obviously looking for a seat and spotting the vacant one at Timius' table made his way over and asked Timius if he might join him. Timius agreed and the stranger sat down and waited some minutes for the waiter to attend him. During this period, Timius was able to study the man. He noticed that although the man was well groomed and that his clothes were clean, it was obvious to Timius that this state was not normal or easy for the stranger. There was something indicative to Timius that the man had been able to keep his dignity at some expense and difficulty. The man's eyes portrayed a state of loneliness. Timius was sensitive enough to detect that the stranger, who tried to act in a dignified manner in the company of other customers who were obviously men with careers and businesses, tried to give the impression to any onlooker that he was totally accustomed to this kind of atmosphere.

Before the man ordered broth made basically from sheep's trotters, he had placed his hand into the side pocket of his robe and fumbled with something momentarily, obviously checking to see that he had sufficient money. Timius knew that the sheep's trotter broth was the cheapest meal on the menu, and the man also ordered the cheapest wine.

"Will that be all, sir," asked the waiter.

"Yes, thank you, that will be all," replied the stranger, adding, "I am not very hungry tonight.

Timius felt this was not true because even though there was chattering going on around him, his hearing was sensitive enough to hear the man's tummy rumbling, which indicated he was ravenous. The manner in which he drank the broth, without any bread to soak into it, was proof that this was so. He drank thirstily from his beaker of wine and, as he placed the empty vessel on the table, Thengus approached to talk with Timius.

"Well, young man," said Thengus, "have you enjoyed your meal?"

"Very much so, thank you, Thengus." "The broth was delicious and the bread was crusty and fresh. It just melted in my mouth."

"You disappoint me, young man," said Thengus admonishingly.

"Why, why do I disappoint you?" enquired Timius.

"Well, I thought after so many years of army food you would have at least tried the delicacy of the night. The stuffed quails are absolutely delicious. I can vouch for that and, as you may well know," he added jokingly," the *Latium Rest* is famous throughout the Empire for this delicacy. You can eat some more food surely, a young strapping fellow like you?"

"Well, I suppose I could, but I didn't want to appear greedy among all these noble people."

"Never mind about them," said Thengus, "I'll ask the waiter to bring you a dish of stuffed quails, and I am sure you can wash it down with some good wine. Stay where you are. I'll have it sent out to you."

Timius nodded bashfully in agreement. From the corner of his eye, he noticed the stranger looking at him. There was an odd sort of expression on his face which prompted Timius to ask Thengus to send out two platefuls of the delicacy.

"Ah, you want two, now, do you. I thought I would make your mouth water."

"Yes, I would like the other helping for my friend here."

The stranger was amazed to hear this and tried to tell Timius that he did not wish to be included, but Timius brushed aside his opposition. When Thengus had gone, Timius knew that he had placed the man in an embarrassing situation, especially when the man said, "Please, young friend, don't include me. I have had quite sufficient to eat, and if I have a heavy meal I will to be able to sleep well.

"Of course you will," Timius responded, "and besides I would like company while I am enjoying the delicacy; and since I am paying for it, I insist that you join me."

"That's very kind of you, young man. I am most grateful for your generosity."

They both enjoyed the meal thoroughly.

The stranger introduced himself as Cornus Albius and alleged that he was a merchant's representative who had come to Velitrae on business at the behest of his employer. The untruthfulness of this statement became apparent when he asked Timius, during their conversation, whether Timius could advise him of any place in the town where he could make himself comfortable without paying the expense of a bed in a room. Timius was quite confused with this request and did not quite understand what the stranger was saying, until he explained that he was really looking for a storehouse, or some such facility, where he could sleep on straw or some empty sacks. He would even be obliged if Timius could tell him of any comfortable spot in the town's parks where he could sleep under the stars, his excuse being that he never slept comfortably in a bed provided by a rest house. Timius could not help him because he was preoccupied with his own theory concerning Cornus's strange attitude. Timius was convinced that while the man tried desperately to give one the impression of an air of well-being he was, nevertheless, concealing the true situation. Timius had tremendous admiration for the man's attitude and understood completely. Here was a man who, he was convinced, had nothing in the world, not even friends or relatives, but who was trying hard to keep his dignity.

If the truth was known, this man was probably unemployed. Timius thrust himself on the man's privacy by offering to ask the inn keeper, Gaius Apuleius to rent him the only other vacant room, for which he himself would pay. Cornus was reluctant to accept this offer, but inwardly he was eager for a helping hand. Timius also went on to say to him, as obliquely as he could, that if the man was not satisfied in his employment as a representative, he would be willing to introduce him to the pottery manager, Dodimus, whom he had never met himself, the following morning, which would allow Cornus to ask Dodimus for a job. Cornus only half-agreed to both suggestions because he was too sensitive to give Timius the impression that the young man's conclusions were absolutely correct.

They parted company to their respective rooms that night, both knowing inwardly that they understood each other.

"I shall be forever grateful to you, Timius, for what you are doing for me, and let me say that whatever the future holds, I trust earnestly that I shall some day be able to do some small service for you. Thank you kindly and goodnight."

Timius rose early the following morning and enjoyed a hearty breakfast of coarse wheat biscuits soaked through with warm milk. This was followed by a healthy portion of fruit juice, and it was while he was sipping the fruit juice that it occurred to him that if he was to pay a visit to Dodimus accompanied by his new found destitute friend, Cornus Albus, he would need to furnish an excuse to validate his visit. Certainly he would convey Marcus's compliments to his ex-employer and benefactor, but he would need to have something more material to take with him. A fair-sized jar of one of the best and most palatable wines would be the answer. Yes, this is what he would do, he would buy a jar of wine and take it with him, and this would be his excuse.

He quickly checked the remains of his money and found that he was reasonably sound financially, after which he hastily made his way to the market place of Velitrae. It was not long before he was proffered what was allegedly the smoothest delicacy ever produced from the local grape by a wine merchant who did not need any lessons in salesmanship. Timius bought the jar of wine. He made sure the stopper was firmly in the bottle before he slung it over his shoulder by the cord affixed to it. He made his way hurriedly back to the *Latium Rest*. On his way he passed a small jewellers, and it occurred to him that since it was the real reason for his return to Velitrae, although his hopes of meeting her were undoubtedly forlorn, however, he felt if he did have the opportunity of meeting his young friend Tricia, it would be rather thoughtless of him not to present her with a little gift.

In the jewellers shop he selected a gold bracelet which comprised a chain to which were attached consecutively three small coins minted in the reign of Tarquinius Superbus, the last monarch of Rome before the inception of the Republic. This item of jewellery was the best he could afford. There were many others there he would have liked to have bought, and some were most exquisite; so was the price. He was now ready to keep his appointment with Cornus Albus.

He entered the dining room of the inn and looked around to see if he could see him, but he was not there breakfasting among the other residents. He went up to the room that Cornus had occupied the night before, but there was no response when he knocked on the door. He went back to the dining room and enquired of one of the assistants who knew nothing of the gentleman, but the second assistant he asked, informed Timius that the gentleman he was enquiring after had hurriedly left that morning without even ordering a morsel of breakfast. Timius was absolutely disappointed that somebody whom he had offered kindness to had left without even saying farewell to him. Anyway, he thought, he would put it down to experience, and never again would he be taken in by first impressions. There was nothing for him to do now but to make his way to the pottery in the hope of seeing Dodimus.

Timius did not hurry, but made his way to the pottery quite leisurely, absorbing all the trivia and other places of interest on his way. When he arrived at the pottery, he asked an officious looking gentleman if he cold be given the opportunity to see Dodimus. Timius had timed his arrival to coincide with the hour of mid-day, assuming that at this hour the activity throughout the pottery would be somewhat ebbed.

"Do you have an appointment to see the manager?" asked the official.

"No, I'm sorry I have not," replied Timius apologetically.

"Well, what is your business?"

"Well, I have a message to give to him personally from a very old and close acquaintance of his."

"Very well, come with me. He shouldn't be too busy at this time of day to see you."

"As the official said this, he led Timius along a short corridor to the manager's office. When they entered the office, Dodimus was browsing through some official papers, and the official interrupted him by introducing the young visitor. The official did not know the young man's name, but merely explained to Dodimus that the young man wished to see him personally.

"Very well," said Dodimus to the official, "you can leave us."

Dodimus then turned to Timius and said enquiringly, "Well, young man, what is it you would like to see me about?"

"Well, sire, I am sorry to intrude on you—"

"What did you say your name was?" asked Dodimus, "I didn't catch it."

"Did you say your name was Issimus of Lissimus? By what name are you called?"

Timius replied, "Sire, there's an old saying in the legion; *'People may call me what they like, so long as they don't call me late for pay'* my name, sire, is Timius Arbutus!"

This remark tickled Dodimus and he burst out laughing.

When he composed himself, he said, "I'm sure I have seen your face before."

"It is possible you have, sire, because I have had this face a long time."

Again, Dodimus burst out laughing, but when his humour subsided he continued, "If you have come for a job, I am afraid I cannot offer you one, because the last vacancy I had in our offices was filled this morning by a man who claimed to have had a reasonable amount of sales experience in Rome. The only other vacancies I have are for the assistants to the potters, and the pay for those jobs is very low, but if you are willing to take one of the jobs we will be very happy to have you work for us."

"Timius was dumbfounded with this offer of work which he was obviously unable to accept. He explained the purpose of his visit, and Dodimus apologized profusely for being too presumptuous. He handed the jar of wine he had bought for Dodimus to him. He insisted on opening it but was persuaded not to do so by Timius. Timius reminded him that the wine was a present for both him and his family from Marcus Piritus. However, Dodimus did break open a smaller jar of wine, and during their conversation, they both enjoyed its contents. After Timius had completed his business with Dodimus he made his way towards the park near to the gorge. Timius sat on the marble bench, alongside the pathway nearly opposite to the approaches to the gorge. He was undecided whether to go into the gorge and while away a few hours and look over one or two interesting spots to help in cherishing his childhood memories.

He remembered that he had not paid a visit to the last resting place of his dear mother. This he would do first thing the next morning. He drove off the temptation to go to the gorge with the excuse to himself that there were several days over the next two weeks where he would have the opportunity, weather permitting, to do so. He decided to sit where he was and relax. Whether his friend Tricia would come along or not he did not know because it was over three years since he visited this spot where he had last seen her. He was sure that her early evening walk routine would have, by now, changed. She would be three years older and either betrothed or married to someone.

Whomever she was betrothed or married to Timius could be sure that he would be a person of good standing. After relaxing for nearly three hours, during which time he enjoyed the spectacle of several swifts darting about catching the midges that were leaping high into the sky from the surrounding bushes and shrubs he decided that he would pay her a visit. He felt that there would be no harm done in calling on her, assuming of course that she was still at the address she had given him, if only to say hello and pay his complements. After all, he promised he would, should he find himself in the vicinity again. Besides he had a present—the bracelet he bought—to give her, if only for old time's sake.

The door of the Roussus's home was answered by a woman in her late twenties, who was very smartly dressed. When Timius explained that he had come to see the young maiden by the name of Tricia, he was asked to remain where he was on the step of the veranda, so that the woman could go along and fetch her. While Timius stood there for what seemed to be ages, he became very apprehensive and nervous and felt like calling the whole thing off. His nervous state reminded him of the time in Noricum when he was presented with his citation, but in this instance there was no compulsion for him to remain. However, it was not long before Tricia appeared and when she saw who it was her eyes and mouth opened wide in astonishment.

"Timius," Tricia greeted him, "I didn't expect it to be you."

"Have I disappointed you?" he asked bashfully.

"No, no," she stuttered, "certainly not. I am just very surprised and overjoyed to see you again. Would you like to come in?"

"No, because I don't wish to intrude," Timius replied and continued, "I was just passing by, and thought it would be pleasant to stop and offer you my compliments."

"Thank you," replied Tricia, "but you will not be intruding. Please come in."

When they entered the house Timius was introduced to her mother. She had a very kind face; stout and probably in her fifties. The woman who answered the door was Tricia's elder sister, Sonia. Tricia's mother asked him, "Will you be joining us for supper, Timius?"

"No, ma'am, as I explained to your charming daughter, I was just passing, and I thought that it would be in order to offer her my compliments. After all, it is over three years since we met, and that also was only in passing."

"Do you have another appointment?" asked Tricia.

"No, I do not have another appointment. I am on vacation from the legion and time is my own for the next two weeks and . . ."

"Oh, then you must stay for supper," interrupted Tricia's mother, and I will ask the servants to lay another place at the table. Supper will be soon, so you will not have long to wait. I am sure you must be hungry?"

"Thank you kindly, ma'am, he replied, "and I sincerely hope I am not imposing."

"Come along, Sonia, and we will see you, young man, at supper," Tricia's mother said as she and her other daughter left the room.

"Timius and Tricia sat down and, to make conversation, he asked, "Are you keeping well and happy?"

"Yes, I am, very well, thank you," she replied.

"Then your husband must be treating you kindly."

"Husband!" exclaimed Tricia.

"Yes," said Timius, "If you are not married, you must surely be betrothed?"

"Neither," she responded, "I am still independent and mistress of my own destiny."

"You surprise me," said Timius.

"Do I?"

"Yes, because I would have thought a charming and lovely person like you would have been married long ago."

Tricia paused a moment and then said, "My father has tried to get me betrothed on two occasions to young men he thought suitable, but I refused to hear of it. They accused me of being only interested in books and studying."

"That sounds interesting, pray tell me what do you study?"

"Well," Tricia replied, "you might think it very silly, but I spend very long hours studying the religions and cultures of the people who live in our Eastern provinces, and I find the subject fascinating. From time to time I also study the adopted religions of our glorious homeland, but these are not as interesting as the Eastern religions."

How enchanting, he thought, and he told her so. "Someday I would love to discuss this more fully with you, as there is so much you could teach me about the subject because religion does not particularly interest me."

"That's probably because you haven't read sufficient about religion and the part it plays in our lives every day: anyway enough of this. What was life like at Noricum?"

"Oh, not much, you know, just the usual life in the legion. It was rough at times and sometimes very cold, but apart from that I haven't much to complain about. But changing the subject and before I forget—I have something for you."

Timius handed her the bracelet. Tricia was overwhelmed with it, and as they were called in to supper by her mother, she was studying the coins closely, having placed the bracelet around her wrist.

CHAPTER XXIII

Sentit animus se vi sua, non aliena, moveri.

CICERO

The mind feels that it moves by its own force, not by that of another.

WHEN THEY ENTERED the small dining room, Timius noticed that the table had been laid with place settings for six persons, and before he could even begin to wonder who else was dining with them that night, two men smartly dressed in their togas entered the room from the antrium, busily engaged in conversation. The elder of the two men was tall and sturdily built and balding rapidly, whereas the younger man gave the impression that he held down quite a high position in state administration. Tricia's mother gently ushered Timius towards the two men to introduce them. The elder man was Tricia's father and the younger her brother-in-law, Sonia's husband, whose name was Tetrianus Felux.

After a few perfunctory remarks they all seated themselves, and the meal commenced. It was nothing elaborate but one that formed a routine menu in their diet. During the meal Timius learned that Tetrianus, who was older than him by several years, was employed by the local municipality in an administrative capacity. The way he tended to brag about his responsibilities gave Timius the impression that he must surely be one of the very senior members of the municipal administration. The conversation during the meal centred on family affairs and local current events. Most of the conversation took place between Messrs Roussus and Tetrianus Felux. The women intermittently discussed some intricacies connected with needlework and tapestry and some personal matter concerning close friends. Timius felt like a duck out of water because he could not join in or contribute anything to the conversation, until Tetrianus turned to him and asked, "Did you say you were a legionary, friend?"

"Yes," replied Timius between chewing a mouthful of sweetmeat.

"What legion are you with?" asked Mr. Roussus.

"I am not with any legion at the moment, sire. In fact I am at the moment in transit. I have these last three years been with the Fourth Legion and am shortly to be transferred to serve under the eagle of the Ninth."

"I see," said Mr. Roussus. "Were you in Rome with the Fourth Legion, or elsewhere?" he asked.

"No, I wasn't in Rome, sire, I was stationed in Noricum with the Fourth Legion, and they are still there."

"Ah! I see. Did you enjoy the life in Noricum?" he asked.

Before Timius could reply, Tetrianus interrupted by saying, "Of course he did, father-in-law. You should know that. Haven't you heard all the stories that are told about the legionnaires serving in the provinces?"

"Yes, I have heard some. But are you trying to tell me there are others?"

"Yes, of course there are," explained Tetrianus as he went on to explain: "these fellows in the legion are well known to enjoy themselves thoroughly, and for the enjoyment they receive tributes and monthly donations from the Emperor's office, not to mention some of the loot they pick up. I am told they also spend most of their time flirting with the local girls. And many of them, believe it or not, marry the local harlots," he added disdainfully.

Mr. Roussus replied, with a mouthful of food, "I can't say I blame them." He swallowed the mouthful and then continued, "We must remember that these fellows joined the legion to shirk family responsibility and responsibility to the community."

At this moment Tricia spoke out quite indignantly: "With respect father, I think you and Tetrianus are most unkind and very wrong in your assumptions. I think there is something you both need reminding of strongly," she continued by saying, "If these fellows whom you speak of so disdainfully did not offer their services to Rome and the Empire in the manner in which they do, you and I and thousands of others throughout our glorious empire would not be enjoying supper in the security and peace of mind that we are today. These fellows, after all, give their whole lives unselfishly for our sake. Let's not forget that."

"I see we have upset young Tricia with our comments," said Tetrianus.

"Come along, my child, you must not take what we say too seriously. We do appreciate the service they give to us and, as I said earlier, we must not blame them if they do partake of some pleasures during their arduous duties along the frontiers. Is your father in the legion?" Mr. Roussus asked Timius.

"No, sire, he is not! He was a legionnaire for many years but was killed on the German frontier when I was a boy."

"Oh, I am sorry to hear that," he said. "It must be very hard on your poor widowed mother, unless of course she has married again."

"No, sire, my mother also died of an incurable disease when I was a child."

A strange silence hung over the household for awhile until it was broken by Tetrianus who asked Timius in a much more amiable way, "Will you be staying long in Velitrae, Arbutus?"

"Yes, I will for almost another two weeks."

"I am glad to hear that," he replied and enthusiastically continued, "you must come to the local amphitheatre with us one day to watch the gladiatorial and other sporting events that take place in the arena, which I am sure you will thoroughly enjoy. You do like sports don't you?" he asked.

"Yes, I do," Timius replied, "but my passion for sports is in athletic events."

"You surprise me; I thought soldiers took a great delight in being spectators and participants, in blood-letting events.

"No, that is not true, Tetrianus," Timius responded. "Perhaps some do, but the majority do not—at least, not in my experience."

Timius felt that he could have extended the conversation by informing them of his activities on the athletic field during his service with the army. He could have told them that he had been selected and held down the position of cohort foot messenger and also describe to them the many occasions when he had represented the Fourth Cohort in the track events during athletic meetings held within the legion. Moreover, he could have told them that he was considered to be one of the best long distance runners with the legion, and had won many trophies in this event. But he felt that if he did this, he would only be bragging about his athletic prowess, so he refrained from doing so. Instead, in answer to their questions he informed them that at the end of his vacation he would be proceeding to Cyrenaica, where the Ninth Legion was stationed. He told them that he would probably be away for some three years or more. When Tricia heard this, the expression on her face became very solemn and to avoid her true feelings being noticed, she quickly interrupted, "well, the next time you come and see us, don't forget to bring us some baskets of some of those delicious pomegranates for which, I believe, the provinces of Africa have a very good reputation.

"Yes, replied Timius, "of course I will. In fact, I will hire a donkey from the port of disembarkation to carry the load which I shall bring."

Tetrianus interjected by saying, "Once he gets out there he will forget all about the pomegranates."

"Why would I do that?" questioned Timius.

"Well, old boy, didn't you know that the town of Cyrene is simply swarming with beautiful Egyptian girls who all claim to be related to Cleopatra?"

"No, I didn't know that," Timius responded.

After they enjoyed the last of the wine and returned to the atrium, the rest of the evening was spent in general conversation, during which the family learnt a little about their new friend in their midst. He did not tell them very much because he felt that there was not very much to tell. After all, he felt his few experiences of life would be of no interest to them and besides they were really only concerned with affairs of a very parochial nature. Anyway, he did arrange to meet Tricia the following afternoon so that they could walk in the grounds of the park before each departed in their respective directions.

*

Back at the Campus Martinus, Timius had still another six days Vacation ahead of him, but there was no alternative other than to return to the camp in Rome, because firstly his friend the hotel proprietor, Gaius Apuleius, was unable to furnish him with a room for more than two weeks, and secondly, he had very little money left. He did not have sufficient to pay for accommodation at another inn for even one more night. The jar of wine, the bracelet, and the unexpected cost of his benevolence to the stranger Cornus Albus had depleted his funds considerably. He had no regrets though because he felt that the enjoyment gained from such expenditure was well worthwhile. Permission for him to stay at Campus Martinus was granted to him by the senior Praetorian centurion, who was in charge of day to day administration of the camp. But there was a condition attached to it. Timius was required, like other men using the camp for lodging purposes to partake in camp fatigues from sunrise to sunset. For their labour they received free lodgings and food. He accepted this situation cheerfully and while he was now busily engaged in sweeping up the courtyard surrounding the headquarters building, his thoughts wandered over the events of the past few weeks, and in particular the many happy moments he had spent in the company of his new-found girl friend, Tricia. There were other moments he also remembered that were not pleasant but he realized that he must always take the rough with the smooth, and he would not concern himself too much over those less happy moments. He had had the opportunity of meeting Tricia almost every day of his vacation after his first visit to her home. Each day was spent walking through the nearby park or sitting under a shady tree deep in discussion of various subjects that were of interest to both of them.

There were also two occasions when she accompanied him to the cemetery, where he was able to lay a small bunch of flowers on the remains of his mother's grave. Her grave was now only identified by a roughly hewn stone onto which was inscribed her name. Tricia had promised that she would make a point of visiting the cemetery and placing flowers on the grave on his behalf at fairly regular intervals. She would pluck the flowers home-grown in her family's lovely little garden.

Part of her interest was to tend to the variety of shrubs and flowers that grew in their garden, and when Timius was shown around it he expressed his deep desire to have one day in the not too distant future a home of his own and a garden, but he added, "I know nothing about gardening."

"Never mind," Tricia replied. "Once you start growing flowers and shrubs you will learn many botanical intricacies of keeping a lovely, well-tended garden."

"I'm not so sure about that, but would you show me how to begin with it. You could also pass on to me some tips. I promise to be a good pupil," he said.

"I would love to do that. When do you hope to achieve that?"

He paused a moment before replying, "Do you know I haven't given it much thought. In any case I shall need a fair amount of money to purchase a house with a garden of my own. So it will really mean continuing in the army for a few more years until I have accumulated enough savings and increased my terminal gratuity until I am in a position to afford it. But while I have been speaking to you I have made up mind that this is what I shall do, come what may. My whole aim now will be to save and get myself a small property just so that I can have the opportunity of having you visit me for lessons in botany."

"What a wonderful aim, Timmy," she replied. "Please don't ever lose sight of it."

"I shall not, don't worry," he replied. "But what about you would you keep your word?"

"What do you mean?" asked Tricia.

"Well, by that time you will probably be married to some young man who is most worthy of you and in the process of raising a happy family."

"That might be so," she replied, "but the way I see things at the moment, it is most unlikely. So please do not refer to that subject again."

"Very well, I will respect your wishes, and I promise to be a good pupil."

"Good!" she exclaimed, and added, "as long as you are not bumptious like that brother-in-law of mine, Tetrianus."

"Oh! Tetrianus, laughed Timius. "He amuses me. He is a very clever man, but it's a great pity that he hasn't really seen anything of life. One can only pity his sort."

"Pity him? I despise him!" she exclaimed.

"No, you must not despise him, because," Timius continued, his type are only bumptious because of their parochial attitude to life, but once they start seeing the real world, they soon loose their big headedness."

"No, I cannot agree with you," she said, "and may the gods be thanked that men with his kind of attitude to life are not administrating the provinces and colonies. If they were, they would sure to rebel against Rome. As it is they are not happy to be subjected to Roman repression."

"Repression!" exclaimed Timius. "Why do you use that word? After all Rome has given them civilization, peace, and prosperity and at some expense, might I add."

"Yes," she replied and continued, "that it so. They have done it inhumanely. Rome has deprived them of their freedom and introduced to them some of the bad traits of Rome itself."

"I don't understand. Please explain what you mean," queried Timius.

"Well, for a start Rome has deprived them of the free practise of their religion, and in order to achieve her aim Rome has oppressed them inhumanely, and I am sure it is people of the likes as Tetrianus that have been the perpetrators of this policy."

"No, I cannot agree with you, Tricia, my dear friend. My view is entirely different, and I beg to differ with you."

"Well, what is your view Timius?"

"I am not an expert on the subject, but I have always believed and been led to believe that there are two things that are sacrosanct to the low Roman attitude to life. You find running right the way through our civilization and the civilization we have taken to other unfortunate people around the world are firstly our attitude towards the human spirit. Rome, as far as I know, is primarily concerned with humanity—hence the system of jurisprudence that we all hold with the highest regard. Secondly, though equally important in my view, is tolerance of religion."

"Tolerance of religion!" she exclaimed. "What nonsense! Do you not realize there are many who have held strong religious views and have been executed for their views?"

"No, I cannot believe that," Timius said, shaking his head. "I cannot imagine for one moment that their religion had anything to do with it, because there are three principles by which Rome measures her religious tolerance. Do you know what they are?" he asked.

"Yes, I think I do," she replied then asked, "but you tell me what they are?"

"Well, firstly, the foreign religious cult must not upset any of the truly Roman cults. Secondly, they must not possess any political undertones. They must be politically acceptable. Thirdly, they must be morally desirable. If a foreign cult did not satisfy these conditions, and if those that practiced these cults did so to a degree of fanaticism; those people would be regarded as undesirable toward the stability of Roman administration. Therefore, each foreign religion must satisfy these tests, and if they do, they are acceptable and, as you well know, many foreign religions have been adapted and adopted as our own."

"Tut-tut," she said, "this is all very well in theory, but it doesn't work out in practice."

"Well, my dear, I cannot argue with you further, because I do not know enough about the subject to do so."

Timius had had many such discussions on religion and politics with Tricia, and he remembered each conversation clearly, as though they were taking place at the present time. They both found themselves extremely attracted to one another, but until the next time they intended to meet, he must devote some time to reading up on these subjects so that their conversation could be more interesting. He had only taken two meals at her home and declined the invitation to accept any more, especially after the occasion when he was insulted by Tetrianus. Tetrianus had asked him where he was staying in the town, and when Timius had told him that it was at the Latium Rest, Tetrianus had replied. "Could you not have picked a better place than that? The Latium Rest hasn't got a very good reputation around here. It is reputed to be the cheapest lodging house in Valitrae and frequented only by those men of ill repute."

Timius was livid with the remark and lost control of his temper. He blurted out in anger, "If the people who frequent the Latium Rest are disreputable then thank god they exist, because if you are an example of the well bred and better type then I would sooner spend my time in their company than yours. Besides the proprietor is an old friend of mine and an extremely hospitable man, and may I add, he is a man of very good character, and how dare you say otherwise. Moreover, I could not afford anything else, and if I could have done so, I would not care to seek accommodation in any other place where I would be compelled to associate with your type."

Timius got up from the table, excused himself, thanked his host kindly and walked out. Tricia ran out after him and was full of praise for the way in which he had answered Tetrianus's accusation.

"It's about time somebody put him in his place. My god, I have tried on a number of occasions, but he is too thick skinned for any of my remarks to penetrate. Good for you, Timmy. You're a person after my own heart."

"After a moment Timius spoke his thoughts aloud, "I'm sorry about that Tricia. My behaviour was disgraceful. It was ungracious of me to behave like that, especially since Tetrianus was not the host. Please apologize for me to your dear mother and father. It was wrong of me to lose control in that fashion."

"Oh, don't worry, did you not see the glint in father's eye when you spoke. I am sure mother and father were on your side."

As a result of this Timius was too embarrassed to accept any further invitations from Tricia's parents.

Timius was in the camp dining room on fatigues for which he had been detailed early that morning. The mid-day meal was over, and the small detail he was with had been ordered to scrub the floors of the big hall. He was on his knees, busily scrubbing away with coarse cloths, when he began to realize how unsightly his appearance must be. His hair was dishevelled, and he was sweating. His hands and arms, up to the elbows, were full of grime and likewise were his knees. The bottom of his fatigue tunic was also damp and grimy. He thought how different it was from the last day he met his dear Tricia. On that day, he had smartened himself up and had gone to meet her near the tiny shrine to Juno situated at the entrance to the park. He had made a real effort to make himself especially presentable. She was a little late coming that day and while he waited he studied the beautiful frescoes which comprised of vine leaves surrounding impressions of satyrs and bacchanals. While he was studying these frescoes he could hear, coming from a distance, a haunting voice, singing a love song. The singer repeated the same chorus of the song over and over again, until Timius found that he also was able to hum the melody. When he looked over to see who it was that was singing so beautifully, he discovered to his surprise that the music was coming from an empty building that was in the process of being prepared for the arrival of new occupants. There was a hive of activity around the building, and it appeared to Timius that the singer was working on his own and keeping himself company by singing.

Very soon the one he had waited for joined him. As he scrubbed the floor he could not forget how very lovely she looked. Her small kindly face looked fresh, though a little melancholy, caused perhaps by the thought of his impending departure. That was how he wished to interpret it anyway. Tricia was wearing a pale brown dress, tied at the waist with a purple cord, and he noticed the hem of her dress was cut into a zigzag fashion, which was edged with purple. Her delicate silk stole was the same colour as the cord tied round her waist. She looked an absolute picture, and he only wished there and then that they could go away somewhere together and forevermore. This could not be so because life is not a dream, but a reality.

That evening as they walked through the park, Tricia had asked him if he had noticed many changes in Rome. He informed her that he had not, simply because he had not spent very long in Rome and had certainly not toured the city at all, however much he would have like to do so.

He remembered asking Tricia, "Why do you ask? Are there many changes to be found? If there are, I would not be able to tell the difference because I do not know Rome at all."

"Well, I just wonder, Timmy. I was really wondering if there was any change in the attitude of the people of Rome."

"What makes you wonder that?"

"Well, as you are aware no doubt, the general of the Praetorian Guard, Lucius Elias Sejanus, is now in overall control of the city."

"No, I did not know that," was Timius' reply. "But does the fact that he is in charge make any difference?"

"Well, yes. Apparently he has collected together all his friends and supporters and placed them in important positions in order that his policies would receive the utmost support. He has also ruthlessly disposed of all critics and opponents of his policies, and it is rumoured that many of the ordinary people of Rome are fearful of expressing themselves freely on topical issues, lest they offend Sejanus or his henchmen."

"But what about Tiberius?" asked Timius. "What is he doing for Jupiter's sake?"

"Oh well, he is a crusty old man who has retired to the Isle of Capri and has delegated his responsibilities of First Consult to Sejanus. The way things are going it is feared that Sejanus will succeed him if he should die, and if that happens Rome will regret the day that Lucius Elias Sejanus was granted the powers of a delegate to Tiberius. Rome will be ruled by a tyrant and our history, unfortunately, is marred by the deeds of tyrants."

"I see your point of view," said Timius.

Tricia had become rather carried away with her emotions and replied sternly, "It's not much good you seeing my point of view, if only you fellows in the legion knew what was going on and tried to keep yourselves abreast of current affairs, you would all be able to do something about it."

Timius has been surprised by her sudden outburst and, turning to her, said, "What can I do about it? I am only a lowly legionnaire."

She hesitated a moment and then said, "Forgive me, I am sorry for the explosion of my feelings, but I did not mean you personally. I really meant the legions as a whole, but then I do suppose that the ordinary soldiers in the legions are not aware and are never really made aware of Roman current affairs. They are only there to do a job and to do it well."

"That is so," agreed Timius. "But tell me, are you not in favour of our present constitution? Do you not like the senate's authority being proclaimed through a *Princeps?*"

"No, I do not," she replied. "I am a Republican at heart, and I shall always be a Republican."

"Well, we have a Republic now," rejoined Timius. Tiberiuis, after all, is only the First Consul and so was his predecessor, Augustus."

"How naïve you are, Timius? After all, the First Consul of *Princeps*, as you prefer to call him, is only another name for Emperor and Rome now prefers to refer to her colonies and her provinces as the Empire, and you cannot dispute that."

"No, I'm afraid I cannot."

They stopped on the path along which they were walking and Timius turned to face Tricia. As he did so he clasped her hands in his and looking into her eyes, he said, "Tricia I like the stuff you are made of. You are full of spirit and a noble Republican at that."

She laughed a little, replying as she did so, "Don't be silly, you must forgive me for getting emotionally involved in politics."

He then looked down at her hands and noticed that she was wearing the bracelet he had given her and after a moment with a slight frown on his forehead, he said, "I think I make a mistake giving you that bracelet."

"For goodness sake, why?" she replied.

"Well, the coins of which it is comprised were minted during the reign of Tarquinius Superbus, and now that I know your feelings toward monarchy and kingship, have I not made a mistake?"

"No, of course you have not," she replied. "Do remember," she continued, "the kings of Rome were expelled over five hundred years ago, and though I hold Republican ideals, I do not live in the past. I live very much for the future. That is how you must be also."

"Very well, dear friend, very well," he agreed.

That evening, after their walk, he asked if he could go to her home to apologize personally to her mother and father for his outrageous behaviour that memorable night.

They were both very understanding when he did so, and informed him casually that Tetrianus had received notice that his application to the foreign office, in the Civil Service, had been accepted, and that he was excitedly looking forward to service in a foreign country. They also informed him that their daughter, Sonia, was busily making preparations to accompany him and her mother added, "So you see, my dear Timius, after a spell of foreign service, he might well return to us a changed man and have much better understanding of the work at large."

*

The dining room fatigue detail had finished scrubbing the floor of the main hall. They were now in the last stages of the task, in that they were scrubbing the entrance. Timius found that he could not forget his beloved Tricia, and when he thought about the last moments he had spent in her company, tears welled in his eyes. He remembered her asking him if he would ever return to Velitrae and if he did to promise that he would not hesitate to go and see her.

"I give you my word, my dear, I promise faithfully that unless something unforeseen happens I will come and see you. I can assure you also that I will never forget you, nor will I ever forget all these many happy days and moments I have spent in your company."

Tricia then asked him if he would communicate with her and, as she did so, she spoke very tenderly.

"Yes I will, of course I will," he assured her, "but please try and understand that I am only an ordinary soldier, and we do not have all the facilities that the much more senior members of the legion have of communicating with our friends and loved ones."

Her face took on an expression of complete tenderness as she asked, "Do you consider me your loved one, Timius?"

To which he replied, "Yes, I do, I do indeed."

They kissed each other gently before he departed, as Timius promised again that he would return.

As Timius returned to his dormitory the significance of the attire Tricia was wearing on their last evening together suddenly occurred to him. The purple embellishments to her dress signified purity and chastity, and the thought of this added to the love and tenderness he now felt towards her.

CHAPTER XXIV

Annui fugiunt.

OVID

Years flee.

THE MEN WERE sat in groups around small camp fires, warming their hands and chatting among themselves. They were on the quay at the small port of Brindisium, and the sun had set some two hours earlier. Timius, Marcus, Cyrus, Lipsius, and Protius were talking among themselves rather more excitedly than the others in the small group of which they were part. It was to be their first experience on board ship. Each had by now got over the emotional experiences of their vacation, although Cyrus and Marcus did have periods of depression. Both felt they were very much in love with Praetorian Officer Carpus's daughters, Lygia and Julia, respectively. The one hundred and fifty men, which comprised the relief party, on its way to the Ninth Legion in Cyrenaica had earlier paid their respects in a short form of worship to the god Neptune at the little temple situated near to the quayside. It was practice for all those sailing abroad from Brindisium to honour the god Neptune prior to their departure. After their act of worship they had all partaken in an evening meal and were now merely waiting to board the three ships tied alongside the quay. They had been informed that they would sail at around midnight when the tide turned because the ships used the current of the ebb tide on which to begin the voyage. Time passed very quickly, and before long the relief party were aboard the ships with their packs, armour, and accoutrements.

Each ship carried fifty fully armed soldiers. In addition their was a small crew of regular seamen and among the crew was a seaman trained in the art of medicine. He was known as the *capsari duplicaris*. In addition to the crew, there was a complement of twenty sturdy slaves who were used as oarsmen. The oarsmen were not expected to row the boats throughout the voyage because their routine was broken by the hoisting of a stout sail from the main mast of the ship and also by relief oarsmen selected from the soldier passengers. The object of using the soldiers on board for this task was not primarily to relieve slave oarsmen but as a means of providing them with exercise throughout the voyage that was considered essential for their fitness.

In addition, the soldiers were used on galley duties and for the general cleanliness of the vessel. This included scrubbing the decks daily. Within the cramped quarters of the ship it was necessary that the soldiers were kept busy throughout the day because sometimes a voyage could last weeks on end. The voyage from Brindisium to the port of Cyrene, weather permitting, would take three weeks. During these three weeks Timius and his companions experienced the arduous task of an oarsman confined to a ship of the Roman navy for months on end. How lucky Timius thought he was to be a legionnaire. He felt that had he been a slave, subjected to these conditions, he would have attempted to escape even though it meant death if recaptured. Soldiers who had been used to the freedom of the countryside during their marches from garrison to town, or visa versa found it difficult to abide with such cramped conditions and at the end of their three week voyage and their eventual landing at Cyrene, disembarkation took place not with just a sigh of relief but a tumultuous cheer that they were back on *terra firma*.

The relief troop found on their arrival that the climate had turned warmer to that which they had been used to in Italy. The change was gradual, but now it was noticeably different. As the troop marched through the town of Cyrene, small crowds gathered along the pavements of the streets to cheer them on. It would seem to a newcomer that even the locals of this distant province of North Africa were delighted with the sight of a troop of Roman legionnaires. This was very true here in Cyrene because it was one of the least troublesome provinces of the Empire. On arriving at the fortified garrison the newcomers had found that the geographical layout of the fortifications, the planning of the buildings, and the general routine and training programme were no different to any other garrison.

The garrison at Cyrene was surrounded by wheat fields and fruit orchards, and the only difference here in the routine of the soldier in comparison with the routine at the Danube garrison in Noricum was that turns were taken by each and every soldier in tending to the fields and orchards. The Roman soldier had been trained in farming methods in addition to his military tasks and those of general engineering. Farming duties only ever took place in garrisons which geographically permitted farming to be carried out on an extensive basis. The time of the soldier was fully occupied from dawn to dusk and there were very few free days during which he could relax and make use of the very few facilities that the town of Cyrene offered. Some areas of the town were strictly out of bounds to the soldier. It was an excursion into such an area that Timius and his companions soon found that their two years stay in Cyrenaica was brought abruptly to an end.

During the past two years, Timius had received and had replied to a total of eight letters from his beloved Tricia. Each letter reduced the distance between them, and it was plain to him that he was now very much in love with Tricia. Her letters indicated clearly to him that her feelings toward him were reciprocal. In her last letter she had described to him her annual pilgrimage with the family to Rome and the Temple of Diana. She had assured him that everything would be all right for him, because she had consulted the Sybil who had foretold the future favourably. This cheered him up enormously. Both Cyrus and Marcus had also communicated frequently with their girl friends at Larcia, but unlike Timius, they had planned marriage on their return. The plans for their marriages gave to them renewed impetus to saving as much money as possible.

Arranging a marriage was, in their situation, rather easier than it would have been for Timius, because both Cyrus and Marcus, during their stay at Carpus's home, had become very familiar with the family. Timius on the other hand could not really consider himself on full familiar terms with the Roussus household. Besides the Roussus household had given him the impression that their daughter Tricia would be best advised to cultivate a growing friendship with a young man of patrician birth. This was not so with Carpus and his wife, Lucia, as they were an ordinary plebeian family. Timius knew that the only way he could bridge this class gap, in order that he might ask for the hand of Tricia in marriage, would be by the nature of his character alone. He had neither money nor position in life to assist him. His ability, education and reliability were the only characteristics he could offer. He had to place a profound reliance on his character and personality. If successful he would be privileged and honoured to live the rest of his life in the company of his beloved Tricia.

Timius had now taken his turn at the oar because on this particular night the wind had dropped completely which meant that the large sail of the ship was hanging limp from the main beam of the mast. It was just gone midnight, and he knew that he would not be relieved of the duty for at least another four hours. Each stroke of the oar dipping and rising was done in unison with the other oarsmen, some slaves, some soldiers, to the steady beat of a drum played by a crew member who was seated on the lower deck facing the oarsmen. The steady rhythm had to be properly timed by the drummer to take account of any swell or roughness on the surface of the water that might have an effect on the torque of the stroke. Timius had been rowing only a few moments when he decided to ask the drummer, who appeared to be a well-travelled man, what things were like generally in Syria.

"Wonderful place, soldier, it's absolutely wonderful there," answered the drummer.

"Oh, I am surprised," said Timius, having to speak above the swishing of the oars. "We were told that service in Syria was always regarded as some kind of punishment posting. So tell me the truth, please, what's it like there?"

"I've already told you," retorted the drummer. "It's a wonderful place." After a moment he added, "When you get there you will find there is one blade of grass every hundred miles."

Timius's face fell with this remark, but the remark caused the other oarsmen to burst out laughing. This remark sounded a little bit ominous to Timius, but then, he thought, how could this be so when the Sibyl had foretold that things would be all right with him, as he had been assured by Tricia.

The Roussus family had made their annual pilgrimage to the Temple of Diana, and on these occasions the family stayed at a rest house near to the city centre, and it was customary for them to spend five days in Rome. One day was spent at the Temple where Mr. Roussus would offer sacrifices to Diana, and the remaining days enabled the family to visit the variety of shops and stalls in the forums, the theatre, and the library. If there were major events taking place at the amphitheatre, such as chariot racing, gladiatorial contests or other displays, they would make a point of visiting the circus. The family enjoyed their annual visit to the city, although Tricia often inwardly prayed that no event would be programmed for the amphitheatre during their visit, because the events which took place were rather repulsive to her.

After the usual sacrifices at the temple, on this occasion she had asked permission of her father to proceed to the adjoining sibylline vestry of the temple to seek the sibyl's prophesy. Naturally her father remonstrated with her, but after some persuasion by her mother, he relented and, moreover, to the extent that he offered her twenty sesterces from his own pocket. She knew that the cost of the service provided by the oracle would be much less than twenty sesterces—approximately fifteen—because her friend at Velitrae had informed her of this.

But then she thought that perhaps inflation would have increased the cost of the oracle's service. She hoped it had not because with the remaining five sesterces she planned to have the lobes of her ears pierced a second time. So that she could wear two earrings in each ear lobe. She had noticed that this was now fashionable among Roman women, and since she had a passion for gold jewellery, Tricia felt that it would be a most worthwhile way of spending the remaining money. Perhaps she might even be able to persuade her father to buy her another set of gold earrings more fashionable than her other sets. Tricia's mother accompanied her to the vestry while her sister Sonia decided to accompany her father to the nearby library. He was interested in reading the latest publication of the last work of Cicero.

As they entered the vestry there was a tablet affixed to the wall, just inside the door, requesting visitors to shut the door and to place their money, fifteen sesterces, in the receptacle provided. The person seeking the prophecy was also instructed to go to the middle of the small hall and stand perfectly still until called on to speak by the sibyl. Before doing so they were asked to ring a small bell to draw the attention of the sibyl to their presence. The little hall was dimly lit and neither Tricia nor her mother could see the motives or frescoes incised into the walls and into the pillars that supported the roof of the chamber. Her mother remained near the doorway and sat down on a rough wooden chair that was provided. Tricia stood still and patient in the centre of the chamber and, as she did so, her eyes began to get accustomed to the dim light which was provided by two oil lamps on the walls to the left and right of her, two directly in front of her and one suspended some three feet above her head. In the dimness of the chamber, she could now discern fairly clearly that the lights which had been placed on brackets on either side of the wall to her front allowed one to see what appeared to be a raised platform. Partly drawn across the platform were two yellowish curtains which did not meet in the centre, but which in fact left a gap in the middle at a slight distance from which she could see the outline of a raised marble seat. After about some ten minutes, and just as she was about to give up her venture, to invoke the sibyl, she noticed in the gap between the two curtains a slim figure of a women whose face she could not see very clearly sat on the marble seat. In a few moments the figure began to speak, and Tricia was taken aback by the sound of the sibyl's tone of voice.

It had a metallic-sounding tone, but the diction was clear. The metallic tone of her voice was obviously caused by the acoustics of the chamber.

"Have you paid your donation to our goddess Diana?" the sibyl enquired.

"Yes, I have," replied Tricia.

"Then tell me, what can I do for you, my child?"

"Great oracle I come to seek your prophecy regarding the future of my loved one."

"Where is your loved one?" was the response from the sibyl.

"He is in service to the Emperor, the Senate, and the Roman people in the province of Cyrenaica."

"Is he the commandant of a legion and if so what legion is he serving with?"

"No, great sibyl, he is not the commandant, he is a legionary with the Ninth Legion."

"Then I am sorry, dear child," replied the sibyl, "but unless he holds the rank of a dignitary I cannot foretell his future, or the future of any individual legionary."

Tricia was disappointed with this reply; thanked the sibyl, and began to withdraw despondently from the spot where she was standing towards the exit. As she did so the sibyl spoke again, saying, "Stay where you are my child, do not move yet, because while I cannot foretell the future for any individual legionary, I can foretell the future of a legion. But this will be of little concern to you, because it is practice in the Roman army that a soldier does not remain with any one legion for the full extent of his service."

"That is right," replied Tricia, "I understand that."

"All I can do," continued the sibyl, "is to prophesy to you the future of all our noble legionaries, and this I shall do if you are willing to hear it."

"Yes, indeed, I would appreciate your general prophecy regarding our legionaries."

"Very well, dear child," said the sibyl, "but my prophecies I can only tell to you in poetic fashion, so please listen carefully."

The sibyl then commenced her prophesy thus:

> *O noble soldier you will tread,*
> *O'r weary miles to earn your bread,*
> *And serve your Caesar loyally*
> *Discipline to totality.*

Caesar's tasks you will perform
Gruelling but considered norm'
In battle, many you will face
Valour will be your humble grace.

Senators in their debate,
Will care not much for your fate,
Patricians, plebeians and those who are freed,
Expect from you great deeds

O noble soldier no defector,
O noble Roman the world's protector.

In winter white so bleak and cold,
Hungered and fatigued you will be bold,
Fighting or marching each measured mile
Your training will have served you in style.
Through desert sands you'll tread your sandal,
The stars at night will be your candle
Thirsty, hot perspiring,
Steadfast you will remain and still aspiring.

Your cries of pain they will not hear,
Be you far or be you near,
'is on your comrades you rely,
In anguish they'll not pass you by.

O noble soldier no defector,
O noble Roman the world's protector.

Whatever your tasks you'll play your part
Though some may tend to jerk your heart,
Cruelty's high upon your list,
Unquestionably you'll do your best.

You will be called to sacrifice
An alien God that bears no vice,
Your judgement will be hesitant,
To the unfolding future you will look distant.

Cruelly treating, cruelly slaying,
Duty bound for Caesar's paying,
Diligently and without malice,
Shamelessly you'll drink from the chalice.

O noble soldier no defector,
O noble Roman the world's protector.

In years to come this non event,
Will be looked on as heaven sent
Caesar's power and Jupiter's shrine,
Will be only worthy of decline.

Jurisprudence and oratory,
In support of stability,
Abundant in materialism,
But will not protect from barbarism.

But Roman soldier long remembered,
When the Empire had been dismembered
With shield and sword all resplendent,
Civilization is on you dependent.

O noble soldier Roman soldier,
Nothing for you but for you to shoulder

"Thank you, great Sibyl," Tricia said hesitantly, "thank you very much. I am most grateful to you for your time and patience."

She withdrew from the chamber to rejoin her mother.

"Well, are you satisfied with the Sibyl's prophesy?" her mother asked.

"No not quite," replied Tricia, "because I cannot fully comprehend it. It will take me quite some time to work out and digest the meaning of the Sibyl's words."

"That was a fat lot of good then, wasn't it?" her mother remonstrated. "You pay all that money and then don't understand a word that has been prophesied."

"Oh mother, don't be like that. It is not that easy to understand a Sibyl's prophesy."

"Very well then, if you think you have spent your money wisely, so be it."

Tricia then informed her mother that she still had five sisterces left and her plan on how she wished to spend it. Again there was some heated words spoken between them, after which her mother acquiesced and accompanied her to the nearest jewellers. For the remainder of their stay in Rome and for months thereafter, Tricia pondered the Sibyl's prophesy. She slowly began to understand its meaning and the only doubt that remained was the time scale for which it applied. The power of Caesar and of Rome and the temples of their beloved gods could come to an end either tomorrow or many centuries in the future. So it was a doubt she was unable to clear. She wondered why oracles were never very precise about the time when events were likely to happen.

*

Timius and the other oarsmen had now been rowing some three hours, and since the muscles in his body were not attuned to this form of exercise, his arms, back and legs were beginning to ache. The steady beat of the drum was getting on his nerves, but he gritted his teeth and made up his mind that it was something he would simply have to endure. After all, his four companions had blamed him for placing them all in their current situation. He clearly remembered that evening some three weeks ago which began so cheerfully. It had been a day free from duties for all of them, and they had all decided to pay a visit to the town of Cyrene, where they had been on quite a few occasions previously. Their evening began at a well appointed inn at which they had all enjoyed a delicious evening meal. After the meal they retired to the anteroom to relax. They enjoyed their many games of dice which Cyrus seemed to win each time because he was a cheat, and they had drunk several jars of a very fine wine. Late into the evening Cyrus came up with what sounded like a wonderful suggestion. He was quite enthusiastic about it and had reason to be. After all he had gained the most winnings from the games of dice. It was Cyrus's suggestion that they should sneak into the out-of-bounds area of Cyrene unseen by the town patrols, which were provided by a especially selected detachment from the legion. This detachment was made up of men who were inclined to be boorish and brutish in their attitude. When they had reached the out of bounds area undetected, they were approached by a Cyrenee wearing a long loose robe with a small green scull cap perched on his head. He half whispered as he said, "You Romans looking for pretty girls, yes?"

"No, we are not!" exclaimed Marcus. "We are just exploring the area."

"Yes, you explore the area, but something tells me you explore for pretty girls," he insisted. "If you each give me one dinarii, I will take you to a house where there are plenty of very beautiful Egyptian girls who will entertain you all night long. If you want they will bring you plenty of wine and dance for you. But if you don't want, then they will willingly do other things for you."

The man's Latin was not very fluent, but they all understood exactly what he meant. After contemplating the proposal, it was with Cyrus's slight persuasion that they agreed to pay the man and accompany him. He took them through a back alley which was hardly lit at all and then through a courtyard surrounded by low-lying buildings and thence into one of the buildings. In the building he introduced them to a group of about a dozen young women who were heavily made up and wearing excessively scented perfume, yet very scantily dressed. All the girls clustered around the five young men. It was Protius who made the first choice of the most beautiful Egyptian girl present. He was quickly followed by Lipsius, who did not want to be left out of making a selection at the earliest opportunity. After each young man selected a companion for the night the remaining girls withdrew to another room, leaving the company of the men and the girls to enjoy themselves without their presence to spoil it. More wine was brought to them and each of the party drank their fill and amused themselves generally. It was now time for each couple to withdraw to their selected apartments in the building and, as each did so, a payment of ten dinarii was handed over to the female partner.

The room that Timius entered with his partner was furnished in the same way as all the other rooms in the establishment used for this purpose. Apart from the bed, there was a cupboard in which the occupants could hang their clothes, and there was also a wooden pedestal on which stood a jug of water and a bowl. Each room had a small oil lamp sufficient to provide whatever light was necessary for an apartment of that size. Timius and the girl sat on the edge of the bed sipping the wine from the beaker, which each had taken into the room. The conversation between them was sparse.

She told him that her name was Shamin and that she enjoyed her work. It was quite fun, especially when newcomers to the district brought their custom to the house, such as he and his friends. They merely talked in general, and when they had drunk their wine, she asked Timius if he was now ready for bed. He nodded bashfully and they both stood up. She did not take long undressing, and after she had removed her bodice and

scanty pantaloons, she nonchalantly placed the garments at the foot of the
bed. Timius by now had only undone his cord tied round his waist, having
slipped off his sandals. As he did so, his eyes fell on the two garments that
Shamin had placed on the bed. By now she was lying stark naked on the
bed, smiling at him. She was very dark haired, and Timius thought how
extremely attractive she looked, but when his eyes fell on the garments there
was a sudden jolt to his conscience. He immediately thought of his beloved
Tricia back in Velitrae and, in particular, that purple-edged gown that she
was wearing the last night he had spent in her company. He could not go
through with it with Shamin and hastily began to retie the cord around his
waist.

Shamin was astonished to see him act that way and asked, "What's the
matter with you? Aren't you going to stay the night?"

He could detect a note of anger in her voice, presumably because she
had lost the means of earning seven dinarii, which he would probably
demand she return to him, but Timius replied, "No, no, Shamin, it's not
that. I think you are very beautiful, but I have changed my mind. You can
keep the money, and what's more here is some more for the inconvenience
I have caused you."

He placed a handful of coins at the foot of the bed as he put on his
sandals. She was not content with this and, jumping off the bed, ran to
the cupboard and quickly put on a robe, screaming as she did abuses in
her native Egyptian language. Timius begged her to stop screaming and
said very quietly that he was now leaving. But instead she ran to the door,
opened it, and ran out in the main hall, shouting "Rape, he has raped me,"
at the top of her voice.

At this the rest of the building seemed to come alive and the hall was
soon filled with many of the other occupants, including his four companions,
who wondered what it was all about. Dumbfounded with what was going
on, Timius ran out trying to explain to them the cause of the commotion.
Very soon a group of eight legionnaires with swords drawn entered the
building. They were men from the guard cohort of the Ninth Legion who
were on a tour of duty in the out-of-bounds district as part of their town
patrol beat. The leader of the group very soon silenced the babblers, and
before they knew what was happening, all five of the young Romans were
being marched under escort back to the encampment. As they walked down
one of the better lit streets, Timius noticed that his companions who had
been giving him black looks were now grimacing. From their expressions he
knew he had upset them, and this was something he did not wish to do, as

he valued their friendship; but because of his high mindedness he had got them all into trouble.

When they arrived at the encampment, the five of them were immediately placed under close arrest and spent the rest of that night in the encampment guards quarters to await being called to appear before a senior officer of the legion the following morning to answer the various charges that would be brought against them. In the cell of the guards' quarters, recriminations were raised against Timius by his companions for his inept action earlier that night. Cyrus and Protius were thoroughly annoyed with him for the unsatisfactory situation in which he had placed them.

"Do you realize that tomorrow we are going to be charged with not only being out of bounds but also being caught in a brothel?" said Cyrus angrily.

"I'm sorry, Cyrus, I didn't mean this to happen because I did nothing to warrant such a despicable outburst filled with untrue accusations by that slut of a woman," replied Timius.

"What the hell happened," Protius asked angrily.

"Nothing," replied Timius, "absolutely nothing," he affirmed.

"Well, what was it all about?" asked Lipsius who was also very annoyed.

Timius then related to them, as calmly as he could, what had happened. Marcus then asked what made Timius change his mind about going through with it.

"I really don't know," was the untruthful reply. "I just did not want to go through with it."

"You were bl . . . . Scared that's the truth of the matter," Cyrus piped in.

"No, I was not scared," retorted Timius.

"You surprise me," said Lipsius. "You haven't even got a girl friend back home; so what on earth scared you, I would like to know."

"I was not scared," rejoined Timius and continued "and while we are on the subject of girl friends, haven't any of you got consciences? After all," addressing Lipsius, "you and Protius are supposedly betrothed to very fine young ladies and there's Cyrus and Marcus who give one the impression that they are head over heals in love with the daughters of Praetorian Officer Carpus."

"What's that got to do with it?" replied Cyrus. "What does it matter, neither of the women are here with us now and would have no idea of what we do unless you go and blab when next you see them."

"Timius shook his head slowly, then said, "Don't worry old friend, I will not tell them. I will not tell anyone because it's none of my business what you do and, as I have already told you, when I withdrew from Shamin's room I did so with the intention of waiting for the four of you in the hallway. I intended there to be no fuss and bother about it. I was not to know that she would react so petulantly and untruthfully."

"Well, as soon as she began behaving that way you should have changed your mind again and stayed the night," Lipsius stated.

"I suppose I should have done as you suggest but it is too late now."

"Why don't you shut up with all your excuses," said Cyrus abusively.

"They are nor excuses," retorted Timius, "and let me remind you fellows about something. Do you remember Gemulus?"

"Yes, we do," they replied in unison, "what about him?"

"Well, what happened to him?" asked Timius, "don't any of you remember what happened to him?"

He paused for their replies but none was forthcoming, so Timius went on, "You fellows have very short memories, don't you? It was only a few weeks ago that Gemulus was shipped back to Rome for discharge from the army because he had contracted a severe dose of pox which was incurable, and he is only one of many others that have been discharged for that reason. Just think, any one of us could find ourselves in the same boat."

Nothing was said for a few moments after Timius's outburst.

Cyrus broke their silence by saying, "Shut up, Timius, and go to sleep. We'll sort this out in the morning. God help you if we land ourselves on a six-month's spell of cookhouse fatigues. You will get a bucket of cold water thrown over you.

The following morning the five of them appeared on the said charges in front of the second in command of the legion, Commander Paetus. After he read out the charges, he asked them, "What have you to say in your defence?"

There was total silence.

Commander Paetus then continued, "Let me remind you despicable lot that the town of Cyrene has been and continues to be a peaceful settlement. We have the cooperation of the majority of the local population, but there are agitators among them who will seize on any misdemeanour of us Romans to further their aim, and no doubt it is news throughout the town that one of their fair maidens—albeit an immigrant settler—was raped last night in a dastardly fashion and, moreover, within the walls of a brothel. I'll accept that I cannot believe this to be true, but our behaviour has not been impeccable, and in order to satisfy the local people that such dastardly misdemeanours are frowned upon with the utmost severity by the Roman authorities, all of you are to be shipped out of the province at the earliest. You will join the next relief party that is sent from this legion to that of the Twelfth Legion in Syria. You will regret the day that this happened when you arrive in Syria, and until your departure, you will all remain in solitary confinement during silent hours, and you will be engaged in hard labour during working hours. You are all dismissed."

Until their embarkation the arguments and bad feeling between Timius and his companions continued, but the night before their embarkation Cyrus, Marcus, Lipsius, and Protius decided that no earthly good would be served in maintaining their animosity towards Timius. They had all realized that the terrible fate of Gemulus and others had been spared them even though their service in Cyrenaica had come to a sudden end with only the prospect of service with the Twelfth Legion in Syria ahead of them.

The Twelfth Legion had gained itself an unworthy reputation. It was purported to be a legion that comprised of Roman legionnaires who had been posted to its strength as a form of punishment. The remaining Roman citizen legionnaires were those drawn from the nearby provinces of Judea and Bithnia and each of these nationals was extremely nationalistic in custom and attitude while enjoying Roman citizenship. Attached to it was also a very large force of Syrian auxiliaries who were ruthless adversaries of any enemy on their frontier. The Twelfth Legion and its commanders were feared to an extreme degree, as they were also men of ruthless devotion to military methods. Throughout the Roman army the Twelfth Legion was infamously referred to as 'the terrible Twelfth' and service with the Twelfth Legion meant servitude and not the accepted form of service.

CHAPTER XXV

Libertas, dulce auditu nomen.

LIVY

Freedom, a name sweet to hear.

TIMIUS HAD SPENT several turns manning the oars, as had his companions and other members of the troop aboard the ship. His first shift at the oars, at the commencement of the voyage, was spent rowing alongside an African man, a member of the slave complement of oarsmen on board. Thereafter each time it was Timius's turn for rowing duty he tried to seat himself alongside the same man and share the effort on the oar. The ship was fitted with five oars, protruding on each side of the hull and each of the large oars was propelled by two men; one a slave, and the other a legionnaire. This ship had been fitted with three large sails, which meant that the number of oars required could be reduced in number. On the first shift, at the commencement of the voyage, when Timius tried to make conversation with his rowing companion, partly to kill time and partly to break the monotony of the incessant drum beat, the man's response hurt his sensitive feelings. Timius had only tried to be friendly by talking in generalities, but the man only grunted in response. However, he was a strong, well-built individual who took most of the strain of the rowing and Timius being much slighter in stature was grateful for this, although it was not an arrangement that had been worked out previously between them. The effort of both the oarsmen was relative to each person's strength. It was on the second shift that Timius began to learn more about his rowing companion. The dark-skinned man must have sensed a feeling of genuine amiableness in his rowing companion, and his response this time was not so offensive. Timius introduced himself to his rowing companion by telling him his name and the name of the township in Italy where he was born. He then asked the man, "What is your name?"

The man did not answer, and Timius turned his head to look at him. His face was expressionless, and this showed through clearly because he was very clean shaven and without a hair on his head. When the man looked at Timius to reply, Timius noticed that slightly above his left eye was a festering sore. Timius had also noticed previously that there were festering sores dotted on both his arms which could not be covered in any way by virtue of the fact that the tunics worn by the slaves, as it was with soldiers, were short sleeved. Timius had attributed this to the conditions under which the slaves worked. The lower deck on which the rowing took place was a humid, ghastly place for any human being to work.

The man replied in a very deep voice, "My name is Mucta Wahabis."

"I am very pleased to know you," said Timius, and he meant it, because he was pleased that he had responded to his question. He continued as kindly as he could for fear of not upsetting the man, "Where are you from Mucta and how long have you been doing this job?"

Again, there was no immediate response, but after a while he said, "My home was in a little village in Numida until you filthy despicable Romans came and thrust me into bondage."

This remark upset Timius, and he remained silent for a while, not knowing what to say, and Mucta continued, "You Romans must have no conscience or feelings for humanity at all. As far as I am concerned you are the scum of the earth."

"I am sorry you feel like that," said Timius, "but even though you consider me a piece of scum, I consider it a privilege to sit alongside you to take my turn in the rowing. I have no ill feelings toward you, my firend, but only respect."

"Respect," exclaimed Mucta, "you b . . . . Romans don't know what the word means. My respect was snatched away from me in Numidia, three years ago, and I shall never regain it now."

"I cannot agree with you Mucta," said Timius. "Whatever we do, you can still retain your dignity and respect if you wish to, and pleased try and remember that not all of us Romans are alike. There are good and bad among us, you know."

"That's what you think," replied Mucta with a note of bitterness in his voice. "Do you know, up to some three years ago, I was happy working in the fields, near to my village, when the Romans came. I was happy with my wife and teenage daughter and you bastards came along and upset the whole of my life."

"What happened," asked Timius.

"I will tell you," replied Mucta sternly. "The Roman authorities were looking for volunteers to recruit for the auxiliary force, and I was selected. I refused to serve that despicable lout Tiberius Caesar, and for my sins I was shackled and taken to work in the nearby quarry. My house was burnt down, and my wife and daughter were transported to Rome to serve as slaves or concubines to our Roman masters. Five months ago, I was dragged out of the quarry and marched to the port of Cyrene in shackles. This is because they wanted strong men whom they considered no better than animals to serve as oarsmen on their ships; and here I am now."

There was a long silence, broken only by the constant rhythm of the drum. Timius was extremely upset to hear how cruelly his rowing companion had been treated and told him so, as sincerely as he possibly could. Thereafter their friendship grew, but at the same time respecting their circumstances. Both respected one another even though Mucta was a slave and Timius a legionnaire. Both performed the same tasks during the voyage but each new his station in life.

It was after they had been on the voyage nearly three weeks when Timius seated himself beside Mucta and was asked by his rowing companion, "Tell me, friend, when you came down from the upper deck, did you notice that the wind was strengthening?"

"Yes, I did," replied Timius excitedly. "Why do you ask?"

"Well, if the wind becomes stronger we will be relieved, perhaps halfway through the shift."

"That's exactly what I was thinking on my way down here," responded Timius.

"Don't get too excited about it, though, friend, because if we run into a storm, you will know all about it. You'd wish you had never been born."

"Oh, come now, Mucta, surely it cannot be as bad as that."

"No, perhaps I am exaggerating."

"But tell me, Mucta, have you used that medicine I brought down for you?"

"Yes, I have, friend, and it has certainly eased the irritation on my arms and forehead."

"Good, I am glad to hear that," said Timius cheerfully.

Timius had a habit throughout his career of being able to scrounge whatever he could, whenever he wanted it, and from whoever was able to provide what he needed. He now had the reputation among his companions of being a scrounger. He had been able to scrounge some medicine from the *medici duplicaris*, and when he had handed it secretly to Mucta, Mucta was most grateful for the kindness of the young Roman.

During the first two hours or so of rowing, the oarsmen began to feel, on occasions which became much more frequent, that on the down-stroke of the oar, the oars were not dipping into the water, and this was indicative to them that the ship was riding swells which had begun to gradually develop on the surface of the sea. The wind also had now increased to a point where they were ordered to rest on their oars. Very soon the oarsmen on the rowing deck could hear orders being given to lower the main sails. They could not hear the wind very well on the rowing deck, but nevertheless the sound of the wind was now reaching their ears, and under normal conditions, there would be no sound of wind at all. This was ominous. Soon the drummer left his position to report on deck and returned very quickly to instruct them to make haste either to their cramped quarters or to positions of safety on the upper deck. The unexpected end to the rowing shift was what Timius had been looking forward to excitedly, and he quickly made his way to the very camped quarters at the rear end of the ship.

Gale force winds were now blowing and the sea had developed an enormous swell. He had been advised by Mucta that although the Mediterranean was reputed to be a calm and placid ocean, when it was disturbed, it became extremely angry, and this was one of those occasions. Throughout the day and night, the ship rode the storm, but was tossed about on the rolling swell like a piece of discarded drift wood. Crew members and passengers could only keep themselves from falling over each other and over other obstacles, causing injuries to themselves by desperately clinging on to any device or fitting that was near at hand.

It was a traumatic experience for all on board, and by the time dawn was about to break, they had ridden out the storm which had begun to subside. Many were desperate to clamber to the upper deck, not only to relieve themselves over the side of the ship, but also to vomit their guts out. Timius was one of these, and when he reached the edge of the deck, he leaned over the barrier and almost fell head over heals into the ocean. He felt terribly ill and lay at the side of the barrier in between moments of having to get up and repeat the performance. He was not the only one, there were several others doing the same thing, and quite near to him were Marcus and Lipsius. After about three hours, Timius began to recover, but Marcus and Lipsius were in a horrible state. They were even trying to vomit while lying on the deck.

Very little substance was now coming out of their mouths, just a greenish liquid, and the way in which they were heaving made Timius feel very sorry for them, but there was not anything he could do, as all his strength had been sapped. He merely sat at the edge watching them with his protruding eyes and sunken cheeks. He felt a hand on his shoulder, and turning around quickly, he looked in to the face of Mucta Wahabis. Mucta crouched down beside him and placed an arm around his shoulders.

"I've brought some dried bread for you, friend." As he spoke, he produced a piece of dried stale bread from the bosom of his tunic.

"Thank you, Mucta," said Timius weakly, "but I cannot eat anything now. I just don't feel like it."

"Enough of that," interrupted Mucta, "you must eat it. You must force it down you."

Again Timius shook his head violently, declining the offer.

"I am serious," said Mucta, grabbing hold of the back of his neck with his right hand.

Timius was so weak that Mucta's grip was, inclined to hurt him. Mucta was a very strong man, and Timius had often admired his height and build. He was very broad shouldered with a beautifully proportioned physique, and he towered above Timius. Timius often thought that Mucta had the physique of a god.

"You must eat this bread. I insist, because if you don't you will not have the strength to make it to the rowing deck in just a few hours, and if you are absent, the authorities on board will have no sympathy or mercy on you. They will tie you to the main mast and have you lashed. I am not exaggerating, friend. I have seen it done with other soldiers," he assured him firmly.

Timius forced the bread down his throat and made a desperate effort to keep it down. Mucta then moved over to Lipsius and Marcus and propped them up against the barrier, likewise forcing bread down their throats, as he had just done with Timius. They were most annoyed with him and, in between mouthfuls, cursed and swore at him. Indeed, they were very offensive. Timius crawled over to his friends and, although he could hardly speak from weakness, he tried to explain to them the importance of eating the dry bread and trying to digest it just to try and keep up their strength, or what little of it they had. They soon calmed down and forced the bread down. Mucta then made his way along the deck on his hands and knees and persuaded one or two other similarly affected soldiers to eat some of the bread.

When Timius joined Mucta on the rowing deck for his shift, he was very, very weak and, as he sat alongside Mucta to take up the oar, Mucta quietly advised him to pretend that he was rowing and that he himself would take the strain. Towards the end of the shift, Timius began to feel much better. Strength started returning to his body. He very humbly thanked Mucta for his help and understanding.

They were only four days away from arriving at their destination and, that night, after Timius had played a game of dice with his companions until it was too dark to see which way the thrown dice were landing, he spent a few moments on his own, pacing the deck slowly. The sea had become very calm, and there was hardly a breath of air, the three sails hanging languid at the mast.

He stopped a few yards from the prow of the ship and leaned on the barrier to look at the water. Below him and slightly to the rear, he could see the oars from the deck below dipping in rhythm into the water, and as they emerged after each stroke, the wet surface of the blades glistened in the moonlight. The moon was, in its first quarter, surrounded by a myriad of stars. As the bow of the ship cut its way through the surface of the sea, the wash from the bows sparkled as though it also contained stars of its own.

What Timius was seeing was the deposits of phosphorous, which was a natural substance of the ocean. This fascinated him, and he tried to compare the sparkling wash with the sky above him, with its many stars twinkling away in the midnight blue sky. He thought of those nights when he would walk Tricia home after spending an enjoyable evening in her company, and he wondered whether she had ever remembered the topic of their many conversations when she looked at the starlit sky from her garden. He was deep in thought, trying to recapture those wonderful moments, but he was also a little bit uneasy about the conversation he had had on the last rowing shift with Mucta. Mucta was very depressed that shift, and Timius concluded that the man was obviously thinking about his wife and daughter. He had asked him outright if this was the reason for his sullenness.

"Please don't talk about my family," Mucta retorted, "I am trying desperately to forget them."

"But you must not forget your wife and daughter," Timius chastised.

"Yes, I must, and I am sorry to appear so sullen, but like you the other day, I am not feeling very well."

"Are you sea sick?" queried Timius.

"Sea sick definitely not. Sea sickness will never affect me again," he said assuredly. "It's these damn sores on my arms and on my body that are irritating me."

"Have you used all the ointment I brought you?"

"Yes, friend, I've used all of it."

"I see, well, I will get you some more. I'll try and get you enough to last you a few weeks."

"Thank you kindly, but please don't risk getting into trouble."

"Don't worry about that. That's of no consequence. I'll scrounge some more for you.

After a while Timius asked, "What was your daughter's name, Mucta, and what was your wife's name?"

"I asked you not to talk about my family," Mucta replied angrily, "but since you ask, my daughter's name is Shamin, and she was snatched away from me when she had just passed the age of sixteen, and my wife's name is Jazmina, and it was a terrible sight to see them both dragged away by those Roman bastards." He hesitated a while then added, "Your bloody countrymen."

This last remark caused Timius to remain silent and then, as if speaking his thoughts aloud he responded, "It's strange that you should tell me that your daughter's name is Shamin because it was through a girl whose name was also Shamin my companions and I are where we are now—on our way to commence duty at a punishment posting with the terrible Twelfth Legion."

This statement aroused Mucta's interest and he asked, "where did you meet the girl Shamin?"

"Where, well it was in a brothel at Cyrene."

"Was it?" said Mucta and continued, "Describe her to me."

Timius described Shamin the best way he could, but he was sure his memory was playing tricks on him. Too much had happened since then. He told Mucta all the details as best as he could of that awful episode, but quickly added, "Please don't associate that bitch with your daughter of the same name, because the Shamin I am talking about was an Egyptian."

"Well the pimp who took us to the brothel told us that all the girls there were Egyptian, and he also told us that the proprietor of the establishment was Egyptian."

Very few words passed between them after this conversation and it was only later that Timius realized the terrible seed that he had planted in Mucta's mind. However, they still remained on amiable terms, and Timius made an effort to seal their friendship by persuading the *medici duplicaris* to give him a container of ointment, which he gave to Mucta.

*

Timius's heart was pounding rapidly as he stood to attention alongside Marcus and Lipsius outside the office of the officer in command of the Sixth Cohort. They were guarded by four other duty guards of the day, but Timius could not understand the reason for this small show of force because they would not dare to attempt to escape and, in fact, if they did, surviving in the barren countryside would be almost impossible without the help of Syrian natives and nomadic Arabs. He had come to realize how true the words were, although jokingly said at the time, when the drummer on board the ship had replied to his question concerning Syria that it was a place with only one blade of grass growing every one hundred miles.

He and his companions had now been in Syria for nearly fifteen months and during that time they had all resigned themselves to the hard life that was forced on them in service with the terrible Twelfth. The camp of the terrible Twelfth was situated some twelve miles from the old town of Palmyra, and apart from one visit to the township which seemed to be a conglomeration of market places and a focal point for the nomadic traders, they had not ventured beyond the campus. Very few men of the legion had done so. Life with the Twelfth was very hard indeed, and the soldiers spent the majority for their time on training exercises, in which they constantly practiced battle formation and, more importantly, survival with very little food and water for days on end, beneath the hot blazing sun of the day and the cold chill of the night that penetrated to the marrow of their bones.

Water was a commodity that was extremely short, and most of the time when they were not training they would have to take their turns in assisting the qualified engineers in the laying of a new and more imaginative aqueduct that was in the process of being built between a lush oasis, some eight miles north of the camp, to the town of Palmyra with a distributor to provide much needed water to the Roman encampment.

Besides training and providing labour for the engineers, Marcus and Lipsius had an additional job of assisting the fletchers and bowyers in the camp armoury. Cyrus and Protius were employed in the camp kitchens, whereas Timius continued as he had done with the Ninth, and previously with the fourth Legion, as messenger runner. He found it soul destroying and exhausting running in the heat of the Syrian plain, but it was often the instruction of his superior officer that such training would take place under these conditions. This was imperative, and it was impressed on him that if their Parthian neighbours ever decided to attack the Syrian province, they would not do so at the coolest part of the day, and consequently the whole training of the legion was carried out during the most uncomfortable and hottest part of each day. They had experienced many sand storms, where the sky would become darkened, as though they were experiencing the dense fogs of the German forests, but the contrast here was in the humidity that such sand storms brought about. The humidity and darkness would last sometimes for days on end, and in such a climate, their water skins were of much more importance to them than their weapons. A legionary's water skin had to be jealously guarded. On exercise, even their eating utensils could not be cleaned with the use of water.

Dry sand was used as a cleaning material and there was an abundance of that. Timius remembered the first day that he and his companions had seen a camel. In fact, they had seen three camels being led heavily laden with merchandise by their owners, quite near to the area in which they were training. Marcus had asked a veteran what kind of animals they were, and after such laughing and joking with his companions, the veteran soldier enlightened Marcus and his companions with the history of the camel. He told them that when Octavian had marched at the head of his legions against Cleopatra, that while he was crossing a very sandy stretch of desert on the borders of Egypt, he had become angry with the way his horse, and indeed, all the other horses of the legion, had faltered in the deep sea of sand.

Octavian immediately sent instructions to the Senate that they would set up a committee of designers and that they would design a horse that would be capable of negotiating the desert sands and also be able to travel long distances without water. Therefore, they were advised the camel was a horse designed by a committee. They thought the story quite funny and did not know whether to believe it or not. Despite the arduous nature of the service there was a tremendous sense of humour among all the men of the Twelfth Legion. Without humour life would have been absolutely grim. The officers of the Twelfth Legion had reputations that would make a new recruit to the army tremble in his sandals. They were stern, harsh men, but they were also men that commanded the highest respect from the troops. The smallest misdemeanour was severely punished, and it was no wonder why Timius had once again found his knees trembling.

He could not understand any element of severity of the crime he had committed together with Marcus and Lipsius. What they had done was quite innocent and a natural human reaction to the situation. However, when the centurion had explained to them the seriousness of their act, they could well understand how easily and unwittingly was their health and the health of their comrades placed in danger. They were now to face the consequences of this act of innocence, which had occurred the previous day.

A maniple, the Sixth Cohort a subdivision of the legion lead by Centurion Cletus, was returning from a week-long training exercise. The remainder of Sixth Cohort would be returning to the encampment in two days time, and the necessity for a maniple to return in advance of the remainder was in order that the advanced party could take up duties along the perimeter of the Roman fortification. Guard duties in and around the perimeter of the encampment was a regular but necessary feature of legion life. The maniple were now some three miles from the camp when Centurion Cletus ordered a halt. The halt served two purposes: one was to allow the troops a chance of taking a much needed rest after the long afternoon march, and the other purpose was so that they could tidy themselves up so that when they marched into camp they were smart and at attention. The spot where they were ordered to halt was a regular halting place along the dusty hard road that led the ten miles distance from the training area.

Alongside the road, were boulders and rocks which were regularly used as seats for the weary troops and on one side of the road was a gradual embankment leading to a wide gulley which stretched some distance beyond. It was one of the very few undulating features of the barren terrain.

In the mid distance of the gulley stood some roughly assembled dwellings made from a variety of materials by its inhabitants. As the troops of the maniple rested and quenched their thirst with the remains of the water in their water skins, a few of the inhabitants of the makeshift commune began to appear and walk towards them.

Whenever the troops stopped at this spot the same activity would occur; so it had been decided to avoid this place for a rest whenever possible. Instead, they were invariably marched much nearer to the camp to a spot where the fortifications were visible. This time Centurion Cletus decided to call a halt to the march at an earlier juncture, because his maniple had on this occasion marched from the furthermost point of the training area some distance of over twenty miles without a stop and the troops under his command were beginning to show signs that they were suffering from fatigue. The inhabitants of the commune slowly gathered in a group towards the base of the embankment. There were a few other stragglers limping and one or two crawling their way towards the group. As they approached the embankment they called out in pleading voices, "Bread, please give us some bread."

It sounded as though they were wailing in unison. Lipsius had never experienced a halt at this spot; so partly out of curiosity, he walked over to the edge of the road until he was able to look down towards them from where he stood. Marcus soon joined him, because he was also inquisitive. When Lipsius heard their plea for bread, he pulled out the remains for some from his ration pannier, and he was about to approach the group down the embankment to hand them the bread when a cry went up from those assembled: "unclean, unclean."

Lipsius was stopped in his tracks because the cry from the assembly was as though they were warning him. Very soon, Marcus dragged him back to the edge of the road. They looked at each other, wondering what was wrong with the people in the group who were begging for bread—yet warning them to keep away. Without saying anything to each other, they both broke the pieces of bread that they had in their possession into smaller pieces and threw it over to them. The group of lepers scrambled for the bread as it was thrown.

Suddenly Marcus was astonished with what he saw take place, and in his astonishment called out, "Timius, Timius, come quickly!"

"What's the matter, Marcus?"

"Come over here—quick; there is something I want to show you."

Timius ambled over quite nonchalantly from where he was resting. When he arrived at the side of Marcus, Marcus said to him, "Have you any of your bread left?"

"Yes, but it isn't very much."

"Well, don't be bloody mean throw it over to those poor wretches over there."

"Fair enough then, but is that all you called me over for?"

Marcus replied agitatedly, "No, of course not, idiot. Look at that man over there."

"What man are you talking about?"

"There, that big dark skinned man." He pointed the man out as he spoke.

"Well, what about him?" asked Timius.

"Who does he remind you of?" enquired Marcus.

"I've no idea," said Timius, still quite agitated that he should be dragged away from his resting place.

The big man was looking at them from the small group, and Timius suddenly realized whom Marcus was referring to.

"By Jove, you're right, Marcus, that man, I am almost sure, is Mucta Wahabis."

"Don't be silly," Lipsius interjected, "Mucta would still be rowing to and fro across the Mediterranean."

"I don't—"

Before Timius could finish the sentence, they heard the harsh voice of Centurion Cletus call out. "Get away from those bloody lepers and come over here to me, the three of you."

Obediently, they began to do as they were told, but as they were about to leave, Lipsius noticed that the dark man whom they had thought was Mucta gently waived to them as though he recognised them. The three soldiers soon received a dressing down from the Centurion, who informed them that by placing themselves even some twenty yards from the lepers they were endangering themselves and their comrades and that he had no alternative but to charge them with this offence immediately on their return to the encampment.

After waiting some considerable time they were marched and ordered to stand to attention in front of the cohort commander, the admonishment they received was in similar vein to that which they had received from Centurion Cletus. The commander was stern in telling them that he would accept no excuse for their behaviour. As punishment the three of them would join the special troop which would march to the city of Jerusalem in two weeks time, where they would remain for the duration of the governor's presence in the city as his bodyguard, after which they would return to the Twelfth Legion encampment. Not one of the party felt that this punishment was as severe as they had fully expected. In fact the three of them felt that it would be rather light relief, with perhaps some excitement thrown in, to say nothing of a visit to the city of the Jews. They had heard tales about Jerusalem and many of them seemed thrilling—especially from veterans who had been there on several occasions. However, those veterans had only been to the city during the course of duty, and it was not easy for them to know whether their tales could be believed or not. They recalled having heard a lot of exciting things about Palmyra, but Palmyra was a disappointment to them. It could not have been otherwise because the only opportunity to visit that town was on one occasion a year or so after their posting to the area. The consolation of this posting to them was that the change of air and the change of scenery would be beneficial to them. They might even get an opportunity to browse in the market place in Jerusalem.

CHAPTER XXVI

Fortuna ludum insolentem ludit.

HORACE

Fortune plays an insolent game.

"BOTH YOUR CLOTHING and equipment are absolutely filthy. It stinks!" shrieked Centurion Culpurnius, as though he were announcing this statement to the whole world. He continued shrieking, "Is not your kit bloody filthy? Answer me."

"Yes, sire," replied Cyrus sheepishly.

The centurion gazed at him admonishingly for a few moments before turning his head towards Protius, who was in the next position in the dormitory to Cyrus.

Again he shrieked, "You bloody kit is worse than his. In fact I daren't come near it. I might become contaminated."

The centurion then turned to face two other soldiers who were standing the opposite side to Cyrus and Protius.

"You two," he pointed to them, "collect all their kit immediately and throw it right outside the door. I am not going to have any stinking kit in this dormitory."

The two soldiers immediately obeyed the centurion and quickly gathered up the kit of Cyrus and Protius and promptly carried it down to the far end of the dormitory and threw it outside the door, where it landed in the dust. The centurion then ordered Cyrus and Protius to have their kit ready for a further inspection on the following evening.

He said, "It had better be clean otherwise the pair of you will be for the high jump,"

He quickly turned on his heel and marched out of the dormitory without proceeding further to inspect the kits of the remaining few in the dormitory. Cyrus and Protius were upset and dejected and could not understand the reason for the centurion's outburst. It seemed to them, and indeed to all those present, that they had been picked on for some reason or other.

An inspection of the soldiers' clothes and equipment was carried out one evening a week while they were in the encampment. This did not happen too frequently because the legionnaires spent most of their time either on training in the huge training area some miles from the encampment or assisting as labour on engineering projects. Each cohort took its turn in either training or engineering on a rotation basis, but they also took a turn in carrying out guard and other duties within the encampment.

The kit inspection consists of each soldier laying all his change of clothes and equipment—apart from that which he was wearing—on a blanket uniformly on the stone floor of the dormitory. Each dormitory housed eighty men, and in the Palmyra encampment of the Twelfth Legion, no beds were provided for the troops. The climate was so hot and humid that to sleep on a blanket placed on the stone floor afforded them the most relief from the intense heat. In addition to the kit inspection the previous evening the remainder of the time was taken up by interior economy. This meant that the soldiers in the dormitory were required to scrub the dust-covered stone floor on their hands and knees, and also clean the dust from the stone walls of the building.

None of the soldiers enjoyed this routine and found it exceptionally irksome. Any light relief that they could think of from this irksome duty was readily pursued. The previous night of this particular inspection Timius, who had a floor position alongside Marcus, had quite playfully picked up the orthopaedic sandal belonging to his friend. Marcus was in the process of cleaning his sandals, and Timius tried to hide that which belonged to his right foot.

Marcus spotted him and tried to snatch it away from him. Timius quickly threw the sandal to Protius whose ground space was in the opposite row. Marcus irritated by this limped over to Protius to try and retrieve his possession, but as he reached Protius, the sandal was thrown through the air and caught by Cyrus who was some twenty yards away. Marcus continued to limp but this time towards Cyrus and, as he did so, Cyrus threw the sandal back to Protius. This went on for a while with Marcus going to and fro between the two protagonists. The rest of the men in the dormitory, on seeing what was going on, began to take sides; some were cheering Marcus, and the others were cheering Cyrus and Protius.

The fun and games came to an abrupt stop when Centurion Culpurnius entered the dormitory. He was in charge of this dormitory and soon put an end to the frivolity. Marcus was no doubt relieved at the intrusion of the centurion, but he held no hard feelings towards his companion, although he was annoyed for being made the centre of the frivolity, because they had often mucked about or played around in such a manner. Centurion Culpurnius had made a mental note of the two soldiers who were the cause of the frivolous behaviour in the dormitory and had decided to take retribution on them at the earliest opportunity. The kit inspection provided such an opportunity.

The standard of cleanliness of the clothes and equipment belonging to Cyrus and Protius was no worse than any of the others he had inspected that evening. He used it as a means of punishing them for the previous evening's event. Such an outburst from a centurion was quite common not only in the terrible Twelfth but in the other legions of the Roman army. It was one means of them maintaining the fear for them from the troops under their command. The admonishment and remarks levelled against offenders always took an exaggerated form.

The next evening the two offenders once again laid out their kit at the appointed hour for inspection by the centurion. They knew that whatever extra effort they had put in to cleaning their kit would be of no avail, because they had been singled out for punishment and there was no escape. The only matter now to be decided was what form the punishment would take. Both Cyrus and Protius were very much relieved when the centurion, after admonishing them in more exaggerated terms, ordered that they should report immediately to Centurion Sextus to be placed on the list of troops selected for the extra guard duties in Jerusalem. They were delighted to know that they were to join Timius, Lipsius and Marcus in the troop bound for Jerusalem, but Centurion Sextus was an equally harsh officer, who would give them no respite throughout the performance of their duty while under his command.

He was an extremely tall, gaunt man and a model of physical fitness. They had been given to understand by veterans who had been placed in the same position on previous occasions that he would expect as high standard of physical fitness from them as he himself was capable of attaining. They were told that the march would be harsh and wearisome to an extent that they would wish they had never been born. That is why volunteers for the Jerusalem duty were never forthcoming. Soldiers accused of various offences, near to the time when it was necessary to provide the extra guard in Jerusalem, were selected to make up the detail. All thoughts, all plans of enjoyable pastimes in the City of Jerusalem were quashed by the tales reported by veterans of earlier excursions. Soldiers of the Jerusalem detail were fortunate if they were even granted a few hours of undisturbed sleep, let alone recreation. The sternness of Roman authority was prevalent and had to be seen to be so in the city during the Jewish festival of the Passover.

The Jews were extremely nationalistic and religious, and their emotions overflowed during such a festival. Therefore, the authority of Rome had to take the form through the discipline of the Roman contingent, as a reminder to them.

On the night before their departure, Timius took time off from packing his few personal belongings to write a short note to Tricia. He informed her in his note that he had been selected for special duty, lasting for a short period of three weeks in the City of Jerusalem. The communication was written to give the reader the impression that only the best were selected for this duty and the duty that had fallen regularly on the Twelfth legion was one that had been regarded in the highest esteem.

He was in no doubt that she would be pleased to hear of the progress he was making in the army. Communications from the soldiers of the legion would be conveyed by the troops to Jerusalem from whence they would be despatched to Cesarea for onward transmission to Rome. His companions also followed his example that night and had penned a few lines to their loved ones back in Italy, being conscious of the fact that by the time their communications had reached their respective destinations they would all be back here in the encampment at Palmyra as full participants in the regular routines.

The troop assembled at dawn and after a cursory inspection of their equipment by the two centurions in charge, the tribune who was in command of the contingent then ordered the legionnaires that their rations for the march were to be packed away quickly in their panniers. The rations had been brought to them by a fatigue party from the ration stores. It comprised mainly of portions of bread, dried fruits, a small portion of salt and a healthy portion of millet. These rations were to be supplemented on route by the purchase of other fresh fruits, but the absence of fresh fruit was prevalent in that part of the world. There was a goodly abundance of dates, both fresh and dried, pomegranates and cactus apples. Their rations would be supplemented by such fruit as and when the centurion in charge of the cohort was able to purchase the items from local dealers.

Centurion Festus inspected each man's water skin to ensure that the skin was water tight and filled to full capacity. Centurion Sextus was the senior centurion in command, but he was subordinate to Tribune Marcellus. The two centurions and the tribune were mounted on horseback for the march and they looked a picture of military resplendence in their uniforms. The remainder of the troops were required to march, and Centurion Sextus had informed them before they set off that they would be expected to march at least thirty miles a day until they reached their destination. There would be only one stop at mid-day, so that they could quench their thirst from their water skins.

They would not partake of any food during the march, and any man that flagged on the march would be severely flogged by him personally at the first opportunity. In addition, that individual would also be flogged again thrice over on their return to the base at Palmyra. The discipline of the Roman army was so severe at all times that it made the soldier wonder whether he was serving some sort of cruel sentence for some crime he had committed unwittingly. Many contemplated desertion. Many contemplated defection to the barbarians or to the ranks of the locally raised armies of the client kingdoms, but very few ever went through with such ideas. They knew that if they were caught they would be treated unmercifully by the officers of the army and find themselves cruelly scourged before their execution. Desertion and defection were unspeakable crimes in the Roman army, and not tolerated under any circumstances. Any form of cruelty to the offender was permissible as far as the officers were concerned. Consequently the discipline of the Roman soldier was total.

Within the hour the troop was marching past the place where three weeks earlier Timius, Marcus, and Lipsius had been reprimanded severely for throwing pieces of bread into the hands of the hungry lepers. The troop were being led by the Tribune and Centurion Sextus, who were both on horseback and bringing up the rear of the contingent was Centurion Festus. The troop marched in a column of four ranks, and Timius was on the outside rank nearest to the gulley. In front of him marched Protius. As they passed the spot, Timius recalled the incident of three weeks earlier and glanced over to his left, quite naturally, not expecting to see anything; The site had not changed at all as far as he could remember it but the sound of their marching feet began to disturb the leper settlement, because he noticed a few heads protrude inquisitively out of a few of the doorways of the little huts.

Standing some distance from the huts, and at a place between the road and the beginning of the settlement, he noticed a figure of a man that jerked his memory. Quite near to the man were two other figures and all three were looking in the direction of the troop. The man standing on his own was the big dark skinned man whom Marcus, on the last occasion they had seen him, was convinced resembled Mucta Wahabis. Timius's eyes rested on the man a few seconds. He was also now convinced that it was Mucta. Timius could not understand how a man like Mucta could now be associating with those poor creatures.

When he had taken leave of Mucta at the Port of Saleucia which was the outlet in the Mediterranean for the City of Antioch, Timius and his companions were aware that the possibility of seeing the slave oarsman again was very remote. Timius wondered whether the sores that he had seen on Mucta's arms and legs, and the odd smattering on his forehead, for which he had given Mucta the ointment, were the first stages of leprosy. This had very likely been the cause of his discharge from slavery.

Timius's thoughts were shattered by the shrill voice of Centurion Festus shouting at him. "Look to your front."

Timius was momentarily startled and looked around, only to be shouted at again by the Centurion.

"Yes, it's you, you idle man, I am talking to. Look to your front."

Timius did exactly as he was told and concentrated on the march.

The troop could see, ahead of them in the distance, a small caravan of merchants leading their heavily laden camels out into the distant horizon, but actually on the horizon they could also see what appeared to be a dust storm. They all hoped that it was not approaching in their direction, because they knew the discomfort of marching through a dust storm, and that would have meant marching incessantly without a break in order to clear the storm area. This was not to be so fortunately, because at midday they stopped at a spot unsheltered from the hot sun but which was strewn with boulders. Each soldier wearily made his way to or near one of the boulders to rest and drink from the water skins. Timius could not get comfortable, so he sat on top of one of the rocks. The heat penetrated his tunic and caused his backside to burn. Anyway, it was as comfortable as any other place, he thought. He took a piece of cloth from his tunic pocket and began to wipe the perspiration from his brow and from behind his neck. As he was doing this, he was interrupted by a call from Cyrus, who was seated on a boulder quite near to him.

"Watch out, Timius, there's a snake behind you."

Timius, quite startled, jumped to his feet, his helmet in one hand and the piece of cloth in the other. The reptile slithered over the rock on which he had been sitting and very soon other soldiers began pelting it with stones, until it lay at the foot of the rock bleeding and lifeless.

"By Jupiter, that was a close shave," exclaimed Protius, "we were nearly sending you on your way to the gods."

"You are quite right," agreed Timius, quite shaken because he realized that the snakes in that part of the world were poisonous, and a bite from the reptile would have not only caused him intense pain, but it could have been fatal within a few hours. The excitement soon died down except for Marcus, who approached Timius, and placed his right arm around his shoulder.

"That was a close one," Marcus said quietly.

"Yes, I know it was very close."

"Well, you should concentrate on what you are doing." Marcus continued then added poetically,

Timius sitting on a rock picked his nose
Along came a viper and got him to his toes
Oh! Timmy said, that's not fair
Ah, said the viper, "I don't care."

The few soldiers in close proximity to them laughed loudly when they heard this recitation from Marcus, but Timius was not very amused, and only reacted by telling Marcus to shut up. Since childhood Marcus had always found a unique way of describing an event in poetic form.

The troop had been on the march nine days when, on the morning of the tenth day, when the soldiers had been mustered to commence the march again, the tribune spoke to them, while mounted on horseback, and informed them that they would make temporary camp at the site they were to occupy that night. In his judgement to proceed further would only lead them into what appeared to be a frightening dust storm which they could see ahead of them. Throughout the march the dust storm was visible to the troops, but it was apparent from the beginning that it was moving gently in the same direction and to the left of them.

The tribune knew that since they were approaching the extreme and northern most boundaries of the Palestinian province, the terrain would become hillier and this would serve as a trap for the storm. It was his judgement that if they could make camp for a day or two, the storm might spend itself completely, and so enable them to avoid it completely. He knew—although he did not disclose this to the troops—they were making good time, and two or three days of rest would not be unwelcome to those under his command. However, he did inform them that although they were on Roman provincial soil, there were still marauding bands of natives hostile to the Roman presence, which they would have to guard against. This meant that small details would have to be sent out from time to time to patrol an area some two miles radius to their tiny encampment. Three horses had been brought with the compliment and served as pack animals carrying a few small tents to serve as protection from the hot sun if the necessity arose. The use of the small tents was made on a strict rota basis.

On the evening of the third night, Marcus approached Timius who was sat with others around a camp fire made from dried scrub collected from the surrounding area, and said to him very quietly, "Timius, please don't think that I am being affected by the sun, or suffering some strange kind of sun stroke, but I want to ask you something."

"What is it Marcus?"

Protius, who was near Timius, pricked his ears up and tried to listen in to what Marcus was about to say. He had been gazing blankly into the embers of the fire—as had Timius before Marcus interrupted his thoughts.

Marcus then said, "You might also be interested Protius in what I have to say, but again, please don't think the sun is driving me mad. It certainly is not," he emphasized.

"Well, what is it you have to say," asked Timius.

"This morning when we went out on patrol, and when we reached the extremity of the boundary, did you notice anything in the distance?"

"No, I cannot recall seeing anything," replied Timius.

"Nor did I," Protius interjected.

"Then I must have been seeing a mirage."

"What did you see?"

"I am sure I saw a man coming in our direction along the road we had marched three days ago."

"Strange that you should say that," said Protius, "because I thought I saw someone."

"Yes, come to think of it," Timius added, "I do recall having thought I saw someone but attributed it to being just imagination. The man seemed very much like Mucta."

"Yes, that's what I thought," said Marcus, and Protius nodded his head in agreement.

"I wonder why he is following us, if that is what he is doing."

"I've no idea, Marcus. I suppose it is possible that he feels a bit alienated in the leper colony and has decided to move to another where they would make him a little more welcome, or to perhaps one where he would be able to obtain extra food. After all, he is a big man with a large appetite."

"Yes, but what explanation do you have for his particularly following our troop?" asked Protius.

"It is only conjecture," replied Timius, "but again it is possible that he is following us at a distance in the hope of picking up scraps of food that we are all inclined to just leave behind when we strike camp each morning."

"Yes, that is quite possible; yes indeed, that is possible," agreed Marcus.

"Have you any food left that you will not need tomorrow night?" Timius asked Marcus. "And what about you Protius, have you any left?"

"Yes, I have a piece of bread," replied Protius.

"I've a small piece of bread and half a pomegranate," Marcus added quickly.

"I've a handful of dates," said Timius.

They made their way unobtrusively away from the camp fire and the others who sat around it, and with a piece of sweat cloth laid flat on the sand, they placed the dates, the bread, and half a pomegranate in the centre of the cloth and then tied its ends together to form a small bundle. This they laid near to the prominent rock and with a small stick they wrote in the sand, near to the rock, to Mucta from your Roman friends.

"Let's hope the wind doesn't blow this message away," said Timius.

"More importantly, let's hope the centurions do not see it in the morning, otherwise we'll never get away from the Twelfth Legion.

On the morning of the fourth day, the order was given to strike camp and the troops were on the march again. Timius, Marcus, and Protius had informed Cyrus and Lipsius of what they had done, but Cyrus was pessimistic. He felt that some desert rat or other animal would have a good feed on the food they had left behind and he felt that they had all wasted their time. Lipsius agreed wholeheartedly. He was also pessimistic and felt that by the time Mucta arrived at the site, if indeed it was Mucta, the food would be swarming with families of scorpions.

The night of the thirteenth day, the troop made camp again. They were two miles outside the city of Jerusalem, and before they were dismissed, the tribune, with the two centurions at his side—and all three mounted on horseback—addressed the soldiers. He was very stern in his address and intended that it should have the desired effect. Before speaking, he demanded their keen attention to what he had to say:

"Tomorrow morning we shall strike camp an hour before dawn. I am fully aware that you are all looking forward to reaching the palace of Jerusalem. Mainly so that you can all immerse yourselves in much needed baths. I am also aware that after our long march, your clothing and equipment have become deteriorated in standard. When you arise tomorrow, you will make every effort to clean yourselves up and to smarten up your equipment.

I insist that this will be done, and I do not care a damn about the excuse that you have marched many miles these last twelve days in hot and dusty conditions. When we march into Jerusalem, you will march at attention, and I demand the highest standard of bearing from each of you. You are all Roman soldiers, and you are now in a province that is not wholly conciliatory, or acceptable, to the Roman rule. Your bearing must indicate to the onlookers that Rome is supreme. Throughout your duty in Jerusalem, I demand the highest standard of discipline. You will be alert at all time, and any man shirking, to whatever degree, will be most severely dealt with by me. You will find that we will be in Jerusalem during the days of one of their annual festivals. It is during this festival that the Jews are inclined to become naturally high spirited, just as we are during our festivals. This is the time when nationalist agitators do their best to stir up the crowds of visitors to the city in their efforts to cause maximum disruption.

I need not remind you that the disruption is aimed at the continued rule of our illustrious Emperor. You will not, on any account, get involved in the merrymaking or religious festivities. I demand that you keep control of yourselves throughout, although I am aware that at times you will probably be faced by bands of high-spirited people who will mock and poke fun at you. Their aim of course will be to break your spirit. They must not succeed. Self-control and self-discipline will be the order of the day. Any trouble-maker that you might recognise in the midst of these crowds, you will arrest and bring to the palace immediately. You will not associate yourselves in any way with the people of the city. You are here to do a job of work, and do it you will, even though you might be, at times, placed in a situation of extreme provocation.

Finally, before we march off tomorrow, we will be joined by a tiny complement of auxiliary musicians comprising of trumpeters and drummers. They will lead us through the gates of the city and into the palace. We will follow them, and behind us will follow the three standard-bearers.

You can carry on now Centurion Sextus."

Sextus smartly saluted the tribune and instructed the men to fall out. He told them to prepare to enjoy their evening meal and advised them that, since darkness was falling, they would have to leave the cleaning of their equipment until daylight. He also advised them that they would have time to do this because the musicians were not due to arrive until some four hours after sunrise.

*

The last few days had seen a complete change of scenery. The men were now in hilly country, and from time to time they could see orchards of oranges, grapefruit, and other fruits growing on the hillsides. They had crossed over the River Jordan near to a place named by the natives as the waters of Merom. There the soldiers were given permission to bathe in its cool waters. The route of their march then took them along the shores of the sea of Tiberias, but they were not given time off this time for bathing. One of the veterans of the legion had informed newcomers to the expedition that they should consider themselves highly honoured because their camp site this night was situated only some five hundred yards from the well known local site called the Tomb of the Kings.

"You lot are bloody lucky, aren't you? You are going to spend the night sleeping alongside royalty. Don't get any big ideas during your dreams of playing the part of King Herod, because Centurion Sextus will very soon raise you to the lofty heights of a king by sticking a spear up your backside," the veteran said laughing to himself.

It was now dark, and the soldiers were relaxing, sitting around small campfires. Some were stretched out on their backs taking a well-earned rest. Suddenly there was a shout from one of the soldiers, which was followed by a painful groan. The soldiers seated at the campfire nearest to him, who heard the noise, jumped up and rushed to the spot where he lay. "What's the matter," they asked.

Still groaning with pain, he replied, "I have been bitten by something."

A couple of his companions helped him to his feet while another ran to the fire and grabbed a piece of burning wood to provide more light at the spot where his companions had laid him. Some thought a snake had bitten him, but they soon discovered that it was not a snake but a scorpion, as the creature tried to scamper away out of sight. It was about two inches long and one inch across, as could be seen from the other torches brought to the scene—with a grey green back and sand-coloured legs. Its tail was amber in colour and curved up over its body. They soon killed it, but by this time the victim's arm was beginning to swell, so a tourniquet was quickly applied and tied at the soldier's, elbow. He had been bitten on his right forearm.

One of the soldiers endeavoured to suck the poison out of the bite, which could hardly be seen in the half-light of the burning wood torches. Another suggested pouring some wine over the wound. This they tried, but there was little relief from the pain. A small handful of salt was then placed on the bite and, where it had fused with the wine, it lay caked to cover the spot. The soldier felt that this last remedy did provide some relief. He was then assisted to another more open spot and was advised to lay still and try to sleep it off. Back at the campfire the incident had caused some consternation because it was ironic that a veteran, like Sotorius, should be bitten by a scorpion. Sotorius had been with the Twelfth Legion nearly three years and, during that time, he had developed the art of catching scorpions by snatching them by their tails and dropping them in a ring made of fibre string, some two foot in diameter, dipped in oil. The oily string would then be set alight, and the frightened creatures would fight and sting one another to death. This always provided entertainment for many members of the legion.

Sotorius was in his thirteenth year of service in the army, and none of his companions throughout, who had served with him in Gaul, Tunisia, and Thrace, had never known him to be seriously affected by any kind of illness or disease. He was as hard as nails and expected the same tenacity from each of his comrades, but during the night his two close companions who were asleep on the ground, on either side of him, were disturbed by his loud groaning. His companion Cassius rolled over near to him to see what was wrong with him. He found Sotorius shivering under his blanket and shaking like a leaf in the high wind—yet his face and forehead were wet with perspiration. As he shivered and shook, he kept tossing from side to side.

His other companions soon came over and pulled his arm out from under the blanket, and in the dim light of the dying embers of the fire, near which they had decided to sleep that night, they could see that the swelling on his arm had not taken a turn for the worst, but his two companions after contemplating the situation for some moments, decided that they should seek the assistance of the *medici*. Novus decided that he should go to get him to attend to Sotorius. He was not away long and the *medici* soon arrived on the scene—with his *capsarii* slung over his shoulder—grumbling under his breath at having his sleep disturbed. The roughly made bandage was removed from the bite wound, and the *medici* placed a small poultice comprising some medicinal salt over the wound in order to draw out the poison. He then bound the swollen forearm properly. From his *capsarii*, he took a bottle of a form of narcotic and gave some of it to Sotorius to drink.

He then laid the veteran's head gently back onto his pannier, which he had been using as a pillow and, as he did so, he said, "That should settle him for the night and—,"

They were interrupted by the voice of Centurion Festus as he loomed above them.

"What's going on here?" he demanded.

Novus and Cassius quickly got to their feet, followed by the *Medici*. Centurion Festus had also been disturbed by the incident and demanded again, "Well, what is going on here?"

"Sire, Legionnaire Sotorius was bitten by a deadly scorpion earlier tonight, and he is suffering cruelly from its after effects, and I have just attended to him," replied the *Medici*.

"Attended to him!" he exclaimed. "I don't believe it," he continued, "I will not have one of my soldiers let a little scorpion obstruct him from his military duties. You can tell him tomorrow morning that if he isn't back on his feet and smartly forming himself in the ranks, I will consider him a sissy, and he will be dealt with accordingly when we return to Palmyra. By Jupiter, he will never act or behave like a sissy again. Tell him that, will you?" he said sternly as he walked away.

The following morning Sotorius was far from well. He had a devil of a job putting on the leather wrist bands. His delirium the previous night had sapped him of all his strength, and he felt quite ill, but bearing in mind the ominous message passed to him by Centurion Sextus, from Centurion Festus, he tried desperately hard to behave normally. He was a sick man, and he knew it and could not wait for the march to begin which would end soon after when they entered the praetorian in Jerusalem. It was mid-morning when the small assembly of musicians arrived and the troop was mustered for the final ceremonial march into the city. Their equipment was clean and their helmets, *pilums* and other insignia glinted and glistened in the sunlight. Any onlooker would consider that these were a fine body of men and the Roman would regard them as a fine example of their illustrious empire.

During the preparing and personal cleaning in preparation for the march, Sotorius gave his comrades the impression that all was well with him when they had asked after his health. He did not want to tell them that he was feeling ill because after some initial sympathy they would soon overlook his true state of health—and make no allowances for it for by doing so it is possible that they would draw unnecessary attention toward him and this is something he did not want to happen because Centurion Festus was a man of his word. While on the march, Sotorius had decided to summon all the energy he could and subconsciously apply himself to the task in hand. He was a trained and highly disciplined soldier and this was not difficult for him. Discipline and self-control came quite naturally to him. He marched in the left hand outer rank with his eyes fixed to a point at the back of the helmet of the soldier in front of him. To take his mind off his illness he tried to remember and go over the many happy and equally many unhappy moments he had experienced in the army.

As the troop approached Agrippa's wall, at the northern end of the city, to their left and running at right angles to the road on which they were marching was a well-worn dust track which converged with the road at the entrance to the city gate. The troops could see that they were not the only procession entering the city. Coming along the dust track was a band of some fifty or more people who were local natives joined together for the purpose of joining the festival. Although the music from the trumpeters and drummers was loud and stirring, the troops could hear shouts and chants of jubilation emanating from the native procession. Some were waving small branches cut from fig, or other, trees in the vicinity, while many others were waving branches of palm leaves. None were carrying any emblems or insignia but used the natural products of nature to simulate such ceremonious regalia. They were a happy and high-spirited crowd, obviously intent on enjoying the festivities. The troop was now just beginning to enter the gate of the city wall, and the band of natives stopped to allow them to proceed. The leader of this band was seated on an ass. He was dressed in a sand-coloured robe, and he gave one the impression that he had an air of confidence and complete control over himself and his followers. One could also create an impression that here was a man surrounded by a few followers who had perhaps joined him from the many villages through which he had passed challenging the power of Rome as symbolized by the Roman troop on its way into the city.

Sotorius's thoughts were broken by the new sounds he heard, and he looked up and to the left, from where the sound was coming. His eyes met those of the stranger seated on the ass, and momentarily each held the other's gaze. It was in that moment that Sotorius experienced a strange phenomenon. He quite suddenly realized that the medicine applied to his wounded arm by the *medici* had worked wonders. The ill effects of the scorpion's bite had disappeared, and he felt a complete and sudden change. It was indescribable. He was completely amazed to feel that he was no longer ill, but fully restored to his old self. What a wonderful *medici*, he thought, what a clever man. He promised himself that, at the first opportunity, he would make sure that the man who had attended to him the previous night would allow him the privilege of buying him a large beaker of wine. He would make a point of doing that.

The troop was brought to a halt in the quadrangle in front of Antonia's praesidium—the garrison adjacent to and on the north side of the Temple of Solomon. This is where the troops would be barracked during their tour of duty in the city, as this was the headquarters and palace of the procurator. Before being dismissed to their quarters the troop was split into details of eight legionnaires and each detail was given its respective hours of duty and points of the city that would come within their patrol. They were once again warned against fraternizing with the locals and advised not to become indulgent in the festivities.

CHAPTER XXVII

Quis hic est homo que ante aedes video.

PLAUTUS

Who is this man whom I see before the house?

IT WAS ONE hour past midnight when the turbernia, to which Timius had been assigned, had been dismissed from their duty shift which, on this occasion, had been spent at the gate of Gennath. They each ambled into the small dormitory to quickly remove their equipment and settle down for the night. Their duty shift had lasted eight hours and the troop from Palmyra had been split up into groups of eight soldiers, which were referred to as a turbernia, and each turbernia was accommodated in a small dormitory adjoining the praesidium. The facilities of the dormitory were very sparse. In the middle of each dormitory stood a small wooden table accompanied by a bench, and in the middle of the table stood an oil lamp. These were the only furnishings, and the troops were required to sleep on the stone floors. They had become accustomed to the latter in the encampment of the Twelfth at Palmyra. The dormitories were served by a Thermae, the only luxury provided for the detachment of troops. Timius and his companions had spent many hours relaxing and discussing generalities in the tepidarium and fridgidarium of the Thermae baths in their off-duty hours.

When they arrived in Jerusalem, four days previously, each member of the troop—aside from veterans of previous excursions—had experienced a feeling of excitement, but just four days in the city had dampened all their enthusiasm for the continuation of the detached duty that lay before them. On their tours of duty—and they had discussed the matter frequently—they had found an air of resentment towards them from the city population, but they were sensible enough to realize that the resentment was well founded.

The Roman attitude towards the Jews was abrasive and, in the past, many Jews who had openly shown their resentment had been quickly and cruelly executed. A stage had been reached where the slightest provocation from a Jew resulted in execution. The previous governor of the province was an extremely cruel man and his successor, the Procurator Pontius Pilate, showed no mercy on his foreign subjects. The Jews were nationalistic and deeply religious and guarded the beliefs of their monotheist religion tenaciously, whereas the occupiers were profligate in their practice of polytheism. The occupying power had erected statues to the Emperor and to the past heroes of Rome and, moreover, statues of their gods in almost every crook and cranny of the city. This was abhorrent to the Jews, whose religion dictated that no statues to gods or men of great deeds should be erected because, by their very nature, the Jews considered these to be an oblique form of worship.

The Temple of Solomon was an inspiration to them in their religious attitudes, and the high priest and elders of the temple were allowed to pursue their autocratic rule over the religion.

There were some desensitizers of this rule merely because the hierarchy of the religion did not reach such lofty heights through religious servitude and progress, but by hereditary means. They claimed to be the descendants of Moses, their deliverer from Egyptian bondage. But it was the Roman and the auxiliary troops, representing the power of Rome in their midst, that they focused their constant resentment.

Those Jews that tried to work in harmony with their oppressors were shunned and held to be collaborators. This was the attitude at that time prevalent in the city and the province as a whole, and it was an attitude that had found its beginnings in the not too distant past. Despite this Rome considered it imperative that the province of Palestine should be part of the realm of the Roman Empire. The province had provided Rome with a settled and civilized corridor to its two more important provinces of Egypt in the south and Syria in the north. Despite its reputation for being a troublesome province it was essential to maintain control of it—even though oppression had to be stretched to its limits. Humanity was the prime concern of Rome but in order that the kind of humanity that the Roman believed in should prevail, it was necessary to cruelly oppress dissenters of the Roman way of life and Roman civilization.

"Come on, you lazy bastards, on your feet!" shrieked Centurion Festus as he rapped the table with his vine staff. "You lot are required at Pilate's consular straight away, so get a move on. I can't wait for you all bloody day," he shouted. "Come on!" he shouted again impatiently, "and you will need full sentry dress, so get a move on."

It was the early hours of the morning, and the troops had been roused to especially undertake a duty in Pilate's chamber. They were annoyed at having been awakened at this unearthly hour, and their annoyance was aggravated by the fact that it was only some four or five hours earlier that they had completed a duty Gennath. They thought that this was most unjust, and it was any wonder that no soldier from the terrible Twelfth ever volunteered for detached duty in Jerusalem—an annual event. The procurator, Pilate, had returned to Jerusalem for the feast of the Passover. The Roman governor normally resided at Ceasarea, but it was considered to be important from the point of view of etiquette and good manners not to mention the endorsement of the occupying powers presence to be in the capital during the celebrations. It was also considered to be part of the wisdom of Roman policy that the Roman governors, however much they were detested, try and identify themselves with facilities of local provincial population. Besides the presence of the local governor dictated the presence of additional troops as bodyguards to the consul, which was a convenient way of ensuring that additional troops were at hand in case the excitement of such festivities occasioned seditious disturbances. Pontius Pilate was an extremely able administrator and commanded the respect of the cunning Judean, King Herod. He was tactful and diplomatic in his dealings with the Judean leadership and fully aware of the delicate situation that existed in this province. Herod's power over his people was absolute, but he was subordinate to Rome, and it was essential that Herod's alliance be maintained. This was done through diplomacy and cajolery. There were many dissenters of Herod's rule, also, and Roman cruelty was given sanction.

The soldiers quickly rubbed the sleep from their eyes and dressed themselves ready for duty. Throughout the past four days, they had been constantly subjected to sentry duties in and around the focal points of the city conurbation. Marcus and Lipsius were moaning and groaning at being selected for the Jerusalem detachment, whereas Timius and Cyrus accepted it as merely additional experience. Protius was abusive under his breath and the other members of the contuburnia were equally abusive under their breath. The other four members of the conturburnia were Jarvius, Dolba, Petrano and Tagus, who had all seen many more years' service in the army than Timius and his companions. Their mumblings and grumblings began to rub on the nerves of Cyrus, who promptly told them to shut up and get on with it. He went on to remind them that during their tours of duty there had been many beautiful Jewish girls who had looked at each of them in a way that could only be construed as an invitation which they could not accept, and as far as he was concerned this was a greater annoyance than the duty itself. On one occasion during the past four days Cyrus had remarked to Protius that he thought the local girls were beautiful.

Cyrus was most amused when Protius had replied, "I agree with you, but do you not know that when the local girls begin to look attractive and beautiful, it is time we were returning to Rome; we've been out here too long."

The maniple assembled in the tiny quadrangle outside the praesidium and after Centurion Festus had satisfied himself that the troop was present and ready to march to the main section of the palace he reported to the tribune who had approached them on horseback. The tribune, who also looked annoyed at being disturbed this early hour of the morning, indicated his satisfaction. He, too, like the eight men in the troop, looked tired and frustrated. He spent the previous evening in the baths, after which he had joined other officers in a drinking session which went on into the late hours of the night. He certainly gave the appearance that he had indulged himself in a bout of heavy drinking. The tribune halted his horse in front of the small troop and immediately began rather impatiently to inform them of the purpose of their very early call to duty that day.

"The noble procurator, I am told, has just tried and sentenced a murderer who is to be executed after day break, and I am informed that he is at the moment trying two other criminals who have committed a felony. These damn Jews are a bloody nuisance, and they are a hypocritical lot of swine as far as I am concerned. Anyway, let us proceed."

Turning his horse round, he led them away. During the short march to the consular, the troops could not stop yawning, and their morale was at low ebb.

The troop entered the quadrangle of the procurator's consular and they were detailed to march inside the chamber and relieve eight of their colleagues who had been on duty all night. As they marched up the steps of the consular, they were passed by a troop of auxiliaries leading out two criminals who had obviously just been sentenced. The troop entered the consul chamber, smartly saluted their colleagues of the previous duty, and took up their positions. Their colleagues of the guard they relieved marched away. Nothing happened for a while but from where they were standing, they could hear the voices of a group of people, possibly Jews, which gave them the impression that something was afoot. Very soon, the procurator entered the chamber from a side entrance, followed by two assistants, and sat down on a marble seat while two assistants took up their positions on either side of him.

The procurator was dressed in a white toga with a red cloak cast about his shoulders. The red cloak was edged with a Grecian key border and he wore a chaplet of gold laurel leaves on his head. This symbolized his office. The procurator looked weary and fed up. He had obviously had a busy night attending to administrative matters and during the more recent hours the administration of justice. The next prisoner to be brought before him would be dealt with severely now that he was in this present belligerent mood. The procurator asked his assistant to bring in the next prisoner. While they awaited his arrival, which took only a few moments, Timius gazed around him and concluded that the consular was a cold and foreboding place. Timius and Lipsius had taken up positions to the right of the marble seat, while Cyrus and Marcus positioned themselves to the left of it. The tribune and centurion were in attendance to the procurator, whereas the remaining four members of the troop had taken up their place near the entrance of the chamber. Very soon the offender—who appeared to be in his early thirties—walked slowly to the spot before the procurator's seat. He was followed by two members dressed in their religious regalia, representatives of the Jewish Sanhedrin. The offender stood motionless, his eyes cast down on the stone floor in front of him. His eyes seemed to be positioned close together on his face with his eyebrows almost meeting. He had a very dark complexion and his nose was aquiline. His hair was black and dishevelled and his beard unkempt.

The sand-coloured homespun robe he wore hung loosely from his shoulders. Timius noticed that he was slightly built and about five feet seven in height. He also noticed that his garment was badly in need of repair, and the need to replace it was imminent. There were no sandals on his feet, and he carried no possessions with him. He had obviously been relieved of all his belongings before being brought to trial. The two spokesmen for the Sanhedrin were now flanked on either side of him, and they, too, stood equally motionless, as though in a religious pose. Very soon a legate and two lectors entered the room, and the assistant began to prepare to take notes as a record of the trial on a waxed tablet. The procurator appeared to be more irritated and annoyed at being summoned to sit in judgement over such a puny individual who now stood meekly before him. He looked around momentarily and then questioned the prosecutors of the offender.

He asked impatiently, "Well what is the crime for which you bring charges against this miserable offender?"

One of the spokesmen replied, "Sire, this man before you had committed the crime of blasphemy, for which we are justly offended. He has caused the most unspeakable offence to the Jewish nation."

"Has he?" asked Pilate. "In what manner has he blasphemed?"

"Sire, he offended the priests in the temple by insulting them over the manner in which they practiced and preached our holy religion. He claims that he is the Son of God and our rightful king. He has also caused disruption in the temple by scattering the tables and monies of the honourable burgers. Furthermore, sire, he has encouraged sections of our community to oppose the ancient rights and practices of our religion by preaching the misinterpretation of ancient and accepted philosophies of our forefathers and profits. These, sire, are some of the many charges we wish to level against him."

Pilate fidgeted for a moment, clasping his hands and then re-clasping them before saying, with a strong note of irritation in his voice, "this is a matter for your high priest Caiaphas to deal with not for me. I am only concerned with crimes against the state. Take him to Caiaphas; don't bother me with him."

The accused man throughout the exchanges said nothing. He remained motionless. He then looked around him slowly at each of the soldiers facing him. His eyes met those of Marcus, and they gazed at each other for a few moments. Marcus looked away quickly because there was something uncanny in the man's eyes that made him feel quite humbled. Suddenly an inexplicable peace seemed to settle on him.

After a moment the Sanhedrin spokesman once again continued with his accusations, as though there was a need to communicate with the procurator.

"Sire, we also accuse him of sedition."

"Sedition, did you say sedition?"

The spokesman nodded his head,

"I cannot believe this wretch of a man is capable of acting in a seditious manner."

Pilate now looked at the man with a fearsome expression on his face. "What have you to say to this charge?" he demanded.

The accused did not reply.

Pilate immediately got to his feet and, turning to the guards near to him, ordered, "Take him away and give him a scourging. That will teach him a lesson not to treat Roman authority contemptuously.

He turned on his heel and strode through the exit of the chamber. The legionnaire, Jarvius, obeyed the command and roughly pushed the accused man forward and towards the rear of the chamber where there was a colonnaded entrance leading into a small courtyard once used as the solarium for the praetorian. It was now used for a different purpose, because erected in the middle of the courtyard was a roughly hewn stone pillar to which was embedded an iron ring. When the prisoner had been taken into the solarium, the lector stripped him of his robe and shackled him by his wrists to the iron ring which was already set about two feet above his head. The shackles of the prisoner made him half-reach towards the pinnacle of the pillar. The lector then called to the assistant to bring him a scourge which was promptly handed to him. The scourge was a finely developed implement of torture consisting of ten leathered thongs fastened securely to a cane. Each thong was knotted in its centre and at the end. Wrapped around the end were strips of lead. It had been developed to inflict maximum pain on the recipient, and any prisoner who survived a scourging was in severe pain for a number of days and sometimes weeks after. Many did not survive a scourging, and usually at the end of a punishment, a prisoner would cry for mercy. It was considered to be a most horrible punishment next only to that of crucifixion.

The prisoner's robe was roughly stripped off him and lay at his feet as the *lictor* began the punishment. With each stroke of the implement laid on his back, the prisoner winced. Those soldiers who were witnessing the punishment for the first time were horrified. Perhaps few were even shocked at the extent to which Roman authority would go in order to maintain control of its less obedient subjects. The scourging continued for about twenty minutes until the frail body of the victim sagged and lay against the pillar, his wrists still shackled by the chains. The lector then released him from the iron ring that held his chained wrists, and his body slumped to the floor. Timius and the other guards present were appalled to see the damaged and bleeding back of the victim. The scourge had cut deep into his flesh, and he was ashamed that the illustrious state for which he was a minor representative, together with his colleagues, could stoop so low as to inflict such inhuman punishment on an individual who appeared to be so inoffensive, and, in his opinion, could not possibly and by any stretch of the imagination be a threat to the power of Rome. Timius also had the strange feeling that even the noble procurator had attempted to brush the accusation of sedition aside and to only sentence the man to the scourge to appease those who had levelled such monstrous accusations against the accused.

The prisoner lay for a short while where he had slumped but was very roughly grabbed by the wrists and by the hair on his head and dragged to his feet. He could barely stand. The lector then dragged him with the assistance of Legionnaire Dolba, who prodded him in the back with his *pilum*. He was dragged, pushed, and roughly persuaded to make his way back, under guard, to the spot in front of the procurator's seat to await further deliberations. Pontius Pilate re-entered the chamber and once again seated himself comfortably on the marble seat.

He looked straight into the man's face and after a moment asked him, "Well, have you had enough? Do you now repent and ask for our mercy?"

The man did not reply.

"I see you are one of the more obdurate types that we meet occasionally."

As he spoke, the two spokesmen from the Sanhedrin returned to the chamber from the main entrance.

After they had bowed and saluted the procurator, one of them spoke and said, "Sire, would you please forgive us for imposing on your valuable time and asking you to administer true justice, but it has come to our ears that the prisoner before you has also made claims to be the **King of the Jews**. We consider this to be extremely dangerous."

Pilate was astounded to hear this further accusation, but replied, "I think this is a matter which comes under the jurisdiction of your King Herod."

"This is so, sire, in normal circumstances, but the man before you is not a Judean but a Galilean, and as you are fully aware, the province of Galilee is outside the jurisdiction of the noble King Herod.

There was a long silence while Pontius Pilate contemplated the new situation before he began to speak. There was a sombre note in his voice when he began.

"Your prosecutors' earlier charges of sedition and blasphemy are more serious than was I led to believe. You are charged with sedition of the most serious kind against the state. You are charged with rebellious incitement. What have you to say in your defence?"

The prisoner answered for the first time since his arrival.

"Sire, it is true that I have admonished the elders of the temple for the hypocritical manner in which they preach and practice the religion of my father who is the living God, but I have not preached rebellion against the authority of the state."

His voice was calm and clear.

"What then have you said that has been the cause of such serious charges brought against you?" asked Pilate.

The prisoner remained silent.

"Come on, come on, I need an answer!" Pilate said impatiently.

"Sire, I have directed my followers and friends to give unto Caesar what is Caesar's and unto God what is God's"

"Is that the truth?" Pilate asked.

"Sire, *I am the truth.*"

Pilate said nothing for a moment not knowing what to make of this pitiful individual's reply. He then asked the question, as though speaking his thoughts out loud, because it was not addressed to anyone in particular.

'What it truth'

Turning to the spokesman of the Sanhedrin, Pilate expressed his displeasure at the lack of evidence produced so far in support of the charges and gently admonished the accusers. He said, "I cannot see any wrong in this man. What evidence have you that he has incited his followers to rebel against the power of Rome?"

"He had been wandering throughout the countryside and villages, preaching rebellion and propounding blasphemous theories. In this he has been abetted by a small group of men who are his close associates. We have not as yet been able to arrest these men. They were hiding in the garden of Gethsemane—last night when we caught him,"

Pilate looked at the prisoner for a few moments and said nothing. His eyes then roved in an upward direction, as though he were silently studying the golden rays of the sun, which began penetrating the upper windows of the chamber. The spokesman then added a further allegation to those already made. "He also claims to be the son of God."

"What god are you talking about?" Pilate exclaimed impatiently.

"Our God, sire."

Pilate grunted his understanding and then asked the prisoner, "Are you the son of God?"

"Who do you believe I am?" asked the prisoner very calmly.

Pilate took exception to this reply and stood up abruptly and walked over to the prisoner and, in his annoyance, struck him across the face with his right hand. The prisoner flinched slightly but soon regained his composure.

Both Pilate and the prisoner's eyes were fixed on each other for a few moments and the momentary silence was broken when Pilate, with his face only a few inches away from the prisoner, asked in a deeply tormented manner, "Who are you?"

The man did not reply. Pilate sat down and, turning to the representatives and crowd present, said, "Earlier this morning I sentenced a murderer to death. I understand his name was Barabbas—*Barabbas was a brigand.* It is customary that if the situation occasions it, I should release one of the condemned prisoners in honour of your festival, which I understand is a symbolic representation of your people's freedom from Egyptian bondage. Go quickly and ask your people whom they would like me to acquit, Barabbas or this Galilean?"

The representatives of the Sanhedrin quickly withdrew. Pilate continued to fidget uncomfortably.

The representatives soon returned in to the presence of the procurator, and Pilate. The latter getting more impatient, asked them, "Well, well, what did your people say?"

"We have consulted the people sire—"

Pilate interrupted them, "Yes I know all that, but what did they say?"

"Sire, they have asked for the one called Barabbas, and are demanding the crucifixion of the Galilean who claims to be the King of the Jews."

Pilate's expression was one of shock and disbelief.

'King of the Jews, eh' he repeated under his breath, and then he asked the accused, "Are you the King of the Jews?"

The Galilean again replied calmly and clearly, "You have said I am the King of the Jews."

Pilate was amazed at the courage and confidence of the man before him, and his uneasiness grew. He turned sharply to his assistant and demanded angrily, "Bring me some water—bring me some water!"

The assistant quickly ran into a side entrance leading to the chamber and returned with a small bowl of water. A towel was placed over his left forearm.

The procurator washed his trembling, perspiring hands and, as he did so, looked straight at the representatives of the Sanhedrin and said with a tone of remorse in his voice, "I wash my hands of this whole affair."

Those present could detect in his manner a sense of disbelief that the religious adherence of the Jewish faith who had contrived out of mendacity to bring this man to trial on the flimsiest evidence should not be satisfied with the punishment that had already been applied, but were demanding the prisoner's execution. Pilate's sense of disbelief caused him to take a further step in trying to exonerate himself in this most despicable episode by rising to his feet and clutching the right shoulder of the man whom he had just tried and led him away to the main entrance of the consular. At the foot of the steps, which led to the consular, were a group of Jewish nationals. Some appeared to be suffering from the after-affects of drink while others stood solemnly in their midst. The rumblings from the small crowd died away as Pilate stood before them with the Galilean at his side. He himself now put the question to the crowd. "Am I to release the one called Barabbas, or am I to acquit this Galilean?"

There was still silence from the crowd. Again Pilate asked sternly and in a clear voice, "I ask you again. Am I to release the one called Barabbas or this Galilean? I demand an answer!"

Many in the crowd cheered and shouted. "Release to us Barabbas."

Pilate, although half-expecting the reply he received, was dumbfounded. As far as he was concerned the matter was closed.

He finally ended it by saying to the crowd, "I present to you your king, *the King of the Jews*".

He turned and beckoned the guards to take the Galilean away. Marcus and Cyrus stepped forward and were quickly followed by Lipsius, who grabbed hold of the Galilean and forced him down the steps. Pilate re-entered the chamber and, as he passed Legionnaire Arbutus, who was also making his way towards the main entrance, Timius heard him say to his assistant, "That man is certain to be a greater danger to Rome dead than he ever was alive."

Timius also recognised the face of the assistant to whom Pilate had spoken. He never forgot a face, no matter how many years had passed since he last met that person, and he was astonished to realize that the face he had seen was that of his childhood friend Ciatus. Ciatus did not recognise Timius, as he was too engrossed in what his master was saying, but when Timius reached the top of the stairs, there was a commotion going on around the Galilean. One man i the crowd was forcing onto the head of the Galilean what appeared to be a copy of a Roman chaplet, but it was made of thorns. As he pressed the chaplet onto the condemned man's head, blood trickled down his face and down the back of his head, and this was causing the man's hair to become more matted than it had been previously. Centurion Festus was making an endeavour to calm the excited and fanatical crowd.

They were crying in mockery, '*Hail, King of the Jews.*"

Many ran up to him and spat in his face. Centurion Festus called out to Timius and the other guards to come quickly and on their arrival, near to the condemned, they were able to force back the crowd by presenting the sharp end of their *pila* to them. Meanwhile assistants in the praetorian had fetched a wooden beam.

This they lifted onto the back of the Galilean and secured it place by tying each of his arms from under the arm pits to the beam. Timius was instructed by Centurion Festus to tie a length of rope around his waist, after which he was instructed to drag the prisoner out of the gate of the praesidium courtyard. The tribune mounted his horse, but Centurion Festus remained on foot, his sword in his right hand and his vine staff in his left. The other members of the guard were also instructed to draw their swords. It was obvious to them that they would need both weapons—*pilum* and sword—to keep away the jeering and mocking crowds—even spectators who took a delight in seeing a condemned man dragged through the narrow street of the city to the place of execution.

"Come on, now, let's get him up there," should Festus, "and keep the crowds away."

Timius dragged on the rope and pulled the prisoner behind him. The prisoner was followed by the lector armed with a whip. The whip was laid across the man's back as a means of persuading him forward. The tiny procession was now on its way through the gates of the praesidium. This was the second procession that had passed through the gates that morning. Earlier two criminals condemned to death for felony had been dragged out in a similar fashion by auxiliary troops. As he passed through the gates, the realization came to Timius of why veterans of the terrible Twelfth avoided excursions of detached duty in the city of Jerusalem during the festival of the Passover.

CHAPTER XXVIII

Ibam foete Via Sacra.

HORACE

I was going by chance along the sacred way.

THE EVENT IN which the soldiers—forming the Conturburnia—and their two superior officers was the end result of collusion and conspiracy. The man who had just been sentenced to death by crucifixion by the Roman procurator was pitifully innocent of the charges brought against him. He had been charged with blasphemy; he claimed to be the Son of God. This was the allegation against him when he was taken to the high priest of the Jewish temple to a man by the name of Caiaphas. The sentence Caiaphas could impose on him would have been a sentence requiring the harshest repentance practiced within the Jewish faith.

This was insufficient for the conspirators. After all he had openly accused them of corruption and had done so within the walls of a temple held in the highest esteem by followers of the faith. The allegation that he had claimed to be the King of the Jews was one within the jurisdiction of King Herod. Herod knew that the ultimate sentence for such a claim was the death penalty but, again, since the accused man was not a citizen of his domain, such a penalty was outside his jurisdiction. Ultimately the final act of ridding the citizenry of this troublemaker would involve something more serious to bring the alleged crime within the domain of the Roman authority.

The allegation of sedition was the ultimate crime that could be levelled against a citizen of the Roman province. The evidence of such lay in the manner in which the Galilean had aroused his followers. Pontius Pilate being forever concerned with satisfying his masters in Rome in his just administration of the province was left little alternative than to acquiesce with the man's prosecutors. The procurator had quite recently been embroiled in matters concerning the province and Rome, the result of which was his admonishment. He did not seek to repeat such an episode, and the easiest course of action open to him, whatever his personal feeling, was motivated by trying to maintain a balance between his own authoritative rule and the provincials on whom he relied for their good offices.

He was a tired and troubled man, and this attitude was prevalent throughout the short trial of the Galilean. Normally, Pontius Pilate would have dealt with an offender hastily and sentenced him swiftly, but on this last occasion the element of hesitancy had crept into the proceedings, of which he was naturally in sole charge. He had felt that the severe punishment of scourging would suffice to rid him of this petulant offender, but this was not so, as the accusers, he discovered, demanded nothing less than execution. Their demands were qualified with an execution combining torture of the most serious and most painful nature. Crucifixion was the only penalty that the prosecution councils and its supporters would settle for. Thus, troubled and tired, he met their demands. The matter was closed for the Roman procurator.

The procession had passed through the gates of the praesidium and along the narrow road leading out through the walls of the city. It had become crowded with sightseers. Many perhaps were visitors to the city for the festival who had never seen the spectacle of a condemned man being led away to meet his ultimate end. This was a spectacle the majority enjoyed, and it was a pleasure in which they could indulge in the early hours after sunrise. Spectators in the crowd had heard the rumour that the condemned man had made claims of being the King of the Jews—thus the explanation for the chaplet of thorns that he was wearing. The jeering and mocking continued and grew fiercer with every step that the man, accompanied by his captors, took. Some even were bold enough to disregard the soldiers' *pila* and swords, which were being used to keep them away from the prisoner, to step in front of him in order to spit in his face. The soldiers present were appalled by such despicable behaviour, and felt that it was sufficient for the man to be condemned insidiously, with no need for the crowd to behave in that way.

The prisoner fell, and the jeering and mocking increased. The lictor, using his whip, lashed the man while he lay on the road. Timius pulled on the rope with both hands, having replaced his sword in its scabbard temporarily. The man dragged himself to his feet, the wooden beam still lashed to his outstretched arms, and with some persuasion from Protius's sword, he dragged his feet forward again. Timius was disgusted to see the expression on the faces of those in the crowd. In the midst of this turbulent episode he closely studied some of those in the crowd lining the street to the left and right of him.

His eyes rested on a small group of five men who appeared to be noblemen. They were dressed in white togas and were obviously Roman citizens. He noticed that each was carrying a scroll and a leather pouch under his arm. They were the Roman tax collectors who were now in the city manning a registration office for the purpose of collecting the personal tribute imposed on the citizens of Jerusalem and its surrounding district by the Roman Emperor. These men were also amused with the spectacle, and Timius could not help wondering at the shallowness of human feeling, even from his own countrymen.

He was jerked back to reality with a sudden pull on the rope. Again he sheathed his sword and tugged on the rope to try and assist the prisoner to his feet. He had fallen again. Some members of the crowd quickly ran over to where the prisoner lay and spat at him while he struggled to get to his feet. The *lictor* this time used his whip to drive them back and, having done so, turned his attention on the prisoner and lashed him unmercifully. His threadbare robe was becoming shredded from the strokes of the whip. Timius lost control and within a few paces pushed the *lictor* away.

He was absolutely furious and shouted at the *lictor*, "Can't you leave him alone. He'll never get up if you keep whipping him."

Marcus was soon at his side tugging Timius away. The *lictor* glared at Timius and shouted above the din, "Dare you talk to me like that. I will deal with you later."

Timius got the message and decided to carry on with what was his unfortunate duty. The enthusiasm and gusto of the soldiers was now being sapped, and Festus, realized that if they did not get the man to the place of execution quickly. The execution party would loose control and the crowds would soon tear the prisoner apart like hungry wolves. He urged them on frantically, and Timius dragged the man at the end of the rope as hard as he could without letting him lose his balance. The prisoner was bleeding—the sweat was mingling with the blood that was running down his face from his forehead. He had also taken a stroke of the whip across his face. It was, therefore, a horrible mess. He could hardly see where he was walking—through the blood and matted hair—when a woman quickly broke away from the crowds, ran up to him and wiped his face with her handkerchief. She was thrust back into the crowd by Cyrus.

The execution party and prisoner were approaching the gateway in the northern wall of the city. Their progress had become slightly more hurried than at the outset, and it was becoming noticeable that the jeering crowds were dwindling. Following the party was a small group which did not give the onlooker the appearance of spectators. The countenance of this group was one of sorrow. Timius could feel that the prisoner tied to the end of the rope he was pulling, was becoming weaker because it felt as though the dragging on the rope was caused through the man's faltering, weak, steps.;

If the rope could have supported him, the prisoner would have used the rope for that purpose. Again Timius was pulled to a halt because the man had fallen. The *lictor* continued to use the whip but not as unmercifully as on previous occasions. Even the *lictor* knew that the man's strength had been sapped. Very soon a man stepped out from the crowd and, approaching the *lictor*, asked the officer something. The stranger was of medium build with short black hair and was wearing a brown tunic. Timius saw the *lictor* direct the man to Centurion Festus, and he then saw Festus nodding his head as though agreeing to some suggestion. Timius and Livius were called over by the *lictor* who instructed them to untie the beam. This they began to do, and as Timius knelt down beside the prisoner, he felt the coarse stones of the road abrasive to his knees. Livius untied the prisoner's left arm while Timius released that part of the beam from his right arm.

The prisoner's arms were numbed with pain, and they fell limp on the beam. Timius clutched the prisoner's right hand so that the beam could be taken from behind his shoulders. As he did so, the prisoner clutched Timius's hand tightly, and in that very brief contact which was in the form of a rough handshake Timius immediately recognised that the hand he was clutching was the hand of a friend. Prior to this incident, Timius felt, as he was certain his companions did, that the whole episode was tormenting to him, but at this moment torment was banished from his mind. He was astonished to feel completely at peace. He had a duty to perform, and he knew that he would perform it to the best of his ability. He felt that there was no need now to be emotional about it, because in that momentary handshake, Timius knew that the prisoner understood that he was only carrying out the duty of a Roman soldier. There was no personal animosity between the prisoner or any of the soldiers.

The stranger from the crowd assisted Timius and Lipsius to get the prisoner to his feet, after which he picked up the beam and carried it behind the prisoner and out of the gate of the city. Once outside the gate, the party turned left, and in front of them, they could see the small hill known by

the local population as Calvary. This was the site where executions were
carried out. They could see erected on top of the hill scaffolding made from
sturdy beams of wood. Timius looked round briefly and apart from noticing
the agony on the prisoner's face, he also noticed at the rear of the small
group following the party, four men dressed in religious regalia. These men
were following the execution party to report back to the high priest the
completion of the act. As the party marched up the hill, Timius had to
drag the prisoner more fiercely because the incline of the hill was sapping
the last ounces of strength out of his body. At last the party arrived at the
place of execution. It was a gruesome place, and Timius felt that this was
the most grotesque experience he had ever been called on to encounter since
joining the army. Little did he know that there was worse to take place,
but there was one consolation—he knew the prisoner understood his—his
companions and officers—feelings and exonerated them and by knowing
this his remorse was somewhat alleviated.

The scaffolding comprised three stout beams which were one feet across
by eight inches in width, bedded firmly into the ground. Each beam rose
to a height of twelve feet above the ground, and protruding to a height of
about two feet from the horizontal face of the centre beam was an iron
dowel about two inches in diameter. Although the two outer upright beams
were fitted with similar dowels, these were not completely visible because
their lower part was hidden at the centres by the horizontal beams which
now rested on the upper face of each of the upright beams and for which
the dowels provided a fitting. The dowel passed through previously drilled
holes in the centre of the horizontal beams, and to these beams were lashed
the arms of the two convicted prisoners who had earlier been brought to this
place of torture and execution. The ankles were also lashed with a strong
rope to the respective perpendicular beams. It was in this hanging position
that they now found themselves; the agony of a slow death hung over them.
Sometimes it took days for a condemned man to die while hung in this
manner. But in order to speed up the process considerably, the legs of the
prisoners were broken, bringing about death within eight hours. The two
prisoners had suffered this fate.

The upright beams stood approximately six feet apart, and standing
at a distance of one foot to their rear were a row of four other upright
beams of the same width and depth as those already described. At the back
this set of four upright beams were three feet higher than the three that
were in the forward position. These were also firmly embedded into the
ground, and two of them stood in the middle distance between each of the

upright beams in the forward position while the other two flanked the row of the shorter beams at about eight feet away at either end. Across the top of the taller upright beams ran a single, and what appeared to be continuous beam, to form a supporting frame. This horizontal continuous beam acted as a gantry over which ropes were slung. The prisoner, whose arms were already lashed to the a beam across his shoulders, was hauled up a respective upright beam until the centre hole of the horizontal beam slid over the dowel forming the shape of a 'tee' Two wooden ladders rested aimlessly against the frame and fixed to that part of the protruding dowels above the horizontal beams were pieces of stiff papyrus on which was hastily scribed the crime of the prisoner.

The execution party, on their arrival at the site, observed another rowdy group approaching the place. This group comprised mainly young men who were not only shouting and balling obscenities, but were also armed with either staves or short lengths of wood, which gave the appearance of cudgels. The tribune in charge of the party felt that there was something ominous about their arrival but he was also aware of the safety in numbers of his own highly disciplined troop and the auxiliaries that had arrived earlier and were now aimlessly standing around awaiting the death of the earlier victims.

He dismounted from his horse, and Centurion Festus did the same. The centurion glanced up into the sky because he could see, above the site, a small flock of eagles circling in anticipation. Centurion Festus ordered the Roman soldiers to strip the robe off the prisoner. The prisoner stood there naked and the cuts from the scourge were now clearly visible across the whole of his back. His back was completely covered with congealed blood. The man that had carried the wooden beam up the hill for the prisoner was now told to lay it on the ground.

He carried out his instruction, and a cheer went up from the recently arrived rowdy mob. The prisoner was forced to the ground and made to lie on his back. Cyrus and Dolba were then told to drag him until his deeply cut shoulders lay on the surface of the beam. Ropes were then passed to Timius and Marcus so that they could proceed to lash his arms to the beam. As they attempted to do so a rowdy chorus rose from the mob as they waved the staves and cudgels in the air: 'Nail him! Nail him!'

Timius and Marcus hesitated and looked to Centurion Festus for his reactions. The tribune, realizing the mood of the mob, and wanting the least amount of disturbance, nodded in agreement to Festus. The *lictor* called to Timius, "You, over there."

Timius glanced up at him, not knowing whether the *lictor* was referring to him, "Yes, it's you I am talking to. You're the cheeky bastard who had the audacity earlier to tell me my job. Go over to the centurion in charge of the auxiliaries and get some nails and a mallet from him, and bring them here quickly. Go on—don't look at me like that. We haven't got all day to wait."

Timius did as he was bid and ran over to the auxiliary centurion. The auxiliary centurion wandered over to a donkey, which they had brought with them as a pack animal, and from one of the panniers handed Timius six or seven stout iron nails and a heavy iron headed mallet. Timius ran back with these to the *lictor*.

"Right, you hold the nail while your friend over there," he said pointing to Marcus, "can hammer it home into the beam."

"Yes, sire," replied Timius.

He crouched over the part of the beam on which the prisoner's arm lay limply, forced the man's palm open, and placed the point of the nail into the centre of it.

"Not there!—you stupid bloody idiot—it will rip his hand apart—put the nail in the centre of his wrist."

Timius did as he was told.

"Go on, hammer it home," he instructed Marcus.

While Timius held the nail in position it took Marcus only three strokes of the mallet to drive the nail through the prisoner's wrist and into the wooden beam. As it penetrated home blood from the man's wrist squirted out onto Timius's breast plate and Marcus's greaves.

"Now do the same with the other wrist the other side," bawled the *lictor*.

The prisoner quietly groaned in agony as the other nail was driven in. Timius and Marcus were then instructed by Festus to lash the man's arms with the ends of two long ropes while Protius and Lipsus were told to sling the other ends across the gantry beam. When they had done this they were told to go behind the wooden scaffolding and for two men each to grab hold of the loose ends of the ropes that were now dangling from the gantry beam and haul the cross member, to which the prisoner's arms were nailed and lashed, up until it came to rest on the upper face of the centre upright beam. They did this and the prisoner groaned more loudly as the back of the beam to which he was nailed slid up the forward face of the upright. The cross member was hauled up until it was nearly touching the gantry. Dolba and Jarvius were told to climb up the ladders and steady the cross member until the hole which was drilled in it was centred with the dowel.

When this was done, the men who were putting their weight on the ropes were instructed to release their hold. The cross member slid down the dowel and came to rest with a thud. The prisoner yelled out in agony because his wrists, through which the nails had been driven, took the whole weight of his body.

Each groan or yell of agony from the man brought a more frenzied cry from the mob. The *lictor* now walked to the front of the prisoner and crossed the prisoner's feet and held them in position while he instructed Timius to bring another nail and place it in the centre of his left foot behind which his right foot rested. Marcus was told to bring the mallet, and very quickly, though clumsily, he drove the nail home until the prisoner's feet were pinned tightly to the upright beam. Again the prisoner groaned in agony. Petrano and Tagus collected a piece of stiff papyrus from Festus, on which was scribed the letters **INRI**. Tagus climbed the ladder and to the uppermost part of the dowel protruding up from the cross member nailed the inscription.

The mob was not satisfied: they began cheering, jeering, and mocking; and some even began to throw stones at the man on the cross. The tribune allowed them their moment of satisfaction for about half an hour and then felt that enough was enough.

He mustered his soldiers and those of the auxiliary troop and walked slowly over to the jeering mob, the *lictor* whip in hand beside him, and bellowed to them. "If you do not leave this place straight away, many of you will find a *pilum* or a sword through you. I warn you, get out of it; you have had your fun for the day. If you wish to stay, I demand that you remain absolutely quite and peaceable, otherwise you will regret it."

The jeering died down because the unruly element in the mob realized that the Roman's word was no bluff and that the Romans would not hesitate in executing troublemakers. Very soon the crowd dispersed leaving a few silent spectators.

The troops were disbanded and made their way aimlessly to sit among some rocks to the rear of the hill. As Timius and Marcus wandered over to the rocks they were stopped in their tracks by a yell from the *lictor*.

"You, soldier, come over here!"

The *lilctor* was talking to Timius. "For your insolence to me this morning, you will stand guard on this wretched victim throughout and until we leave. You will be joined by another soldier who will be relieved from time to time."

Timius obeyed and, as the *lictor* made his way over to the rocks, he noticed the victim's bloodstained robe lying on the ground, where it had been stripped from him. He bent over, picked it up, and went on his way. Marcus suddenly came running forward, *pilum* in hand. As he ran, Timius noticed that his limp was far more pronounced than it had ever been. He thought to himself, poor Marcus, if your limp does not improve, they will discharge you from the army. Marcus had spotted a vulture which had settled on the gantry beam above the victim on the centre cross. As he approached the scaffolding, he thrust up his *pilum* and frightened the bird away. It took to flight, screeching its annoyance, and a strange thought occurred to Timius. It was analogous to him that the eagle should represent Rome picking on the victims of its Empire; but, then, he knew that unlike the vulture, Rome did not only take its pickings, but gave to the Empire an enormous amount of good. As instructed, he took up his position as sentry to the centre cross. Marcus had been detailed to accompany him as the first relief and Marcus stood a few feet away from him. At the foot of the centre cross, Timius could see, directly beneath the man's wounds, small pools of blood over which the dust was settling.

CHAPTER XXIX

Hanc viam si asperam esse negem, mentiar.

CICERO

If I were to deny that this road is rough, I should lie.

THE DISPERSAL OF the soldiers caused the unruly element in the mob to take advantage of the situation, and they began their jeering and mocking again. There were loud shouts of laughter as they amused themselves at the three wretches who hung on the scaffolding. The mocking obscenities were in the Hebrew and Aramaic tongue. Even the sacerdotal element dressed in their robes of religious office had joined in the mockery. Their remarks and sarcastic calls were directed at the victim who hung from the central position of the scaffold. Flies were buzzing around his limp and beaten body, and groups of flies had also settled, making a feast of the open wounds. Saliva was dripping from his mouth, and it was mingled with blood as it dripped onto his matted beard and chest. Timius and Marcus exchanged looks because they were beginning to feel that the mob was getting out of hand. Eagles continued to circle overhead. Their anxiety was soon allayed with the arrival of two more of their colleagues and four auxiliary soldiers onto the scene. Centurion Festus had recognised the changing mood of the spectators from where he had been resting and sent the troops to join the sentries. The mood of the spectators became slightly subdued. Suddenly, the man on the centre cross shouted out a phrase in his native tongue, Aramaic. A hush fell over the spectators but was soon broken with their laughter because whatever it was the Galilean had said caused them some amusement.

Petrano, one of the soldiers sent to join Timius and Marcus, called over to one of the spectators, who had appeared to remain silent throughout, and asked, "Do you speak Aramaic or Hebrew?"

"Yes, I do," replied the spectator.

"Well, tell me, what did this King of the Jews cry out? And I want the truth."

"I always tell the truth to you Romans."

A likely story, thought Petrano. "Well?"

"He asked his father in heaven to forgive you all," replied the spectator.

Neither Marcus nor Timius could understand the full meaning of such a plea, and they raised their eyebrows interrogatively, but there was no further explanation of the meaning of the phrase when asked to explain by Petrano.

"I am glad to hear that it was not some insulting remark about Caesar or Rome. I can assure you," he continued, "if it had, his last moments of life would have been made more difficult for him."

There were three small groups of people comprising about fourteen in all, standing around at the edge of the hilltop. They were silent and merely gazed up at the criminals and innocent victim nailed to the scaffold. Timius thought that they were probably the relatives or close friends of the condemned man, and Timius wondered why none of them had come forward to either defend, or even plead, for the life of the Galilean when he was being tried. Perhaps none of them had any association with him, and it was probable that this man was all alone.

Timius's eyes wandered over the heads of this group, and in the distance, he could see the tops of the buildings of the city. Beyond the city he noticed a heavy dust cloud gradually moving in their direction. The dust storm that they had evaded throughout their march from Palmyra looked as though it would finally get the better of them. Perhaps they would be back at the praesidium before it finally enveloped the city and its surrounding district, thought Timius. As his eyes wandered back to the spectators in front of him, he noticed standing beyond the silent group a tall well-built man with the hood of his robe covering his head. From where Timius stood, he could discern that the man was very dark skinned and his clean, shiny forehead was just visible. Timius's heart raced with sudden excitement as he called Marcus over.

Marcus limped over to Timius and said, "What's the matter, Timius?"

"Look over there," he said, pointing his finger to the man in the distance. "Can you see him?"

"Yes, I can," replied Marcus, "but what about him?"

"It looks very much like Mucta Wahabis."

Marcus looked hard at the man to see if he could also recognise him and quickly replied, "By Jove, Timius, you're quite right. That is old Mucta. What on earth is he doing here?"

"I should like to know that too," replied Timius and quite spontaneously called out above the babble of the crowd, "Mucta."

He paused and called again, "Mucta, come over here. It's your friends Marcus and Timius."

From where they stood, they could see that he gazed at both of them momentarily but turned around slowly and walked down the hill.

"What did he do that for?"

"I don't know," replied Marcus, "he is probably frightened of us and who can blame him? We are bloody executioners, aren't we?" he replied with a note of shame in his voice.

"Yes, I suppose you are right, old friend. But did you notice something."

"What?" Marcus asked.

"Did you notice as he turned away when the hood of his robe slid off bearing his head, his forehead was completely clear and shiny?"

"Yes, I did, but what is the significance?"

"You've a short memory, Marcus. The last time we saw Mucta his forehead was completely covered with sores."

"How right you are, Timius. How strange it all is, but I had better get back to the other side of the scaffold."

As he said this, Marcus limped away. It was now nearly midday, and the spectators were beginning to disperse. Perhaps they were aware of the thickening dust cloud that was hanging over the outer edge of the city. The two victims who had been strung up earlier in the day were now dead. But the third victim again cried out.

In response to his cry, one of the auxiliary sentries on duty went over to the pack animal and fumbled awhile. He then returned with a wadding of cloth stuck to the end of his spear. The cloth was dripping with some sort of fluid. He then raised the spear head up to the victim's gaping mouth and thrust the sponge into it. After he removed it, Timius walked over to him and asked him out of curiosity, "What is it that you put on the sponge at the end of your spear?"

The auxiliary looked around and replied, "Oh that. Haven't you seen that done before?"

"No."

"Well, sometimes we give it to them to dull the pain. It's a very coarse wine, or one could call it vinegar."

"Well, I didn't know that," replied Timius.

Timius realized that the Galilean had obviously called out in agony, and the auxiliary had mercifully administered a form of anaesthetic to him.

Marcus had for some time been replaced by Protius, who was his relief, but when Protius joined Timius, the latter had noticed that he was not completely steady on his feet. The reason for this was plain because, as Protius explained the officers and soldiers in the wings and—out of sight of the scaffolding—had begun to drink some of the wine brought to the site on the pack animal—by the auxiliaries—and from this had ensued a round of gambling.

Timius was grateful to Protius for bringing him a beaker of the coarse wine. He had been terribly thirsty and although it was horrible stuff to drink it did help quench his thirst. The unruly mob and the sacerdotal element had now departed, leaving only a few silent spectators behind. Timius' thoughts now turned to his last vacation spent in Velitrae. He hated being here and hoped that this would be the first and last time he would experience this ordeal. He remembered the happy moments he had spent in the company of his loved one, Tricia, and wished that she could be here with him.

He wondered what she was doing and what she would think of this dastardly episode. He knew she would be absolutely outraged at the event and even more upset to know that he, Timius Arbutus, had participated in it. He promised himself that he would never tell her of it and would do his best to forget the episode. His thoughts were broken with the sound of trumpets and drums which were leading a troop of auxiliary troops through the gates of the city.

He could just see out into the distance the bronze instruments glistening in the sunshine. The sound of the music stirred him as he was quickly reminded of the fact that he was a proud legionary of the illustrious Twelfth Legion. His thoughts were also broken with a call from Marcus, who came limping over to him. He could tell that Marcus had also had a fair share of drink, but Marcus had come to him to borrow some money.

"Timius, have you any money on you?"

"No, I haven't, Marcus. We were mustered so hurriedly, early this morning that I left what little money I had behind. Where is your money?"

Marcus bowed his head in shame and exclaimed that he had lost it all gambling. Timius felt sorry for him, but quickly realised that he had the gold coin given to him years ago, still wrapped in a piece of papyrus in his tunic pocket.

Timius got it out of his pocket and handed it to Marcus, saying, "I have just remembered I have this gold coin, and you can borrow it if you wish."

"Thank you so much, Timius old friend, I'll never forget this kindness."

When he pulled out the papyrus envelope with the coin from his pocket, Timius also felt another small envelope. He pulled this out also and opened it carefully. Before he finished opening it a man approached him and asked, "Soldier could I see your friend?"

Timius quickly looked round to see where Marcus was, and before Marcus disappeared out of sight, Timius called out to him. Marcus came limping back quickly.

"What is it you want?" Marcus again asked, impatiently.

"This man would like to see you about something."

Marcus, turning to the man, said, "Well, what it is you want?"

The man hesitated a moment before answering, "Soldier, would you please ask your officer if he would be so kind as to let us have the garment that our master was wearing."

"Which master are you talking about," asked Marcus abruptly.

Pointing to the Galilean, the stranger replied, "Our master who hangs crucified in between those two criminals."

"What do you want it for?"

"Soldier, it is the only possession my master had, and we would like to keep it in his memory."

Marcus said nothing for a moment, but as he turned on his heel to return to join his colleagues, he said, "Very well, I will ask the tribune."

The man moved back to join his friends.

It was now nearly three hours past midday, and the sky was darkening with the dust cloud. Marcus ran back to Timius, limping badly, and excitedly returned to him his gold coin. He explained to Timius that he had lost it thrice over to Centurion Festus and had now won it back and more besides. Timius remembered he had not completely opened his second envelope, but he remembered to ask Marcus what response he had received to his request on behalf of the stranger for the Galilean's garment.

"Oh, yes, I did ask, but since some of the gang lost all their money in the betting, we decided to gamble over the garment. The tribune said it would be a worthy prize because it belonged to the *King of the Jews*. We are still gambling over it."

"I had better tell the man then," said Timius with a disappointed note in his voice.

Marcus returned to his colleagues and took the relief soldier Dolba with him. There was no need for all of them to be on sentry duty now.

Timius put the coin away and opened the second envelope and was quite surprised to see the little dried daisy he had picked when he was tied, ready for execution, in the barbarian's encampment at Carnuntum. The little daisy and its companions had been company for him during his ordeal, so he thought it would be a nice gesture to place the daisy between the feet of the Galilean hoping perhaps it would give him solace also. He did this and then returned to tell the man who had asked for the Galilean's garment that the tribune had refused to release it. The man and his companions were extremely disappointed, but thanked him and asked him to convey their thanks to his colleague for making the request on their behalf.

When Timius returned to his duty post at the scaffold, Cyrus had arrived on the scene. Cyrus asked if the Galilean was now dead, but was informed by Timius that this happy release had not yet occurred. Cyrus then explained to Timius that he had been sent to relieve him for a very short while so that he could join the others for a drink and a morsel of bread. He was absolutely famished, but his appetite had left him. He joined the others, who were all seated on the rough, dusty ground, still gambling. Centurion Festus handed Timius a chunk of bread and passed him the jug of wine from which to take a swig.

When he had finished and was about to return to his post, the tribune stood up, dusted himself down, and asked, "Is the Galilean dead yet?"

"He wasn't when I left, sire," replied Timius.

The tribune then studied the heavens above him. He was concerned about the approaching dust storm and felt that there was a need for him and the troops in his command to return to the praesidium as quickly as the situation permitted. The tribune instructed Lipsius to follow him. Timius led the way back to the scaffold, followed by the tribune and Lipsius. When they arrived there, the tribune walked to the front of the scaffold to study the dying man. He was anxious at the length of time it was taking death to overcome the man. He looked about him again and realized that the storm was soon about to break, and only some quick action on his part could bring this matter to a close. His instructions had been that he was not to leave the site with his troop until the victim was dead.

"You will have to use the point of your sword, legionary Vegitus." Lipsius didn't know what the centurion was referring to and looked at him askance.

"Go on, do as you are told. Pierce him through with your sword. Let's get it over with," he directed impatiently.

Lipsius drew his sword and without further ado reached up and thrust it into the side of the Galilean. The man rolled and rolled his head. Blood squirted out of his side, and Lipsius stepped back to avoid it. Lipsius then returned to rejoin his colleagues, but the tribune strode around the gallows to satisfy himself that the other two criminals were dead. He returned and quite nonchalantly placed the palm of his right hand onto the upright beam on which the Galilean was hanging to lean on it momentarily. The drink was having a slight affect on his bearing. Some blood from the pierced side of the Galilean dropped and landed on the back of his hand and his wristlet. He frantically withdrew his hand and equally frantically tried to rub the blood off with his left hand. Timius noticed that the tribune seemed noticeably troubled. The tribune quickly looked up at the man hanging above him and strode away to join the others.

The sky overhead became thickened with the dust cloud, and the strength of the wind began to increase. It was not long before the atmosphere around Timius became choked with the fine dust churned up by the swirling wind. Jerusalem was no longer visible from the hilltop. Visibility was down to a mere twenty, or thirty, or so yards. The wind increased in ferocity, and a flash of lightening broke through the opaque sky, followed by a loud clap of thunder overhead. Timius could feel large drops of rain penetrating the atmosphere around him.

He moved nearer to the scaffolding and leaned on the central upright beam with one hand to steady himself. He noticed there was hardly anybody in sight. The auxiliary sentries had now run for shelter. He wanted to do the same, but he had been ordered to remain at the sentry post throughout. Some twenty yards in front of him, and in the greyness that surrounded the site, he noticed four people still present. They were crouching on their knees in an effort to protect themselves from the dust and large rain drops that were bearing against them all. As he peered at them, he realized that three of the four who were crouching were men and a few yards in front of them—also crouched over—was a woman. Her head was covered with a shawl, and he could just discern that she was trembling with the effects of the storm. Timius walked over to her slowly and stood in front of her. Her head was bowed. He reached over his shoulder with his right hand and unbuckled his red cloak. This he gently placed over her shoulders. She raised her head and looked up at him and with a wan expression thanked him.

Timius replied, "That's all right ma'am, you need it more than I."

"What is your name, soldier?" asked the woman.

"Me ma'am, I am Timius Arbutus," and he added proudly, "I am Legionary Timius Arbutus of the Twelfth Imperial Legion of Rome on detached duty at Antonia's praesidium."

"May you be blessed, soldier."

Back at his post, he decided to follow the example of the four people he had just left, and he crouched down on his knees at the foot of the central beam. He found he was comfortable in that position so he placed his helmet more tightly on his head, to prevent it being carried off by the swirling, whirling wind. He then stood up because he thought in present circumstances it was wiser for him to be on his feet just in case he had to run for shelter. As he straightened himself, he looked up at the Galilean. His head was sagging forward, and Timius could no longer see the marks of dripping blood that had oozed from his head. Timius eyelids were caked with flying dust mingled with the rain. He rubbed his eyes to clear them and looked back at the Galilean. His eyes were closed and covered, as was the rest of him, with dust and rain. The Galilean's eyes opened slowly and met those of Timius.

Timius could see underneath the mistiness of the man's eyes that he was suffering absolute agony, and they also conveyed to him the impression that the man was now totally alone. At that moment—memories of the occasions when Timius too had experienced loneliness flashed through his mind. He remembered the occasion when, as a young boy, in Velitrae he had been persuaded to attend the party of the Senator's daughter, he had been subjected to humiliation by his friend Ciatus and the other boys and girls who were guests at the party. He remembered the loneliness he felt when he was informed of his father's death; he remembered the loneliness of the day he departed from Larcia, and he remembered the loneliness of many other occasions since. He fully recognised the condemned man's desperate plight and tried to convey to him his understanding through the expression in his own eyes.

He also tried to convey his assurance that he, the dying man, was not alone—that Timius Arbutus was there with him. The dying man very, very slowly raised his head with what seemed to be a tremendous and agonizing effort. The nails in his wrists had torn the flesh through which they were driven, and the pressure he had put on his feet in order to raise his head caused the flesh surrounding the nail through his feet to do the same. When his head and eyes were raised to the heavens he called out in a loud voice; it was as though he was crying out for help. His head sagged back onto his chest, his eyes closed, and his mouth sagged open. At that moment, as though by some strange phenomenon the raging storm immediately subsided. Timius thought that this was remarkable, as the storm subsided as rapidly as it had started. By this time, he was soaked to the skin when Cyrus came running over to him.

"What's happening, Timius—what on earth is going on? Is that bastard dead yet?"

Cyrus's speech was rather slurred from the wine he had been drinking as he continued, "I hope so because we all want to get back to the Praetorian; I think we have spent enough time in this godforsaken place."

Timius replied, "Yes, I think he is dead now, so with permission of the tribune we should all be able to leave very shortly." He added dejectedly, "I feel thoroughly fed up, dirty, and hungry."

Cyrus left him to report to the tribune that the man was dead.

During their brief conversation, the Greek—who was the assistant of the tribune—had walked up to the scaffold. He was a burly man with closely cropped hair. His tunic was wet through and droplets of water dangled from his earrings which he was wearing. The Greek had accompanied the tribune all the way from Palmyra. It had been rumoured that the tribune had bought him as a personal slave at the market place in Rome, and during the march from Palmyra the man kept himself inconspicuous from the rest of the soldiers, probably because he recognised his menial position as that of a slave. The Greek was now gazing at the body of the Galilean hanging in front of him. Tears rolled down his cheeks.

Timius walked over to him to try and comfort him and asked, "Did you know that man?"

The Greek slowly shook his head, "No, not properly," he replied, "but I have heard a good deal about him."

"Tell me," said Timius, "is he really the *King of the Jews?*"

"No," the man replied, shaking his head again, "he is **Jesus of Nazareth**."

Their brief conversation was broken by the orders of Centurion Festus calling the troops to muster. Timius turned from the Greek and obeyed orders. The tribune, Centurion Festus and the centurion in charge of the auxiliary troops mounted their horses in readiness to march away. A man approached the tribune and made some form of request. His voice was not audible, but the reply of the Tribune was:

"Yes, you can take the body of the Galilean and do what you like with it. The bodies of the other two victims will be disposed of by the four auxiliaries I have left behind, if none of their relatives want them."

The tribune was about to give the signal to march off but Centurion Festus rode up on his horse from the rear of the troop and brought it to a halt near Timius.

From where he was seated, he bawled at Timius, "Where is your cloak?"

Timius trembled: "Sire, it went missing in the storm."

"Very well, for your carelessness you will be on duty all day tomorrow from dawn to dusk. When we return to the praesidium, report to the stores and have another one issued to you. You are filthy and improperly dressed, and if you lose the second cloak, you will remain behind in this lousy city for the rest of your career.

"Yes sire," replied Timius obediently.

At that moment, the Greek slave made his way to the front of the troop and faced them in a confronting manner. He was trembling with rage and sorrow. Placed over his left arm was the folded garment of the dead Galilean. This had been won by the tribune during the gambling, and the tribune had handed it to his slave for safekeeping.

His face was wrung with emotion as he shouted, "You filthy Roman swine, call yourself Romans, you are too despicable for words. You have condemned and murdered an innocent man, and the burden of that man's death will remain forever on your shoulders."

The tribune seated on his horse was angered and about to severely admonish the man in front of his troop, but he was unable to do so because as soon as his slave had completed his outburst, he turned and ran down the hill towards the city. The accusation of the Greek penetrated the feelings of the troop causing them to silently contemplate the episode of the day. They all felt the truth of the accusation, but they were only soldiers and carrying out the orders of the civil authority.

They marched off down the hill. When they reached the bottom of Calvary, the troop wheeled right onto the road leading to the gates of Jerusalem. Timius turned his head slightly while marching in order to look up at the hill where the scaffolding was visible, and on the scaffolding, the bodies of the three victims were also visible. He very unexpectedly realized something that appeared to him to be most significant. The backs of the victims, hanging from the scaffold, were turned to Jerusalem. He also deduced from the position of the sun—which was now lower in the western sky—Rome was in that direction. By some quirk of fate, the victims' hands were outstretched as though they were about to embrace the City of Rome, which lay many miles to the west and over the sea.

CHAPTER XXX

Quicquid est biduo sciemus.

CICERO

Whatever it is, we shall know in two days.

LEGIONNAIRE SOTORIUS WAS coming down the steps of the troop quarters in the praesidium when he was passed by the men of the Contuburnia who had just been dismissed from duty after the event of the day. He nodded to one or two of them as he passed, but it was Marcus who was the only one of the men to speak to him.

"Hello, Sotorius. How's the scorpion bite? Has it healed yet, and has the pain eased off now?"

Sotorius stopped and acknowledged Marcus, rolling up the sleeve of his tunic as he did so.

"It's fine Marcus. Come and see for yourself. Quite strangely, there is no trace of it at all now.

Marcus looked at the man's arm and replied in a tone of wonderment, You're quite right, friend. I cannot see any trace of it, either."

"Just as I said!" exclaimed Sotorius, "that *medici* was a fine fellow."

"Yes, I agree," said Marcus. "Some of the *poltice-wallopers* are remarkable fellows. They certainly know their business! I'll be seeing you," Marcus said as he walked away.

Marcus had become acquainted with Sotorius because he had spent several shifts of guard duty with the man, but neither knew the background of the other.

That evening, before their meal, Timius and his companions relaxed for nearly an hour in the other ranks Thermae. Timius noticed that while they were in the Coldarium, the conversation was about everything—including his extra duty imposed on him for the following day—but the day's events. Each tried to broach the subject but quickly retreated from any kind of discussion about it. The looks they exchanged throughout the time of bathing and even during the evening meal, of roast mutton and bread washed down with a local wine, were indicative that the event in which each had taken an active role was on their consciences. Each man was friendly, and there seemed to be an atmosphere among them of peace and calm. While it was apparent to each of them that they would need to discuss the event among themselves in order to contribute their own opinion and views none of them would openly broach the subject. Commiserations were offered to Marcus for his apparent pronounced limp, and his companions were concerned that the affliction was getting worse. Marcus did everything to assure them that this was not so, and oddly enough, he now had no ill effects from it at all. They concluded that he was obviously trying to distract their attention from him. The tone of his assurances persuaded his companions to say no more about it. After the meal and before returning to the room in which he was barracked, Timius called at the equipment stores where he was issued with a new cloak. He would need this for duty the following morning.

*

"Come on Timius, come along now, wake up quickly; on your feet, get your clothes on," cried Marcus excitedly.

Timius sat up in his bed, startled by the shouts of Marcus, and began to rub his eyes vigorously. He had spent from dawn to dusk the previous day on guard duty, and when he returned to the praesidium that night, he had been thoroughly exhausted; too exhausted to even go along and have his evening meal. He unbuckled his breastplate, removed his greaves and sandals, changed his sweaty dusty tunic, and flopped exhausted on the bed. He had had very little sleep over the past three days, and he was livid with Marcus for waking him, especially at this unearthly hour of the morning. As he gazed around the room with glazed eyes, he saw his other companions still asleep, though he noticed that each had been disturbed by Marcus.

"Come on, Timius," implored Marcus. "Don't you know it's the day of the resurrection?"

"Oh, shut up," retorted Timius.

"It is the day of the resurrection," he repeated, "and there is someone to see you."

"I'm in no mood for your bloody fun and games, so stop mucking about."

"I am not mucking about; I am telling you the truth. There is a young woman accompanied by a man waiting to see you at the gate; so hurry up and get cracking—they cannot wait for you all day, you know."

"What woman are you talking about? I don't know any woman around here," retorted Timius angrily.

"Timius, my friend, you're a sly fellow, you are. There is a very good looking woman who has called to see you, and, moreover, she has called to see you on the day of the resurrection, and you are acting quite ungratefully, and what is more, you don't even believe what I say! Throw some water over your face and go and see for yourself. And when you go out into the yard, you will notice that the sun is shining brilliantly and the plants in the tube surrounding the courtyard look much more alive than you have ever seen them look since we arrived here."

"The sun is always brilliant around here, and I wouldn't really know the difference in the disposition of the plants, as I have not had time to study them sufficiently," mumbled Timius

"Ah, but the sun is not just brilliant this morning," replied Marcus, "because each sunbeam seems to have a delicate touch about it, and you have never seen plants so fresh and green. The flowers, you will notice, are not only fragrant but seem to be smiling at one. The birds are chirruping gaily and more sweetly; anyway, go and see for yourself, if you do not believe me. You are bound to notice the difference. It's an absolutely wonderful morning."

By this time, Timius had slipped on his tunic, washed his face, combed his hair, and he was about to slip his feet into his sandals, when there was a disgruntled grunt from Cyrus, which came from under the blanket. "Why don't you two noisy perishers shut up!"

Timius picked up his sandals put them on outside the room and walked through he courtyard to the gate. Marcus was quite right. It was indeed a glorious morning.

When he arrived at the gate, the two sentries pointed to the man and woman who were stood outside waiting to see him. He walked towards them and then stopped. The woman had her dark hair covered with the end of the wrap that she was wearing. Her features were very soft and full of expression. Draped on her left arm was a folded red garment and behind her stood a tall bearded man. The man's head was also covered with a hood and in his right hand he clutched a long stick. Timius walked forward again hesitatingly, and when he was quite near to them, he stopped and said, "I understand you wanted to see me."

The woman then spoke, "Are you Timius Arbutus?"

"Yes ma'am, I am. Is there something you want from me?"

"No soldier. In fact there is something I bring to you. I am returning your cloak which you so graciously draped about my shoulders two days ago."

Timius now remembered that moment and replied, "But you need not have returned it ma'am. I have been issued with a replacement," and he added very quickly, "of course, I have had to pay for, so I would like you to keep that one."

"Thank you, soldier, but I have no real use for it and besides, you will most probably need it much more during your service with your legion."

Timius stepped forward and accepted the garment back. It had been beautifully washed and was radiant in the morning light.

"Thank you, ma'am," he said bashfully.

"It's my pleasure," she replied and added, "are you going to be staying here long?"

"I don't know, ma'am, I don't think so now that the feast of the Passover is practically finished. I think we will all be returning to our base in Palmyra."

There followed what seemed to be an endless pause, and Timius broke the silence by saying, "I am sorry about what happened the other day. My colleagues and I are very sorry about what occurred."

The woman bowed her head and said very softly. "You must not condemn yourselves for it. We are all forgiven."

Timius did not know how to reply, but thought he had better take his leave of them, "I had better be on my way now, ma'am. Farewell to you and your companion—and the gods go with you."

"Farewell, soldier, and the way be blessed for you." she replied.

Timius turned on his heel and ran back through the gate in the direction of the dormitory. Before he reached it, there was a shout from Marcus, "Timius, Timius, come here quickly."

Marcus was seated on a protruding part of a plinth which supported a statue. Timius stopped and walked over to Marcus.

"What is it this time? By the way, remember the cloak I lost?"

"Yes."

"Some local folk found it, and one of the women washed it for me and has just returned it to me," said Timius as he approached Marcus.

"Ah, but look at this Timius," said Marcus, excitedly kicking off his sandals.

Timius watched as Marcus strode around the statue, jauntily, and then began to run up and down the courtyard until he was out of breath.

"Do you notice anything Timmy?" he said gasping for breath.

"Yes, I do, Marcus, it's absolutely marvellous! You haven't got a limp. Isn't that a miracle?"

"It is, and I have only just noticed it as we came out of the dormitory carrying our sandals; but you were in such a hurry to get to the gate, I was not able to tell you about it then."

Timius was so happy for Marcus he patted him on the back saying, "Come quickly, let us go and wake the others and tell them about this marvel."

As they ran up the steps, Timius abruptly stopped Marcus and said to him very seriously, "Do you know, friend, this is going to cost you some money?"

"Why do you say that?"

"You are going to have to buy yourself some sandals and throw away those orthopaedic sandals."

"Oh, I see what you mean!" exclaimed Marcus laughingly and continued, "I am so excited about it that I don't mind buying a hundred pairs of sandals.

As they continued up the steps, it occurred to Timius that the limp his friend had put up with these many years must have disappeared at least three days ago and was the cause of him walking with a pronounced limp. A crippled limb which had become whole again—on which an orthopaedic sandal was worn—would have caused this effect.

The gods have certainly favoured you my friend and you should be grateful to them forever more."

"I shall indeed Timius, I shall indeed."

They were about to enter the small dormitory when Timius abruptly stopped Marcus by clutching his left shoulder. Marcus turned around sharply to face him when Timius said to him, "There is something I want to ask you; I have just remembered."

"What is it?" enquired Marcus.

"When you came and dragged me out of bed earlier, you said something about today being the day of the resurrection. What were you referring to?"

"Well," replied Marcus," when I was called over by the sentries at the gate to pass the message to you that visitors had arrived, I walked over to them purely to confirm that it was you whom they wished to see. When I did so I was informed by the woman that today was the day of the resurrection and when I asked for an explanation, thinking that this was some kind of Jewish festival which we are not familiar with, the woman explained that the Galilean whom we crucified a couple of days ago had today risen from the dead, and the woman also confirmed that he had been seen."

"Seen—what do you mean seen? He was dead when we left the hill."

"I am only repeating what the woman said, and who am I to argue with a beautiful woman," replied Marcus.

"Ah, she was probably very close to him and was letting her imagination get the better of her."

"Yes, I suppose you are right."

"Think no more about it," said Timius, adding, "Come along let us tell the others about your good fortune."

The same evening, after they had all finished their stint of duty, they were relaxing on their beds in the dormitory. The sun had set some three hours earlier, and none of the young men were in the mood for a game of knuckle bones or dice. Lipsius reflected aloud as he said, "We should be leaving here in a couple of days and marching back to Palmyra! By Jove, I wish I were returning to Italy because I feel that I have been out in this part of the world far too long."

Each of his companions endorsed his view.

"When will you be leaving the army?" Protius asked Timius.

"Me?—I've no idea. I think I will need to do a few more years to save sufficient money."

"What do you want money for?" Marcus asked.

"Of course I want money," replied Timius. "I have made some plans for the future."

"Tell us about your plans. We are longing to hear."

"Well, I would like to have sufficient money to buy myself a little villa, nothing very elaborate," he quickly added, "surrounded by a small plot of land on which I can grow fruit, vegetables, and a good variety of flowers."

"Well, I didn't think you were interested in horticulture."

"I am not, really, I don't know anything about it, but I would like to learn."

"Why don't you sell some of your personal possessions? The money from the sale of those items, plus your gratuity and accumulated pay should help you realize your plan," Lipsius advised.

"What possessions? I do not have many worthwhile possessions; in fact, almost nothing, when you come to think of it."

"Strange that you should say that, Timius," said Marcus. "Cyrus and I haven't anything either, but I am not so sure about Lipsius and Protius."

The latter friends did not respond.

"Anyway, we are not the only persons in this situation; the Galilean had no possessions, either."

"How do you know?" interjected Lipsius.

"Because one of his friends who was asking to take possession of the Galilean's garment told Timius and me that that was his only worldly possession, and there are probably thousands of other people who possess—like him—nothing at all."

Cyrus nodded his head in agreement and then said, "Yes, I suppose we have a lot to be grateful for. After all, the army does provide us with a salary, our food, and our lodgings, whereas there must be a good many persons who don't enjoy anything like this! Furthermore, we have our health and we have sound faculties and there are many with neither. One only has to look at the leper colonies to realize this fact. While we are on the subject, do you, Marcus, think that the Galilean was guilty of the crimes levelled against him?"

"No Cyrus, I certainly do not. I feel sure the man was innocent."

Timius then spoke, "I, too, am convinced the man was innocent. They charged him with blasphemy, treason, and sedition, and for one, I cannot accept that he was guilty of any of those crimes.

"When I was on duty the day before yesterday," Protius explained, "a couple of the auxiliaries at the gate told us about some very strange happenings and stories concerning the Galilean."

His companions waited patiently for him tell them what these were. After a short pause Protius continued, "Evidently, he was an extremely precise speaker on the subject of the Jewish religion, and he encouraged his followers to bring their faith to life in their behaviour towards each other and towards all other men. Seemingly, he preached that it was not sufficient to merely worship in the temple and offer sacrifices to their god, but over and above this it was important that the morals of their religion must be practiced in their daily actions and behaviour towards others."

"Can you elucidate on this?" requested Marcus.

"I cannot really, because I don't know sufficiently about it. I am only relating what I heard and, as I understand it, although he was accused of sedition this wasn't correct because it bore no relation to what he was teaching. Apparently, he advised his followers that it was essential for them to obey the laws of the state, given to them by our Emperor, however distasteful those laws might be. But at the same time they must also behave morally and responsibly toward each other. Greed, selfishness, and avarice were deplorable and not the way to fulfil the wishes and commandments of their god. It is said that the meaning that lay behind the Galilean's teachings, if understood properly and acted upon, as intended, would give the adherent a better and fuller appreciation of life, including the full appreciation of the wondrous things that surround us all.

"How very interesting," remarked Marcus, "can you enlighten us further?"

The others eagerly awaited Protius's reply.

"I understand," continued Protius, "that he also performed what they call miracles."

"I cannot believe that," interrupted Timius. "What sort of miracles?"

"I don't know all the details, but evidently he brought a dead man to life, he converted water to wine, he cured the lame, and he fed the hungry among many other things."

"I don't believe that," remarked Timius again.

"Nor do I," explained Protius, "but that is what I heard."

"There is probably a simple explanation for all these things," said Lipsius. "It is probable that when all these took place, they were all so beyond the understanding and comprehension of the simple village people that witnessed them that they attributed it to the miraculous powers of a man whose teachings inspired them."

"That is very likely so," agreed Protius. "Perhaps what he was trying to do was help them to have faith in themselves, and do remember," Protius added, "the people that followed him were local people who were confined to a simple way of life, some dejected and with little hope of rising above their station in life. And what he was trying to do, perhaps, was to instil in them the spirit of life to help them rise above their adversities and be responsible for and control their own destinies, to a certain extent. He was endeavouring to put life back into their souls, and that is certainly no crime, not in my opinion anyway; after all when we feel down in the dumps and fed up, our officers and centurions very soon jump down our throats and make us do things which we would otherwise not do, if we had our own way."

"What else did you hear about him?" enquired Cyrus.

Protius thought for a while before replying, "Not much more, except that evidently the basis of his teaching was that one should love his neighbour and forgive and love one's enemies; and it was also his teaching that to do so would apparently help one enjoy a richer life. I don't believe he meant material wealth but believe what he meant was—"

Protius was interrupted by Timius, who said, "That's something I could never do. I could never imagine forgiving the *lictor* for sticking me on extra duty yesterday—and a duty that lasted all day long."

"Ah, but that's it, Timius. That's the basis of his teachings, and it is even said that he forgave us all even after we crucified him."

"Are you sure the man wasn't a crank," Marcus asked after he heard this latest comment.

"No, apparently not," exclaimed Protius. "It has been suggested that he was an intelligent and very level-headed person. He also advised people that to fully comprehend and then practice their religion truthfully they should think nothing of giving up all their material possessions and placing all their faith in their god."

"By Jove, it's not a religion I would like to follow. I wouldn't like to give up everything I have, which is not very much," Cyrus quickly added, "so that it could be divided among some of the lazy good-for-nothings we have met on our travels, and, therefore, that religion is not for me. I'll continue to practice the religion of our Empire—and that is not very often I'm ashamed to say."

"I don't think I could ever do that either," said Marcus, contemplating the comments, "but I can certainly see the logic. It was probably his way of telling people that it was good and right to share their good fortunes with those less fortunate than themselves."

"A far too highly moral pose for my liking, I'm afraid," stated Timius.

"That's it. That's precisely the problem," uttered Protius. "To truthfully follow the teaching of the Galilean—as I understand it when told about them—life would not be easy. In fact, life could be damn difficult, and it is certainly not a religion I would like to follow, either."

"Do you still think the man was innocent, Timius," asked Marcus.

"Yes, I do indeed," replied Timius.

"Then do you realize, old friend, that if we all conclude that the man was innocent, each one of us has the blood of an innocent man on our hands."

There was an embarrassing silence. Marcus broke the silence by continuing. "Don't feel too bad about it. After all, we are soldiers, and he was probably only one of many who we have wantonly put to death or killed in our defence, as part of our duties as soldiers. Besides, as Protius has already said, to follow his teachings would indeed be difficult and that is why perhaps his so called close followers were not at the trial to offer him any kind of support because they must also realize the difficulty of following such a highly moral life."

"I expect the tribune, the centurion, the *lictor*, Dolba, and old Petrano must also feel the same way as we do. In fact, perhaps also Pontius Pilate thought this way too, but there is nothing any of us can do about it. We shall just have to live with it," Cyrus added as his contribution to the conversation.

"Did you say Dolba?" asked Lipsius.

"Yes, I did," replied Cyrus.

"Don't include Dolba. He's too mean, in my opinion, to have any feelings at all. He is not only mean, he is selfish and tight. In fact, I don't think that fellow ever learnt to swim.

"What do you mean? 'Never learnt to swim'?" enquired Timius.

"What's that got to do with it?"

"Well can't you guess?" insisted Lipsius. "He is so tight, he would never drown."

The others found this remark amusing, and all laughed heartily.

"Talking about swimming, I wish we could all go swimming somewhere," remarked Protius.

"I am not too fond of swimming, Protius, because I am inclined to swim like a stone," retorted Cyrus.

"I shall have to teach you to swim, my friend, the next time we have the opportunity."

"I wish you would, because I have watched you in the past and have envied the way in which you glide through the water," Cyrus stated. "When and where did you learn to swim? And where?"

"I learnt to swim before I was one year old," replied Protius. "My father taught me. He used to take me out in a boat on the lake near to our township and just throw me in the water."

"Did you find it difficult?" asked Marcus in amazement.

"As a matter of fact I did not," replied Protius and continued, "the swimming wasn't difficult but fighting my way out of the sack was really tricky."

When this last comment registered Protius' companions laughed their heads off and Marcus rejoined with one of his impromptu poems

> *Baby Protius tied in a sack*
> *Was dropped into the water*
> *He was told that he must swim*
> *But not of the intent to get rid of him!*

Marcus' poem brought the evening's discussion to a close in a jovial and light-hearted manner. The seriousness of the earlier part of the evening had now been forgotten. Timius could not get off to sleep quickly, so he lay in bed thinking, and the more serious points of the evening's discussions were being tossed about in his mind. His thoughts were concentrated on the Galilean and the compassion on the man's face, even as he was near to death, had become impressed on Timius' mind. He would never forget those moments. Some of the things he had heard, related by Protius, needed further thought. He discarded the report that the Galilean had allegedly performed miracles. This, Timius thought, was pure heresy, around which exaggerations had been woven, and indeed if this was not the case, surely the man was a sorcerer and those that had rumoured it were obviously right.

Timius tried to apply simple logic to one of the statements that had been uttered by the Galilean at the trial. He had stated to the procurator that he had exalted his followers to give to Caesar what was Caesar's and to give to their god what truly belonged to their god. Timius saw nothing illogical at all in this statement.

After all, he thought if the people did not obey the laws and regulations of the state, and lawlessness was allowed to flourish, the result of that state of affairs would be anarchy. The more he thought about it, the more he realized that laws and regulations could never please everybody all of the time, and however repugnant some were, nevertheless they were obviously instituted to preserve the fabric of society, and the society that lived within the parameters of the law could be assured of security from which would naturally follow a measure of prosperity.

Anarchy, on the other hand, would only bring chaos, greed, and eventually bloodshed. The civilization that had been and still was so costly in human life would be wasted. There would be nothing to put in its place. He knew that justice for all is the most difficult ideal to achieve and that the Roman way of life, even though it was forcibly imposed on Rome's provinces, was the best they had at the present. He felt that even the most repugnant regulations could in due course be repealed, provided society reached a state where the existence of them would be totally unnecessary. Failing this, the alternative method of replacing such regulations with those that were more justified was by simple argument, debate, and persuasion.

This was the Roman way and the Roman way was the enlightened method of development. He continued to think where religion played its part and concluded that while the Emperor and the Senate provided the laws and regulations by which all peoples must live, they could not successfully regulate attitudes and the morals by which they should live. This is where religion played its part. He felt that most of the religions practiced throughout the Empire, however variant their methods of worship, nevertheless postulated codes of morality that were in the main adhered to by the people. Perhaps this is what the Galilean was trying to put across and quite logically the man must have known that religious order could not possibly exist in a situation where anarchy abounded.

A disciplined race of people would be a god-like race, and, in being so, they would create the framework through which the less fortunate members of the community would not be forgotten. What part had he to play in all this, he thought—not very much. He was a disciplined young man, as were his friends. But he had often rebelled against the regulations of the army by breaking the rules. This was more out of mischievousness than malice. With this consolation in mind, he decided to try harder in future and obey his superior officers. He felt he had had enough of defaulters and that he would try to behave himself. After all he remembered that when he was a little boy, his mother constantly implored him to do as he was told. He would try his best in future, and these were his last thought before he fell asleep.

CHAPTER XXXI

Caesar, properans noctem diei coniumxerat neque iter intermiserat.

CAESAR

Caesar in his haste had joined night to day and had not broken his march.

THEIR ARRIVAL BACK at the encampment at Palmyra was an exciting event. Lipsius Vegitus informed Timius, Marcus, and Cyrus that two relief cohorts had arrived just ten days previously, and with them had been brought messages and letters for the majority of the troops in the encampment. The two cohorts had crossed over from Sicily to Carthage and had marched the whole length of North Africa, through Egypt and Palestine, with their arrival here eight months after their departure from Rome. He excitedly informed his companions that each were fortunate to have a letter awaiting them for collection at the headquarters building. He was quite amused when he told them that he had also received a letter, but thought, at the time, that he was more fortunate than others to have received two letters until he discovered, on opening it, that the second letter was addressed to his namesake, Lipsius Tagos, who had been with the others in Judea. Lipsius Tagos treated the error good-naturedly, and had informed Veg that there was nothing of very much importance for him to take umbrage.

"Why have we two more cohorts added to the legion?" asked Cyrus.

"Well, as I told you," replied Lipsius Vegitus, "they are relief cohorts, and those of us who have been here—and I just don't mean here—in Syria but really away from Rome for over three years, are to be relieved, and we are to return very shortly."

"What do you mean, 'those of us'?" exclaimed Marcus.

"Exactly what I said; our names are on the list to join two cohorts that are to return to Rome," answered Veg.

"Are you sure?" queried Cyrus.

"Yes, of course I am sure. When you go to the headquarters building, each of you will see your names on the list. But don't get too excited about it," he added, "because that was the good news. I now have some bad news to pass on to you."

"Come on, come on," said Marcus impatiently, "let's have it."

"The two cohorts that we will form part of will have to march back to Rome, and this is going to take us over nine months."

"Can't we march faster?" joked Timius, "or even run?"

"Evidently not, we have been given to understand that we will be carrying out road repairs and other maintenance work along the route and this will take us at least the whole of nine months before we have the pleasure of crossing the Tiber," answered Veg.

They digested the news for a moment, and then Marcus added consolingly, "At least none of us will get bloody seasick again."

"That will be a consolation, too, because had it been otherwise our dear old Mucta Wahabis would not be there to wet nurse us now that he is not a slave on board ships."

They were pleased to hear the news, and even the thought of foot-slogging it to Rome could not mar their pleasure of the thought of leaving Palmyra. On the way to headquarters building to collect their letters, the four companions hurriedly related the events of their detached stay in Judea. They assured Veg that he had not missed anything worthwhile, and he had probably been better off remaining at Palmyra. Lipsius Veg, on the other hand, could not agree with them because the very dry conditions that were unusually prevalent before the troop departed to Judea had become progressively worse. The weather was going through one of its more freakish moods and they were all soon to find out the discomfort that was produced by the extremity of the Syrian climate.

The list was hurriedly studied by Timius and his companions on entry into the headquarters building and they were overjoyed to see that their names appeared on the list. However, they were not too happy to see included on the list, and heading it, the names of Tribune Marcellus Gallilo and Centurions Flavius and Festus. The tribune was an officer who behaved in the manner to which he was accustomed, that is his family background and upbringing evident in his character.

He gave one the impression that he was pusillanimous and even placid, but this was because he had little dealings or contact with the troops under his command, but as was the generally accepted custom, he ensured that his orders were transmitted and carried out through his subordinate centurions. It was they who added the fire to the orders initiated by the tribune. The promulgation of his own orders by himself was not a matter that concerned him. The four companions had had a taste of the severity of the centurions' when properly applied. Each had only just escaped the application of their respective vine staffs across their backs. They shuddered at the thought of having to spend at least another nine months under the command of Tribune Gallilo and Centurions Festus and Flavius.

As they were returning to their dormitory, after each had collected his respective letter, it was Marcus who was to remind them of a seemingly trivial event that had taken place in Jerusalem.

"I wonder what happened to the tribune's slave Demitus," asked Marcus.

"I had forgotten all about him because, come to think of it, he didn't accompany us back from Jerusalem," answered Cyrus.

"Perhaps the tribune got rid of him after his unprovoked outburst when we began to march away from that hill of crucifixion," joined in Timius.

"That is a possible explanation Timius," replied Marcus, "the man was a miscreant, and it is possible the tribune handed him over to some galley master."

"That would be a harsh penalty for a mere indiscretion on the man's part," rejoined Cyrus.

"Maybe so," replied Marcus, "but then the tribune could not possibly have a disobedient slave at his side and accompanying disciplined troops. He would set a very bad example to the troops."

"I can't quite go along with that theory," Timius piped up, "because he must have been disobedient on a few other occasions even while we were in the city."

"Yes, you are right," agreed Marcus thoughtfully. "Remember the two nights we heard him shrieking with pain as he was being flogged?"

"Yes, you're right," both Timius and Cyrus replied.

"Well then he had obviously run away and who could blame him," said Timius, "after all, from all accounts, he was an extremely well-educated young man from a good family background and a man of sound character. To live the life of a slave to a Roman tribune must have been most degrading for the man. I believe he was sold into slavery for proffering his views on Roman administration, or shall we say maladministration as far as he was concerned."

"Ah, Greeks always think they are better than us Romans. They can never get over the fact that Rome denuded them of their Empire," Cyrus remarked impatiently.

When they arrived at the dormitory, they decided to clean themselves up before relaxing and reading their letters. Each collected an iron bowl to take to the artesian font provided for the men's ablutions, but on their arrival they were told that the water was rationed. The severe weather necessitated this action. They were to find during the days before their departure, that the situation had become so severe that washing water was not to be made available. The water in the encampment was conserved for drinking purposes only.

Fortunately, the weather caused strong winds to blow continuously and collected up by the winds were tiny granules of sand, which were to have the blasting effect on any obstacle. The eating utensils were cleaned after each meal by merely hanging them out on stout lines in the wind. The effect of the sand granules and the strength of the wind sand blasted the utensils until they were clean and shining.

Without washing water, the troops found life quite unbearable. Their clothes were covered with fine particles of sand, and even their blankets in the dormitory gave the feeling that they were impregnated with sand. Many of the troops developed sores on the exposed parts of their bodies, and the only remedy, or even curtailment of the sores spreading to other parts of the body, was the application of salt. The *medici* issued out large quantities of salt to the troops on the basis of a daily ration, and they also advised that it should be applied to the affected parts generously. They also advised that it was necessary not to overlook the application of the dried salts to their unaffected parts.

Timius developed sores all over his face, and throughout each day, he prayed earnestly to the gods that these would not turn to leprosy. He could not forget the fate of his old and dear friend Mucta. But then Mucta had been cured, and perhaps Mucta also applied salt as the remedy. Timius thought that it was the will of the kingly gods who dwelt in heaven to impose such severe weather on the terrible Twelfth Legion for the act of some of their members who committed an innocent man to death. The sores on his face probably their means of taking revenge on him personally.

Marcus and Cyrus informed Timius, after each had read their letters from their girl friends, that Lygia's and Julia's father, the Praetorian officer in charge of the latrines at Larcia, had been experiencing spells of ill health, but they were assured that he was now making a gradual recovery. They both joked about the unpleasant odours from the latrines as being the cause of his deteriorating health. Although Timius also joined them in jocular remarks, it was merely a veneer of his true feelings for Carpus, because during the years he worked under Carpus's guidance he had cultivated a deep respect for the man and now considered him to be one of his dearest friends.

His letter from his beloved Tricia warmed his heart because he was beginning to feel the uselessness of trying to maintain any kind of relationship with a young girl of that calibre in his present circumstances. The tone of her letter was pleasantly affectionate, and it was evident that she had not yet married. She told him excitedly that she had had her ears pierced for the second time, and when he read this, he thought it would be a wonderful idea to surprise her with a pair of unique gold earrings; perhaps a design not commonly found on sale in either Velitrae or Rome. He would make a special effort to keep a look out for such a pair. She also told him about consulting the Sibyl while on a visit to Rome and from the prophecy of the Sibyl advised that he should take great care of himself.

'I implore you, dear Timius, please do not get yourself involved in any situation that may have a religious connotation to it. The prophecy is ominous,' she wrote.

Timius thought before he read on and related the incident in Jerusalem to the prophecy of the Sibyl, but he quickly concluded that Sibylline prophesies were pure hokum.

The letter was ended by her saying, 'My dear Timius, as each day passes, I think that I shall receive news of the arrival of the illustrious Twelfth Legion in Rome. Each day I look forward to seeing you, and no matter how long you are away you can rest assured that I shall remain here in the hope that you will soon return. I place all my trust in the merciful gods that they will bring you back to me safely.'

Timius read the letter through over and over again, and he was very pleased to hear that she had continued with her passionate interest in the religions of the Empire. She told him that she had spent many, many days since his departure in the religious section of the library and that this was the subject in which her interest was most keen. Timius was happy that she would be able to enlighten him on the subject. He felt it would be interesting to know something about them, and his deepest desire was to get back to Velitrae as quickly as possible. He even contemplated desertion but rejected this idea immediately, because he knew that on his arrival at Velitrae, if he told Tricia that he was a deserter, she would have nothing more to do with him. It was considered gross immorality in Roman society for one to desert one's duties, however repugnant those duties were, and she was a well-bred Roman girl. Her reaction would be no different to any others faced with the same situation.

Nearly a month had gone by before the two cohorts departed from Palmyra. Timius had made a real effort to keep out of trouble for fear that his name would be deleted from the list. He also made a supreme effort to keep himself clean, so as not to allow the spread of the sores on his face to other parts of his body. He did not want to jeopardize his chance of returning to Italy, and had his skin disorder deteriorated, repatriation would have been withheld from him. When they departed the encampment—and fortunately for those remaining behind—the weather was beginning to moderate.

There was even the possibility of some rain. The soothsayers in the district had studied the entrails of various birds and animals and had predicted the end of the extremely hot spell with the on-come of rains. Even though the soothsayers' predictions could not always be trusted they caused the morale of the troops to rise. The military commander and the senior civilian administrators of the district had planned a special project of engineering to enable water to be brought to the encampment from springs some ten miles away. Work would commence as soon as conditions permitted, and the vast majority of the legion would be devoted to this engineering task, even at the expense of combat training. The administration was not going to be placed in the awful predicament of lack of water again if there was the possibility of preventing such a situation. To main discipline in such circumstances was difficult, and penalties had to be harsher than under normal conditions.

The route of the march mapped for the two cohorts under Tribune Gallilo would take than north into Cilicia and then west into Lycaonia. They would then proceed north again, through Galatia, and west again, through Bithnia. It was planned that they would have a long stop before crossing the Bosphorus and proceeding north westward into Meosia. The last province through which they would march before entering Italy would be Illyricum.

They were told that any of those falling sick or injured on the way would be disposed of into legion encampments that had been set up in vicinities throughout the route. Those disposed of would be replaced by other legionnaires who were equally deserving of a return to the home province. There were many maintenance tasks that would need to be performed all along the route, and each man was expected to work hard and put the maximum effort into the job. Those who shirked would be severely dealt with because they would be infringing the right of their comrades of an early return to Rome.

Each member of the cohorts knew the exact circumstances in which he was placed. He was made fully aware of the seriousness of the instruction. It was also mentioned that there was a distinct possibility that they would have to face the attacks of marauding bands of barbarians and local insurgencies. They would be expected to fight to the death. The illustrious name of the Twelfth Legion would be upheld at all cost. With this message imprinted on their minds, the troops of the two cohorts began to tread the long and weary miles.

Before leaving Palmyra, the men of the two cohorts were advised that any letters they wished to write to their kinfolk back in Italy would be transmitted. There would be no other opportunity for them to communicate with Italy and its provinces during the march. Timius and his companions took this last opportunity of writing their letters.

Marcus and Cyrus replied to the letters they had each received form Praetorian Officer Carpus' two daughters while Timius wrote to Tricia. Like the others, he informed her that they were due to leave Palmyra any day and would be marching to Rome. He did not hold out much hope of their arrival before the space of at least nine months from the date of his letter, and he added affectionately that he was looking forward to seeing her again more than anything else in the world. He assured her that his future plans of owning a tiny villa, surrounded by a small plot of land, was still very much in his mind, and it was to this aim that his main thoughts and efforts were now concentrated. He informed her that he was saving very hard and doing his best to behave himself. He did not want anything to jeopardize his plans. As a forlorn hope, he mentioned his longed for dream of her joining him in his comfortable but simple villa.

Throughout the march, his thoughts did not stray far from his plans although the variety of countryside through which they passed was of tremendous interest to him. He paid special attention to the changing climatic conditions of each of the countries through which they marched—also to the vegetation that resulted from the physical and climatic variations. Syria was hot and dry and desert-like conditions prevailed through most of the country. The climate was arid and continued to prevail into Celicia. Lycaonia, Galatia, and Bithnia were where the scene of changed physical conditions occurred because most of that land comprised of a plateau-like terrain.

The weather was cooler, but the vegetation not much greener to that of Syria. A good measure of aridity was prevalent. It was not until they had marched into the vast expanses of flat land which was found in Moesia that the vegetation changed to any degree. Here there were vast flat lands of tall grasses, dotted profusely with copses of trees. During the march through Moesia Timius could well imagine how the legendary tales surrounding the Thracian horsemen had grown up.

This to him appeared to be ideal country for the horsemen and it had been said that the Thracian horsemen would fly swiftly into the wind, straddling their beautiful animals which were sleek and fleet of foot. Every time the breezes blew strong he wondered if these legendary cavalry men would appear—riding towards them swiftly—on the wind from nowhere. The horsemen of Thrace believed to have been born 'in the saddle', and the untold legends that were often told about them and which he had heard throughout his army career, especially while sitting around campfires at night, had set fire to his imagination.

Each cohort marched at a distance of a mile apart, and each cohort dragged behind it five carts each drawn by four horses. The carts were heavily laden with camping equipment and equipment needed to undertake the engineering maintenance tasks along the route. Several stops were needed for this and sometimes meant camping in parts along the route for periods of two weeks at a time, in order that repairs to the road and to bridges and viaducts could be carried out. All the men worked very hard because they were all equally keen to return to Italy.

Centurion Festus was in charge of the First Cohort, of which Timius and his companions were members, and Centurion Sextus was in command of the Second Cohort. Because each cohort was separated by a distance of one mile it was necessary to maintain communications. The purpose of separation was military and defence, for if any one cohort was attacked by marauding bandits, a messenger was quickly despatched on foot to the other cohort that could be on the scene and at their assistance within a short time.

Two messengers were therefore chosen from each cohort and Timius was one of those. This meant that every fourth day he would need to place his combat accoutrements in the care of the driver of one of the carts that followed the first cohort and run to the second cohort, deliver any communication, and return the same day. Thus communication was maintained. It was whilst they were marching through the grasslands of Moesia that Timius imagined he was one of the Thracian horsemen. It was normal practice that the distance between each cohort could be covered by a messenger within an hour—the return trip taking less than an hour—but Timius, imagining himself to be one of the legendary horsemen and flying with the wind, covered the distance on one occasion in less than half an hour. His penalty for doing this was that when his turn came along he was instructed to run his communication both in the morning and in the late afternoon. This caused the other members of the troop to find the whole episode amusing. Timius took it all in good fun because he loved running and he loved his imagination playing tricks on him in this fashion. The tribune held the young man in high regard for the spirit he was showing, and on the occasion that Timius accidentally tripped and sprained his ankle, it was the tribune who had asked that the young man should be detailed to be in his attendance until he had fully recovered to take up his messenger duty again. This meant taking the tribune hot water for his ablutions and taking him his meals from the cohort camp field cookhouse. Timius did not mind this because the tribune never spoke to him. He merely nodded his acknowledgment each time the service was provided.

He was an aloof man who rarely mixed with the troops. In fact, Timius noticed that before their arrival in Jerusalem the tribune did spend some of his time among the troops, and he clearly remembered the day during the event at that hill called Calvary when the tribune even condescended to join the other members of the troop in a game of dice. Since the days of Jerusalem, this officer had become very reserved. Many of the troops did not even know he existed. The troops had now crossed the border of Moesia and were in the province of Illyricum where the terrain became more rugged.

The countryside was dotted with hills, and there was a profusion of rocks and crags. The hills were covered profusely with an endless variety of shrubs. They camped the night, after marching ten hours into the province of Illyricum. Timius collected the tray of food served up for the tribune and made his way to the officer's tent, which was made of pieces of animal hide sewn together and held up in the middle by a stout pole forming a bell shape some five feet in height. The outer and lower edges of the tent were pegged down firmly into the ground. As he walked to the tent he noticed the brilliant sunset in the West, and he wondered if his dear Tricia was also watching this very same sunset that was causing the sky to become so picturesque.

He was pleased that this would be the last occasion on which he would have to provide this service. His ankle was now fully repaired, and he was ready to take up his messenger duties again; his first communication run would be in the morning. Timius approached the tent and noticed the entrance flaps were drawn down.

He stood outside the entrance and called out in a manner that would be sufficiently audible to the occupant, "Sire, your evening meal is served."

Timius waited a moment, and was suddenly startled when the tribune came charging out. He stopped abruptly in front of the entrance, his eyes penetrating into space, and then shouted, "Stop it! Stop it!" he kept repeating, "that man is innocent," he yelled. "Stop it!" he yelled again.

Timius was dumbfounded. What had come over the tribune, he wondered. The officer's tunic was dripping with sweat and sweat was pouring down his face, and Timius spoke:

"Sire, are you—?"

The officer interrupted and retorted, "Were you there?"

Timius did not answer.

"I ask again," the officer bawled. "Were you there?"

Timius did not know what to say as the officer stared at him—yet through him. The tray was now shaking in his hands, and he had spilled some of the broth from the bowl onto the tray. The officer turned round and walked back into the tent. Timius did not know what to do. He had no idea how to react. He just stood there aghast. The officer quickly turned, wiped his face with his handkerchief, and flopped down on the stool that was stood outside the tent entrance and cupped his face in his hands.

"Sire, is there something that is troubling you?"

With his head still cupped in his hands the officer shook his head.

Timius asked again, "Tell me, sire, is there something troubling you?"

"No, there isn't really," the officer replied. "Just leave the food in the tent and go."

Timius did as he was told, and as he emerged from the tent, he saluted the officer to depart when he was called back. The officer asked him again.

"Were you there?" Then he said—as if to himself—"No, I don't suppose you were! If you were," continued the officer, "you would understand. I was drunk most of that night, and even during the trial, I was under the influence of drink. Perhaps had I been sober I could have said something in the defenceless man's favour, but you wouldn't understand, would you, soldier, because you were not there. You can go now."

After leaving the tray in the tent Timius retired to collect his own portion of the evening meal. He then quietly told his companions about the incident and asked them to vow that they would not say a word to anyone else.

"You don't need to ask us to keep quiet about it," replied Cyrus. "In fact several of the other fellows know about it. Many have heard him shouting strange things during the night. He seems to have constant nightmares."

"That's right," said Marcus. "I believe he shouts at the top of his voice asking the same old question; 'were you there' and none of them know what he is talking about."

"I expect the hot sun of Palmyra has affected his brain. He is probably going insane," rejoined Cyrus.

"Don't say that, Cyrus. Perhaps there is something troubling the poor man, and there is nobody that he can really talk to about it. At least we have friends, but that poor man hasn't anyone he can confide in, because of his military station."

"Forgive me, Marcus, I suppose you are right, old friend," agreed Cyrus.

The following morning at sunrise, the troops of the cohort were assembled in readiness to commence the march. Timius was despatched with messages to the Second Cohort, and Centurion Festus reported to the tribune to receive any special instructions that were appropriate for that day.

"Centurion, now that we are in the province of Illyricum, don't you think it would be a good idea if we recommenced the practice of sending out our small reconnaissance party ahead of us?"

"I don't think that will be necessary, sire. We discontinued that practice during the march through Moesia, and I really don't see any need to institute it again. What made you think of doing so?" enquired Festus.

"The thought crossed my mind principally because Illyricum has a reputation for restlessness and insurrection."

"I see your point, sire, but I think you are forgetting that this province is well policed by two reputable legions—the Tenth and the Eleventh—and I think we can rest assured that the commanders of these legions would have taken all necessary steps, by means of patrols and other necessary measures, to control the situation," replied Festus.

"Yes, I see what you are driving at," agreed the tribune, although he was unconvinced. But however much control the commanders might have over the situation, the unrest still continues and, in my opinion, will not lessen until they replace the governor. The Procurator Cattulius is a most unpopular man in this province, and the last I heard Lucius Illius Sejanus was thinking of replacing him."

"I agree with everything you say, sire, but I still do not think that the situation warrants sending out reconnaissance parties. As you are well aware," continued Festus, "we have a highly trained and disciplined body of troops who will be able to handle successfully any group of bandits that might take it into their heads to harass us."

With this assurance, the tribune let the matter rest and the march commenced.

Timius met the Second Cohort and reported to Centurion Sextus. He was delayed for nearly an hour because there had been a problem caused by one of the carts—accompanying the troop—turning over because of a soft shoulder in that particular stretch of track. There were no messages to take back to the tribune because all was well, so Timius hastily ran back trying to make up the time lost due to the minor incident. When he finally caught up with the First Cohort, he was astounded to find his colleagues in complete disarray. The cohort had been ambushed and attacked by a fairly large group of bandits. Eight of the soldiers were dead, and a further thirty-two were wounded.

According to the accounts he heard, the fracas did not last long, and there were thirty dead insurgents whose bodies were piled in readiness for quick burial. Of the thirty soldiers who were wounded, he was shocked and extremely said to hear from both Protius and Lipsius, that Marcus and Cyrus were two of the severely wounded casualties. Timius tried desperately to get a detailed explanation from them of the severity of his two friends' injuries, but they could not tell him much. Marcus and Cyrus were in the care of the *medici*. He ran over to where they lay, each covered in their respective cloaks, and although they were not unconscious, neither was able to speak, nor did they even recognize him.

They had been administered with strong doses of morphine. Timius implored the *medici* to tell him the precise nature of their injuries, and from what he heard, there was very little hope for either of them. One of the bandits had rolled a boulder down the side of the hill which landed on Marcus, pinning him to the ground. The *medici* was fairly certain that the young man's back had been broken. A spear launched by another bandit had penetrated the right side of Cyrus's chest. The only hope here was that the young man's lung had not been punctured. Very unconvincingly, Timius posed the question to the *medici*, "When will they be well again?"

"Well again, did you say?" replied the *medici*. "Frankly, I don't think there is any hope for either of them: surely the gods would have smiled on them, if they live until first light tomorrow, and if they do it will only be a matter of time before they close their eyes in a permanent farewell."

Timius lost control and bawled at the *medici*, "Don't talk like that. My friends are good and strong. They'll get over it. I swear to you they will; they will not give up so easily, and don't let me hear you speak like that again."

The *medici* was surprised at this admonishment and said nothing, continuing with his medical work.

Timius returned to the company of his other two friends, Protius and Lipsius, and broke down and wept when he reached them. They comforted him as best they could.

CHAPTER XXXII

Si vales, bene est.

CICERO

If you are in good health, all is well.

AFTER THE INCIDENT of the treacherous ambush, the cohort on instructions from the tribune moved away from the area to safer ground only a short distance from the place of the attack. The area chosen was one that would provide a means of defence, because it was the instructions of the tribune that the cohort should encamp for a few days to allow the less injured of his troops to recover. Little hope was held out for the four young men who were severely injured, and two of the four died on the first night in the encampment. Timius, Protius, and Lipsius, were extremely distressed at the unfortunate tragedy that had befallen Marcus and Cyrus. They were in the care of the *medici* and both lay side by side wrapped in blankets beneath a goat skin awning hurriedly erected to provide some shelter from the elements.

Timius, Protius, and Lipsius visited them frequently, but both young men were so heavily drugged that their visitors were never sure whether they recognised them. On one such visit, Centurion Festus passed by to enquire about the progress they were making. The *medici* was not hopeful, and to this report, the centurion merely responded by advising the three visitors of the sick men that they had better urge them to make some sort of quick recovery or else the cohort would have no alternative but to leave them behind to perish. This was tantamount to the abandonment of two able and loyal soldiers, which caused their companions to seriously consider desertion. Fortunately, on the morning of the fifth day after the attack, when their three companions visited them, Cyrus and Marcus were beginning to wake from their unconsciousness. The three young men were extremely pleased to see some change for the better occurring and attributed it to the glorious early morning light that the great Apollo had shed over a darkened world.

The *medici* was persuaded to report the excellent progress that the injured men had made in rather exaggerated terms to the centurion. He was very pleased to hear this, and the others wondered why a man who was considered somewhat heartless had this change of attitude. He ordered that they be placed on one of the carts, where space was hurriedly made by piling some equipment elsewhere. When the cohort assembled to march, they were told that they would need to make a detour and that they would now march to the township and port of Salonae. They were told the reason for this was to enable them to see to it that the two seriously injured men could be placed in the care of the port military authorities for onward transit to Rome, where it was hoped that they would receive proper medical attention.

This was a noble act on the part of the centurion, but not every member of the troop believed this to be the case. It had been rumoured—and rumour is the swiftest of tests—that the real reason for the detour and the call at Salonae was to enable the centurion to report to the military authorities the inability of his commander to carry out his duty. The tribune's nightmares had become increasingly worse and the blame for the mistake of not sending out a reconnaissance to reconnoitre the area was totally and wholly the tribune's error. The tribune did not shirk this responsibility, but rumour also had it that he was dissuaded from taking the necessary action—against his better judgement—by Centurion Festus.

Many realized that although the tribune was suffering some mental malady, he was certainly in control of all his faculties. At the port of Salonae the tribune, as fully expected, was replaced and quickly put on the list by the authorities for transit to Rome.

Timius, Lipsius, and Protius spent their last hour in the Port of Salonae in the company of their two injured friends. Both had regained some of their former spirit, and they all planned to celebrate their full recovery when it eventually occurred by attending the games at the circus in Rome. This was agreed and sealed. Marcus was looking forward to it very much and was confident that it would not be too long for them to wait. His attention was suddenly taken by the presence of a small spider scudding across the blanket that was wrapped around his legs. Timius spotted it also and was about to flick it away, when Marcus stopped him. "Don't do that, Timius, let it run away on its own."

"Why do you say that, it is only a little spider," replied Timius.

"Haven't you heard the old saying?" queried Marcus.

"No, what saying?" asked Timius with an enquiring look.

'*If you want to live and strive, let a spider run alive,*' quoted Marcus.

Timius chuckled and said, "Oh, Marcus, you will never change—you and your poetry. I am going to really miss hearing it until we meet again in Rome. But we had better be going now otherwise the centurion might order us to the boats as galley slaves. Farewell, Marcus, and to you Cyrus, we'll be seeing you both very soon. Promise us that you will look after yourselves because if you are not fully recovered by the time we meet up again in Rome each one of you will get a thick ear from me, I promise you both that."

Each of their friends then hugged the injured men as a gesture of farewell before joining the assembled cohort to march off under the command of a new tribune by the name of Sulpicius.

When Timius left Marcus and Cyrus, he was encouraged by the slight progress they had made. Marcus was in terrible pain, and this was given away by the glazed look in his eyes and his wan, drawn expression. Cyrus had obviously lost a lot of blood, and his cheeks were hollow and the furrows on his brow deeper. He was optimistic about their recovery, but the edges of this optimism were rubbed off when he next saw them in suburban Rome. Their future in the army was precarious.

He was able to meet them again, but not until spending at least a day seeking them out after the arrival of the two cohorts in Rome. The march from Salonae to Rome took over six weeks. Timius missed his two companions terribly, and to add to his distress and to that of Protius and Lipsius was the fact that Tribune Sulpicius treated the men, under his command, contemptuously. Many miscreants—and even for the slightest errors—were punished severely. Floggings were administered relentlessly.

Timius continued to do is duty as a messenger runner for which by now he had received the nickname Mercury, and the tribune had felt that he was becoming a little too bombastic about it. This was not true. Timius had always loved running and had always set himself targets of achievements in the distances and times he endeavoured to achieve. For this, he was made to carry messages sometimes three and four time a day. Naturally, this sapped his strength, and there were two occasions when because of exhaustion, he had returned later than usual. For this he was subjected to a lashing. The new tribune was younger than his predecessor—and much shorter and smaller in stature.

Timius recalled a remark once made by Cyrus when he had been in an argument with another legionary who had the same sort of build as the tribune; he said, 'short small people you will find are invariably pompous and bombastic. This makes up for their physical deficiency'. Timius realized how true Cyrus's words were in relation to the man who had subjected his fellow soldiers to such contemptuous disregard for their feelings and dignity. Apart from a few skirmishes which they had encountered from insurgents during the march through Illyricum, the remainder of the march was uneventful. On their arrival in Rome, they marched to the Campus Martinus. There they remained a day before being instructed to take a well-deserved vacation. The soldiers were very disappointed when they were told that the vacation would last for a mere week. They had all expected a vacation lasting at least four weeks. But they had been informed that there was good reason for this.

Timius spent as day making enquiries around the military establishments in and around Rome, in his efforts to seek out the whereabouts of Cyrus and Marcus. He was successful in that he was advised to make enquiries at the medical centre, which formed part of the Campus Tarquinius. There he had received permission to pay his two friends a visit. His other two friends Protius and Lipsius, had hastily made their way to their respective homes. Timius did not have a home to go to, so he was the one person who could afford the time to enquire after Marcus and Cyrus whereabouts and progress.

Marcus and Cyrus were delighted to see him, and both had made considerably good recovery. He related to them the event of the march from Salonae, and they in turn informed him that they had been honoured to receive two visits since their arrival in Rome from the daughters of Preaetorian Officer Carpus. Timius learned that Praetorian Officer Carpus was now quite a sick man, and he only wished he had the time to go to Larcia to see him again. They also informed him, among other things, that it was not now the practice to officer the college with only selected men from the Praetorian Guard.

Other men and other ranks with distinctive service but were not fully capable of active service, were now chosen to serve at the college. They joked about the possibility of each of them one day returning there as members of the staff, but Marcus pointed out that in their state of health the only possibility that lay open to him and Cyrus was being discharged from the service permanently, and Timius was too fit a soldier to be tucked away in the back woods of a boys' institution. Marcus and Cyrus expressed that they would like to return to the college as staff members, but this possibility was out of the question. Before leaving, Timius said to Marcus, "Old friend, you amaze me, you really do. What made you get flattened by that rock? Couldn't you get out of the way of it?"

"I tried to but jumped the wrong way, and it bounced straight on top of me. That is the *amazing* thing about it."

"What I really meant was," said Timius, "that it was only about twelve months ago that you were able to discard your orthopaedic sandal, and now you cannot even stand up straight."

"Yes, Timius, that thought had passed through my mind. But, anyway, cheer up, old fellow, because the physicians have arranged for me to be fitted out with an orthopaedic breast plate," joked Marcus in his reply.

Timius promised faithfully to keep in touch with them. How he would do this he had no idea, but he would find a way. From Rome, Timius travelled to Velitrae, as though he were being beckoned to that city by some invisible force.

On approaching the Tabernae Latium Rest, he noticed a small bush of some sort of shrub hanging from a pole outside the entrance to the building. He realized the significance of this and concluded that his old friend Alpulius must be losing business, because the bush was displayed to attract custom. Alpulius confirmed this when they met and informed Timius that several Tabernaes had opened up in the town, and each was vying for customers. Apulius was extremely pleased to see him again and extended a wholehearted welcome to the young man. Timius insisted on paying the full fee for the lodging, although Apulius remonstrated with him about it. The man had obviously grown older, and his physique was much frailer. The problems of running the establishment had begun to tell on him. Thengus who used to be in charge of the kitchen was now the day-to-day manager in charge of affairs of the establishment, and he was quite overcome that Timius should want to return to this particular inn when there were so many others more worthy of a young legionnaire who had proudly returned from overseas service.

Timius spent hours in discussion with both Thengus and Apulius, and the following morning he committed himself to paying a visit to the Rousus household to see his beloved Tricia. He was quite apprehensive about the visit; apprehensive of the kind of welcome he would receive. He tried to imagine the manner in which Tricia would have changed and wondered even if she would have the time to spare to speak to him for a few moments. But, however, he decided he would go—come what may.

On his way to the Rousus household, he remembered that in her last letter to him she had mentioned that she had had her ears pierced for the second time. He also remembered that he had promised himself that he would buy her a pair of earrings to present to her when they next met. The streets of the township were crowded, and after jostling through the crowds of shoppers, he managed to find jewellers in which he selected a pair of gold earrings which he thought would be suitable; they were a simple circular type of the purest gold that was available on the market. He did not pay too much attention to the reasons for the shops being unusually busy, although he had been told by Apulius that most people were now in the throes of preparation for the festival of Satanalia.

When he arrived at the Rousus household, the tiny courtyard in front of the house was quiet. There were only small birds hopping around in search of food. He apprehensively knocked on the door and waited. There was no reply, and he thought perhaps that all the members of the household were also out shopping. He knocked again and this time the door was opened. Tricia's mother opened the door to him but was slightly vague in her attitude.

She obviously did not remember him as she asked, "Yes, what can I do for you?"

Timius stuttered out his reply, "I'm sorry to trouble you, ma'am, but I was passing this way and decided to call and see the young lady Tricia."

"I'm sorry, but I am afraid she is not here at the moment, she is in Rome with a friend—a young man by the name of Ciatus—and we are not expecting her back for at least four days."

Timius choked back the disappointment, and his mind began to race. He repeated the name Ciatus over and over again in his mind, and very hesitatingly answered, "I see, ma'am, so I had better be on my way."

"But wait a minute," Tricia's mother called as Timius was about to walk away, "but who should I say has called to see her?"

Timius Arbutus, ma'am," answered Timius, stopping in his tracks.

"Timius!" she exclaimed. "You have been here before, haven't you?"

"Yes, that's right, ma'am, but three years ago."

"How foolish of me to have forgotten you—would you like to come inside?"

Timius was choked with what he had heard and, making suitable excuses, beat a hasty retreat, promising to call again on the fifth day.

He wandered aimlessly for the next two hours, because he could not accept that the Ciatus who had accompanied Tricia to Rome could possibly be the same Ciatus of his childhood days. It could not possibly be the same Ciatus because Timius recalled having seen him in Jerusalem at Antonio's Praesidium some twelve months earlier, if in fact the person he saw there was Ciatus—he was almost sure it was him. Nevertheless, he could not get this out of his mind. All this was a terrible disappointment to him, and he decided to walk it off by wandering down to his childhood playground in the gorge. After spending most of the afternoon there, he called in at the cemetery to pay his respects at his mother's resting place, before proceeding to the inn.

Again he was disappointed; he remembered the site of his mother's grave, but the simple stone on which her name was inscribed and the area of the grave were now overgrown with grass and weeds.

There were some other graves in an equally unattended fashion, but most of them gave the appearance that they were well attended to by relatives or friends. He searched around until he found a suitable length of branch to use as an implement to clear some of the overgrowth, and promptly set about the task. He did not hear the footsteps of the approaching keeper and was startled when the man asked him, "What are you doing, young man?"

Timius jumped up. "Oh nothing, just trying to clear the weeds from my mother's resting place in order to make it look more respectable."

The keeper nodded his head, as though he understood and then said, "Using that kind of implement will take you all day. Why don't you have it properly attended to in future?"

"How do I do that for I am not here most of the time?"

"Do you not live here in Velitrae than?"

"No, I don't, I do not live anywhere. I am a soldier and can only come here on the very odd occasion; when I do, I try always to pay a visit to this spot out of respect to my dear departed mother."

"If you paid me some money, I would look after it for you," suggested the keeper.

Timius put his hand in his tunic pocket and offered the man some coins. The keeper took it, and counted it and advised the young man that it would pay for twelve months of his service. Twelve months was too short a duration, as far as Timius was concerned, as he did not know when he would be able to return to the cemetery again, but he could not denude himself of all his money lest he leave himself with no savings at all. He remembered the gold coin. He took it out of his pocket and offered it to the keeper. "If I gave you this, how many years service would I be buying?"

The keeper took the coin and examined it closely, before replying, "If you were to give me this, I would promise to attend to it for at least five years."

Timius didn't know what to say. He hated the thought of parting with the gold coin that the old man, many years ago had given him. He was sure, though, that it was the least he could do for his mother and his father—buried in an unknown grave somewhere along the Rhine Danube frontier—would undoubtedly approve of this gesture of his, were he still alive. Timius agreed and good heartedly parted with the coin. The keeper and Timius shook hands, and the bargain was sealed.

That night when he was in the room at the inn, to pass time away, he decided to count his money to ensure that some of it could be put away as regular savings. He had paid for the room and his meals for the rest of the week in advance, so that was no problem. Entertainment while he was in Velitrae did not bother him. He was in no mood for it anyway. He then went through some of his other belongings, including those he had left in the care of Apulius. There was the begging bowl, the old lire, and the broken musical pipe. To this he added the small bag of gum Arabic and the clean cloak which he had not worn since it was handed back to him by the woman in Jerusalem. These belongings he would again leave with Apulius. He tied up the bag and placed it in the corner, and made his way to the dining room of the inn for his evening meal.

It was his last day in Velitrae, and Timius decided to pay a visit to the Rousus family to see if Tricia had returned from Rome. He was anxious to see her, although the apprehension of the meeting filled his thoughts. He planned to go immediately after breakfast, but decided to postpone it until the weather changed. It was a shocking inclement morning; the rain was pelting down on the roof tops, and the sky was black with heavy rain clouds; it was as though Neptune had, in his fury, raised his chariots out of the ocean and driven them fiercely over the Velitrae skies. By noon, however, there was a break in the clouds and brilliant sunshine warmed the atmosphere of the town. Timius excitedly took this opportunity to make his way to the house in which Tricia lived. He had spent the last few days quite aimlessly; he had wandered round the gorge, the cemetery, and spent a fair portion of the time mingling and losing himself in the crowds of shoppers that bustled through the commercial streets with a view to losing his sensitive feeling of being lost. Many enjoyable hours had been spent in the company of Pulius and Thengus in long general discussions, but Timius was aware that they were both men who had their own affairs and work to attend to, so he tried hard not to prolong the discussions. He did not want to impose on their hospitality, so he grasped any opportunity that arose which would give him a means of extricating himself.

At the Rousus house Timius felt his heart racing, as though it was going to beat itself out of his chest, and it took some effort for him to pluck up the courage and knock on the door. He could not understand why he felt like that because, after all, he had only come to pay his friend Tricia a fleeting visit. After some moments, the door was opened and Tricia was standing there in front of him. There was a natural look of complete surprise on her face, and she remained speechless. Timius did not know what to do to break the silence, but Tricia did this by saying, "Timius, what are you doing here? You didn't tell me you were coming," and, breathlessly added, "mother did say you called, but she led me to believe that you would not be returning. How lovely it is to see you," and with this she quickly stepped forward, placed her arms around him and hugged him tightly.

Timius responded and was immediately invited into the house. Tricia led him into the little garden at the rear of the house and insisted that they sit alongside each other on the bench, so that he could relate to her all that had happened since their last meeting. Timius explained he was only in Velitrae for one week and that this was his last day there. Tricia was extremely disappointed to hear this but was anxious for him to tell her of some of the events of the long march from Palmyra. Timius related all that had happened and told her about the severe injuries sustained by his two most devoted friends, Cyrus and Marcus.

Tricia was most sorry to hear that his two friends would most certainly have to leave the legion.

Timius continued by asking, "When I called the other day, your mother told me you were in Rome with a young man. I am so happy for your sake"—as he was speaking, his voice faded into almost a whisper, as if he were speaking to himself—"that you have met a young man whose company you enjoy."

Tricia looked slightly surprised at this last remark and interrupted him by saying, "Oh, Ciatus, you mean Ciatus, of course. Well, he took me to Rome to meet a few people whom he thought would be of some interest to me."

"That's right, your mother did tell me his name was Ciatus."

"Yes, his full name if Ciatus Portunus, and I met him some weeks ago when I was in the library. I went there as I usually do to browse through some literature concerning Greek religion when he approached me and expressed that he was also interested in religion and was in the midst of trying to read through some of the texts of the Jewish faith."

"I see," said Timius. "You have both obviously a mutual interest."

However, he could not get over the fact that the Ciatus she was talking about was the same Ciatus who was his childhood friend. He felt it prudent not to mention this to her at all because it was of no relevance. After a while, she detected that her explanation needed some amplification, so she went on to tell him that Ciatus had returned some seven months ago from Judea, where he had been a junior member of a fact finding mission sent to the province on instructions from the Senate. It was while he was there, and in the course of his duty, he had met and heard, on several occasions, a Jewish teacher who was preaching to the local people. Ciatus had become most impressed with what the man had to say. He was mostly impressed with the simple logic of the man. Ciatus had felt that this man was the intellectual and moral leader of the Jews and through his teachings had come into conflict with the religious hierarchy, which was indeed only an arm of the state.

Timius listened to what Tricia had to say intently, and after she had finished, he asked, "What was this man's name; but before you answer, please remember that the Jews are notorious for producing teachers, or people who claim to be prophets, at will."

"Yes, yes, I understand all that Timius, but from what I have heard from Ciatus, and a few others who were introduced to me in Rome, this man was totally different. He is considered by those closely associated with him as being divine, and the morals of his teachings torment the foundations of our beliefs."

Timius said nothing for a moment, until he repeated his question; "you haven't told me his name."

Tricia lowered her eyes and after a momentary pause answered, "He was a Nazarene from the province of Galilee, and his name was Jesus."

Timius' mouth sagged slightly open, and the colour drained from his cheeks. Tricia looked up at him and noticed this and enquired, "Is anything wrong?"

"No."

"Are you sure?"

"I'm absolutely sure."

She could not understand this, but let it pass. Timius felt a little embarrassed and decided it was an opportune moment to present her with the earrings. Tricia accepted them excitedly and placed them through the newly pierced holes in her ear lobes. They both enjoyed the pleasure of that moment, but Timius felt that it was time for him to depart. He felt it would be wrong to impose on a relationship that had grown up between Ciatus and her.

"Must you go now, Timius, why don't you stay longer?"

"No, I really must go. After all it would not be fair for Ciatus to arrive and find me here with you."

"What's Ciatus to do with it?" she asked impatiently. "If you think that we are on the verge of becoming lovers then you are greatly mistaken. We share a mutual interest in religion, and that is as far as it goes.

"You say that as though I were implying something. I was not, but do remember that you shall have the pleasure of his company on many more occasions that you should be able to see me and your affection is bound to grow into love."

"What nonsense you speak, Timius. That will never happen because, although Ciatus is a very pleasant young man, I could never grow to love him. I am not even fond of him; he is just a friend. My fondness and affection is reserved for only one person."

Timius did not want to exacerbate the situation, but was longing to know who that person was, although from the tender expression in her face as she spoke, there was no mistake as to whom she was referring. He stayed the rest of the day in her company, and they talked about many subjects. When the time came for him to depart, he did so feeling depressed and dejected. He explained to her that on this occasion, although his vacation had been short, there was the very strong possibility that the special order they had received to return to Rome, after only one week, was indicative that the mission planned for them would not be one of long duration and that he would return quickly.

They parted company sharing this hope and assurance and longing for their next meeting. Timius promised faithfully to keep in touch with her at every opportunity afforded him. Tricia in turn promised him that on his next vacation, she would arrange with her mother for him to stay at their house instead of at the inn.

They embraced and kissed each other before parting, and Timius said to her, "I hope the *other person* will not mind too much my way of saying farewell."

Tricia did not reply, but smiled shyly.

Timius returned to the Tabernae via the cemetery. He was eager to know whether the caretaker had carried out the work of attending to his mother's resting place, as arranged. He was satisfied with what had been done. The area of her grave had been cleared of weeds, and a few clumps of primroses had been planted. He felt pleased with what he had seen and knew that she would also be pleased that he had not forgotten her. He felt sure that both his mother and father were now part of the happy gathering of the true somewhere in Elysium.

He returned to Rome the following afternoon, having left Velitrae the previous night. Timius had heard of a baggage truck leaving for Rome when its driver called at the Latium Rest for a drink. He was able to persuade the driver to give him a lift back to the city for a handsome reward. He had planned to return to the campus early afternoon, in order to spend a little while in the company of Marcus and Cyrus. Throughout the journey—and even now—his thoughts were constantly concentrated on his beautiful friend whom he felt caused him pangs of distress on parting again. Timius was walking across the courtyard in the Campus Tarquinius deep in thought when a loud voice jolted him back to reality.

"You, soldier, come over here at once."

Timius looked around to see some ten yards away from him a tribune and centurion in full military uniform standing facing him. Before he could respond the centurion bawled at him again, "Yes, it's you I am talking to. Come over at once and at the double."

Timius did as he was told. The centurion studied him and looked him up and down and then said to him, rather sarcastically, "Don't you usually salute an officer when you see one?"

"Yes, sire," replied Timius obediently.

Timius had not seen the officer pass him as he walked along deep in thought.

"Why did you not salute as we passed? You are not a new soldier are you?" he rasped sternly.

"No, sire, I am not."

"Well, why didn't you salute the officer as we passed?" commanded the centurion again.

Timius excused himself by replying, "I did not realize it was an officer who was in your company, sire."

"Well, young man, you have been in the army long enough to realize that if something moves, you salute it. If it stands still, you clean it, and at the moment there are plenty of dirty cooking utensils that do not move on their own volition that require cleaning in the cookhouse. Report there straight away, and I will see you there when I do my rounds. Don't stand there, get on with it," he yelled.

Timius saluted smartly and ran towards the cookhouse. He was most annoyed with himself because this meant that his chances of seeing Marcus and Cyrus before the cohorts assembled for their next mission had now gone. His only hope was that Lipsius and Protius would have a chance to pay Marcus and Cyrus a visit. He wondered if they were back and wished that he could only make contact with them but even that was a forlorn hope now.

When he returned to the barrack room late that night, Lipsius and Protius both told him that they had paid a visit to their old friends. They mentioned the fact that both young men were now making steady progress, but they held out little hope that Cyrus and Marcus would be fit for active duty for a very long time. Timius resigned himself to not seeing them again for many months.

When the two cohorts assembled the following morning details of their next mission was made known to them by Tribune Sulpicius. There was a spate of unrest in parts of Illyricum and although Governor Cattulius had been replaced quite recently, the unrest continued, but the new Governor had taken administrative steps to alleviate the discontent. The two cohorts were therefore required as supplementary troops for the Tenth Legion, and when things settled down in the province, they would return. He felt that they would only be away some two to three months, but in his bombastic manner, he added that he wished their duty would last a few years. He ridiculed their standards of discipline and bearing, but he was the type of man who was bumptious enough to ridicule any and everything. They would march to the port of Truentum and would embark on vessels that would take them to Salonae. That was their brief and he told them that they could regard the mission as having now begun.

CHAPTER XXXIII

Nil nostril miserere.

VIRGIL

You pity me not at all.

THE UNREST IN Illyricum was founded on the maladministration of Governor Cattulius, who was a nobleman who had gained a reputable position in the Senate through his constant support of Sejanus. Sejanus, then, by the way of a reward, had bestowed on him the governorship of the province. His administrative ability and approach to local jurisprudence was sadly lacking in tact. He had felt that by imposing exorbitant tribute on the provincial people he would be favouring the wishes of his master in Rome. After nearly two years of his governorship, this policy and the harshness in the way it had been imposed had become the cause of his undoing. The local population were restive, and no action was taken to allay their feelings of repression. Therefore, insurgency was rife, which had now given in to banditry of the worst sort.

Bands of insurgents had begun looting the villages, and Roman establishments had been put to the torch. The Tenth Legion was stretched in their resources to cope with the situation. They were responsible for keeping the border properly patrolled and providing numerous patrols to control local uprisings in addition to the pursuit of bandits. Many of the leaders of these groups, when caught, were executed by crucifixion without trial. Rome realized the extent of the folly brought on by maladministration, and in their wisdom had recommended that the governorship of the province should be handed over to one Terence Curtius.

The procurator, Curtius, immediately put policies into action to remedy the situation, but ne knew that it would take some little while for his policies to filter through. The economy of the country was on the verge of collapse, and this had to be dealt with expeditiously, but it would not be possible until the restlessness had been quelled. Terence Curtius was an administrator of experience. His whole life had been devoted to administration; he was a just and worthy governor to be put in charge of the affairs of a country facing near chaos. The ability of the man had earned for him a noble reputation, and the Senate at Rome was now relying wholly on him to bring about the return of law and order and a flourishing economy.

Timius and his other companions in the maniple were sitting around the dying embers of a fire. The remaining flames were dancing their last dance of life. They were all relaxing after a long night patrol which took them up and around the varied contours of this hilly and rugged part of the country. The faint beams of dawn could be seen very gently filling the sky in the east. The two cohorts had arrived at Salonae and immediately were marched to the Tenth Legion headquarters. From there they were despatched to a north westerly district some thirty miles from Salonae under Tribune Salpicius with Centurions Sextus and Festus at their head. They had been on patrol duty of the district for over one month and had been confronted by gangs of terrorists on numerous occasions.

Many soldiers of the two cohorts had lost their lives because the enemy used the hilly and rocky terrain as cover for surprise hit and run tactics, which was the only way they could get the better of disciplined Roman soldiers. The fighting spirit of the Romans nevertheless prevailed, and each felt that this type of tactic was not the respected type used by the barbarians further to the north and east who habitually confronted the Romans in their headlong confrontations. Whatever tactics Rome's enemies used, their determined efforts were no match for the indomitable Roman military machine.

Very little conversation passed between the soldiers as they sat around the fire awaiting the break of dawn, but the stillness of the early morning was broken by the mournful shriek from a soldier sitting next to Timius. A spear had pierced his chest, and although his companions jumped to their feet in a state of shock and astonishment, there was nothing they could do for Tagus. He was dead. The accuracy of the spear had pierced his heart. The soldiers immediately ran for cover in the dawn light and heard orders being shouted from Centurion Sextus to go on the attack.

The enemy was seen darting from rock to rock on the small embankment to the north of where the maniple had rested. On sight of them the Roman soldiers began their pursuit.

Each soldier launched his spear when a member of the terrorist gang presented a target. Many were able to retrieve their spears, but those that were unable to do so unsheathed swords and daggers and pursued the enemy to confront him with hand-to-hand combat. By the time the sun had risen in the east and its golden rays had lit up the morning sky, several of the terrorists—and it was assumed all of their gang—had been killed. Five Roman soldiers had lost their lives in the fracas, and there were two severely injured. A continued search was made of the area for any other terrorists still remaining.

Timius went over the brow of the hill, sword and dagger in hand, and then slipped a little way down the bank of its north face. He controlled his fall by clutching the stumps of a tree felled previously. He looked down below him and some twenty yards away he noticed, coming along a well-worn pathway that circled the hill, a young dark haired man wearing a sand coloured tunic and clutching a bundle which appeared to be his possessions.

The approaching stranger immediately darted behind a rock alongside the pathway to take cover. Timius thought that the stranger had probably seen him and taken fright, but in fact the young stranger had seen other soldiers of the maniple silhouetted on the brow of the hill. These soldiers spotted him and ran down to where he was taking cover and dragged him away from the shelter of the rock. Sticking the point of their swords in the small of his back two of the soldiers that had run down were now forcing him forward and back up the hill for questioning. He was their captive and if he was a bandit he would usefully disclose to his captors the tactical plans of other gangs, especially under torture. Timius recovered himself and joined the others. When the soldiers had assured Centurion Sextus that all was now clear, they assisted in burying their dead as ceremoniously as they could under field conditions and then set about burying the dead terrorists in shallow graves.

While this was going on, eagles continued to circle in the sky above. The men were then marched back to cohort headquarters, the proud possessors of a captive terrorist. When they arrived at cohort headquarters, Centurion Sextus forced the young captive forward, using the point of his sword, and into the presence of Tribune Sulpicius. As he did this, Timius was able to get a good look at the young captive's face and immediately recognised him. Beneath the young man's beard, his features were recognisable as those of Tribune Galilo's slave Demetius. Two of the soldiers were detailed to be his body guard, while the others were dismissed to relax and eat their oatmeal biscuits. Timius joined Lipsius and Protius to keep their company during their relaxation period. This was broken by the screams from the captive that were coming from within the vicinity of the tribune's tent. The prisoner was being tortured. They heard the centurion's voice call to two other soldiers. Timius stood up to see what was going on—was spotted by the centurion—and was called over as well. When he reached the spot, he and the other two soldiers and the two bodyguards were given instructions.

"Five of you and the centurion will take this man out of my sight and you will hang him to a cross. He is a terrorist and we will make sure that by the time the hot mid-day sun is overhead he would have provided a worthwhile feast for the eagles."

The captive pleaded; "Sire, I am not a terrorist. I was merely travelling to find my master whom I think is in Rome. My master is Tribune Marcellus Galilo. I deserve his punishment for running away from his service when we were in Jerusalem, but I tell you honestly, I am not a terrorist. I know nothing of their ways, nor do I know anything of their targets or tactics."

"Ah, so you are Demetius, are you?" asked Centurion Sextus.

"Yes, sire, I am," replied the badly beaten captive.

"Yes, I remember you did run away from your master, and you have come to join the terrorists—is that correct?" he enquired insistently.

"No, sire, I did not," insisted Demetius.

Timius was moved by the young man's plea and decided to intervene on his behalf, "Pardon me, sire might I say something?" asked Timius.

"What is it?" was the angry reply from the tribune.

"Well, the facts as stated by the prisoner are true in that he was not a member of the attacking force which we have just successfully repelled. I saw him come down the track, below the hill, and then hide. He was not armed.

The tribune momentarily glared at Timius, before replying, "That does not excuse him from the fact that he escaped from his master—a crime deserving execution—take him away and string him up," ordered the tribune.

"Come along—let's take him away," instructed the centurion, adding, "There are enough trees around here from which we can construct a makeshift scaffold."

"Pardon me, sire, might I again say something?" Timuis asked.

The tribune stopped abruptly at the entrance to his tent and turned angrily to face Timius who was beginning to try the officer's patience.

"What is it, this time?"

"Sire, with respect, might I be excused from this task."

"Why?" exclaimed the tribune.

"Because I feel the prisoner is innocent of the charges—you are condemning an innocent man to death," replied Timius, as respectfully as he could. Timius could not forget that he was party to the execution of an innocent man in Jerusalem, and this had played on his conscience ever since.

"Do you—Do you indeed," retorted the tribune. "You dare question the instructions and orders of your superior officer. No, you cannot be excused," he said emphatically.

Timius was stunned at the officer's merciless arrogance. He coldly but firmly replied, "Then, sire, I am compelled to disobey your order!"

"Have you lost your senses," asked the tribune petulantly.

"No, sire," replied Timius.

"Then I order you again, join the others under the centurion, and execute that prisoner."

He looked towards the prisoner as he said this, standing akimbo—his legs astride.

"No, sire, I refuse."

The tribune was in a foul temper when he heard this, a blatant act of disobedience. He ordered the centurion to disarm Timius and have him tied up, adding, "When we arrive at legion headquarters in a few days time, you will be court-martialled for refusing to obey an order given lawfully by your commander.

On the instructions from the centurion, Timius was disarmed and taken away by two other soldiers, who tied him to a tree with stout ropes. Meanwhile, the prisoner was led away for execution.

The tribune entered his tent and re-emerged almost immediately. He then called out to the centurion and execution party.

"Centurion, wait, bring the prisoner back here."

The centurion did as he was bid and was then informed by the tribune, who said, "I have changed my mind. Tie the prisoner up to a tree too. When we get to headquarters we will hand him over to the authorities, so that they can return him to his lawful master, who can have the pleasure of dealing with him in whatever fashion he chooses. I am sure his master will like that."

"Very well, sire, as you say," replied the centurion obediently.

Until their arrival at legion headquarters in Salonae, Timius was kept under close arrest and bound hand and foot. He was humiliated by being ignored by all the other soldiers in the cohort, who had been instructed to ignore him, because it was said that he was a coward who did not have the courage to go through with a lawful order to execute a terrorist.

He was fed scraps of food which were the paltry remains of the meal, but he was comforted by the thought that on every occasion, that either Protius or Lipsius came into any contact with him, the looks they exchanged impressed on him the fact of their admiration and understanding of the motive behind his blatant disobedience. Timius knew that he would receive a fair hearing at the court-martial that faced him. Even if he did not, he was proud of the thought that through his intervention an innocent man's life had been saved—for the time being anyway.

Had he not intervened, he was sure that a stay of execution would not have been granted by the obnoxious tribune. He began to wonder how cruel fate had been in that his whole upbringing and throughout his service as a legionary it had been impressed on him, as it was on all the other legionaries in the army, that it was important for each to stand their ground in defence of justice. This he had done instinctively, and for this he was now condemned to face a trial by court martial. He fully realized the seriousness of the charge against him, and his only hope of succeeding in his defence was to plead the justice of the case as he felt it at the time. He would rely wholly on the indoctrination he had received with regard to justice. He did his best to maintain his dignity throughout the coming days until he faced a court martial with the General of the Tenth Legion presiding.

At the hearing, Timius was alone. There was no officer provided to plead his defence, because it was considered that the crime of disobeying a lawful command given by a superior officer, in the face of the enemy, was a crime of the most heinous nature that any soldier could commit. Whatever the motives of the soldier, there was no defence in such circumstances for disobedience. As he stood there facing the officers who comprised the tribunal, he understood fully how that poor man felt back in Jerusalem, when he had faced the charges levelled against him by Pontius Pilate and the members of the Jewish Sanhedrin.

That man had no defence consul, either. But he set an example to all who followed him in that he maintained his dignity and did not retract from the injustices that were levelled against him. Timius felt that if he could only minutely follow that man's example, he would have good reason to be proud of himself, whatever the outcome. He was sure that the general and his colleagues on the tribunal were fair minded and just men.

General Nemitor's expression was grave as he sat at the table with two officers (junior to himself) on either side of him. He was dressed in full military regalia, as were his colleagues. Sitting apart from them and to the left was another gentleman dressed in a toga. He was the civilian justice advisor to the legion. Standing to the left of Timius was Tribune Sulpicius and Centurion Sextus. The general opened the proceedings by asking Timius, "Are you legionnaire Timius Arbutus?"

"Yes, sire, I am," answered Timius, his knees trembling.

The general then asked the tribune to state the charges proffered against the accused. He then asked the centurion for his version of the events. The centurion reiterated the statements made by the tribune. After listening to the statements intently the general looked straight at Timius and said, "You have heard the charges proffered. Do you deny them or otherwise?"

Timius paused before answering in a trembling voice and quaking in his boots, "No sire, I do not deny them."

He did not add any more to the statement, hoping that he would be given the chance to do so later in the proceedings. The general nodded his head and then began to speak in a sombre voice. "You have not denied the charges and therefore there is little more for us to do but to pass sentence. This is the most serious form of disobedience that a soldier in the army of our Empire can commit. The extreme severity lies in the fact that it was committed in the field of active service and in the face of the enemy. Whatever your motives, they are of no consequence, because we cannot in any circumstances excuse them. It leaves me now with the most unfortunate task of passing the supreme sentence. You are condemned to death, and you will be executed by a party of specially selected archers at dawn tomorrow. That is all!"

When Timius heard this he absolutely froze and was unable to move. The two escort guards had to assist in dragging him away from the headquarters office. His legs were like jelly beneath him, and when they dragged him into the warm afternoon light, the brilliance of the sun overhead had no affect on him at all. Its very existence did not matter to him. He was dragged back to the stockade and forcibly pushed into the cell that he had occupied for two days and two nights before the hearing. After a while in the cell, he slowly began to recover from the shock and immediately fell on his knees in the corner of the cell, near to his small kit bag, and wept for what seemed like hours.

He gradually regained control and began to think seriously about the penalty that now faced him. The light coming through the little barred window near the top of the cell wall was beginning to fade. The horrible realization fell on him that when the light began to shine through that window again his life would be non-existent. There was nothing he could do now. He had endeavoured to practice all the virtues preached by Rome throughout his life, and it was most ironic that when the test had finally come to put the virtues into practice, he had been condemned to death for doing so.

How cruel life was, he thought, but life was only cruel because certain men could not recognise the virtues of justice and fair play and, moreover, they could never recognise the truth when they were faced with it.

The door of the cell opened and a guard entered carrying a small meal cake on a platter and a bowl of broth. The guard said nothing as he placed the meal on the floor for Timius. Timius thanked him as he left the cell. He had no appetite but he thought he had better each something because it would take his mind off the awful situation in which he now found himself. The guard re-entered to remove the empty utensils and to light the tiny oil lamp that stood on a small shelf on one of the walls. Again Timius thanked him for this service. Some hours passed by before another guard entered the cell. He stood there at the door and gave Timius some news. "There are two friends of yours waiting outside to see you. Do you wish to see them?"

Timius nodded.

"Very well, I will send them in, but my instructions are that they can only remain a short while."

Protius and Lipsius were ushered in and the door locked behind them. Both young men gazed at Timius where he was slouched in the corner, absolutely shocked with the outcome of the court-martial. Their expressions were extremely solemn, and after a while, they rushed to him, grabbed hold of him, and brought him to his feet.

They both embraced him to express their pity for him and Lipsius said, "Timius, we are shocked to hear this news. What made you do it? Why did you have to be so damned obstinate over speaking up for the slave?"

Timius replied very softly, "Don't ask me, I don't know why. Perhaps it was because I felt that it was right, but I did not think that I would be condemned to death for it, but that's of no avail now is it?"

"Timius, could you retract what you said in your statement? Could you plead forgiveness and mercy?"

"No, I cannot do that. It is too late for that now."

"You could try," implored Lipsius, "because General Nemitor is reputed to be a very fair man. Perhaps he had no alternative in imposing the sentence he passed on you. He has to set a disciplinary example to all the other men in the legion. But if you pleaded for mercy and forgiveness, he might just send you away somewhere to prison or something like that."

"No, dear Lipsius, I was not even asked what my motives were, so it is no use now trying to plead forgiveness; it's too late. But thank you both for coming to see me."

"Timius, when we received permission to come and see you, the tribune instructed us to take away your personal belongings. He also asked to whom you would like to leave your personal belonging to—which member of your family; so you had better tell us?"

"Protius, I have few belongings worthwhile, and they can do what they like with them because I have no family to leave them to, so you can take them."

Lipsius, meanwhile, picked up Timius's bag and started slowly emptying its contents. There was very little in it except for a small bag of salt, a leather pouch containing fat for washing; a tunic, a pair of sandals, a spoon, and a small scroll. Lipsius unravelled the scroll and began to cast his eye over it. The expression on his face gradually changed as he came to the writing on the scroll.

He walked a few steps to where Protius and Timius were standing and said excitedly, "Timius, here's your chance. This citation, have you read it?"

"Yes, I read it long ago when it was given to me, but it doesn't mean much really."

"I think you are wrong there. Read it again; you have the right, if this is anything to go by, of appealing to the highest authority in the Empire, in the event of you having recourse to it. This is it," he insisted. "This is the time you need to use it."

"What good would that do," replied Timius dejectedly.

By that time, Protius had also read the citation and added excitedly, "You can appeal direct to Tiberius Caesar. This is your right and you never know, you might just catch Tiberius in a merciful mood, and there is a slight possibility that he will give you a reprieve."

"Go on, Timius," they urged in unison. "Just give us the word, and we will go and see the duty officer straight away."

"Very well, my friends, if you both insist, I suppose it is worth a try, but time is getting very short. It will only be some few hours before dawn breaks."

Both his companions hugged him and patted him on the back before hurrying to the cell door and calling to the guard to let them out.

The next few hours were torture to Timius. He was on *tenterhooks* wondering what the dawn would bring. He did not sleep that night, and when he heard a distant cockerel crowing, he knew his life was nearly at an end. It was only a matter of time now before the arrows from the archers' bows would pierce his body. The door was suddenly opened, and Timius stood up and braced himself for the event. They had come to march him away to the place of execution. The duty officer was present, accompanied by the two guards. He stood facing Timius and looked him up and down before saying, "Be thankful, the gods are on your side. The general had demanded a stay of execution, and your appeal to higher authority has been accepted. After morning assembly, you will be taken to the offices of the procurator. If he grants your permission, your appeal against the death sentence will be heard in Rome.

Timius breathed a tremendous sigh of relief and politely thanked the officer who marched out of the cell immediately.

Throughout that day and until the early part of that evening when he was taken, bound, into the presence of the procurator—apprehensive of the advice given to him by his two companions about using the Dictum of the Citation with a view to saving his own life—he had little hope that an appeal would succeed. There was little spirit left in the young man, but he felt it would be foolish to give up trying and trusted that he would be given an opportunity to explain the reasons for refusing to obey a lawful command of a superior officer.

He admired Protius and Lipsius for their tremendous fidelity in urging him to take every opportunity afforded him, and for their sake he felt he must not now give up. This was the spirit in which he approached the questioning that ensued from his presence at the offices of the Procurator.

Terence Curtius, the recently installed governor of Illyricum, was seated at the desk and behind him stood his assistant administrator. Both men were dressed in flowing togas and dotted around the walls of the office were armed guards. Lying in front of him on the desk was a folio which he was busily reading when Timius was brought into his presence. Also on the desk a little to the left of the procurator, was a scroll which Timius recognised to be his citation. The document was a little frayed at the edges and the dumbbells to which it was attached were worn through constant handling when packing and unpacking his bag. His wrists were bound behind his back but apart from this he was not tied by the leg or the waist. The procurator looked up at him and studied him carefully before speaking.

He spoke in a calm slow and understanding manner when he said, "You, Timius Arbutus, were rightfully charged by a court-martial for failing to carry out a lawful command of your superior officer. You were sentenced and condemned to death. You now rely on a citation awarded to you, many years ago, for bravery beyond the call of duty, which has given you the means of appealing to the highest authority in the Empire. Are those the facts?" asked the procurator.

"Yes, sire, that is so," replied Timius, as courteously as he could.

"What were your reasons for refusing such a lawful command?"

"I can only briefly tell you, with the utmost respect, that it was over twelve months ago that I and my companions and the officer in charge of our troop were ordered and directed to put a man to death whom we all later, in our considered view, thought to be innocent of the charges proffered against him. We duly carried out our orders, and since that day the act which we committed has lain heavily on our consciences.

Timius paused for a while, and Terence Curtius prompted him, by saying, impatiently, "Go on, tell me more, I am interested."

"Well, sire, after an attack on a group of my cohort, some two to three weeks ago, there was an innocent man—a young Greek—who was captured by some of my colleagues in the troop and was accused by the officer in command of being one of the ring leaders of the terrorists. I knew this was not true, sire, because I had seen this man come onto the scene of the attack unarmed and from a different direction, and I can vouch to all the mighty gods on high that he was not a terrorist. I recognised him to be the runaway slave of the tribune who was in charge of the execution party of the man crucified that I mentioned previously. This Greek captive was originally condemned to death without any trial by the tribune who was in command when we were attacked. I was ordered with others, under the direction of a centurion, to carry out the execution. Knowing that the young captive was innocent, I could not go through with it, and I requested to be excused. I was refused permission to be excused, so I in turn obstinately refused to carry out the order."

The procurator said nothing for a while, and then when he spoke he said. "I admire your principles soldier, but both of us are aware that to refuse to obey an order, however repugnant, from your superior officer, is a most serious crime. However, I have studied your record and, aside from many recalcitrant acts that you have committed throughout your service which, may I add, I consider to be a normal record of a spirited soldier, the rest of your record speaks very well in your favour. I am, therefore, giving my permission that your appeal to Tiberius Caesar be granted. I am not sure," he continued, "whether you will in fact be able to be granted a hearing by the Emperor himself, because I understand the Emperor spends most of his time at Capri. However, General Sejanus, who is now in command at Rome, will probably grant you a hearing, but I cannot guarantee that Lucius Elius Sejanus, our honourable general, will show you any mercy. He is a military man, and all military considerations are of prime importance to him. However, you will have to take a chance on that, and under the circumstances that is all I can do for you. This is a military matter and can only be dealt with by the military authorities or by those delegated to do so.

"Thank you, sire. I am most grateful for your understanding."

"That is all, now, you can leave," he added quickly, with a slight smile crossing his lips, "My very best wishes and hopes go with you."

Timius thanked him again before he was ushered out of the building by the guards. He was then told by other officers—who were part of the establishment—that he would have to remain in custody for between ten days and two weeks before being taken under escort to Rome. He would have to slave on the galley that would take him from Salonae to an Italian port, from where he would be taken to Rome.

CHAPTER XXXIV

Tremit artus.

VIRGIL

He trembles in his limbs.

TIMIUS WAS LYING quietly on a makeshift straw bed on the floor of the dungeon in which he was imprisoned. He had been brought to the centre of the government, situated on the Palatine Hill. This was the Senate chamber where the Emperor's palace and the high offices of the Empire stood. This is where he had hoped to finally know whether his life was to be dispensed with worthlessly. There were no furnishings in the dungeon, with only a small oil lamp for company, day and night. He had been there for four days, after being forcibly transported by galley to the port of Truentum, and then by a military vehicle, drawn by two horses. He had no idea how long he would have to await the outcome of his appeal to the Emperor. He was not even sure if the Emperor was present in Rome, because his escort had not conveyed any information to him at all.

Timius had lost a good deal of weight and was beginning to feel quite ill. The trauma of the experience was having its effect and, added to this, was the effort he had put into the work of an oarsman in the galley during the voyage. He was made to row sixteen hours a day for nearly ten days. The food he had been given was of the poorest quality, and there was no friendliness shown to him by any of his escorts. They were obviously under strict instruction not to fraternize with him.

He had had plenty of time to think over the situation in which he found himself and his admiration, which he had held for many years, for the Roman justice and fair play was beginning to fray at the edges. He had admired the manner in which Rome had administered justice to its peoples and the peoples of the provinces; he had admired the tenets of Roman jurisprudence, and he was relying heavily on the character of a general who he hoped would exercise justice towards him. There were many occasions e had admired the manner in which Rwhen he thought about his beloved Tricia, but felt that under the circumstances there was no alternative for him than to put her out of his mind. After all, whatever the outcome, there was no hope of him ever seeing her again. Those were his conclusions, but, nevertheless, he could not stop thinking about her and wondering how she would react placed in such a situation and, indeed, wondered what her impression would be of the state of affairs that now surrounded him—the death penalty hanging over him. He also thought frequently of his friends Marcus and Cyrus. He wondered how their recovery was progressing and cherished the memories of their happy times together. Although they were foremost in his thoughts, he did not forget the noble advice given to him by his two other companions, Protius and Lipsius, but wished that he had rejected their advice because he felt had he done so his ordeal would be over—instead his state of acute anxiety persisted. He cherished their good intentions, and perhaps they were also wondering what the outcome of his appeal would be.

Timius was deep in thought when he was jarred back to reality by the clanging from the dungeon cell door being opened. In the dim light he could discern portrayed in the doorway four men dressed in military uniform. One of the guards was carrying a lighted torch. They crossed over to where he was lying, and he recognised one of the men to be a centurion. Timius sprang to his feet when they approached him and as he did so, the centurion said, "Come along now. Your time is up, the consul will see you."

Timius began to tremble and the hairs stood up on the back of his neck. He did his best to control his feeling and partially succeeded. The centurion continued by explaining, "General Elius Sejanus is not in Rome. For your information he is in Herculanium and the Emperor himself is still resident in Capri. Luck is not on your side," he advised, "because you are to see that idiot of a man, Claudius. He has been delegated with the powers to attend to military affairs here in Rome during the absence of General Sejanus! I am sorry, soldier, but your days are numbered."

Timius' heart sank into what seemed like a bottomless pit, but he had to simply recover to face the military consul. He was marched up the steps of the dungeon and then through some corridors of the building above it. He noticed it was a beautiful building, and even the corridor floor was laid out with beautiful marble mosaic. His mind was racing too fast to absorb any of the beauty that surrounded him and continued this way until he was forcibly ushered into the consul chamber. The consul was dressed in a wine coloured toga, and was seated at a marble table. He looked up at Timius, instructing the centurion, as he did so, to remove the bonds from Timius' wrists.

"Your n-n-n-name, soldier, is Timius Arbutus. Is that c-c-c-correct?" asked the consul.

"Yes, sire, it is."

"Cen-Cen-Centurion w-w-w-will you b-bring in Tribune Galilo r-r-right away, please."

"Very well, sire," answered the centurion.

The centurion was gone for a few moments, and in the meantime Claudius explained to Timius that he had read the charges proffered against him and also the report sent him by Procurator Terence Curtius. He informed Timius that while he admired the principle behind his refusal to obey a lawful command of a superior officer, nevertheless such disobedience could not go unpunished. He would have to treat the matter with the utmost seriousness.

He also informed Timius that he had sent for Tribune Galilo because the reports showed that Timius had spent many months under the command of the honourable tribune, and before deciding the case he was anxious to obtain a testimonial of his conduct from the tribune. Timius expressed his understanding. The consul stood up from his chair and moved over to the side of the chamber to collect a silver goblet of wine. He did not walk, but limped. The stuttering of the man and his limp now convinced Timius that he had met this man, the 'idiot of the Palatine Hill'—as many called him—somewhere before. His mind began to race in trying to remember when this was. Meanwhile, Tribune Galilo had entered the chamber and Claudius sat down at the marble table. The tribune saluted the consul smartly and remained standing—awaiting questioning. An administrative assistant leaned over the consul and whispered something in his ear.

The consul then looked at the tribune and said, "I understand y-y-you have been sick. Ah-ah-are you will enough now?"

"Yes, I am, sire, thank you," replied the tribune respectfully.

"This soldier you see standing here, h-h-has been cha-charged with disobeying the order of his superior officer. He was c-c-c-condemned to death by a court-martial and has made use of the authority given to him in a c-c-citation to appeal for his life. I w-w-wish to know what k-k-kind of a soldier was he when under your command?"

The tribune waited a moment before answering, and when he did, he informed the consul that the soldier was one of the most diligent and obedient men who had served under his command. He spoke highly of Timius's conduct, but agreed with Claudius that to disobey a command, given by a superior officer, was a most serious military crime.

"I understand from the r-r-report that he refused to take p-part in the execution of the captive named Demetius. I also understand that the said Demetius was once your personal slave, who escaped from you in Jerusalem. I also am led to believe that he has since been returned to you."

"Yes, sire, that is perfectly true."

"You ha-have no doubt dealt, by now, with the runaway slave and perhaps even had him properly disposed of?"

The tribune did not answer until he was prompted to do so by Claudius.

"He is still with me, sire, and is now a freed man. Perhaps you will understand better if I explain that even after being given his freedom, Demetius insisted on remaining in my service."

"How s-s-s-strange—what caused you to f-free him?"

The tribune explained further, "Sire, my slave Demetius was overcome with emotion at an incident he witnessed while with me in Jerusalem that caused him to run away. He was disgusted with my part in it. He has since repented and decided on his own free will to return to me from halfway across the Empire not knowing whether by doing so he would lose his life, as he almost did, had it not been for the young soldier standing here in your presence. Demetius was brought to me bound hand and foot, and he was wholly repentant of his act. He begged my forgiveness."

"That is quite n-natural of a runaway slave, but why free him? Why did you n-n-not p-p-punish him—or s-s-send him p-packing as a galley slave?"

"A very good question, sire, but I decided to forgive and free him," replied the tribune.

"But why did you decide to do that?"

"With respect, sire, may I tell you that the incident in Jerusalem, about which I spoke earlier, was one where I was in command of a small body of troops of which our prisoner here was a member. We were ordered to execute, by crucifixion an intellectual and moral leader of the Jewish people. I was partly drunk at the time and unquestioningly saw to it that the execution was properly carried out. I later heard, and this has been substantiated many times by others who were present, that the condemned man had the strength of character to forgive us, his executioners, even as he was dying in agony; with respect sire, I am a Roman. That man was a Jew—if he could have the strength of character, a mere provincial, to forgive us his executioners; then I as a noble Roman would be failing everything the Empire stands for if I could not find it in me to forgive a runaway slave, who after all was only searching for his freedom.

Claudius pondered the explanation for a while before replying, as though talking his thoughts aloud, "How noble and magnanimous of you to reach that decision. That will be all, tribune, you may leave now."

The tribune saluted and departed.

Claudius again got up from his seat and filled his goblet with wine. He turned to Timius and said nothing. As he sipped the wine from the goblet, some of it began to run down the side of his mouth. Timius then remembered where he had met him previously. He did not know how to approach the consul on the matter and wondered if, indeed, he ought to. He felt he had nothing to lose, so without being asked, Timius spoke, "Sire, may I say something that you may consider of little importance?"

Claudius sat down again, saying impatiently as he did so, "Yes-yes-yes, what is it?"

"I seem to recall, sire, that I met you many years ago under completely different circumstances."

"D-did you. You p-p-probably did. I have m-met many people. What is s-s-significant about that? T-t-tell me, where and when did you meet me?"

"Sire, I remember when I was a little boy, and my father and I were passing through the township of Narnee, he needed to go and hire a horse. He left me seated on the low wall of a villa to care for our baggage while he did so. You, sire, then came and sat down beside me, and we conversed. You invited my father and me to visit you on the Palatine Hill. I then remember sharing my orange with you."

Claudius said nothing, but the thoughtful movement of his eyes were indicative to Timius that the noble consul remembered. Still saying nothing, Claudius stood up and limped around the table, as though he were impatient about something. He then stood up straight and facing Timius, said to him, "I am returning you to the dungeon, because I need time to think this matter over. I will send for you when I have decided."

Timius was thoroughly disappointed to hear this. His ordeal had not ended. He felt it would have been a happy release if the consul had rejected his appeal. Instead now he would have to spend hours, perhaps days, while the consul deliberated his fate.

It was not until the following afternoon that the centurion and three guards marched Timius back into the presence of the consult. The palms of Timius' hands were wet with sweat and he felt cold shivers run down his spine. This was the moment he had waited for—the decision whether he was to live or die. He found the consul seated at the marble table with his assistants standing behind him. The consul stuttered as he pronounced his decision.

"I-I-I have deliberated this m-matter very carefully and very s-seriously and h-h-have decided to grant you a reprieve. Perhaps the honourable Sejanus will not look very kindly on my decision when he hears of it, b-but that is m-m-matter I shall need to face. H-h-however, I have decided that your crime shall not go unpunished. The enquiries I h-have made inform me that there is a vacant post for an official at the Augustan institution for sons of members of our military forces. This institution is s-s-situated at L-l-larcia. You are b-b-banished from military service for the next seven years. After which, the s-s-situation will be reviewed. Your r-r-release will depend on your conduct over these years. You w-will be confined—and I mean conf-f-fined totally to the institution throughout that p-period. You w-will be taken there under escort at the earliest opportunity. I have also d-d-decided that you s-shall forthwith receive twelve strokes of the l-lash across your back. That is all."

"Thank you, I am deeply grateful to you and shall honour you forevermore."

"N-never mind that—t-t-take him away, centurion."

Timius was taken down to the dungeon. His tunic was ripped from his back and twelve strokes of the lash duly applied. It was absolute torture to him, but he was grateful that his life had not been taken from him.

The immediate pain resulting from the lashing caused Timius to think acrimoniously about the consult. He thought that the stuttering, limping, and reputable idiot of a man was cruel to the extreme to have him punished in such a manner, but during the two days that followed, the pain eased slightly because the dry salt that had been rubbed into the wounds was beginning to have its effect and Timius was able to think over calmly, in the quietness of the dungeon, the whole circumstances of the trial by the consul.

He concluded that the man had little choice but to inflict some kind of severe punishment on him in place of the death penalty from which he had been reprieved. He recalled the expressions on the crippled man's face during questioning him and the Tribune Galilo that he too was somewhat tormented by the whole affair and despaired of the position that had faced him. His whole position and attitude were indicative of the man's deep understanding of the predicament in which the prisoner in front of him was placed. The sentence he had finally imposed would be regarded by his superiors, Sejanus in particular, as appropriate for the offence particularly in view of the fact that he had granted a reprieve. Therefore, Timius decided that he would not judge Claudius harshly. In fact, his gratitude that he expressed to the man was done so in sincerity. He now considered himself extremely fortunate and humbled by the whole affair, but as his thoughts began to turn to the future they were full of misgivings. Seven years was a long time to be confined.

Of course, he had been confined to Larcia for a longer period, but that was during his childhood and into his early manhood. It was more acceptable then, but now that he had travelled to some distant corners of the world, and had experienced some wonderful moments, also some harsh periods, the thought of having to remain at Larcia was too horrid for him to contemplate. Moreover, he would never see his beloved Tricia again—at least if he did, she would be settled down to a family life of her own and the lovely memories of the past would only be memories. He would have to take control of his thoughts and put her out of his mind completely.

There was Marcus and Cyrus, there was also Lipsius and Protius—in all probability he would never see them again unless they knew of his whereabouts and paid a visit to the institution to see him. Memories are short and, in a matter of months, they would forget all about him. The only hope that was left for him was the one where he might cultivate new friendships among other members of the staff at the institution. He would just have to make the most of it.

Early on the afternoon of the third day, Timius was taken out of the dungeon and, under escort, taken to the Campus Martinus. There he would be issued with fresh clothing for which he would have to pay out of the army salary still owing to him because it was practice that the legionnaires made good from their own pocket clothing and equipment that required replacement. The tunic he was wearing was nearly in shreds, and he felt quite embarrassed being marched from one end of Rome through the quarter in which the Campus Martinus was situated. He felt as though the whole world had their eyes on him. The streets were busy but the passers-by really took practically no notice of this non-event. Timius could not help being sensitive about it and was very glad when they reached the gates of the Campus. He was then taken to a large store room where clothing and all kinds of other equipment needed by the army including pots and other metal utensils were stored for issue and distribution.

He was taken into a fairly large room, where half-way across there was a sturdy wooden counter, with a space at the end which served as access. There he was again tied by the wrists and ankles and told to sit on a bench until he was called. His escorts left him and proceeded to go behind the counter to try and obtain some form of refreshment. From where Timius was seated, he could see across the counter and to the racks that were fixed the wall. The racks were filled with equipment of all descriptions. Between the counter and the racks, he noticed two rows of tables, and sitting at one table was a man in civilian attire busily checking off some kind of a list. The man looked up and gazed over at Timius. Timius noticed this and moved his head to gaze elsewhere. When he looked across again the man was still gazing at him. He placed the instrument which he was using to write with on the table, stood up, walked through the access in the counter and came up to Timius. He stopped a few feet from Timius and bowing slightly said to him, "Excuse me, my friend, but have we not met before?"

Timius looked at the man closely and replied in the negative. He had had so much on his mind recently and even at this minute that he could not recall, nor did he have the faintest idea, what the stranger was talking about.

The stranger persisted, "But, my friend, I am sure we have met before. I can never forget your face."

"Well, if we have, I certainly cannot remember where and when. I'm sorry I don't know you."

The stranger looked rather surprised but relented quickly and said, "You probably don't remember me because something very serious troubles you. Would you remember if I told you that my name is Cornus Albius.

Timius did not reply for a moment and instead studied the man before saying, "No I'm afraid I do not remember you."

The stranger quickly sat beside him and grabbed him by the shoulders saying, "Let me tell you, friend, I remember you very well, and you are one person I shall never forget. You are Timius Arbutus.

Again Timius replied, "I am sorry but I still do not remember you," and he added quickly, "I have met so many people that I cannot remember all of them so you must forgive me. Tell me, where did we meet?"

"Let me remind you," said Cornus. "I shall be brief about it. There was one night, some years ago, when I sat opposite you in an inn called the 'Latium Rest' in Velitrae. You very kindly treated me to the delicacy of the evening's meal, and then you also paid for my accommodation for the night. At that time I was near to bankruptcy and could only afford a bowl of soup and some bread. To tell the truth I was destitute—I was a broken man. You not only paid for the meal and my accommodation for the night, but you told me about a pottery in the township, managed by one named Dodimus. You offered to introduce me to the manager the following morning. But if you recall, I left early that morning without saying a word to you because I thought it would be ungracious of me to impose further on your kindness. However, I proceeded to the pottery and used your name and the name of one of your friends whom you mentioned, and whom I have not had the pleasure of meeting, Marcus Piritus, in order to introduce myself. I will say no more but to tell you that I am now the chief sales representative for the pottery, which is the purpose of my visit here, in order to carry out business on behalf of the manager, Dodimus. I am also a happily married man, with two lovely young twin boys and a comfortable home. All these things I owe in no small measure to you. Now do you remember me?"

"Yes, yes, I remember you now," replied Timius without very much enthusiasm in his voice.

"Tell me, Timius, what it troubling you. What trouble are you in—your hands are tied behind your back, and your feet are tied, and your tunic is ruined. Tell, me what has happened? Perhaps I would be of help if you are in trouble."

"I have been in trouble, but it is nearly over," replied Timius despondently. On the insistence from Cornus Albius, Timius explained the whole episode, and Cornus listened throughout intently.

He was most understanding and asked Timius, "Is there anything I can do for you, my dear friend, anything at all? Before you answer let me just remind you that whatever you ask will be comparatively little for me to do in comparison for what you did for me. Would you like me to pass on a message to your wife and family, for example?"

"No thank you, Cornus. It's very kind of you, but I have no wife or family. I have no one to whom you could take a message.

Timius quickly added, "Yes, there is. If you are returning to Velitrae, perhaps you would take a message to a young woman with whom I have been friendly for some years."

"Yes, indeed, I will do that. What is the message?"

"Would you ask her to pay a visit to the proprietor at the Latium Rest whose name is Alpulius and ask him to dispose of the few belongings I left in his care—he can dispose of them any way he wishes for I have no further use for them. They are somewhat worthless anyway."

"Yes, I will do that," agreed Cornus Albius.

Timius then gave him the address of his beloved Tricia, to which he replied, "Is there anything else you would like me to tell her?"

Timius said chokingly, "Yes, please tell her that there is little hope of me seeing her again, and it will be pointless us keeping in touch at all. Just wish her the very best of luck for me."

Cornus Albius did not say anything for a moment but looked into the eyes of Timius before he asked, "Timius, my friend, do you love this young woman?"

Timius waited a moment before shaking his head.

"Are you being honest with me?" asked Cornus. "In fact are you being honest to yourself?"

Timius paused and then answered, "Yes, I am being honest. I try always to be honest and perhaps that is why I am always in trouble. I try too hard to be an honest man."

"I understand Timius. But have you heard the story of the Greek philosopher Diogenes?"

"No, I have not," replied Timius enquiringly.

"Well, let me tell you. Diogenes was seen to be walking around in broad daylight, holding a lighted candle in front of him. A passer-by stopped and asked him, *'Are you looking for someone or something, sire,'* and the old philosopher replied, *'Yes I am.'*

'Well who are you looking for?' The passer-by enquired.

To which Diogenes replied, *'I am looking for an honest man.'*"

Timius nodded his head saying, "Yes, I understand the point you make."

Cornus Albius continued, "You must not despair my friend because seven years is not a long time and it will soon pass."

"That might be so, but when the years have passed and I leave the institution, I shall be useless for anything in the outside world. In fact I shall be so out of touch that it will take me a very long time to resettle somewhere." He quickly added, "That's my problem, and I shall have to get over it some way or another."

"Don't worry about it, friend. I shall keep in touch with you and perhaps come along to see you from time to time. I will even bring my wife and two little boys to see you when they are old enough to travel. Furthermore, when you leave the institution, you will be welcome to the hospitality of my humble home for as long as you like until you find somewhere to live. I will give you my word on that, and I will not go back on it.

"Thank you Cornus. It is extremely kind of you. I will look forward to seeing you too; when we can converse at length under different circumstances, I hope.

"Most certainly we will, my friend."

Their conversation was interrupted by the arrival of the escorts. Cornus Albius stood up and embraced Timius and patted him affectionately on his back, saying, "I'll be seeing you, friend, be sure of that."

Timius was about to be taken away into the store room to be fitted out when Cornus returned rather quickly, as though to tell him something he had forgotten. He brushed past the guards, stepped over to Timius, and whispered in his ear, "Tell me, friend, that young woman in Velitrae, is she betrothed to you?"

"No, Cornus, she is not."

To which Cornus replied, "Ah, but you do love her don't you?"

Timius did not answer and Cornus was asked politely by the man who was in charge of the guard to leave the prisoner alone and not to fraternize with him. Cornus agreed obediently and gave Timius a final wave.

After Timius was fitted out with a fresh set of clothing, he was taken under escort to the camp baths, after which, escorted by his four guards, he was marched away to the headquarters building so that the man in charge of the escort could collect the instructions detailing his disposal to Larcia. The instructions were simple. They were to escort him to Porta Collina and from there a wagon would be provided to take them to Narnee. From Narnee they would proceed on foot to Larcia, and after delivering him into the hands of the principal in charge of the institution, they would return to the campus. The four men of the escort were fully armed and fully dressed in military uniform.

They were also given sufficient rations to carry in their bags to last them the journey to Larcia. Timius was also given a bag full of rations, but he was dressed simply in a dark green tunic—tied at the waist—and a pair of sandals. During the march to Porta Collina and through the city of Rome, his bag containing his personal belongings and rations were slung across his chest and over his shoulder and his hands tied behind his back. To his waist was tied a long rope, the other end of which was held by one of the guards. They marched through the centre of the city and the sights and the sounds brought many happy memories back to Timius. Among these was the memory of a letter he had received form his beloved Tricia telling him that she had come to Rome accompanied by her parents on one occasion, at which time she had had her ears pierced twice. He remembered how he nearly forgot this event but fortunately did not and was able to present her with a pair of earrings on their last meeting.

He became acutely aware that he was now thinking about her again, and he simply had to reject all thoughts of her from his mind. He knew it was no good remembering too much of the pleasant past, as it would not help him over what lay in store for him in the future. His attention was drawn by the man in charge of the escort drawing the attention of this tiny group as they approached the square of the Temple of Jupiter, the greatest and the best, that a member of the nobility was approaching them.

"Watch out, soldiers, here comes Caligula."

The man in charge of the escort had noticed a litter over which hung a white canopy being carried by four slaves coming in their direction. At the head of the procession marched a soldier—wearing a leopard skin headdress—carrying the emblem of Caligula on a staff in front of him. Beside the litter walked two officials dressed in white togas and behind the litter was a small military guard comprising ten soldiers. Caligula was dressed in an orange-coloured toga. He was busily chatting in turn to the assistants walking alongside the litter. When the tiny procession approached the group of guards, escorting Timius, the man in charge of the guards halted the tiny escort ordered them to face the litter, so that they could pay their respects. This was a compulsory practice when any member of the royal household passed troops on the march. Caligula ordered the litter bearers to stop. And the whole procession came to a halt. He was eating what appeared to be an overripe peach, because the juice from the fruit was running down the side of his mouth. He then addressed the man in charge of the escort. "What have we here today? Another slave for the arena, or are you taking him to feed the rats of the city after execution?"

"No, sire, we are escorting the prisoner to his place of banishment."

"Banishment!" exclaimed Caligula. I've never heard of it. That is not customary Roman practice is it?" he asked disdainfully as he bit into the peach. "After a while he asked, "What has the despicable man done to deserve such an easy punishment?"

The man in charge of the guard answered respectfully and briefly. "Sire, he refused to obey an order from his superior officer, on the field of duty and in the face of the enemy. He was sentenced to be executed, had the authority to appeal to the Emperor himself, who is, as you know, absent from Rome, and his appeal was dealt with by the honourable Consul Claudius. Claudius has granted him a reprieve and instead imposed a sentence of seven years banishment from the Legion."

"How very interesting." said Gaius Caligula biting into the peach.

Throughout the short exchange Timius stood smartly to attention, but with his head slightly bowed, gazing at the ground in front of him.

Caligula bellowed at him, "You, prisoner—look at me!"

Timius looked up and gazed into his eyes.

"Think yourself lucky that you were dealt with by that idiotic, stuttering uncle of mine. Had I dealt with you, you would surely have been thrown to the gladiators in the arena to be used for target practice. When Lucius Elias Sejanus hears of this, he is sure to take issue with the honourable idiot Claudius. Take him away, out of my sight."

The man in charge of Timius's guard marched the tiny escort away, but Timus could not help feeling hurt at the remarks made by that bumptious man Caligula. His attitude concerning Claudius was indefensible, and if the Empire had to rely on his sort for its leadership there would be little hope left for it. Throughout the journey to Narnee, Timius' thoughts returned to the brief meeting his tiny escort troupe had had with Gaius Caligula. He could not forget the odious and insulting attitude of the occupant of the litter, nor the manner of the two aides who walked beside the litter. On one occasion when the escort troupe was taking a well earned break from the bumpy ride in the cart that had been provided for part of the journey, he overheard his escorts voicing their opinions about the honourable Caligula—none spoke kindly of him—in fact it was expressed that if the legions relied on the likes of him for their leadership there would either be large scale desertions, defections, or mutiny. Timius heard the name of Caligula mentioned several times in general conversation during his service and now realized the justification for the disrepute of the man. He also realized the enormity of his fortune in that his appeal should have been heard by the honourable Claudius—the thought of Caligula sitting in judgement over anyone was repulsive.

At the time of meeting, Timius thought he recognized the face of one of Caligula's aides—that of the person who had stood nearest to him. He had tried to put an event, or an occasion, to the face ever since the meeting, and it now suddenly occurred to him who it had been—it was Tricia's brother-in-law, Tetrianus Felux. Tetrianus, he remembered, had been the cause of his outburst at the meal table on one occasion when Timius had visited the household and had been invited to dine with the family. He remembered the occasion well and concluded that the man was well qualified with his pomposity to be the aide of the bombastic Caligula. Timius recalled that there was talk at the time of Tetrianus entering the administrative field—thanks be to Jove—there were many worthy and able administrators who did not fall into his category.

CHAPTER XXXV

Regna, honores, divitiae, caduca et incerta sunt.

CICERO

Kingdoms, honours, riches, are frail and fickle things.

NIGHT FELL WITH her darkened arms embracing the world. Timius lay on his blanket in the compound of the military outpost northeast and outside the town of Narnee. It had been arranged that they would make the rest of the journey on foot before the break of dawn. The cart and the two horses were left in the care of the officer in charge of the outpost, and after the evening meal Timius was tied hand and foot and forcibly thrown on some straw—covered with a blanket—near the stables.

He could see the stars glittering above him and wondered what would be in store for him at Larcia. He had not given much thought to it up to now, because his thoughts rested mainly on his good fortune at being released from the death sentence. Moreover, the long and terrible ordeal had affected his health adversely. He felt completely run down and thought that he would only have sufficient strength in his limbs to reach Larcia. Perhaps after a few weeks there he would recover and spring back to life again, but then he realized that it would be a life of confinement; seven long years of it.

On their arrival at Larcia it was midday. Timius was marched into the office of the senior disciplinary administrator of the institution. Timius had been into that office many times before when he was a pupil and fully expected to see Praetorian Officer Paulo. He wondered what Paulo would say of his return, particularly in these circumstances, but he was soon disappointed. The officer into whose charge he was handed was a man by the name of Viridus. Viridus was not a Praetorian officer, nor was he a man of centurion rank. He was a junior officer. Timius concluded that the man in his late forties was rather supercilious.

He did not seem to have any feelings at all. When he asked Viridus as respectfully as he could the whereabouts of Paulo he was brushed aside with a remark that Paulo had retired and his whereabouts were no concern of his. The soldier in charge of the escort troop formally handed his charge over to Viridus and departed.

Viridus spent some time lecturing Timius on the routine of the institution, which Timius realized had not changed at all since he was here as a pupil, and he went on to stress the importance of his good behaviour throughout his stay, warning him that any breach of discipline, however, minor, would mean his immediate return to Rome and the death penalty. The orders handed to Viridus had contained such a warning. Timius gave his superior a solemn promise that he would not break the rules nor deviate from the routines that had been laid down. He would endeavour to show that his behaviour would be exemplary. After the lecture, Viridus informed Timius that they had better now go to the principal's office to report in.

When they reached the main part of the building in which the principal's office was situated, Timius was told to take a seat on the bench in the hallway. He did as he was bid while the officer Viridus reported to the principal. While Timius was seated on the bench, he clearly recalled the day, when he was a little boy, sitting on that very bench and gazing about him wondering what was in store for him whilst his father was busily engaged in discussions with the principal, Artimeses.

Time moved by slowly, and after a while, a man emerged from the principal's office, walked straight passed him and him and out of the building. After about half an hour had elapsed the same man returned and entered the principal's office—still Timius waited anxiously. It was well past noon, and he wondered what was happening. The door of the principal's office was opened and the officer Viridus called Timius in. Timius felt relieved that he was finally being dealt with after waiting so long. He did not know who the principal was and again half expected to see Artimeses. Again he was disappointed. Artimeses was not there. The principal was seated behind the desk on which a few documents lay. He was a gaunt, grey haired man and was introduced to Timius as senior citizen Xanos. It appeared to Timius that he was of Greek extraction, but unlike Artimeses, his whole dress and manner was that of a Roman.

"Officer Viridus tells me that he had informed you of the circumstances of your stay with us here. Naturally I welcome you, but I shall watch your behaviour most closely. I feel, however, that you can be trusted. But do not break my trust," said Xanos sombrely.

"Sire, I thank you for the welcome you have extended to me, and I give you my word that I will not break your trust. I will endeavour to serve—"

Timius's reply was interrupted by a knock on the door.

"Come in," instructed Xanos.

The assistant Timius had seen leave the principle's room earlier had returned to the office to announce, "Sire, the maid-servant, Jasmina Wahabis, is here with your food."

"Oh, thank you, send her in please," said Xanos.

A very dark skinned and delicately featured woman entered the room carrying two pewter bowls covered with a cloth. She walked over to a table that set aside against the wall and gently placed the tray on the table. She respectfully bowed, was thanked by Xanos and left the room. The name of the woman, announced by the assistant, shot through Timius's mind like a thunderbolt. Could it be, or was it the wife of Mucta Wahabis, but before he could collect his thoughts Xanos spoke again, as though he was speaking to himself. He was addressing Viridus as he said, "Do you know that woman has been an extremely loyal and diligent maid servant ever since we bought her services from the slave market in Rome. Both my wife and I have offered to free her but she has refused saying that freedom to her now was pointless. She had lost both her husband and her daughter—we know not where."

He then spoke to Timius and said, "I don't know what the authorities have in mind with this institution, but they seem to be foisting inactive and recalcitrant personnel on to me. In three weeks time we shall be expecting the arrival of a man who is to fill the vacancy of senior disciplinary administrator—a man who has been very sick—one by the name of Tribune Galilo. There are also two more vacancies to fill and again they have offered me two soldiers who are recovering from battle injuries but I am told they are both ex-pupils of this institution and here I have in front of me a soldier who is to serve a seven-year banishment posting."

Timius was confused, bewildered, and excited with the information he had just been given. He did not know what to say or if, in fact, an answer was required of him, so he decided to remain calm and say nothing. He was even more stunned to hear the next piece of information when Xanos said to him, "Your main duty while here in the institution will be that of a junior official with the full responsibility of taking care of the latrine troop. It was most unfortunate for us that very recently we lost the good and loyal services of Praetorian Officer Carpus, who died—may his soul rest in peace.

You will be taken to a small quarter where you will live, but you will be required to take your meals in the main dining room with the boys. You will not be joined by any of the other officials because they are all married men and have their meals in their own homes, but during the meals you will keep an eye out and assist the duty officer. Do you understand?"

"Yes, sire, I do," replied Timius.

"Officer Viridus will now take you to your quarter, where you will settle in for the rest of the afternoon. We will see you again in the main dining room for the evening meal. You may leave now."

Timius was taken to his quarter by Viridus who gave him cursory information about the tiny building which comprised two rooms, one of which was a bedroom and a small room that could be used for cooking, and another room to be used for his ablutions. There was also a tiny veranda and a store house adjoining the building. At the rear was a fenced-in piece of land—very overgrown with weeds and bramble—and in front of the veranda was a small garden—with a fence round it—which had not been attended to for many months.

It was quite a well-appointed spot, and at the foot of the back garden ran a trickling stream. Timius remembered this stream because he used to go and splash about in it as a boy. After Viridus left him Timius took stock of the place. It was very sparsely furnished. There was a bed, a wooden stand on which stood a pot bowl, a table, four chairs and a big wooden cupboard. There was nothing else in the building apart from a few cooking utensils. He paid no attention to the cooking utensils because he would not need them. The stone floors were covered with rough fibre matting. There was a small fireplace in one of the rooms and a bench placed against one of the walls. Logs had been cut and stacked outside the veranda, and when Timius saw these it reminded him of the day when he and Marcus were caught stealing the axe from the woodman. He sat on the bed and collected his thoughts. He decided that every spare moment that was granted to him, he would work hard and get his little home properly cleaned to provide him with the comfort he now so badly needed. He would also clear up the back yard and try to grow some wild flowers. Seven years was going to be a long time for him, but this would give him a world in which he could lose himself.

That night, while lying in the bed before extinguishing the oil lamp, Timius began to realize that this was the first night in many weeks that he was alone. Previously he had either been watched over by a guard in a dungeon cell or a prison cell, or at a military establishment. It was also the first night that his hands and legs were not bound, and he found this freedom very comforting. He soon became used to the quietude of the little quarter. Even prior to being arrested, he had never known what it was to sleep without company of others. The strangeness of his surroundings kept him from sleeping for some while. Throughout the night he heard intermittently the sounds of the horns being blown by the farmers on the hillsides. These sounds were not strange to him. He had grown used to them years ago, and the mournful sound reassured him that he was now secure. His one fear was that of oversleeping and he promised himself that in due course, when he had cleared the patch of land behind his quarter, he would seek permission to keep a few chickens and would make sure he had a couple of cockerels among the birds. He could then rely on the early morning crowing to wake him in the mornings. Meanwhile, he would have to try not to sleep too deeply, and decided to relight the oil lamp so that its flickering flame would serve that end.

For the next few days Timius applied himself to his duties diligently, but he had given some of the comments made by the Principal Xanos some careful consideration. Firstly, he thought about the two soldiers who were ex-pupils of the institution and servicemen who were due to take up their posts in the very near future. He felt almost certain that they would be Marcus and Cyrus.

To confirm this fact he raised the question when he paid a visit to his dear old friend Carpus's household to offer his widow and two daughters his condolences. Both Lygia and Julia, who had paid a visit to Rome to see Marcus and Cyrus, informed Timius that rather than take a medical discharge from the army, both young men had volunteered their services to fill the vacant posts at Larcia. Timius was excited to hear the news because he knew it would be just like old times again, marred only by the fact that he would have to make an extreme effort not to get drawn into mischievous deeds with his two lifelong companions, which would jeopardize his future. He also thought very carefully about the maid-servant who had brought food to the principal's office. Again he was convinced that the woman was the wife of his other dear old friend, Mucta. He knew Mucta was free of his bondage but was not certain of his whereabouts or even if he were still alive. Mucta had been a leper but Timius recalled that the last time he saw Mucta he appeared to have been cured of the disease.

The thing that bothered Timius most of all was not being able to get word to Mucta, who was probably still in Judea, that his wife Jasmina was alive and well. Even if he were free, Timius could not think of a way of getting a message to him. The only possibility of doing so would be through

Tribune Galilo so he decided that when Tribune Gallilo arrived to take up
his duties, he would take the first opportunity to discuss the matter with
him. Timius had always regarded the tribune as being a man of honour and
kindness. This was distinctly prevalent when the man had spoken well on
his behalf when questioned by the honourable Claudius. Moreover, it had
been said that Tribune Galilo was an extremely influential man. He was
from a noble family that wielded a strong influence over some sections of
state affairs.

If this was true, perhaps Tribune Galilo would be able to use the influence
of his family to get word to Mucta—how he would do this was beyond
Timius's comprehension—he was clutching at a straw but would be worth
trying, and he would never forgive himself if he did not make the effort.
Perhaps Marcus, or Cyrus, would know of a solution. He would have to wait
and see what the outcome would be. There was one other possibility that
had only just occurred to him. If the honourable tribune brought Demetius
with him, perhaps Demetius would know of a means to make contact with
Mucta. He felt that it would be something worth remembering, when and if
he discussed the matter with the honourable tribune. He must firstly make
absolutely sure that the woman Jasmina and Mucta Wahabis were in fact
bound by matrimony, although there did not seem to be any doubt about
that as far as Timius was concerned.

His first few days at Larcia enabled Timius to learn that most of the
staff, apart from Demetrius the Gymnast, had changed. Two assistants who
worked in the kitchens and who were nearing retirement were also pleased
to see Timius back among them. Praetorian Officer Lictus had retired and
so had many others who were official at the institution when he was a pupil.
The newcomers were not as affable as their predecessors, Timius thought,
because some of them looked down on him in his capacity of official in
charge of the latrines. They were condescending in their conversations with
him. No matter, he would not let this upset him because he was grateful to
be alive and to him that was the most important thing. However, his life was
not fulfilled because the very person who could have brought him complete
happiness was now lost to him. He was extremely saddened about this and
often thought how ironic life could be.

His boyhood friend and rival was now his rival for the hand of the one
for whom he had developed a deep love. The rivalry was caused through
an incident which his rival Ciatus had not even witnessed. Ciatus, he
remembered clearly, had not even witnessed the ferocity of the viper in the
gorge when it hissed angrily at Timius when he was left alone to face it; yet

ARBUTUS 447

it was Ciatus who had received the accolade from young guests at the party which Timius had been forced to attend. Timius decided not to judge life too harshly because he must learn to take the rough with the smooth and the ironies of life were too numerous to contemplate at this juncture. When he stood at his post supervising the boys on latrine duty and watched them struggle with the iron buckets to empty them into the lime pit, he felt a tinge of sadness for them. Perhaps this was how Carpus had felt, but Timius had gone through it, and these youngsters also had to learn to go through it. He concluded that if his life since those days had been rewarding for him, these youngsters may also find life rewarding after their training at this institution, when their turn came to face life as adults.

Timius finished his evening meal, buckled on his red cloak, said good night to the kitchen assistants, and strolled out of the dining room and into the night. It was dark with a myriad of stars twinkling above. The moon was just beginning to rise on the horizon, and, as he strolled down towards his quarter, he could hear the crickets screeching and some frogs croaking. He could also hear the farmers' horns being blown on the hillsides. He took a leisurely walk, deep in thought about Marcus, Cyrus, the Tribune, Mucta and remembered that he must write a note to Protius and Lipsius explaining to them his good fortune through following their advice. About a hundred yards from his quarter, he could make out the outline of it against the night sky and trees behind it, but he noticed something strange, but quickly brushed it aside and walked on. Timius had noticed that the oil lamp appeared to be alight and shining through the main doorway of the quarter. He attributed the light to the moonbeams shedding their light across the grounds.

As Timius came nearer to the quarter, he began to realize that the light coming through the doorway could not be caused by the moon. He walked on feeling a little apprehensive wondering what had happened—he quickened his step slightly. As he drew nearer he could see plainly that the oil lamp had been lit and silhouetted against the light coming through the doorway was a figure of a person seated on the step of the veranda. Timius's heart began to flutter—he wondered who it could be—and when he was quite near to it, he realized the silhouette was that of a woman because the figure had a wrap hung loosely over her head.

Timius moved closer and was abruptly stopped when a voice said to him, "Hello, Timius."

Timius wondered for a moment as he could only just see, in the dim light, features of a woman whom he could not quite recognise as the voice gave him no clue. The woman looked very much like the woman over whom he had placed his cloak for protection during the storm at the execution of the Galilean. This woman seated on the veranda was also wearing a cloak draped over her head in the same fashion as the Jewish woman on that hill. He stepped closer and was astounded to recognise the woman to be his beloved Tricia.

After a few moments Timius stuttered as he said, "Tricia, what are you doing here? What brings you here?"

"Aren't you pleased to see me?" she asked.

"Yes, yes I am indeed absolutely delighted to see you," he exclaimed. He rushed up to her and embraced her then kissed her gently. He then sat down beside her and asked her to explain. He was eager to know the purpose of her visit.

"Before I tell you, will you forgive me for taking the liberty of lighting the lamp and also for using this cloak of yours, which I found in your bag, to shield me from the chilly night air?"

"Yes, of course, but never mind about that what are you doing here?"

"Well, Timus," Tricia explained, "your friend Cornus Albus paid us a visit and passed me your message. He told me all that had happened and then asked me, at your request, if I would to the Latium Rest to retrieve your few belongings from the innkeeper Apulius for disposal. I decided not to dispose of them but to deliver them to you in person.

"That's wonderful of you, my love, but I didn't want to impose on you like that. Those belongings are not very important and you should not have gone to all that trouble to bring them here. I am glad to see you though—very, very glad. How long are you able to stay?" Timius asked.

"I have only just arrived—are you trying to get rid of me?"

"No, not at all, I am just anxious to know."

"Do you have to be somewhere else then?"

"No, I do not. I wish you could stay here forever more. But I am aware that you will not be able to do that and that you will probably have to return very soon. Where are you staying?"

"You'll be pleased to hear the Principal Xanos has invited me to stay with his family for a few days. They gave me a meal on my arrival and provided the facilities for me to refresh myself after the journey."

"That's extremely kind of them," said Timius.

Tricia gave a slight shiver and pulled the cloak back to form a hood over her head. She looked at Timius, and by this time, the moon had risen fairly high into the sky. In that dim light, Tricia immediately reminded him of the Jew on that desolate hill outside Jerusalem. He then responded as though it had not occurred to him before by saying, "What on earth are we sitting out here for? Come, my love, let's go in and I'll light the fire to warm you up."

He took her by the hand and into the room to the bench near the little fireplace. He then went outside, collected a few more sticks and some logs, re-entered the room and set about lighting the fire, which did not take long to kindle. When the fire was crackling merrily Timius sat down beside Tricia, and they both sat gazing into the dancing flames. Tricia asked him what was in the bag that she had brought from Velitrae for him. To which Timius replied, "Only a few bits and pieces. Apart from the cloak which you have about your shoulders, a lire and a begging bowl."

Tricia was surprised to hear this, and Timius quickly had to explain how they came to be in his possession.

"Talking about Velitrae," Timius went on, "I'll never forget the day I first set eyes on you. It always reminds me of the famous phrase that the great Julius Caesar supposedly uttered when he landed on the Celtic island of Britain. It was as though 'you came, you saw me, and you conquered me'."

Tricia blushed slightly and replied, "No that is not so. I certainly came, I saw, and then I fell in love."

Timius was shocked and embarrassed to hear this and put his arms around her and kissed her. He then abruptly broke their embrace and shook his head saying, "It's no good, my love we cannot really go on like this. I feel I was very idiotic and too sanctimonious in my actions. Had I kept my place and not intervened in defence of the slave Demetius, there is every possibility that I would have been able to have left the army this coming autumn and then bought a small house, which I would have invited you to share with me. The present circumstances do not allow for us to be together for very long."

"But, Timius, had you have acted differently you would have gone down in my estimation. It was extremely courageous of you to save a man's life at the risk of losing your own. Anyone can turn a blind eye to an injustice."

Timius nodded his head and agreed. He then added, "Yes, I suppose the governor of Illyricum, Terence Curtius, and the honourable consul, Claudius, could have turned a blind eye in my case, and that would have been the end of me."

"How right you are."

After a moments pause, he asked, "Will you be coming to see me again? It is silly of me to ask you that; I cannot really expect it of you. I am stuck here for seven years, and it would be unfair to ask you to wait and share my dream with me."

"Oh, but, Timius, my love, there is no need for us to wait. We can begin to share our lives together just as soon as you wish."

"How can we?" Your parents have not given their permission. Besides, you are not betrothed to me, and, moreover, I have very little to offer you. All I have in life is what you see around you in this quarter—nothing more."

Timius, I am not interested in riches, honours, or privilege. What little we have we will share, and I have some money, and my father also gave me some money to serve as a dowry."

"A dowry!" exclaimed Timius.

"Yes, that's right, don't be shocked. I told him that I was coming here and that we would be married. Naturally, he was sorry to see me leave, but then he couldn't stop me and gave me his blessing."

Timius was quite bewildered to hear this.

"In that case, my love, I will see the principal first thing in the morning and ask his permission for us to be married as soon as possible. They excitedly kissed, but Timius reminded her that his life would be confined to the perimeter of the institution. Tricia did not mind this and suggested that she would take the opportunity of going to the town of Narnee and buying them a few bits and pieces to make their quarter into a comfortable home.

"You are resourceful," said Timius, "and you are so truthful about everything. In fact," Timius continued, "I am henceforth going to refer to you as Tricia the true—just like *Aeneas the true in* **Virgil's Aenied**."

Tricia smiled, embarrassed at these last few words.

"That's right, you are 'Tricia the true', and tomorrow morning my true one, I shall make a definite point of seeing Xanox."

She smiled, blushing, as she said, "Timius, there is no need to do that. I took the liberty of telling him that we were betrothed and that I had come to claim by betrothel. He has given us his blessing and will arrange for us to be married in the temple three days hence on Wednesday."

Timius shook his head in wonderment and replied, "You've thought of everything, haven't you?"

"Naturally!" she exclaimed, "There is no point in waiting about. I love you and you love me, so what's the point in waiting any longer?"

"Quite," he agreed.

Timius then went on to tell her about the information he had received concerning Cyrus and Marcus, Tribune Galilo, and also the surprising information about Jasmina Wahabis. Tricia was intrigued to hear about it all and extremely happy that life together here looked as though it was going to be very pleasant. Timius had spoken to her in the past about Marcus and Cyrus. She also said that she would give the problem of getting a communication to Mucta Wahabis some thought in the hope of finding some solution, although she felt that his plan to discuss it with Tribune Galilo could not be bettered.

After a short pause, a slight sadness came over her face and she said to him, "Timius, before you accept me as your wife, I have a confession to make.

"What is it?" he asked. "What is troubling you?" he asked again.

"Well, my love, I must tell you that I am now a follower of that Jewish teacher, the Nazarene by the name of Jesus."

Timius said nothing. He was quite confused to hear this. He then decided to tell her that he also had something to confess.

"Please don't think too unkindly of me when I tell you what I have to confess. "This Jesus you speak of—"

Before Timius could finish, Tricia interrupted him, "If it is the same Jesus, well he was a divine man who was executed by a party of Roman soldiers."

"That's what I wanted to tell you. I was a member of that party so was Marcus, Cyrus and Tribune Galilo. I crucified him."

She shook her head and replied, "Oh, Timius, don't ever say that."

"But you don't understand, my love, I did."

"Yes, I do understand," she insisted, "you crucified him; they crucified him, you will go on crucifying him, and, in fact, all of us will," she said philosophically, so say no more about it."

"Tricia, you don't understand—"

"Yes, I do, I do understand."

Timius did not know how to continue and thought that if the subject was ever raised again, he hoped that she would never hold it against him for not telling her. He had tried but she just would not accept it. Nothing was said for quite some time as they nestled in each others arms, and Timius broke the silence, as though he was speaking his thoughts, "Do you know my love, only a few weeks ago I was facing the death penalty. As each day went by I expected to be executed that very day. Fortune plays strange games. Here I am now with a little home of my own with you by my side to share your life with me. Soon I shall have my two dearest companions who I shall work alongside again. I shall also be under the command of a man for whom I have the utmost respect. Nobody could be as fortunate as me. I might only be the official in charge of the latrines, but that's good enough for me. I seem to have come full circle. I have escaped death this time, but death is something that none of can go on escaping. One day it will catch up with all of us.

"That's quite right, Timius," agreed Tricia, "I think you deserve your good fortune, and I am sure you deserved the award for bravery that was given to you."

"How did you know about the award?"

"Ah," she said with a twinkle in her eye, "Cornus Albus told me about it, and I also saw it when I entered this house earlier where you had left it, on the window ledge. I took the liberty of reading it, and I feel very proud of you."

"Oh, it's nothing to be proud of," said Timius modestly. "I was only brave because I endeavoured to save my own skin and help poor old Marcus out of a tricky situation."

Timius then went on to speak his thoughts aloud, "We cannot always escape death, as I said earlier. It will come to all of us. Do you know, Tricia, it is the only thing in life that we can be absolutely certain of. There is no assurance more certain than death. Even life is not an assurance."

Tricia shook her head gently and replied, "No, Timius, you are wrong. There is one other thing that we can be absolutely certain of—an absolute assurance."

"What is it?" queried Timius.

"The love of Jesus of Nazareth and I have spoken to a few of those who knew a good deal about him. In his short life he said and did some very beautiful things and **forgiveness** was always high on his list. If we all practised this—regardless of our beliefs or different faiths—the world in which we all live would be a better place."

THE END

Lightning Source UK Ltd.
Milton Keynes UK
UKOW041041270912

199714UK00003B/31/P